JOANNA THE POPE

A Novel by
DANIEL PANGER

Also by Daniel Panger

Black Ulysses

Dance of the Wild Mouse

The Mask of Abraham Morgenstern

Ol' Prophet Nat

The Sacred Sin

Search in Gomorrah

You Can't Kill a Dead Man

JOANNA THE POPE

A Novel by
DANIEL PANGER

Resource Publications, Inc.
160 E. Virginia St. #290
San Jose, CA 95112

Editorial Director: Kenneth Guentert
Production Editors: Scott Alkire,
  Mary Norris, Curtis Gruenler
Mechanical Layout: Geoff Rogers,
  Sharon Montooth
Cover Design and Map: Christine Benjamin
Cover Illustration: Sharon Searle
Production Assistants: Christine Bonnem,
  Allison Cunningham, Catherine Long

ISBN: 0-89390-064-8 (Cloth)
        0-89390-065-6 (Paper)
Library of Congress Catalog Card Number 86-060895

CONTENTS

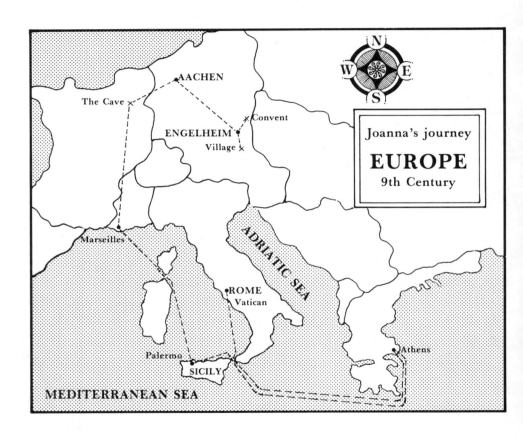

Joanna's journey

EUROPE

9th Century

*For women priests of the future,
one of whom may very well follow
in the footsteps of Joanna.*

From 1400 to 1600 there stood in the great cathedral of Siena, among the other busts of the lawful popes of the Catholic Church, one with the inscription: *JOHANNES VIII, famina ex anglia.** In 1600 the reigning pope, Clement VIII, ordered this bust transformed into a likeness of Pope Zacharias.

* Anastasius the Librarian (d. 886) refers in his chronicle to a Pope Joan — known at the time as John VIII. Later well-known medieval scholars such as Otto of Frisingem, Gottfried of Viterbo, Martin Polonus, William Ocham, and Thomas D. Elmham also made references to a woman who became pope.

I

THE VILLAGE

The peasants, in their cluster of windowless, smoke-filled huts a half day's journey from the city of Engelheim, were startled out of their sleep by a series of terrible screams. Most of the men, taking hold of their cudgels, emerged into the cold night, rubbing their smoke-burnt, sleep-gummed eyes, hacking and coughing. They made a show of brandishing their weapons; several shouted warnings to any brigands or forest dwellers crouching out there in the dark that they could expect no mercy if they dared to approach the huts.

Just a week before a hairy giant of a man had been caught lurking near the village. He claimed to have served the Great Charles as a soldier, and perhaps he had. But the Emperor was dead these four years and too many ex-soldiers combed the countryside slaughtering stray cattle, carrying off women, stealing whatever they could lay their hands upon. This man, as a warning to the others, had been impaled on a stake and left to ripen a little distance from the village.

The screams again echoed through the night, and the men took firmer grips on their weapons and began to form themselves into defensive bands. They were just about to move in the direction of the screams when Rolf the Woodcutter emerged from the widow Gerberta's hut, where he slept one or two nights each week, and declared that the screams came from the edge of the woods where the English monk and his wife lived. A third scream, recognizable as that of a woman, made all the men nod and grin as they relaxed their grips on their weapons.

The monk's wife was giving birth — it was her first.

"With her small bones, God did not intend that fine-mannered Angle woman to bear children," said one of the men with a laugh.

"The little ones often will shame big sows like that barrow of fat you live with," a second man responded.

"Well, we will know who is right in the morning." The first man yawned and started for his hut.

By the time the woman screamed again, all the men were back in their dwellings, arms tightly wrapped around their wives, their breathing settling into the regular rhythm of sleep.

In the isolated hut, dimly lit by a single oil lamp, the monk knelt before his wife. The woman's eyes were shut tight to keep out the burning sweat which had formed pools in the hollows above her cheekbones. The insides of her partially opened thighs were stained with blood. The monk's lips moved in prayer as he made the sign of the cross over his wife's swollen abdomen. Then she screamed again.

It was midmorning before the infant finally struggled from its mother's body. Its tiny hands were balled into fists and the vessels in its forehead swelled as it fought for breath. Blood now was spattered over most of the woman's body and her face looked as if it were made of yellow parchment.

"You have given me a girl," the monk tried to keep his voice from cracking. "A beautiful girl, just like her mother."

The woman rolled her head from side to side and the man took hold of both of her cold hands. Then the woman shuddered and tried to speak.

"I have given her your name, Joanna." The monk brought his lips close to her ear, but she could no longer hear him. The prediction of the peasant was correct. Her bones had been too small.

Except for furtive glances, the peasants kept their eyes fixed on the ground as the monk approached their village. His eyes were hollow, the skin of his face pulled tightly over the cheek bones, giving him the appearance of a man twice his thirty years. A bundle wrapped in a blood-stained blanket nestled in his arms and from the way he carried this bundle, the peasants knew the monk's wife was dead, knew that he came to them for the milk of one of their women. All of his learning, all of his holiness could not save his infant without their help.

He stood before the peasants, his eyes filled with pleading, the bundle in his outstretched hands. Not a word had been spoken. Then the widow Gerberta, whose child still nursed, stepped forward and took the bundle from the man.

Tears filling his eyes, the monk made the holy sign over the baby. "She is all that is left to me of the one who, second only to our Savior, I loved best," he murmured. He reached out and pulled back the blanket, exposing the sleep-softened features of the infant. "Care for

her so that I may yet possess a portion of the one who was dearer than
life to me.''

The woman dumbly nodded.

"I have work I must yet do among the heathens." He touched the
crucifix that hung at his waist. "I go east, but will return for the child
before the passage of two hands of years." He raised both hands, fingers spread wide. He asked the woman her name and she answered in
a hoarse whisper, her face a flaming scarlet. Then he extracted from
deep within his garments a worn silver coin, twice as broad across as
his thumb, and handed it to her. The gathered peasants gasped at the
sight of the coin and whispered to one another. It was the first silver
coin ever seen in that village.

"Two hands of years, Gerberta, and I will return for my
daughter. A child born of such a mother," the monk turned his head
for a moment toward the hut at the edge of the woods, toward a grave
on the far side of the hut he had dug that morning, "a child born of
such a one can bring nothing but the Almighty's blessings on this village."

To this Gerberta nodded and her nods were taken up by others
until all the peasants moved their heads up and down, up and down in
the manner of cattle knotted together in a storm.

One of Joanna's earliest memories was of lying in bed with Gerberta,
her face pressed into the warm soft place in the woman's neck, her
arms and legs tangled with those of Magda, her foster sister. Yet a
sharper image was of the clearing at the edge of the woods where her
real mother lay. Over the years, the women of the village, without
realizing what they did, had converted the rude gravesite into a
shrine.

When the grave was still fresh, the hare-lipped widow had gone
to it to tell the English woman about her son who could not swallow.
"Another hand of days without food and he will die," she whispered
to the mound. "If I lose my son, holy woman," tears dripped from the
woman's eyes, "then who shall care for me when I am too old for
work?" A great vomit of blood and phlegm restored the woman's son
that very night and the women of the village credited the mother of the
infant Joanna with this miracle.

Others visited the grave to beg favors, to gain purification when
their bones were wracked with ague, to complain about beatings from
their husbands. Green from the careful planting of grasses, ringed
with stones carefully rubbed smooth, decorated with wild flowers, the

grave had become a pleasant place where Joanna passed many happy days playing with Magda while Gerberta sat to one side and watched.

Yet at this gravesite Joanna experienced her first taste of bitterness. In deep winter, scarcely in her seventh year of life, she lay in the smoke-darkened hut choked with catarrh, her chest aching with each breath. All night she had been sobbing out "mother, mother," as she clutched at Gerberta, trying to draw warmth and strength from the powerful body. At the first light, Gerberta had wrapped her in a cowhide apron and then carried her coughing and wheezing across the frozen fields to the grave.

"This is your mother, Joanna." The woman lowered the child so that her fevered face was no more than half a span from the snow-covered mound. "You must not call me mother, Joanna, only her." She lay her broad hand with its broken nails and swollen knuckles on a patch of ground swept clear of snow by the wind. Joanna began to whimper. "You are of holy blood, child." The woman's hands stroked the mound with a gentleness it had never shown a lover. "My blood is tinged with cow dung; I am nothing but a peasant. You must never forget this."

For a terrible moment, half delirious with fever, Joanna was certain Gerberta was going to leave her there in the burning cold. Using all the strength of her six years, she gripped the thick muscles of the woman's arm. "Don't leave me here with her." Phlegm filled the child's throat and the rest of her words were lost in gasps and bubbles.

"Say that she is your mother and I only Gerberta," she ordered the glazed-eyed girl. And Joanna forced the required words through coughs and gasps.

In the village, the children of widows called the men who visited their mothers "father," but Joanna never did when Rolf the Woodcutter appeared for his night-long embrace. Not that the little girl did not delight in the huge man's sharp smell, booming voice and bellowing laughter. Not that she did not experience a sense of special safety as his bulk filled their bed to overflowing. But he was always just Rolf. Father was someone out there. How many times had Rolf and Gerberta pointed to the east as they spoke of the English monk. Father was out there doing the tasks given to him by God's own son Christ, and if she were patient and kept her thoughts fixed on him, in time he would return. Father was real, a man who walked and talked like Rolf, who embraced women as did Rolf, who would bring her marvelous presents; but he was not a peasant.

"Ten of me would not equal one such as your father." With a broad grin, exposing his blackish, broken teeth, Rolf would hold up both hands, fingers extended. "The heads of every man in the village are not enough to contain his learning." At this he would deliver a slap to the side of his head, and this invariably made Gerberta laugh. Then her laughter would trail off, leaving her lips softened into a smile as certain thoughts filled her mind.

How could she have been so fortunate to have gained custody of a holy man's child? As a widow with a fatherless infant, she had been among the least of the village women. But ever since that day she was among the most important. The carefully hidden silver coin made her by far the richest. With her eyes fixed on the embers of the fire, she savored thoughts she had never revealed, not even to her closest friends.

When the monk returns from his Christian tasks among the heathens of the east, exhausted by ten year's work, was it not possible that he might rest for a time in her hut? And if as he rested in the hut she gained the chance to give him the comforts all men must have, was it not possible that he might choose to remain for a season? And if one season, why not two? If two seasons, why not three? She knew secrets about pleasing a man for which she had paid Clari, the village crone, a fine fox skin. Given the chance to massage his feet and hands with certain herbs, given the chance to hold the holy man between her powerful thighs until he was spent, given the chance to seek out the tight places in his neck and shoulders with her strong fingers, given the chance to envelope the man with all her womanliness, was it not possible that he might decide to grow old with her in her hut, watching his daughter grow to a woman?

Had there never been a word mentioned of the holy monk, had her mother's grave lain neglected, Joanna would have known she was different from the other children. While boys and girls not yet six years of age joined their parents clearing fields of rocks and stumps, planting, hoeing, and harvesting, she remained with Gerberta, encouraged to play or hunt for colored pebbles along the banks of the river. When other girls were expected to fetch water, gather wood and scrape skins to be used as clothing, Joanna was invited to join the older women and share in their conversation. Those few times when she broke through her shyness and spoke, all would listen.

Any doubts that she was set apart from the other children were put to rest when the hare-lipped widow's son laid hands upon her. Not that it was uncommon for boys whose beards were beginning to grow to catch younger girls out in the fields and attempt to explore their hairless genitals with fingers and mouths. No amount of threats or beatings eliminated these assaults. Those whose daughters were victims made the threats and administered the beatings, while the rest of the villagers just shrugged and mumbled that such things had always been. Yet when the hare-lipped woman's son tore off Joanna's shift, leaving imprints of his sooty fingers on her thighs and abdomen and traces of saliva in her vagina, the villagers rose up as if one man.

Joanna had scarcely fallen into Gerberta's arms, gasping between sobs what had been done to her, before the peasants poured out of their huts, knives and cudgels tightly gripped in their hands. Like hornets stirred from their nest, the villagers swarmed toward the hare-lipped widow's hut. Her son having escaped to the woods, the widow was beaten senseless.

Never was a stag hunted with such precision as was that widow's son. The men fanned out in a great semicircle while the women and boys acted as beaters. All afternoon calls echoed back and forth in the forest. Then just after sunset came the shout that the boy had been found.

Exactly what was done to that boy who had assaulted her, Joanna never learned. She never asked. The villagers never volunteered any information. The hare-lipped widow was alone in her hut. Then one day she was gone.

"Should I be sorry for him?" Joanna asked her mother, brushing some fallen leaves from the head of the mound. "He hurt me and frightened me." She leaned close, softening her voice until it was a whisper. The wind sighed as it blew through the remnants of the hut in which she had been born. "He was cruel and deserved to be punished." Tears filled her eyes, spilled over, then fell one by one on the ground. She pressed her ear against the ground, but the only sound was the sighing wind. "If I pray for him, will you take care of him?" Suddenly sobs wrenched themselves from her chest. "I should have said nothing." She reached out and embraced the mound. "I should have said nothing."

A break in the clouds released a shaft of sunlight that enveloped the grave. A stone flecked with mica picked up a portion of the light spattering a rainbow of colors. "Like the glass beads old Clari spreads on the ground," Joanna thought. The crone read the future by studying the patterns of the beads thrown on the ground.

Joanna eased her fingers into the splashes of color and held them steady as she examined them. Although no dirtier than any other villager's, for no one ever washed, she was ashamed of their grime, of the black half-moons under their ragged nails. Using a piece of broken stick, her hands still held in the splashes of colored light, she dug at the encrusted dirt. Then, tightening her throat so that her voice imitated the hollow and breathy sound of old Clari, Joanna questioned the pattern of colored light. "Will my father come in this many years?" She dropped the bit of stick and spread the fingers of both hands, holding them steady. "It has already been this many years." She curled down the little finger and ring finger of her left hand, leaving the rest extended. The pattern of colored light shifted a little and Joanna picked up the stick and dug at the black half-moons again. "I will whiten my hands for his return," she murmured. Gerberta had once told her a story about a princess whose hands were soft and white.

"How should he know me if I am like all the others of the village?" Her voice grew stronger. An image of a man taller, deeper in the chest, and broader in the shoulders than any man of the village formed in Joanna's mind. He wore a cloak made of red fox skins that reached almost to the ground and a cross fashioned of polished black sticks hung from a chain encircling his neck. "He will enter the village calling out my name." Her voice now was full. "Joanna! Joanna!" Her eyes sparkled and she swallowed several times. "He will go to each hut, pull back the entrance skin and ask if I am inside." In the muscles of her arms and thighs she could feel the excitement that would come to the village at the monk's return — how the women would hide their faces in their hands, how the men with their hands knotted together would shift from foot to foot. "And then he will come to my hut." Her words softened into thoughts. "Gerberta will ask who is there. And he will say: I, the Angle monk, the father of Joanna — I have come for my daughter..."

A drifting cloud cut off the shaft of light and the pattern of colors was gone. A gust of east wind made her shudder.

Then like an ooze of mud, doubt entered her mind.

"Will he take me with him, or again leave me in the village for two more hands of years?" She tightened her fists. "I will go with him, even if he must go back to his task among the heathens. I will make his fire and cook for him. And Gerberta will come with us." She hesitated. "But not Rolf." An image of the woodcutter entering the hut, his face inflamed with drink, forcing Gerberta down onto the bed while she and Magda cowered in a corner, rose in her mind. "No, not Rolf. Only I and Gerberta. I will show him how strong I have become. I will learn to help him with his tasks among the heathens." She imagined gray twisted men and women with parts of their fingers missing, their noses and chins rotted like the wandering leper who had been stoned away from the village. Terrible as were the heathens of the east, she would go there with her father. She would learn from him the mysteries of being a Christian. Although she, as well as all the village, was Christian, she was uncertain what that meant. She had never seen a priest, never been inside a church. Priests and churches were for a city like Engelheim, not for nameless villages. Any traces of religion found in the villages were in the hands of crones like Clari. These old women mixed fragments of Christian prayer together with their colored beads, bits of bone amulets, and potions. And although it was to Christ that they most often directed their supplications, they also turned to other gods, gods known to the mothers of their mothers before the missionaries came carrying their crosses and gourds of sacred water: The gods of the rivers, of the trees, of the stones; gods of the sun, the wind and the rain.

"I will go with him where the most terrible heathens live!" Joanna formed each word carefully, directing them towards her mother's mound. A gust of wind swirled dead leaves and bits of bark against her face. "And I will not wait for him to come to my hut, but I will meet him as soon as he enters the village."

A leaf fragment was blown into her eye, burned for several moments, then was washed away by tears. "But what if he should not be able to find this village?" The thought, like a wind-whipped branch, cracked against her brain. "He cannot have forgotten that it is in the district of Engelheim." To the little girl, it was incomprehensible that anyone, once knowing of the great city about which she had been told so much, yet had never seen, could have forgotten its location. "He will come to the district and start searching." Yet there were many villages in the district, each with its cluster of huts, its cattle pen, its dung heap and grain pit, each indistinguishable from the other. Joanna had once been taken to the village to the north whose smoke could be seen rising over the hill when the air was still. That village, except for the unfamiliar faces of its people, could have been her own. "He will search the district, but how will he know this is the village?" A wave of panic forced the child to her feet. Her eyes darted about wildly. "Two hands of years will have caused him to forget the fireoak." She turned to the east where the great oak, stripped of its bark by a bolt of lightning long before she was born, still stood. "If he has forgotten the fireoak, then how shall he know that this is the village where I live?" A picture of the huge monk, his hand shading his eyes, flashed through her mind — she could see his black cross hanging from its chain. Then like steam bursting from a roasting gourd, the word "cross" exploded from her lips.

As if the monk at that very moment were approaching the village, Joanna tore away two large sticks of what was left of the hut in which she had been born and started fashioning a cross. "I will put crosses all around the village." Her words were orders to her hands. "I will put up so many that my father will see them and know this is the place where his daughter lives."

By nightfall, four crosses were firmly planted; by week's end, more than a score. And the villagers, learning of Joanna's actions, grew fearful, lowered their eyes when she approached, and left gifts of flat bread and hard cheese at the entrance to her hut.

For the next three years, with the regularity of the rooster crying out its daybreak greeting, Joanna tended her crosses. Each day, no matter how severe the weather, she circled the village, raising those felled by the wind, replacing rotted ties of vine; and more and more she was observed standing on high places facing east, her eyes shaded with her hands. But the advent of her tenth birthday did not bring the monk back to the village. As the first snow of winter started to fall, which marked this as the season of her birth, Joanna, her face filled with questions, turned to Gerberta, but the woman gruffly waved the child away, pretending to be busy.

Yet when they were finally in bed together and Magda, her foster sister, was asleep, Gerberta could no longer ignore the girl's desperation. Hiding as well as she could her own disappointment, she pulled her close. "Where your father stays in the east, it may not yet have begun to snow." Her words felt like dust as they passed through her lips. "Or he may have been delayed doing a holy work for Christ, God's son." She forced her voice to sound more certain. "You would not want your father to leave the heathens before his tasks are done, would you, Joanna?" The girl swallowed several times, then slowly shook her head.

"Rolf comes tomorrow evening. We will wait for Rolf."

But there was no need for them to wait. Scarcely had they settled into sleep — the wood in the firepit still smoked — when the skin guarding the door was thrust aside and Rolf entered, snow powdering his head and shoulders, his beard caked with ice. He still carried his ax tightly gripped in his hand. It was this that woke Gerberta in an instant. In all the years he had visited her, the woodcutter had never entered the hut with his ax.

"Get dressed!" the man ordered in a voice so strained that had Gerberta not seen his face in the glow of the embers she would have taken him for a stranger. Knowing immediately that some terrible danger threatened, she shook the girls awake. Then came the rest of his words. "They are burning the village to the east." The woodcutter was unable to control a sob.

"You saw this?" Gerberta tried to control her voice as her hands sought frantically for the leather strips used as foot wrappings.

"I did not see — I met one of the villagers, burned and half-naked. I could do nothing for him."

"Brigands!" The word hissed from the woman's lips as she secured the foot wrappings with thongs.

Rolf shook his head. "Soldiers of the Great Charles — with weapons." Gerberta sucked in her breath. Athough he had died almost 15 years ago, bands of his soldiers still denied that Charlemagne was dead.

"You have warned the others?" Gerberta asked.

Rolf slowly shook his head. "First you and the two girls are safely hidden, then I warn the village." Gerberta stared at the man for several moments, then nodded.

As the man, woman, and two children moved through the sleeping village the dogs started barking, but recognizing them they soon returned to skulking and growling at one another. In the fields away from the protection of the huts, gusts of wind blew sharp bits of ice against their faces and Magda began whimpering. With a backhand blow, Rolf knocked the child half senseless, then tossed her over his shoulder like a sack of charcoal. Joanna fought to catch her breath. The cold air caused stinging needles of ice to form in her nostrils, and her chest ached. From the moment she had been roughly shaken awake by Gerberta to this moment, Joanna had not spoken. The sight of Rolf standing in the hut with steam rising from his leather garments, his terrible ax gripped in his hand, warned her as forcefully as had his vicious slap administered to Magda that this was no time for words. But after they entered the forest she looked up at the woodsman and tightened her grip on his hand as a wordless question.

"It is not safe in the village, my little Joanna." Rolf's mouth was dry and he had difficulty forming words. "There is too much danger. We must hide until it is over." Joanna tightened her grip again — what was the danger? But Rolf shook his head and increased their pace.

Joanna's eyes were glazed with exhaustion when they reached a cave that Rolf had discovered years ago while hunting a fox. Its entrance was hidden by a tangle of vegetation and its condition inside showed that it had never been inhabited by other than forest creatures.

"Here you will be safe enough." Rolf squatted before the woman and two girls. "No one in our village knows of this place so how should soldiers unfamiliar with the district discover it?" The flickering flame of the tiny oil lamp he had lit distorted his features. "Unless I come for you, do not leave this cave for three days and three nights." He held up three charcoal-blackened fingers and stared hard at Gerberta. "And no whimpers!" He shifted his eyes to Magda who tried to stifle her sobs by biting on her fist. "They may pass close to this cave — you may hear them crashing through the underbrush. You may even smell them. But no whimpers, no sound." Magda forced her head to nod. "Do you know what they will do if they find you?" Rolf brought his face close to the child so that his acrid breath was upon her. "They will roast you and eat you." She hunched down until her face was pressed flat against her thighs. The man rose. "No sound. No fires. You have leaves and rushes enough to keep you warm." Then, without another word, after handing Gerberta his ax which had been given to him by his father, and after throwing down his wallet which contained bread and cheese, he was gone.

The first traces of light showed on the eastern horizon as Rolf emerged from the woods. Had his eyes been fresh and clear instead of burned by the cold and dulled with fatigue, he might have detected movement as he glanced toward the brightening sky. Even with his fatigued eyes, had he concentrated his vision on the place where the river curved south, he almost certainly would have seen glints of morning light reflected from breastplates and helmets. But his eyes were now on the village. As he approached its outskirts, he began to shout and within moments all the dogs were aroused — barking, yelping and growling. He continued to shout as he entered the village, not words, just sounds, and this stirred the dogs into such a frenzy that even though they knew him, some tried to bite and had to be fended off with kicks.

Rolf grew hoarse with shouting before all the villagers dragged themselves from their huts. Many, believing their sleep disturbed by a wandering madman, emerged carrying staffs. Dragging a man from under his blanket, away from the warmth of his wife into the icy winter air, deserved a sound beating. But seeing that it was Rolf, they turned their resentment on the dogs, and within moments they were racing in every direction, yelping in pain. Forcing his voice through his burning throat, Rolf told the villagers what he had learned from the dying man.

"You saw the burned village?"

"You saw the soldiers of the Great Charles?"

The woodcutter impatiently shook his head. "I saw the man mortally burned. The flesh of his face and hands seared away. I heard his words. That was enough. The soldiers of the Great Charles have come from the east and will surely descend upon this village."

The villagers looked at one another, some shrugging, several exposing their broken teeth in foolish grins.

"He did not see the village."

"He did not see the soldiers."

Old Clari pointed a crooked finger at Rolf and said, "If we flee our huts and hide in the woods in this bitter weather and then there should be no soldiers of the Great Charles..." The villagers shifted uneasily. "In the woods some of our children will die — the cattle left behind will burst their udders. Do you want us to murder our children, our cattle?"

Rolf hesitated. As they said he had not seen the village, had not seen the soldiers. Was it possible the one he encountered in the woods was a madman who in his madness had fallen into a fire pit?

"The man I met said it was done by soldiers of the Great Charles." There was a hesitant ring in Rolf's voice. Some of the villagers hacked up phlegm and spat on the ground in the direction of the woodcutter, but respecting his size and strength, not too close. A few, muttering curses, started back to their huts. But then a boy who slept in a lean-to next to the cattle pen came running into the village shouting: "Soldiers! Soldiers!"

As if the cowherd's words were firebrands raining down upon the village, the women scattered to their huts to gather up children and possessions. While some of the men rushed to the grain pit, the rest raced toward the cattle pen. But those who had gone for the cattle came running back within moments, flecks of saliva on their lips and beards, their eyes glazed with fear.

"The soldiers are slaughtering our cattle!" gasped the peasant who lived in the hut next to Gerberta as Rolf grabbed hold of his sleeve. "They carry crossbows, swords and spears." The man's voice broke. Then he plunged into his hut and a moment later emerged armed with a scythe, his wife following, carrying her baby in the crook of one arm, the other arm cradling a wooden plowshare. Men and women similarly armed emerged from other huts, all but the youngest children clutching some sort of weapon: sharpened sticks, shards of broken crockery, flint knives.

The villagers gathered around Rolf, their actions and their desperate looks declaring him to be their leader.

A formation of soldiers, swords unsheathed, came over the rise to the east. As they approached, they beat the hafts of their swords against their shields, creating a terrifying din. Another formation suddenly appeared to the north. The peasants, as if driven by a gust of wind, shifted in a mass toward the southeast, as Rolf with single-word commands and powerful shoves tried to form the men into a defensive semicircle.

Screams echoed from the village as several who had taken too long to gather their possessions were trapped by the soldiers and skewered.

Several men abandoned their families and fled for the woods. They were stopped just short of the sheltering trees by a group of soldiers. Grunting like hog butchers, the soldiers hacked away with their heavy two-handed swords. There was no escape. The rest of the village, numbering perhaps one hundred and fifty adults and children, formed a cluster in the stubble-choked field. The men and stronger women, in the manner of wild cattle defending against attacks of wolves, stood shoulder to shoulder in a close outer circle, brandishing their weapons. The rest of the women and the older children formed an inner circle while the several very old ones and all the younger children huddled, sobbing and coughing, in the middle. Although the soldiers facing this cluster of peasants numbered no more than fifty, with their superior weapons, armor, and years of marauding they could have been an army of five hundred. The villagers had no chance.

At times during the course of the morning, when the wind shifted in their direction, the woman and two young girls hidden in the cave could hear sounds coming from the village. Dulled by the distance and blended with the murmur of the forest, these sounds were difficult to distinguish. They might have been the bleating of a distant flock of sheep or the bark of young foxes or the cry of hunting hawks.

"Have the soldiers come to our village?" Joanna whispered after a high-pitched cry that was almost human. Until now, Joanna had lain motionless without speaking, her eyes staring dully into the recesses of the cave. Gerberta stroked the girl's damp forehead with her calloused hand. Magda, who had spent her energy controlling sobs, was fast asleep, her tight fist still in her mouth. Knowing the answer to her question, Joanna pressed her cheeks against Gerberta's soft, warm neck. But here in the cave there were no safe feelings to be found.

"Will Rolf return to us?" How could Gerberta know the answer? Yet the question filled Joanna's throat and had to be asked.

"If he is alive, he will return." Gerberta's voice had grown old. "If he is alive..." Joanna shuddered. "But if he does not return, my little Joanna, you still have Gerberta who will care for you as I promised the holy monk, your father." She hesitated. "It cannot be much longer before he returns to claim his daughter."

With a show of strength remarkable for a child, greater than she realized she possessed, Joanna thrust herself away from the woman, bruising both of them on the wall of the cave.

"He will never come!" The words she had swallowed back again and again now forced themselves out, rasping her throat.

"Rolf?" Gerberta rubbed her bruised arm, more surprised than angered at Joanna's rough action.

"Not Rolf, my father, you ignorant peasant." She wanted to hit Gerberta, to kick her, to bite and spit at her. "My father will never come; he has forgotten." Dry sobs tore at her chest. Then, reaching out for the woman, who pulled her close, she started crying, not caring if the soldiers heard. "My father will not come," she gasped through her sobs. "Rolf will not come. No one will come."

Gerberta cradled the girl and rocked her. Several times she tried to form comforting words, but afraid that sobs, not words, would come, she kept her lips tightly pressed together. Those sounds from the village... How long would it take for Rolf to warn the villagers and return? He had left before sunrise and now it was past midday. Strong as he was, he was no match for trained soldiers. He would never return. The monk would never return. No longer young when he left, now ten years gone... What should be done with the child? What would happen to Magda who has never known a father other than Rolf? What would happen to Gerberta? Unable to prevent it, the woman groaned, and Joanna, now calm, gently stroked her forehead.

A stillness lay over the village as the woman, leading the two young girls, cautiously emerged from the forest. They had remained hidden in the cave the three days ordered by Rolf. Once, during the second day, when a snow-laden branch cracked deep in the forest, they experienced a surge of hope — Rolf somehow had escaped and was coming. Then, nothing, only the sigh of the wind seeking a way through the tangle of bushes and trees.

Hesitating in the shadow cast by the forest, Gerberta tightened her grip on the children's hands as she squinted against the glare of the snow. She examined the wide field that lay between her and the distant cluster of huts. There was no movement. Forcing herself to remain where she was — her feet wanted to run toward that village to see, to know — she strained her eyes through the glare toward the frozen river to the east, then shifted her vision to the fields beyond the village, to the low hills to the north. Still no movement. A wave of irrational hope made her heart speed up. The huts had not been burned, not one. Marauding soldiers always burned the villages they attacked. Yet why this stillness? Why no curls of smoke? Why no movements in the cattle pen?

Placing one foot carefully in front of the other, the woman drew out of the shadows. Her body tense, ready to turn and run back into the woods, she kept checking the wide fields that stretched out before her. Her grip on the girls' hands made them wince. They walked stiffly, like day-old colts. Suddenly Gerberta stopped. Just to the south of the village she could see a large, snow-covered mound. There had never been any mound in the fields bordering the village. She moved in its direction — fifty, a hundred paces, then stopped. It was not yet sharp in her vision, but she knew. No need to approach any closer. No need for the children's sleep to be tortured for all their years by the sight of what lay beneath the light covering of snow.

Circling the village in the opposite direction, refusing to answer the questions etched into the faces of the two children, swinging wide away from the grain pit and the cattle pen, Gerberta headed toward the city of Engelheim. And only when the village was a dot in the distance did they stop to rest.

Seeing Magda still biting on her fist, her chin pressed down against her chest, Gerberta pulled the child tight against her breast. "Cry, my little girl. No more need for silence." The woman felt a pain deep within as if she had been beaten with a club. "Cry, my daughter. Rolf does not care. Cry, cry." But the child remained silent.

"Will we die?" Joanna's eyes met those of the woman. "Will the soldiers do to us what they did to them?" She, too, knew what lay under that blanket of snow.

"The soldiers are gone. They came, did what soldiers always do, and are gone. Why should they return? There are so many other villages waiting for them. No, Joanna, Christ has protected us. We will not die."

"Why only us?" Joanna's eyes held steady, forcing the woman to shift hers away. "Did Christ hate the others — the little children?"

Gerberta passed her hand over her face as if to brush away dust or a bit of spider web. "I am a peasant. How should I know the answer to your questions about God's Son? He does what He does." She shrugged. "He is Christ, the most powerful One, so we must worship Him. We have no choice."

"I will not worship anyone who allows soldiers to kill little children," Joanna whispered. "I hate Christ." Gerberta shook her head. "I hate Christ," Joanna said again. "I hate Him! I hate Him!" Her voice rose to a scream. She looked around wildly, picked up a broken branch and slashed it against a rock. "If I see Him, I will kill Him!"

Gerberta tore the stick away from the girl and clapped her hand tightly over her mouth.

"You must not say such things. If He should hear you, He will throw down a bolt of fire and kill you. Tell Him you are sorry, Joanna. Tell Him you are sorry or the three of us may be dead before dark."

The fear that showed on the woman's face and the terrible urgency of her voice made the child tremble. What if there should be a bolt of fire? Freeing herself of the hand pressed over her mouth, Joanna forced words of contrition from her lips.

"Louder!" Gerberta ordered.

The girl said them again.

"Once more!"

She repeated them a third time. But inside she knew she did not mean them. Given the chance, she would kill the Christ who allowed the murder of children.

II

THE CONVENT

*I*t was late afternoon when they came within sight of the city of Engelheim. Only once before had Gerberta traveled to this place. Her belly already showing the child which grew within, she had walked the distance with the man who was to be her husband. Both of them had grown pale as they saw its towering walls, its turrets, and heard its noise. But they had determined to visit the priest, determined to have their names put down in the sacred records of the church, determined to gain the holy blessings before their child was born. Neither she nor her husband was able to utter a word when they first came into the presence of the priest. But there had been scores like these two peasants that came from the many nameless villages of the district over the years. So, the priest knew the purpose of their visit and asked them no more than their names before intoning the sacrament of marriage.

Forcing her face to appear calm, walking in an almost jaunty fashion, Gerberta herded the two girls toward the city. She had forgotten the violence of the noise — shouts, curses, cartwheels on rough stones, cattle sounds, pounding hammers — and the stench. The foulest hut of the village baked ripe by the summer heat could not match the smells of the city. Still she pretended to be at ease.

"I will take you to the priest, Joanna. Your father is a holy monk and the priest will know what to do."

Stunned by all that had happened and confused by the size and sounds of the city, Joanna remained silent.

"After I take you to the priest, I will go with Magda to a village where I have a brother. If he is alive, he will take us into his hut. Perhaps in that village I will find a husband."

She pulled the two girls close to her as they passed through the gate. The guards spat at them and laughed. Once past the gate Gerberta spoke again. "You are not a peasant, Joanna." The girl whimpered. "The child of such a father cannot waste her life in a peasant village." Joanna tried to form words, but they would not come, only whimpers and occasional sobs as they picked their way through the narrow, twisting, garbage choked streets. She continued to whimper as they ducked the low hanging eaves of decaying buildings and dodged gyrating urchins swinging sticks. But the whimpers and sobs were choked back as they entered the open space in the center of the city where the church stood.

Joanna's mouth fell open as she stared at the church — a structure larger and more magnificent than even those palaces and castles about which she had dreamed; points tipped with crosses rising toward the sky, an entrance guarded by twin iron-studded doors wide enough to allow a yoke of oxen to enter; red-as-sunset windows whose glass was formed in the shape of stars and crosses. It was too big, too threatening. Joanna tried to hold back, but Gerberta tightened her grip and dragged the girl forward.

The priest snarled at Gerberta as, stuttering and choking on her words, she tried to tell him of Joanna's history. He had grown gray and evil-tempered in the service of Christ and suffered from indigestion. He glared at the woman, from time to time bringing a perfumed cloth to his nose. These filthy peasants crawled like lice into his church in a never-ending stream of begging. Was it not enough that he said the mass morning and evening — five times on the sabbath? Was it not enough that he offered all the sacraments without pay? Would these foul-smelling, groveling creatures never cease to plague him? Would they still gather, beseeching, endlessly beseeching, the day he was lowered into the ground? And here was another peasant, offering one of her spawn to the service of the church. Ignorant, stubborn, unteachable, they were worse than useless. Avoiding her pleading eyes, he gestured roughly in the direction of the open doors.

Suddenly, as all the horrors of the past days clotted into a hot mass in her chest and then caught fire, Gerberta's head snapped up, her body straightened, her eyes began to glow like those of a wolf, and she stepped toward the priest. Never had a peasant looked at him this way.

"She is the child of a holy man, a monk!" Gerberta's voice rose from deep inside her body, words distinct. "She is no peasant, to be turned out into the streets, not by a priest, not even by a bishop. I was charged by her father, an English monk, to care for her until he returned. But now all who live in my village are murdered by soldiers of the Great Charles. Who but a priest should I turn to with such a child as this?''

The priest had to listen. Had he not heard rumors years ago of a man who stayed for a time in the district, then traveled east to carry the words of Christ to those Saxons still heathen? He examined the features of the two children. One showed the broad nose, coarse lips and low forehead of a peasant. The other: a high forehead, wide-spaced eyes, a straight nose not unlike his own, and the ears were small and fine. Yet the priest still hesitated. Desperate peasants, eager to give their children to those who will feed and care for them, would say anything. Who could believe the words of a peasant? Even those few who made confession lied.

"Do you have proof of what you say, woman?" The priest's manner was unpleasant, his voice grating.

Forcing her head up, her shoulders straight, keeping her eyes fixed on the priest's face, Gerberta eased her hand inside her tunic. "You ask for proof, holy priest." Her nails tore open a pouch sewn tight years earlier. "If it is proof that you demand, take this." She placed the silver coin given to her by the monk in the priest's hand. "It was the gift of her father when he left her in my arms to share the milk of my breasts. Is a coin of such a value sufficient proof, holy priest?"

In all his years in the service of the church, the priest had never known a peasant to possess other than worn copper grochens. He rang the coin against the stone floor. Its sound was true. He moved toward the open doorway to examine its inscription. It was unlike any coin he had ever seen. The face stamped on its surface and the markings were strange. Turning toward the woman whose waist was hugged tight by the two girls, he opened his arms wide and Gerberta, with a wrench, tore Joanna free and shoved her roughly forward.

Not a day passed during the weeks Joanna spent with the priest that she did not wish for the release of death. The scowling man with his terrible black robe and deep-set piercing eyes terrified her. She froze at his touch, unable to control her whimpering, yet afraid not to submit to his morning and evening embrace. When he taught her prayers, the words choked up inside of her. Then when he shouted and threatened, she was unable to control the tears, and he mocked her.

Alone in her room, finer than any place she could have imagined when living in the village, she longed for the tiny, smoke-filled hut. She trembled constantly as if from cold, although servants of the priest ensured a fresh supply of heated bricks in the hearth.

Had she wanted to escape, the door to her room was always left unbolted and it was only a short passage out to the street through the rear of the church. Yet Joanna made no attempt to leave. Where would she go? The thought of those foul, twisting streets with their noise and confusion made her shudder. But in the half-sleep before sleeping, she would slip out of the window, then like a falcon catch the rising air currents and fly away to the village and her mother's grave. But even in her dreams she was careful not to see what lay in the cattle pen and what made up the large, snow-covered mound.

Often when Joanna was asleep, the priest would carefully open the door to her room and enter. The light from the oil lamp in the passageway was just enough to reveal her features. The fear she always showed in his presence was gone. There was no trembling when he reached out to touch her. Was this child's arrival in the city of Engelheim a good omen? Or was it the work of the Devil? Her fine features and the silver coin proved she was no spawn of peasants. But how many, while claiming to be monks, did black deeds — celebrating the mass at midnight with toads and human blood? Was the English monk a holy man or one of Satan's minions? Was this child of sainted blood bringing with her Christ's blessings? Or was her blood corrupt, carrying a vile contagion?

Again and again the priest visited the child's room late at night, trying to gain from her sleeping features an answer to who she was. Always there was the risk of the anti-Christ, who might be disguised in any of a thousand forms. Those lips perhaps too thin. Did this reveal cruelty? And those wide-spaced eyes, they were not quite human. But that high forehead, seen only on those of gentle birth. This child, from her forehead alone, might have been taken for one as noble as the abbess Brita, and were not the small ears and the texture of the hair also the same?

"I will speak to the baroness," the priest muttered, turning away from Joanna's room. It was always "the baroness" when he referred to the abbess even though the baron, her husband, had been dead since the last years of the Great Charles. "I will tell her of this child of the English monk and together we will devise a method to test if she be innocent or demon."

Except for the bishop who rarely visited Engelheim, the only person the priest both respected and feared was the widow of the baron, now abbess. The priest used to stammer and tremble in the presence of the baron, and a portion of this trepidation had transferred to his widow, modified during the course of the years by a deep respect for her wisdom.

Childless and not yet nineteen when her husband was killed in the service of Charlemagne, she rejected several offers of marriage from powerful noblemen, lived alone for a time in the castle left to her, then took the veil. She still lived in the castle, now a convent, and her authority over its lands, which extended to the very walls of Engelheim and included more than a dozen villages, was as great as her husband's had been. Yet unlike the baron, whose only interest was the practice of arms, the abbess developed a profound reverence for learning. Taught in the first years of her widowhood the mysteries of reading and writing, in time she accumulated a library of more than a hundred volumes, whose study became the central purpose of her life.

The castle, now a convent, loomed over the snow-choked fields north of Engelheim, its turrets entwined with ribbons of mist so that their rough stone construction one moment was visible, the next indistinct, its narrow elongated apertures, once used by archers, now sealed shut by lengths of black oak so that seen from the distance they resembled scab-encrusted wounds, its tall donjon, caked with winter ice, showing near its summit the ravages of an old fire.

Had they confronted a wild boar, dripping foam from its curved brown tusks, Joanna could not have shown more fear than she did when they emerged from a copse of trees and saw the castle. Her body stiffened and she pushed backwards, pressing tight against the priest who had held her locked between his thighs on the broad-backed mare ever since they left the city gate. All through childhood she had dreamed of being taken to terrible places, places inhabited by those tortured souls Clari and the other old women of her village whispered about to one another. This dark stone structure was more terrible than any in her most tortured dreams. Inside those walls there awaited huge horned men armed with clubs and axes, men more vicious than the soldiers of the Great Charles. Of this she was certain. They would take her. She began to gasp. She couldn't let herself think of what might happen next. She had heard about the eaters of human flesh. She had been told about the ones called Jews who celebrated their feasts with the blood of virgins. She fought her thoughts. This terrible priest with his insane eyes was going to offer her as a victim to those inside that stone place. Why else was he taking her there? What other reason? Judging herself as good as dead, she shut her eyes and sagged forward, forcing the priest to tighten his arm around her. And in this way they traveled the remaining distance.

But when they entered the iron gates guarding the castle and she opened her eyes, instead of horned men with matted beards carrying weapons, there were women. Everywhere. One of them, a broad-shouldered woman with slate-gray hair, took her from the priest. Joanna wound her arms around the woman's neck and made her first sound since leaving the city. She sobbed. She would not be killed.

The woman carried the sobbing child into the great hall where the abbess waited.

"Is the child sick?" the abbess demanded of the priest, her high-arched eyebrows drawing together into a frown. At the base of her throat the woman could feel anger rising, ready to spill out if she learned that the priest brought contagion from the city.

"The child is not sick, baroness." The priest struggled to meet the eyes of the woman, but he could not. "My servants tell me the child eats, she shows no rash, and her eyes are clear. No, she is not sick."

"Open her tunic," the abbess ordered the woman holding Joanna. She obeyed instantly. There was no rash and, except for some flea bites which could be found on almost everyone, her skin was clear.

"Let me see your eyes, child," the abbess ordered, but in a voice which was not harsh. Joanna lifted her head, rubbed at her tears with the back of her hand, then forced the lids open. The abbess took a step closer, first examining the eyes, then the other features. *No, this is no peasant child*, she thought. Scarcely aware of what she was doing, she stroked Joanna's forehead. There was something pleasing, almost familiar about the girl's appearance. "Why are you crying, child? Did he beat you?" She gestured toward the priest. Joanna shook her head. "Then why do you cry?"

"I thought I would be killed and eaten." The other nuns caught their breaths and started to murmur. "I thought the priest was taking me to this place as punishment — to give me over to soldiers, to men. I was frightened."

The abbess's lips pressed together and curved down at the corners, giving her face a hard, almost cruel look. Whenever puzzled or deep in thought, her features took on this expression. The other nuns suppressed their murmurs, and the priest stood motionless, waiting. "Afraid of being killed and eaten." The abbess formed her words slowly and carefully. "By men."

With a sudden gesture at the priest, she ordered the man to turn away. Then she had the child stripped so that she might be carefully examined for any special marks or the remnants of a tail. The child's body was free of any suspicious warts or moles. No liquid could be pressed from her breasts that were just beginning to form, and her loins, except for the first vestiges of womanly hair, were without blemish. During the course of this examination Joanna did not make a sound.

"What is the appearance of those men who will eat children?" the abbess asked after Joanna had been reclothed and placed on a high stool. "Have you seen such men?"

"In dreams," Joanna answered in a whisper so soft all had to strain to hear. "They were soldiers carrying clubs and axes."

"Their appearance? What was their appearance?"

"Big. With dark faces and horns."

"Horns!" The abbess sucked in her breath and the other nuns shifted uneasily. "Were there also tails, child? Scaly tails like those of large rats."

Joanna shook her head.

"Perhaps they were hidden under their clothing," the woman murmured. "With such dreams as this, she must be tested. You were quite right," she turned to the priest. "She must be tested."

Two days earlier the priest had spent an entire morning conferring with the abbess. The woman's first reaction had been annoyance when he told her that the child he spoke of had been delivered to his church by a peasant. But as the priest detailed the information given to him by Gerberta, the abbess showed increasing interest. "An English monk," she had said, stroking her chin, a gesture learned from the scribe who taught her in the first years of her widowhood. "Perhaps of the school of the Venerable Bede."

"One of his pupils!" The priest's face had flushed as he thought about the English scholar who in his closing years was honored as the greatest theologian in all of Christendom, whose reputation had only increased since his death so that now most viewed him as a saint.

"Of the Venerable Bede's school, perhaps." The abbess had looked down her nose at the man, making no effort to hide her contempt. "But if your monk was one of his *pupils*, he must have been approaching his hundredth year when he fathered the child. This may have been common in the days of the Patriarchs, but if there still are those who plant the seeds of men in the bellies of their wives at such an age, I have never heard of them."

Every time he had visited the castle since its conversion to convent, whether to give confession or to gain advice from the abbess, the priest had been shamed. His ignorance showed on him as soot shows on a charcoal burner. "I had forgotten that the sainted scholar has been dead so many years," the priest mumbled. "I think of him so often — he lives in my mind." The woman made a snuffling sound. Had the matter not been so pressing, the priest might have offered some excuse and withdrawn to hide his embarrassment. But the chance that this child might be an agent sent by Satan to destroy the Church was of such importance that he steeled himself to the woman.

"I would have had her smothered while she slept when I first realized the peril this child might bring to our mother Church. Why take chances with a matter of such grave consequences? Yet how could I destroy the child of a monk if he truly be a holy man? A monk who carries Christ's teachings among the heathens. Within the body of this child, whose features are as fine as those of any I have ever seen, there may dwell the soul of a saint: father a monk, mother dying at her birth, she may have been sent to deliver us the Lord's blessing, to help prepare us for the end of the thousand years when He will again walk among us. Yet if she should prove to be the anti-Christ..." He had reached out his hand as if to take hold of the abbess's sleeve, then quickly pulled it back. "Is there a test, baroness? You have studied so many learned books." He had motioned toward the shelves of heavy volumes, each wrapped carefully in soft doeskin.

"You were right, holy father," she was saying now. "We must devise a test. There is no calculating the damage the anti-Christ might inflict by gaining entrance to the Church. Satan never rests, always scheming to secure more souls." The woman's voice had risen. "And as you so wisely observed, the anti-Christ can appear even as a fine-featured female child." The priest colored. It was the first time she had ever flattered him. "Yes, holy father, we must devise a test."

Turning away from the priest, the abbess had walked to the far end of the great reception hall, now used as a chapel, and knelt on the flagstone floor before a cross as large as the one on which God's son had been nailed. Formed of unplaned planks, portions of it had been rubbed smooth by thousands of hands in supplication. As she had done several times a day for all the years since becoming a nun, the abbess had embraced the cross with both arms, pressing her forehead and lips against the wood.

The priest had watched the woman. Her passion somehow made him uneasy. He had wondered if he too should pray. After several minutes, the abbess had risen from her knees and beckoned the priest close. "I have devised a test," she said. "With God's help, I have devised a test." Her face was deeply colored and her eyes glistened. "Go to the hangman. For a copper grochen or two he will sell you a length of rope with which a man has been hanged. Then have one of your servants fashion this rope into a doll. Make sure that the doll is well-made, with bits of brightly colored cloth for clothing. We will offer the child a choice between this doll and a cross given to me by a wandering holy man formed of the wood of a tree whose branches once sheltered Christ Jesus as he rested at the shores of Galilee."

The priest had grinned and picked excitedly at the broad leather belt which cinched his tunic. "No child of Satan can take the cross; not a cross such as the one given you by that holy man," the priest's voice rang with respect. "If she is from the Underworld she will embrace the doll."

"If she chooses the cross I will take her," the abbess had said, forming each word carefully. "But if it is the doll which is her choice, I will have her bound and you will carry her deep into the woods and leave her there in the snow for the wolves."

"I, baroness?" The color had drained from the priest's cheeks. "It is a thing better done by one of my servants."

"If this Joanna is of Satan's realm, no mere servant has the strength to destroy her. She will bewitch them and escape. Only a consecrated priest has the power to resist such a one and even he must stuff his ears with wax and keep his eyes averted. If the cross, she is mine to keep. The doll, yours to destroy."

Despite being stripped naked and examined by this strange woman whose high, white forehead gleamed in the rush lights of the cavernous room, Joanna was not upset. Even the attempts to squeeze liquid from her breasts, although painful, did not cause her undue concern. Among women she would be safe, of this she was certain.

She looked around. High on the walls were banners and pennants so darkened by smoke that their markings were indistinct. Behind her was a wide hearth on which glowed a bed of embers, curls of smoke rising from it to the hole in the ceiling. At the far end of the room stood a cross taller than a man, held in place by a length of heavy chain. On each side of the great cross there was a smaller one, each with the cross piece affixed at an angle. She wondered about that. Her eyes continued their search. Except for the stool on which she sat and the rough wood table where she had lain for the examination, the room was empty of furniture.

"I have brought a present for you, Joanna." The strange woman approached, carrying a tray covered by a cloth. "The holy father tells me you have obeyed, so I wish to offer you a reward." The child heard the words as if they came from a distance. What need for presents? It was enough to be safe among these women.

Her thoughts drifted; the flickering of the rush lights and the echoes of the high-ceilinged room caused this. Forcing her eyes to focus she looked at the face of the waiting woman. Her lips were curled down. When Gerberta gave her presents, her body had quivered with excitement. This strange woman stood perfectly still.

Of course it was the doll she wanted. It was carefully made with polished beads for eyes, hair that looked almost real, and such gay clothing, like a bride. The cross was so dark except for its fittings of polished silver. It looked cold. What need had she for a cross? Her thoughts turned for a moment to the scores of crosses she had fashioned and placed around her village. It felt so long ago. So much had happened.

She reached out to the tray, hesitated, then withdrew her hand. Everyone was so still. The nuns standing in the shadows might have been of stone. The priest, his head hunched between his shoulders, was motionless, lips pulled back from his teeth as if in a snarl. What a strange way to give a present?

Easing down from the stool, Joanna bent forward and stared at the two objects on the tray. If they all watched with such intense concern which present she chose, it must be of some importance. The doll could lie next to her in her bed at night. She could pretend it was a little sister. And what comfort would she gain from a cross? She raised her eyes and they rested on the rows of carefully shelved volumes. She knew what they were from the one that lay on the altar of the church. *Why do they offer a girl of two hands of years such a choice?* No girl in her village ever had a doll as carefully made. *But I am not in my village.* Soundlessly, her lips formed the words. *I am with nuns, where there are holy books filled with the wisdom of the world. What sort of place is this for dolls!* She reached out her hand and firmly grasped the cross.

A shudder went through the waiting abbess. Several of the nuns gasped — they had scarcely allowed themselves to breathe. The priest crept toward the door. "You are certain of your choice, Joanna?" the abbess asked. The girl nodded. "Once more I ask, you are certain?" As an answer Joanna pressed the cross against her breast as she had seen the priest do during mass.

With a sudden convulsive movement, the abbess threw the doll into the hearth and within moments tongues of flame sprang up. Clutching the cross so that its edges dug into her chest, Joanna watched, her eyes opened unnaturally wide. As the flames worked into the fibers of the rope body, the doll writhed like the ferret she had once seen chased into a fire pit by a pack of dogs. Tears filled her eyes and she forced back the rising sobs. Had she chosen the doll, would she too have been cast into the hearth? The flames died down. She stared at the charred remains of the doll and it turned into the snow-covered mound in the field outside the village. She felt herself sinking, the stone floor rising up. A pair of hands caught her. Strong hands which lifted her and brought her close to a warm safe place where she could bury her eyes and lips. The skin of this warm place was so smooth. Smoother than any she had ever known. And the woman's hair so fine with the faint scent of flowers. She felt a hand stroking her hands, still tightly holding the cross.

"Keep it with you always, Joanna. Let it guide you. That simple piece of wood speaks to us of the anguish our Savior suffered for our sake. In it there is a greater wisdom than is contained in all the volumes of Christendom. If you will listen, Joanna, you will gain more from that cross in a single day than ever you can gain from all the sisters of this convent in a score of years." Gently easing the child's face away from where it was pressed, the abbess kissed her full on the lips. Then one by one the other nuns approached, each offering a like kiss.

"She is come among us to be our little sister." The abbess addressed the nuns in a soft voice, a voice very different from the one she had used when the priest was present. "I charge each of you to care for her, to teach her the ways of this convent, never to turn her away when she comes to you, but to comfort her, for she is still a child. And I give you permission to share with her the mysteries." The gathered nuns nodded and murmured their assent.

"My name, Joanna, is Brita." The abbess gently placed the girl back down on the stone floor. "Although I am mother superior and must be obeyed in all things, I am called by my name just like any other." Then each nun in turn said her name. Names were important. Among the first words Joanna had learned to say were the names of the villagers. But so many of these nun's names were strange and the echoing sounds and flickering flames of the rush lights made her head swim.

"I am Hildegard, little sister." Soft eyes, voices like singing nightbirds.

"My name is Lorelei, Joanna." Breaths like fresh-picked berries.

"I am called Griselda, little child." Garments that rustled as they moved.

"I am named Elva, dear sister." Hands carefully stroking her cheeks and hair.

"Adelaide is my name." And there were others.

But in their black robes their pale faces blended one into the other; only three stayed fixed in her mind: the abbess Brita; Marla, the woman who had taken her from the priest and in whose arms she had experienced that first rush of comfort; and Wilma, whose harsh-featured face with its sunken cheeks and hairy chin stood out in cruel contrast to the others — Wilma, whose lips were rough and had a bitter taste when her kiss was given.

"Let us offer our thanks to the Almighty Father who has given us this precious gift." The abbess drew Joanna close as she sank to her knees. The other nuns knelt in unison. Only Joanna remained standing, then she too knelt. The roughness of the stone floor hurt her knees. Curls of frigid air made her shiver. Yet these discomforts did not seem to matter to the praying women. Sounds like sighs formed into words came from their lips. She strained to listen, to understand. Her legs grew numb and the cold found its way into her chest and throat. But then Joanna stretched out her arms. It seemed that splashes of light rose up and gathered about the great cross suspended by its thick chain on the far wall of the room. She stared at the cross. It burned as had the rope doll in its bride's dress. It writhed on the wall as had the doll on its bed of embers. "The cross burns," Joanna whispered. The abbess opened her glazed eyes. "It will set fire to the convent." Joanna pointed with a trembling finger. "See how brightly it burns."

"It burns, Joanna, but will not set this castle on fire. Oh, how terribly it burns as did the flesh of our Savior pierced with nails, seared by the merciless sun. It burns to scorch the minds of men, to cleanse our thoughts of sin. It burns. Oh, how terribly it burns. And you too can see these flames, Joanna, sainted child of a holy monk and a blessed suffering mother. You too can see these flames."

The cross which had gained her admission to the convent lying next to her on the thick woolen man that served for a bed, Joanna stared up at the stone ceiling. The heavy sheepskin, tenderly placed over her by Marla, into whose care she had been given, kept her warmer than she had ever been in winter, even those special times when she had snuggled down between sleeping Rolf and Gerberta.

Had Gerberta found her brother alive? Joanna wondered. Would there be a man in that village who would be her husband? What was it that the abbess had said as they took their supper? Something about those who lived in the convent being married to Christ. She had said so many things. And there had been so many questions. What had she learned from the peasants about her father and mother? What were their names? But she did not know their names. Until that moment when the abbess asked, she had not thought of them as having names.

More than any other thing, the abbess wanted to know the details of her Mother's suffering. "The cries, so terrible they woke the village." The abbess had repeated Joanna's words as all the other nuns listened. "Dying without seeing her only child. Suffering as so many women have suffered. Yet although she died, her child lived." The abbess had reached out and stroked her hair. "Yet how much more terrible it must be to live while the one to whom your womb has given life is put to death. Do you know of the Holy Mother Mary, Joanna?"

"Christ's mother?" Joanna had learned of this woman from Gerberta and had learned to pray to her from the priest.

"Do you know of this woman's suffering?" the abbess had asked. Joanna had hesitated, then shook her head. "Among all the women of the world, only Mary did not share conception with a man. Within her womb lay God's own Son conceived by her alone. Of all lives only this life was not tainted by carnal sin. No man gained his pleasure within that sainted woman's loins. Her body remained undefiled while the One who was to be our Savior nestled within. And then her child, grown to a man, nailed to the cross. How much more she must have suffered than any other woman before or since, knowing that the One being tortured was hers alone." The faces of all the listening nuns showed lines of pain and compassion. "And who was it that betrayed Christ? Was it a woman? Who were they that came for him in the garden? Were they women? And the Sanhedrin, that collection of Pharisees and Sudducees who tried him, in that body did there sit a single woman? And who was it that condemned him? Was Pontius Pilate a man or a woman? And was there even one among that band of boisterous Roman soldiers who tortured Him who might have been taken for a woman?" All the nuns had stopped eating as they listened to the abbess, whose speech had taken on a certain rhythm. "And, Joanna, of all who claim to love Him, who was there on that hill as He underwent this crucifixion — who was there to comfort Him? Only women. Only women."

The abbess had stared at Joanna for some time. Finally she said in a choked voice, "Although there are always a few whose lives are saintly, most of the cruelty of this world is brought about by men. It is women who bind the wounds inflicted by their weapons."

Although trembling with exhaustion, Joanna could not force her eyelids to close. Had it been only that morning she had left the city of

Engelheim, the priest's iron arm holding her locked between his thighs as the snorting mare, steam rising from its mouth and nose, made its way carefully along the icy path? She tried to remember the details of the man's features, but like rotted bark they fell away as she reached out for them. Had she ever dared to look directly at the scowling face when his eyes were on her? Only those few times late at night when, sensing his presence, she forced herself awake and opened her eyes a thin slit. He had the power to destroy her — a priest who with a single gesture could send her crashing into Hell. She had felt as helpless as a trussed kid. But unlike the kid she would not beg and bleat. When trapped in the field by the son of the hare-lipped woman, she never begged, never allowed a tear to escape until he was gone. And that terrible night when Rolf took them to the cave, she never made a sound. Even if her chest burst from the pressure she would have held back the sound.

Joanna eased down under the heavy sheepskin. Marla had stroked her hair after she had covered her. She could still feel traces of the woman's touch. Here, within these thick walls among these nuns she would be safe. Safe. Just as she slipped into sleep Joanna sighed. It was not the sound of a child of ten, but that of a woman.

For Joanna, the first months in the convent slipped by almost unnoticed. She had entered when crusted snow lay on the ground, the tall donjon glistening with a coat of ice. Now it was spring. Each day blended one into the other.

Although there was so much to learn, every day's routine was the same. Awakened while it was still dark. Hurried to the chapel by two or three women whose faces were puffed with sleep. Kneeling on the cold stone floor in prayer. Breaking the fast before sunrise in silence. Then the rest of the morning devoted to learning the mysteries of reading, the art of putting down words on parchment. Each nun, taking a turn, offered this instruction. Yet it was always in the presence of the abbess, who, although engaged in study of her own, would offer comment and correction from time to time. The light meal taken by each in her room alone ended the activities of the morning. Then there was time for solitary meditation.

In the afternoon the nuns tended to the many tasks of the convent. Everyone worked, even the abbess: scrubbing, sewing, preparing food for the evening meal, making repairs. Some went into the forest for fuel, never less than three together; one always armed with a crossbow and iron-tipped arrows, the others carrying double-headed axes.

For the tasks of the convent, Joanna needed very little instruction. Her hands were quick. She was strong from peasant life. The afternoon's work done, the nuns gathered for the evening meal which was a celebration. The women laughed, told stories, often sang. After the evening meal came another period of silent thought and meditation, each in her separate room. And to close the day, a long session of prayer in the chapel, interspersed with short readings from the Gospels. Within a week of her arrival, Joanna flowed with the rhythm of the convent.

One morning as she left her bed she found a stain of blood on her thighs. Once in the springtime as she watched a bull mounting a bellowing cow out in the fields, Gerberta told her about the blood that would come: "It is this blood which makes you a woman, Joanna," she had said softly, although there was no one near. "It is a thing not to be revealed to any man. For them, blood is wounds and death. They fear their blood. But for us," the woman's eyes crinkled, "this blood means life. Only for us." Then she told the child what she must do when it first appeared.

Joanna bathed her hands in the pool of warm sunlight. They were so clean — scrubbed with fine sand morning and evening, their nails expertly trimmed by Marla. So different from the hands of the child of the village. "Whose hands are these?" she asked them. The little girl of the village, despite her intention not to have the stained hands of a peasant, had never been able to keep them clean.

"What has happened to Joanna?" she asked softly. She saw an image of the ragged child wearing a peasant's tunic, her hair matted and infested with lice. "Killed by the soldiers of the Great Charles and thrown onto the heap with the others," she answered. She shuddered at the thought of the close, foul-smelling hut, of the vermin which rustled in its thatch day and night, of the men and women of the village with their open sores, their rotted teeth, with breath so foul that you must force yourself not to breathe when they spoke to you. Her eyes lit on a curled, dry leaf resting on the sheepskin cover — how did this ugly leaf find its way into her room? With a sudden, angry gesture she swept it off the bed then ground it into dust with the heel of her sandal. "Don't come," she whispered to the remnants of the leaf. "Don't come." It was spring, and Gerberta had promised to visit in the spring. But now all of that was dead and gone. "Don't come," she said again.

How the abbess became aware of her entrance into womanhood, Joanna never learned. She had been careful to hide all traces of the red stain, had secretly washed the cloths with her own hands, had not whispered a word to Marla with whom she shared other secrets.

"I was scarcely older than you, Joanna, when my father had me betrothed to the baron who was to be my husband. It was when I was first touched with the blood stain of womanhood." The abbess had taken the girl to walk with her in the wide meadow that adjoined the convent. It was the first time Joanna had been allowed outside its thick stone walls. "You did not come among us of your own will, child, as did the others. When they entered this convent, they declared that Christ would be their husband, that no man would have carnal knowledge of them. Now that you are becoming a woman, how will you be betrothed, Joanna? To God, or to man?"

Joanna removed her sandals. The new grass felt soft under her feet. The sounds of the birds singing their spring songs made her head grow light.

"I do not want your answer now, Joanna," the abbess continued. "A matter of such importance demands time for its consideration. I will ask you again at the end of summer."

From the day she had been accepted into the convent to this, Joanna had never considered any life other than that of a nun. That she was presented with a choice, that the abbess suggested the alternative, however remote, that she might form a union with a man, made her uneasy.

"I will never leave the convent, never!" she burst out. "I do not need until the end of summer to give my answer."

"Not another word." The abbess raised her hand. "I order you to consider what your life shall be when you meditate in the morning and in the evening. I order you to do this each day until I ask the question again." The corners of the woman's lips were turned down, her eyebrows tightened together, giving her features an expression not seen since the priest last stood in her presence. She forced her raised hand not to reach out and stroke the child's hair, not to soothe away the distress that made her lips tremble.

Those trembling lips might have once been her own. She had not dared to look at her father when he ordered her betrothed. She stood dumb in his presence. For her, there had been no choice. That there could be a way other than the one declared by her father never entered into her thinking. Had the twice-widowed baron not been killed, she would still be his slave — called wife — if not herself dead. Every time that iron-haired man entered her room reeking of sweat and of the

blood of slaughtered game, she had silently cursed her father. Afraid
to resist her husband's savage advances, she submitted, but each time
it was a form of rape. A remnant of his command had returned his helmet, breastplate, sword, and spurs to her. Stinking of death, their eyes
glazed, their clothing spattered with dried blood, these soldiers told
her how he had been hacked to pieces by a band of Swedish fighting
men. Then they demanded their reward for returning his effects to
her. When one of the soldiers tried to pull open her tunic, she realized
for the first time there was a choice other than submitting. Snatching
up the sword, she struck the man across his face and broke his nose.
Her servants came with weapons and drove the ragged soldiers away.

For several nights after, she had fought her way out of sleep just
to go down to the great hall where her husband's effects lay. Each
time she stared for long minutes at the helmet stained with his blood
around the visor, at the breastplate showing a deep indentation where
a sword had struck. He would never enter her room again, his eyes
reddened with drink, his oak-hard hands spreading her thighs as if to
split her open. Now she was in command. Not if it cost her her life
would she ever submit again. She ordered the sword broken, the helmet, breastplate and spurs beaten into metal lumps. The servants, although they glanced uneasily at one another, obeyed.

If there was one gift she could give to this child, who was so much
like herself as she had once been, it was the gift of choice.

For Joanna, that spring day spent in the field outside the walls of
the convent, although cloudless, felt dark and gray. What a cruel
thing the abbess had ordered — that she consider betrothal to a man:
lie in some filthy hut pinioned beneath a grunting hairy creature. She
had heard Rolf at his work — soft cries like those of a trapped fawn
coming from Gerberta. She had seen other men of the village mounting their women in the fields, on the banks of the river. And always it
was the woman who was pinioned, always the harsh grunting sound
from the man.

Kneeling with the other nuns that evening, she was unable to
hear the words of the Gospels. Her mind was filled with images of
swollen-bellied women forced into this condition by men who made
the animal sounds. She had watched women giving birth, as had all
the girls of the village. Had heard the screams, had seen the blood.
Had felt a churning and a tearing inside as the women writhed and
struggled. Had seen the bloody newborn features flattened, as often
dead as alive. And the abbess had ordered her to consider being
betrothed to a man!

Filtering into her hearing through her dark thoughts came the words: "He died for us," spoken by one of the nuns. "He gave His life upon the cross that we might be saved." Sobs choked the woman. Joanna stared at the huge cross and the remembered images of the tortured women of her village, like wind-blown dust, were swept away into the hidden recesses of her mind. She continued to stare at the cross: "They took the Christ and nailed Him hands and feet." Her eyes began to swim, but she forced them to remain open: "Placed a crown of thorns on His head and thrust the point of a spear in His side, drawing forth blood and lymph." A figure whose features resembled those of the priest, now hung from the cross. His mouth was open as if to scream, but there was no sound. Tears of red from his thorn-torn forehead ran down his cheeks — his wide-open eyes shifting wildly from side to side showed his terror.

She thought of the priest's silent presence in her room late at night. Dragged from her sleep she had not dared to move. And here he was, nailed to the wood so that he could not move. Joanna smiled as she allowed her lids to close over her burning eyes. What was it she had said to Gerberta as they rested in the field, their dead village a speck in the distance: that He allows soldiers to kill little children, that she would kill Him if she ever saw Him. That she hated Him. If any of the nuns ever suspected these thoughts, she would be driven from the convent. Or nailed up in His place. Yet why should these women care if a man be nailed to the cross? Those few times they spoke of men, it was always with a warning sound in their voices. Why do the nuns worship this man? Why worship God the Father? Why worship any man? Why submit to confession from the priest? And the bishop of Rome, called pope, who decides all the questions, the one spoken of in reverential whispers — why obey him? She opened her eyes to the huge cross. Shadows shaped like crouching beasts clung to the wall on both sides of it.

A choice, the abbess had given her a choice: betrothed to God or to man. Christ's bride as was every nun or the wife of a lusting soldier or peasant. Yet if it all was not already decided for her, if she must make a decision, then was it not possible that there were choices other than those two?

"Other choices..."

As the voices of the nuns rising in supplication echoed through the great stone chamber, so these words echoed in her mind. It was as if Joanna had discovered a secret cave, concealed by a tangle of vegetation as had been the cave in which they hid, dark, deep, perhaps inhabited by hungry beasts. But a place in which she might discover... What?

She joined the others in their prayers of supplication, lifting her voice as she called upon Christ to hear her. If those women gained even the slightest suspicion of what she had been thinking...

Wilma, the ugly one, was staring at her. Wilma, who alone of all the nuns she had carefully avoided. Was it only because of the bristles which clung to the woman's pointed chin, like those of an old man? Was it her hooked nose? Could the woman read her thoughts? She tried to see into the woman's dark hollow eyes. Joanna never failed to respond to the woman's touch of greeting when they passed in the convent, but she always lowered her eyes so as not to see the other's face. Had she dared, she would have asked Marla if Wilma was a witch. Wilma's features were so much like those of the old woman who lived apart from the other peasants in the village to the north of her village. She had seen this creature once, when she travelled there with Gerberta: long curved fingernails, hands and face almost black. If clothed in the filthy rags of that woman, Wilma might be mistaken for her. And now Wilma was staring at her. How much of her thoughts did that woman know? Would she betray her to the others?

"Your voice rang like a silver bell when you said Christ's name, little sister," Wilma spoke softly. Joanna had remained kneeling when the prayers were over, waiting for the woman to approach. "And your face, Joanna, like a seraphim who kneels before God's throne." The woman reached out her claw-like hands and stroked her hair. "So soft, so soft," she murmured. "Such gentleness and beauty you have brought to us, dear sister."

Joanna raised her eyes to the woman's face. It was bent close so that no more than the space of two hands separated them. Ugly. Yes, it was ugly. A face that those who saw witches would see as that of a witch. But the eyes were soft. Hollow and dark, but when you looked deep into them and allowed yourself to see, they were soft. And the woman's mouth was tender. All she had seen before were thin lips pressed together to hide the broken teeth.

"Will you allow me to walk with you to your room, Joanna?" There was a break in the woman's voice. Without a word, Joanna placed her hand in the other's hand — claw-like in appearance, yet it was warm and trembled slightly. And hand in hand they walked out of the chapel nodding and smiling at the other nuns they passed.

Her body perfectly still, her eyes fixed on the narrow portion of night sky visible through the window of her room, Joanna fought off sleep. Wilma had covered her and comforted her with as much tenderness as Marla. And she had responded to the woman's caresses as she responded to those of Marla. Strange. All of her ugliness made no difference. How many times when the wind howled across the fields had she held tight to Gerberta as the face of the witch who lived in the village to the north rose up in her mind? Yet instead of turning away in terror she had approached the old woman when she first saw her. Is it that you give power to that which you fear when you turn away? Gain power when you move toward it?

Those times the priest visited the convent to take confession, Joanna had hidden. Only when she heard his mare clatter across the courtyard as he headed back to the city did she dare show herself again. That she would always hate the man she was certain. But why hide from him? The next time he came, she determined she would walk past him, would let him see how little she feared him. Joanna smiled at the sharp points of light fixed unmoving in the night sky. Perhaps the day would come, not yet for awhile, but in time, when the priest would have cause to fear her!

Yet the next time the priest came to the convent, like a contagion terror swept through the ranks of the nuns. His face the color of slate, his breathing labored, his hands knotting and unknotting, the man spoke the moment he dismounted from his sweat-lathered mare.

"An army of soldiers is moving toward the city from the south." His voice rattled in his throat.

"An army?" The abbess pushed her way through the nuns gathered close around the man. "You mean a company, holy father, do you not — fifty or a hundred, such as that which destroyed Joanna's village."

"Would to God it was as you say, baroness." The priest, scarcely aware of his actions, took hold of the woman's arms. "But it is an army, perhaps as many as a thousand. And mounted, baroness. More than half are mounted!"

"Holy Mother of God protect us," said the abbess as her face drained of color. A number of the nuns started praying, their hands clutching at their beads. The rest stood frozen. This was the first time any had seen the abbess show fear. "You say they are to the south of the city?" the abbess asked. The priest nodded. "How far?"

"No more than a half day's journey. Unless they delay for some reason, they will have patrols approaching the walls of the city by late afternoon. And then how should they not send a detachment of soldiers to this convent?" The priest swallowed and frowned. "You must leave this place at once. At once!" He raised his voice. "With God's help they will not breach the walls of the city — within the walls of the city you will be safe."

The abbess turned away from the priest and struggled to steady her trembling lips and clear away the film in her eyes that obscured her vision. If the soldiers reached the convent they would loot it, then burn it. Against a handful of brigands, the nuns might make a defense. Most of them had gained sufficient skill with the crossbow. The walls of the convent were of stone and cauldrons of boiling pitch poured from the turrets would discourage those who tried to scale them. But against trained soldiers fully armed and mounted...

Her face set in a scowl, her eyes narrowed into slits, she turned back to the priest. "We will go to the city. With your permission, we will stay in the church." The priest nodded. "But so that we have sufficient protection from the lecherous vermin who inhabit your city, we go not as nuns, but as monks. And we go armed." With that the abbess barked a series of orders at the women: they were to cut their hair, then shave their pates in the way of the tonsure. The lower portions of their faces were to be covered with cloths as was the custom of those who had taken the vow of silence. Their bosoms were to be tightly bound, their tunics cinched with rope and each woman was to arm herself with the weapon with which she was most familiar — all to carry knives secreted in their sleeves.

Several of the nuns, not yet recovered from the shock of the priest's intelligence, hesitated after the orders were given. As if, by their hesitation, they were transformed into the enemy, the abbess rushed at them with a shriek, striking at their arms and shoulders with her fists. "Are you dumb cattle to be yet standing here?" she shouted. "Are you sows whose pleasure it is to be speared, then butchered?" Saliva flecked her lips. She shoved the women in the direction of the entranceway. "Must I get a whip and herd you!" The abbess had never shown such rage before and the nuns cowered under her onslaught. But the woman's passion jolted them into understanding and within moments they were scrambling after the others to complete her orders.

For Joanna the word soldiers brought back all the terror of that first night in the cave with the animal sounds coming from the direction of the village. Her throat felt as if it were choked with needles of ice. Within her skull powerful thumbs pressed against her eyeballs. When Marla took her by the hand she was scarcely aware of it as she was scarcely aware of what was being done to her as her hair was sheared away with a sharp knife.

"Put bits of cloth between her gums and lips to give her face a coarse appearance," Wilma suggested.

"Darken her eyebrows." Both women were now working on her.

"You are a boy, Joanna," the hatchet-faced woman said as she wrapped strips of leather in a criss-cross fashion around her legs. "You are too young to have the tonsure and to have your mouth concealed because of the vow of silence. So you must be careful to walk like a boy. We do not want anything to happen to you, precious little sister. Marla and I will always be close to you and both of us are skilled with the crossbow."

The sun stood directly overhead as the nuns streamed out of the convent, swords girdled around their waists, crossbows or double-headed axes in their hands; each burdened with a pack containing books and other treasures. But many of the volumes had been left behind, along with most of the cloth and foodstuffs of the convent. The knowledge that before the passing of another day soldiers with blood on their hands, cursing and reeling with drink, might be desecrating the place which had given them so much peace, made the women shudder in spite of the noonday heat.

To the men stationed along the north wall of the city, the appearance of an armed band that was now approaching the gate was cause for wild alarm. Weapons were clashed together, the warning bell struck again and again with an iron hammer, and the shouts of the defending soldiers were taken up by hundreds of others within the city. The best guess had been that the enemy would not arrive until late in the afternoon and and then from the south. Yet here was a patrol approaching from the north. Crossbowmen who had been preparing their steel-tipped shafts in the market square were ordered to the walls by their captains. The great iron-banded doors which secured the gates were swung shut and bolted with heavy beams. Those whose task it was to prepare the boiling pitch lit their fires. And the several knights who lived within the city started marching their retainers in the direction of the gate.

"They are dressed as monks," muttered the sergeant commanding the gate as he strained his eyes through the afternoon haze. He had ordered the crossbowmen already on the walls to prepare their weapons.

"But monks do not travel armed," his corporal, also straining his eyes, replied. "From the way the sunlight reflects, each carries a sword at his waist and all hold weapons in their hands."

"But they are not mounted." The sergeant hesitated to give the order to let fly the shafts. "Only the one who leads them is mounted."

The corporal shaded his eyes with one hand as the other steadied his crossbow. "Unless there is a trick wind, I can take the one who leads them from his horse, I'll wager a copper grochen." He glanced at the sergeant.

"There is no more than two score of them. Let them come closer. Without horses and without armor we can take them all before I can say two paternosters. Let them come closer."

"But if they wear armor beneath their robes?"

"Then we pierce their eyes and throats," the sergeant gruffly answered. "Let them cross the field and I'll wager your copper grochen that I can call which eye my shaft will enter of the one who leads them."

The corporal shrugged and lowered his crossbow.

Suddenly the sergeant sucked in his breath and made the sign of the cross. "It is the priest! The one who leads them is the priest. They are holy monks! And you would have taken him off his horse for a copper grochen." He turned on the corporal, his face blotched with anger. "Sturdy monks to help us defend the city, and you would have killed them."

As the silent company filed through the gates, cheers rose from the defenders along the walls and the knights raised their unsheathed swords in salute. Two score more defenders was not a great number for a city of five thousand, but it was far better to have them within defending the city than without attacking it. Shouts and cheers rained down from the windows of the rickety dwellings as the procession wound its way through the narrow twisting streets. It was as if a battle had already been won with those silent ones in the procession the victors.

The refuse-choked streets darkened by the leaning buildings, some of whose roofs almost touched, brought back to Joanna the terror of the day she entered the city with Gerberta. The odor had been foul enough in winter; now the city was baked by the summer sun and the garbage, dead animals and human waste gave off a stench so powerful that it made her gasp. And all those screaming people — little matter that the noise was cheers, the sound beat into her brain. The convent had been so silent, so filled with peace. As they entered the open square where the church stood, she shuddered and tightened her grip on Wilma's and Marla's hands. She had been so cold during those long days and nights within that church. She had felt so alone.

Still silent, they marched through the great doors into the dark interior illuminated only by splashes of blood-colored light from the windows. But after the doors were shut and secured, the abbess spoke.

"We are safe for the moment." Her voice was brittle, almost harsh. "Yet here in this city, filled as it is with corruption, we must take care not to forget who we are. If needed, we will assist in defense of the walls. At all other times it will be as it was in the convent: instruction and study in the morning, whatever tasks that need be done in the afternoon, prayers after rising and before retiring, and time for thought and meditation noon and evening." She paused as her eyes slowly traveled around the interior of the church. "With your permission, holy father," she turned to the priest, "we will clean this place."

The priest turned his head partially away, then slowly nodded. Except for an occasional sweep by one of his servants, the sanctuary of the church had not been cleaned since a regiment of the Great Charles quartered there together with their horses. The priest had been scarcely aware of its condition, but now with the nuns present, he could smell the sour urine odor, could see the slime coating the walls, the piles of excrement in corners left by dogs and cats that wandered in and out at will.

The women scarcely began their tasks when the alarm bell clanged. Shouts and clashing metal echoed through the city. The nuns looked at the abbess. Several were trembling. "Why do you stop what you are doing?" The abbess made a threatening gesture in their direction. She was so different from that gentle woman of the convent who spoke softly, rarely demanded, never hurried. "If we must work until midnight, this place will be as it was in the convent." Then in a less strident voice she continued. "The walls of the city will hold. With God's help they will hold, and those who defend the city will give a sufficient account of themselves that the enemy will grow discouraged and depart. But for all the time the city is under siege, my sisters, we must live in this place. This is our home. Even if the walls should be breached and it is our fate to die, do we lie in filth for the time that is left to us? It is not the length of our lives that is important, my sisters, but its quality. That is why we are nuns."

South of the city, in the direction from which Joanna had come, beyond the limits of the longest crossbow shot, columns of the enemy soldiers formed. Their appearance at the crest of the rise which fronted the great forest had caused this second alarm. This alarm was not so short-lived as the first when the nuns approached and grew louder each minute until even the iron-throated sergeants could not be heard above the din.

Although only half the number expected — no more than five hundred with less than two hundred mounted — the enemy soldiers still constituted a formidable army. Taking care to remain beyond bowshot, columns marched up and down, holding their shields so that they reflected the rays of the setting sun toward the city. Those who were mounted made a great show of prancing their horses. Peasants, captured in the fields, had been hung on poles above a line of fires. The cries of these slowly roasting men and women were meant to heighten the fear of those within the city. But the cries only hardened the determination of those who lined the walls and silenced the few who might have suggested surrender.

"They are making camp, feasting on cattle which escaped our herdsmen," the priest reported to the abbess on his return from the south wall. His breathing was labored and as he spoke he kept rubbing his chest with his hand. "How we will be able to defend against such a number...." His voice trailed off and he shook his head. "It is God's punishment for the wickedness of this city. We will be destroyed as were Sodom and Gomorrah."

The abbess took hold of the man's hands, a thing she had never believed she could do. "This talk of Sodom and Gomorrah can serve no purpose other than spreading panic, holy father." Her voice sounded soft and contained not a trace of the contempt which had always caused him to cringe. "This city has withstood other onslaughts.

"But not from such an army, baroness, not with so few trained for its defense. Less than three hundred, with no more than half a hundred breastplates and shields amongst them."

"But the walls of the city are high and thick. And it is more costly to attack than defend. If we do not let them scale the walls, we will be safe. They will never breach them." The abbess released the priest's hands. "But if you speak of Sodom and Gomorrah — one such as you who is held in high respect — then those who guard the walls may lose heart." The abbess' eyes bored into those of the priest. "They will take this city only if we fail in our vigilance. One man inside on the parapet along the walls is the equal to three outside on the ground. But let as few as a score of the enemy scale the walls...."

"I will pray that the walls are well defended," said the priest resting his hand on his cross. "And I will say nothing of Sodom or that other place." He turned to walk away, hesitated, then turned back. "But what if they set the city afire with burning arrows? With the houses aflame, how will those on the parapet continue their defense?"

"We will prepare for those arrows. Have them form the street urchins into bands equipped with filled buckets. Station a woman supplied with pails of sand on each roof. Enemy soldiers will burn this city only if we let them.''

Just after sunrise the enemy soldiers started their threatening behavior again. Calculating exactly just how far from the walls they would be safe from the shafts of the most expert crossbowmen, they marched up and down, pounding the hafts of their swords against their shields, shouting in unison, as individual soldiers, from time to time, broke away from the rest to urinate in the direction of the city while making exaggerated gestures with their hands. Four or five times one of the captains of these bands of soldiers, fancying himself a knight, raced toward the city gate with his sword unsheathed shouting challenges for the knights within to come out and risk individual combat. These captains, being well protected with armor and skillful at maneuvering their horses, were able to avoid the shower of crossbow shafts that rained down on them.

Just before noon the enemy soldiers moved backwards part way toward the forest, then lay out in clusters shaded from the heat under blankets stretched between poles.

Although the city had been under siege for almost one full day no one had suffered so much as a scratch and this caused an attitude of celebration to take hold of most of the inhabitants. So far, the presence of the enemy was more an entertainment than anything else, a relief to their lives of hard work and boredom, and they now believed that their walls were high enough, thick enough, and sufficiently well defended so that in time the besiegers would grow discouraged and leave.

"They don't dare approach our walls," the priest greeted the baroness in the most jovial tone of which he was capable. "We have not suffered a single hurt. They must have thought that just showing us their weapons and making their threats would force us into submission. Well, the men of Engelheim will not submit to any threats." The priest started to grin. "One week, no more than two, and they will be gone. If this heat continues it may not take as much as a week. Out there in the fields with little water and enough black flies and mosquitoes, their captains may decide to try some lesser towns to the south or west, towns without the walls and men of Engelheim." As he spoke, the priest patted his belly with one hand while the other hand played with the tassels of the rope which cinched his tunic.

"Only if the earth opens up and swallows them will they disappear as you suggest, holy father," said the abbess in a harsh voice. "I was the wife of a soldier baron, the daughter of a knight whose father before him was a knight. I know enough about the ways of fighting men. The German sun is not hot enough to cause them to retreat. Perhaps the fires of Hell, but not this sun and, if you will forgive me, holy father, they will first drink their own piss before abandoning the siege for lack of water. Perhaps you have forgotten that they lose their manhood if they retreat." She sniffed loudly as her lips curled down and her eyebrows drew tight together. "They are taking our measure, holy father. They are like the man who stretches and yawns before he leaves his bed. They are yawning and stretching, and they will come at us again and again unless the Lord sends down His thunderbolt or the earth opens and they are swallowed down into Satan's realm. Have the urchins keep their pails filled with water, and urge the women on the roofs to stay alert with their buckets of sand."

The priest, emboldened by the abbess being a guest in his church, shrugged at her words as he would never have dared in the convent. Then forcing his face into a weak imitation of a smile, turned and walked away.

The first of the blazing arrows arched over the walls of the city in mid-afternoon. Advancing into the killing zone in units of five, four holding their shields locked together in two tiers, the fifth following in a crouch behind this barrier carrying a bucket of blazing pitch, the units approached the wall, took shelter when possible behind mounds, deflecting as best they could the arrows that showered down, taking an occasional wound in an arm or thigh; then separating the shields for just a moment as the crouching archer let fly his blazing shaft. After several minutes in the killing zone, the unit would slowly retreat, walking backwards until they were in safe territory again. Occasionally a skilled marksman on the walls was able to place his shaft exactly at the moment the shields were opened, thus four or five enemy archers suffered mortal hits in the course of the afternoon. But for the most part this method of attack proved to be highly successful.

The appearance of blazing arrows arching over the walls made the onlookers and loungers retreat in panic into the safety of the narrow streets. At first most of the arrows fell harmless, the enemy units not having approached close enough to the wall. But as the afternoon wore on, a number of the arrows reached the roofs of the houses. These arrows, being short crossbow shafts and holding only a dab of pitch, more often than not were extinguished by the urchins who rushed at them with the same excited cries used when attacking stray cats, although here and there an arrow struck high enough to be out of their reach and by the time the women stationed on the roofs were able to use their buckets of sand, some damage had been done. But just before sunset, realizing that the crossbow shafts were harrassing but not too effective, the enemy captains ordered up their longbow-men. Their shafts carried less distance than those shot from crossbows. Thus the units were forced to approach even closer to the walls and the archers, unable to hold their bows in a crouch, provided a full target as they stood to let fly their arrows. For the little time that separated sunset from dark, unit after unit came up, let fly one or two blazing shafts, then was forced to retreat when the archer was struck down. In this way the enemy lost nine more men, but several houses were set afire within the city and one cluster close to the gate was completely burned.

The tower of flame and smoke drew the nuns out of the church and they pressed tightly together as they watched the crimson reflection in the rapidly darkening sky. Screams echoed from that portion of the city. A alarm bell was frantically pounded with an iron hammer. Since the church stood in the middle of an open space, they were safe from the spreading flames, but rolls of smoke erupting from the narrow streets soon had most of them coughing and gasping. Had there been a wind, much of the southern section of the city would have burned. But as it was, the fire was contained to a cluster of half a hundred dwellings which, after they burned down, provided the rest of the city with a sort of safety zone.

The second day was almost an exact repetition of the first. Columns of the enemy marched up and down shouting and clashing their weapons with challenges from various captains for the knights of the city to come out and fight in single-handed combat.

Just before sunset, the field on which the enemy stood having been cast in partial shadow, a mass of bowmen numbering at least two hundred suddenly advanced into the killing zone and discharged several flights of arrows, then quickly retreated behind the safe line. The suddenness of this movement caught the defenders unprepared — they were in the process of shifting over to the reduced night defense. Eight of the defenders were mortally struck and more than a score of the inhabitants who had moved into the open space behind the walls believing it safe were also struck down. In this operation, not one of the enemy soldiers had been so much as nicked and they set up a great cheer when they saw how successful they had been. Within the walls this sudden shower of arrows gave rise to panic. Those out in the open space rushed for the safety of the narrow streets, several being knocked down and crushed during this frantic retreat. And then the panic swept through the city. The numbers of killed and wounded doubled with each telling. A cat trying to escape a chasing dog and upsetting some crockery was sufficient to rouse an entire section of the city, bringing the men out into the streets armed with whatever weapons they could secure, the women onto the roofs with buckets of sand, the street urchins rushing madly in all directions. So great was the panic in the city that the judgment of the knights and lieutenants in command was affected by it and instead of relieving the soldiers who had been on duty since early morning and were overwhelmed by exhaustion, they kept them on duty, augmenting their numbers by the several score held in reserve. By mid-morning of the next day, as the sun began to turn hot, such was the deteriorated condition of some of the men that one, then another of them fell senseless. It was then that the knight commanding the eastern portion of the south wall sent his lieutenant to the priest, ordering that the armed monks quartered in the church be dispatched to the wall to relieve some of his men.

Perspiration covering his forehead, clearing his throat between every second word, the priest relayed this order to the abbess. "I will go to the knight and tell him you are women," the priest offered. "I will first get his oath that he will keep this secret." As he spoke he kept his eyes averted. "When he learns of your sex he will withdraw his order."

"When he learns of our sex, holy father, we will be forced to barricade this church and defend ourselves from his men."

"But I will get his oath — "

"I have sufficient experience of knights to know the value of their oaths." The abbess flicked an invisible speck of dust from her sleeve as she made a slight sound in her throat. "Let the rabble and the soldiers of this city learn that there are two score women not the possessions of any men living amongst them, and, as I know Christ died for us, I know that they will swill down their pots of mead and beer, then race to this church." As the abbess spoke the priest's shoulders sagged. "I will go to the walls with two-thirds of my women; one-third will remain here in reserve. If through some chance our sex is discovered, we will withdraw and secure ourselves here for as long as necessary."

"What do we do with the child?" Marla took the abbess aside as the other women were rebinding their bosoms, fixing the cloths over their mouths and readying their weapons. The abbess' jaw tightened as she hesitated.

"The child," she murmured, "the child." She looked at Marla her face puzzled. "It will be safer here," she muttered, half to herself, "yet — yet it may be better if she goes with us."

"We will keep her with us at all times." Marla gestured toward Wilma who was rubbing her crossbow string with wax. "Even if it be with our dead bodies, we will protect her." The abbess hesitated another few seconds, then nodded.

During the frantic minutes as the nuns readied themselves for battle inside the church, Joanna, her mind dulled by noise and frenzy, had stood to one side. But as she watched the women rebinding their bosoms, cinching their tunics with leather ropes, testing their bowstrings, giving their swords and daggers a final sharpening, and adjusting their cloths over the lower portions of their faces, her mind began to clear. Then, when Marla came up and handed her a short sword and by this action informed her that she would go with them, her hands and head grew as light as they had those few times when she had been allowed a flask of mead.

Unlike those other times when she had traveled through the twisting narrow streets of the city, for all the minutes it took them to reach the wall, Joanna did not experience so much as a moment of fear or apprehension. Three freshly killed soldiers lay in the open space before the wall and the sight of these three corpses lying in their blood, neglected, their eyes open in a fixed stare, jolted her into an awareness of the reality of her situation.

In absolute silence, their eyes on the abbess for her hand signals, the nuns in their monk's outfits mounted the walls and took their places. Joanna crouched between Marla and Wilma. The place where they crouched was stained with blood and urine which attracted swarms of black flies. It being mid-day, the enemy had retired and except for the cries and groans of several who had been severely wounded and left in the killing zone to die, and the whine of insects, there were no sounds.

Seeing all the nuns securely in place, the knights and lieutenants resting at ease, Joanna inched herself upwards until her eyes reached the level of the aperture through the wall. A haze lay over the field so that it was difficult to see the enemy encampment. But in time, as her eyes got used to the glare, she was able to make out individual soldiers scattered about, some roasting their meat over fire pits, others repairing and sharpening their weapons. In the middle distance they looked no larger than her fingers. Were these the savage ones, the very mention of whose name had caused the faces of the men and women in her village to blanch white? She strained her vision. From the way they lounged about, from their lazy movements, they could have been just peasants from another village. A chance curl of wind brought a murmur of their sounds to her ears — no different than the sounds that came from her village when she rested alongside her mother's grave. Those times, the murmur had soothed her. She had to remind herself

that this was the sound of the terrible enemy. Then the wind shifted
and the murmur was gone. Only the sounds of the buzzing insects
and, from time to time, cries and groans of the wounded down in the
fields. She hunched back down between Marla and Wilma. They
dozed; neither one had closed her eyes during the alarm-ridden night.
The three corpses lay below, their wounds blackened with flies. "How
is it to be dead?" Joanna wondered. She brushed at a fly that was trying to enter her ear. She shifted a little so as to be out of the direct rays
of the sun. Now her eyes rested on the knight in command of this section. He was propped up against the wall directly below, his helmet to
one side, his breastplate unbuckled, his legs sprawled wide so that the
stain of his crotch was clearly visible. His eyes were closed and his
breathing deep and regular, so Joanna made no attempt to hide her
interest. He was ugly, not as Wilma was ugly from irregular features,
but from the deep lines of cruelty etched into his skin around his
mouth and eyes. Even in sleep his face showed a vicious expression.
From time to time dribbles of saliva formed in the corners of his
mouth and his teeth ground together. The abbess had once been married to a man like this. Joanna shuddered and moved her eyes from his
face to his massive chest, then to his arms whose muscles swelled as if
to burst his sleeves. Then she glanced again at the stained crotch, at
the swelling within, and shuddered a second time.

It was still early afternoon and the sun's rays beat down like a heavy
fist. The enemy in tightly massed columns started advancing in the
direction of the gate. No one within the city had expected enemy action in this heat, so that for several minutes after the alarm was given
there were more curses and confusion than effective preparations for
defense. It took a series of vigorous kicks to awaken the captain and
then, befuddled by the glaring sun and the pot of beer he had consumed, he sat rubbing his eyes with his fists asking, "What is happening? What is happening?" as the sergeant who had given the alarm
tried to explain.

The advancing soldiers were halfway across the field, well into
the killing zone, before all the archers were deployed and the banked
fires under the cauldrons of pitch refueled and stirred into flames.
Had the enemy captains ordered their soldiers to advance more quickly they might have reached the base of the wall with scarcely an arrow
shot from the city's defenders. But they were unaware of the conditions within, so they moved slowly, the front rank holding their shields
locked together in double tiers with all their archers following closely.

A hundred paces from the gate the advancing column positioned itself in a semicircle, the locked shields forming a ring of steel, and then lines of archers stood up at command, let fly their shafts, kneeled down to restring their arrows while a second line did the same thing. So thick was the flight of incoming arrows and so deadly the aim that the defenders along the parapet remained crouched, hugging close to the masonry, answering this barrage with only an occasional shaft and that poorly placed. Then the enemy semicircle opened and half a hundred soldiers armed with axes and grapples rushed forward. The commanding knight, having massed archers along the parapet on both sides of the gate in expectation of this assault, at a signal of his hand had them rise in unison and discharge their shafts. Half the attackers were felled before they reached the gates, half of the remainder were pierced as they struggled to affix their grapples, while enemy shafts swept more that a dozen of the defenders from the walls.

A second group of fifty soldiers started advancing toward the gate. But all of these had shields and wore helmets and breastplates, so only ten of them were felled. The rest joined with the remnant whose grapples and axes, embedded in the thick wood of the gate, provided an effective method of mounting to the summit. Holding their shields over their heads, several started climbing upwards, but these were cut down by the massed fire of the defenders. Yet each time these archers on the wall showed themselves, several were certain to be hit by the enemy bowmen protected in the semicircle.

A third unit of fifty advanced to the gate and except for five or six these arrived safely and by pressing close together, holding their shields directly overhead, they formed a canopy of steel which could not be pierced from above. By now the ranks of defending archers on both sides of the gate having been reduced by almost half, the knight ordered a unit of the armed monks to move up and take the place of those who had fallen.

Signaling with her arms, the abbess motioned a dozen of the nuns crouched on the parapet to move in the direction of the gate. The rest were spread out to maintain defense of the east portion of the wall. The dozen nuns who were detached from the rest, now under the direct command of the knight, stood up at his order, let fly their shafts at the enemy soldiers struggling to scale the gates, brought down several of these, but not without losing three of their number to an answering flight of arrows from below.

Additional grapples were swung into place by the soldiers pressed against the gate. As it appeared that a mass attempt to scale was about to be made, the knight ordered the first cauldron of boiling pitch hoisted up. Keeping the cauldron just below the summit of the gate, the knight allowed enemy soldiers to mount until they were within two arms' length of the top with others holding onto axes and grapples immediately below them. Then the cauldron was hoisted another several feet and its contents poured down.

It was as if the boiling black stuff was wind and the soldiers below bits of fluff. The gates were swept clear in a moment with those yet on the ground giving way as their screaming companions fell amongst them. The second cauldron of pitch was ordered hoisted up but was not used, for within moments those who had assaulted the gates retreated back to the protected semicircle. Then for the next half hour each side unleashed flights of arrows at the other. From time to time the protective ring of steel would be breached and a scream would confirm a hit. And those who defended the walls were not without their casualties. Two more nuns were killed as well as five other soldiers.

During the assault on the gates and then while the flights of arrows were hissing back and forth, Joanna remained huddled on her hands and knees protected by the bodies of Wilma and Marla who bent over her, each in turn using the aperture in the wall to fire at the enemy. Her ears savagely pounded during the assault on the gates by the shouts and screams of soldiers on both sides, Joanna kept her arms wrapped around her head, her eyes tightly shut. But with the lessening of the noise and the cheers of the soldiers signaling their victory in beating back the assault, Joanna eased herself into a more comfortable position and looked about.

Down below lay bodies as they had fallen, arms, legs and heads twisted awkwardly — several of those who lay on the ground wore monk's clothing. For some reason Joanna's attention was drawn to the suspended cauldron. Just as her eyes focused on the huge pot from which arose curls of black smoke, an enemy shaft sheared into one of the holding ropes and the fibers of the rope started to unravel.

Joanna glanced down and saw the knight, his lieutenants and several others standing directly beneath the cauldron. Then without a word she sprang up, rushed along the parapet, reached the cauldron just as the rope was about to snap and, using all the strength in her body, thrust against the boom from which it was suspended, causing the boom to swing out just as the rope broke, tipping most of the contents on the far side of the gates. Splashes of pitch burned her hands, one splash landing high on her forehead searing away a portion of skin the size of her thumb. The sergeant of the archers rushed for Joanna, who stood fully exposed, flattening her with his body on the parapet just as a flight of arrows flew over.

Handled by these rough men as if she were made of delicate porcelain, Joanna was handed down from the parapet, resting finally in the arms of the commanding knight. The man's eyes were red, their lids swollen, the pits and creases of his face encrusted with black and twists of hair clotted his nostrils and ears. "Your name?" The knight's breath was as harsh as burning sulfur. Joanna wanted to turn away, but she was imprisoned in his arms which felt like stone.

"You have a name, do you not, boy?"

Forcing her voice deep and rough, Joanna answered, "John."

"Your father's name?"

"His name was John." As she spoke her voice cracked, causing the lieutenants and other soldiers who crowded close to laugh.

"So, John, son of John, I owe you my life, as do half a score of others. Not in all my memory have I heard of a smooth-cheeked boy with arms like sticks who was owed such a debt by soldiers." The knight let out a roar of laughter and handed Joanna to a lieutenant, who examined her then handed her to the next man. Each had to look at her face, feel her arms, examine her small hands. Each made sounds of wonder.

"He is a child," the lieutenant muttered, "fair as a girl, yet if it had not been for him, I would have been given such a bath that I doubt I would have recovered."

"A bath that will give you worse than congestion of the lungs," laughed a sergeant.

"I am no believer in baths, John, son of John," the knight joined in. "I gave my father my oath that I would never take one. If not for you, I would have broken this oath." With that the knight bent down, unhooked his spurs, and handed them to Joanna to the cheers of all the soldiers.

At sunset the enemy soldiers, keeping their semicircular formation, slowly retreated until they were out of the killing zone. As they retreated, every archer along the wall stood up and let fly, shouting insults interspersed with laughs and cheers. As soon as the walls were judged secure, Joanna was lifted astride the broad shoulders of the knight, the spurs she had been given laced to both feet, and then the knight, flanked by his lieutenants and followed by several score of men who carried blazing torches, marched to the center of the city. Word of the bravery of the boy monk had preceded this procession and the roofs of the houses were crowded with cheering men and women. Bonfires were lit in the open spaces. From time to time as the procession wound through the city, one or another woman would rush forward carrying a sick or deformed child, begging for the blessing of the heroic monk. And through it all, Joanna sat speechless, overwhelmed by excitement and confusion. What she had done not two hours since on the parapet of the wall seemed unreal, felt as if it were the action of someone else. The noise and the stench together with the rocking motion of the man on whose shoulders she was riding made waves of nausea sweep through her. But there were moments of excitement as the procession passed through the open spaces with their bonfires and frantic throngs who shouted "John, John" again and again. When she was finally returned to the nuns, who still were on duty at the wall, the moment she was in their hands, overwhelmed by exhaustion, she sank away into sleep without uttering a single word.

For Joanna, the next morning passed as if in a dream. Her sister nuns looked at her so strangely. The abbess came up several times to examine her burns, each time staring deeply into her eyes before turning away. Both Marla and Wilma acted almost as if they were afraid of her. And there were waves and cheers from the soldiers every time she looked in their direction.

"Throw off that monkish clothing and come join us as a fighting man!" the sergeant called out.

"You have proved your balls and won your spurs, John. Small as you are I'll take you for my squire," the knight called to her in his booming voice.

"Let those who have no balls and no taste for fighting be monks," the lieutenant joined in. "Join with us and I promise you, you will have many chances to prove your manhood!"

The dreamlike quality of what was happening grew more pronounced. Joanna tried to remember if it was she who had poured the boiling pitch on the enemy soldiers. Their shrieks pierced her brain like sharp bits of bone. The sun beat down on her, driving into her skull. She pressed her face into the place where the wall and the parapet met, trying to find relief from the cool stone, but there was no relief, as flies and crawling insects attacked her skin. She turned back to the knot of soldiers gathered below and they waved at her again, calling out and beckoning her to join with them. An image of the wild parade of the night before when it seemed that she commanded all the men of Engelheim formed in her mind. Would there ever be a time when she commanded men again? She shifted around and peered out through an aperture in the parapet.

The sun hung directly overhead and the enemy soldiers appeared to be settling down for their midday meal. All morning not one had crossed into the killing zone and only a token few shafts had been fired by either side. Suddenly without warning a mass of over two hundred leapt up and rushed across the fields toward the gate. They made no attempt to protect themselves with interlocking shields, although as they came on they kept themselves separated.

So unprepared were the archers on the walls for this maneuver, they were only able to let fly several irregular flights of shafts before the attackers reached the gates, felling less than a score. Had they been prepared, they might have been able to kill three times that number. Using the grapples and axes still embedded in the gates, the attackers swarmed up. More than a dozen managed to reach the top and scramble over, but these were met by the knight and his retainers and were hacked to pieces.

Under the careful command of the abbess, all the nuns were ordered to mass tight together on the wall just south of the gate. Then, pointing to a group of attackers on which they should concentrate, she gave the order to fire, and half a score of the enemy were swept away. Waiting until all the nuns were ready again and indicating another group of attackers, she ordered a second flight of shafts released, bringing down a like number. By now, less than a dozen still clung to the gates. These were picked off one by one by the archers on the west portion of the wall.

With more than seventy of their number killed or gravely wounded, the enemy soldiers turned and rushed back toward the line of safety, each man for himself. Although their unprotected backs would have made easy targets, the abbess withheld the order to fire. The other archers having nearly depleted their store of arrows, only five or six of the retreating soldiers were brought down.

The failure of this second mass assault signaled the end of the siege. The enemy, reduced in number by more than a third, after a final show of strength during which their shouts and threats were more violent than at the time of their first appearance, turned and made its way south toward the forest.

When the last of the enemy had disappeared in the distance, the commanding knight ordered the gates opened and then led his retainers, followed by a mass of the city's inhabitants, out onto the fields. There was much laughing, as, with shouted coarse jokes, they went from one to another of the fallen enemy soldiers, ripping open the abdomens of those yet alive, hacking off the heads of those who were dead, stripping them of their armor and their clothing. The corpses were then further mutilated by the mob that followed. Sexual organs were cut off and tossed like playthings, severed heads were kicked across the fields by crowds of urchins. The corpses finally were left to the dogs of the village, who were joined after dark by swarms of hungry rats.

By sunset every man and woman in Engelheim who had the strength to hold a pot of beer or mead was reeling drunk. All but the littlest children joined in this drunken celebration, which quickly turned into an orgy of fights and fornication.

It being judged too dangerous to attempt a return to the church during this celebration, the abbess ordered the nuns to remain on the parapet of the wall. Nine of their number who had died, their bodies secured, their faces hidden under cloths, rested alongside them.

Once during the hours they waited, the sergeant of the archers, staggering from drink, followed by half a dozen of his men, came up and demanded that Joanna go with him. "This is your chance to be a man, John!" He held up a pot of beer toward the parapet. "Come on. There are plenty of women on whom to prove your manhood." He made as if to mount the wall but was stopped as half a score of crossbows were pointed in his direction. Then making the pumping motion with his hand, he staggered away with his men.

Exhaustion and the effects of several hundred emptied barrels of beer and mead finally served to quiet the city. Most lay where they were, in the streets, on the roofs of their houses, some hanging half out of their windows. A dozen had lost their lives during the course of the revelry. More than a hundred suffered injuries or wounds. Several houses had been set afire but these fortunately were in the already partially burned out section. But now, finally, the city slept.

Waiting until there were no more human sounds — although at first it was hard to distinguish these from the baying of gorging packs of dogs — the abbess ordered the nuns to get ready. Then assigning two to each corpse of a sister nun and warning all to be on the alert and remain silent, they started moving toward the church. Several times a reveler rising from his drunken sleep and attempting to come at them was felled by the abbess who struck with a heavy, two-handed sword, although she delivered the blow with the flat, not the edge, of the weapon. As they went, swarms of rats scurried into the shadows, then went back to their feasts as soon as they were gone. Often they had to pick their way over those who lay in the streets — at any moment Joanna expected to feel a hand reach up and grip her leg.

The doors of the church swung open just as they emerged from the narrow street into the open space where it stood. The priest, grey-faced, unable to control the trembling of his limbs, gestured them in, making the sign of silence although not one of the nuns had made a sound. But as soon as the doors had been secured, as they were embraced by those who had remained behind, as they carefully laid their dead sisters on the floor of the sanctuary, the women burst into tears. Even the abbess wept. During this display of emotion, the priest stood to one side, clasping and unclasping his hands, frightened that the sounds would invite danger. But then the weeping ceased as the women knelt down, faced the great window formed in the shape of a cross, and began praying.

Morning found some of the nuns still praying; others, exhausted beyond control, had collapsed into sleep where they knelt. And the row of motionless women still lay where they had been placed, some open-eyed and staring, others appearing to sleep. It was this row of silent sisters that told Joanna that it all had been real, that now in daylight with her eyes open, the nightmare would not go away.

The convent was as they had left it; nothing had been touched. The enemy soldiers had not foraged to the north. The nuns could have remained within its walls and been safe. And as they marched into the courtyard carrying the nine corpses, a deep depression settled upon them. Had they chanced remaining in the convent, all would now be alive. From the dark shadows under the abbess' eyes, from the pain that showed in the tight lines around her mouth, it was obvious that she took the full burden of the decision upon herself. As they prepared a crypt for the bodies, again and again pounding into her brain like nails came the words: "If I had only chanced remaining here, they would not be dead. If I had only taken the chance..."

Other nuns, knowing from her expression and from the way she walked what was going on in the abbess' mind, approached, attempting to offer her words of comfort: "Had we not helped to defend the walls, Brita, the city might have fallen." The abbess shook her head. "Another in your place would have made exactly the same decision." The abbess shook her head again. "Had we remained in the convent and the soldiers discovered us, we all would have been slaughtered!" The abbess refused to be comforted.

Although Joanna had been as deeply affected as any of the others when the nine nuns had fallen, and had been as numbed with grief during the time the corpses lay in the sanctuary of the church in Engelheim, now as the nine were lowered into the place of their final rest, she felt almost nothing. She knelt along with the others, her head bowed, her lips moving in prayer, but no sobs broke into her praying, no tears fell into her lap. Perhaps it was just the relief of no longer being burdened by fear. Or it just might have been that she had already poured out all of her grief. Whatever it was, although she appeared to mourn, during most of the ceremony her thoughts were occupied with other matters:

As she had once yearned during the heat of a summer's day for a cool drink from the river — her parched mouth could taste its sweetness — so she now hungered for the silence and privacy of her room. How long had it been? Only a week. It felt like so much longer. Her mind felt choked. Alone in her room she would find relief. She needed to think. Yet the praying and the crying and the ceremony of burial went on and on.

The abbess' face had shrunk around her skull so that it now looked like parchment. Although she kept her hands clasped tight together and pressed them against her chest, she could not control their tremble. The iron determination of the woman which had both excited and frightened Joanna when they first met was gone. From the way her shoulders sloped, from the hollowing of her chest, from the slight tremor of her head, Joanna knew that the woman who knelt by the open crypt staring down was not the same person who had offered her the choice of the holy cross or the doll fashioned from a hangman's rope.

Both Marla and Wilma tried to comfort her as they led her to her room after the burial ceremony was over. Why were they comforting her? she wondered. Couldn't they see that she was strong enough? That she was no longer little, frightened Joanna? That she was changed? Yet she allowed the two women to whisper their comforting words, allowed them to stroke her head, kiss her lips and cheeks, to kneel alongside her bed as she settled down to sleep. *Soon they will learn I am no longer little Joanna,* she thought. *But for now, let them believe what they wish to believe.*

The two women gone, Joanna, who had only pretended to be asleep, opened her eyes and gazed out the high, narrow window. The stars were still there. She held her gaze steady. What were these points of light? ...a black cloth...behind this cloth a great dazzling light, points of light showing through the weave of the cloth a great dazzling light, points of light showing through the weave of the cloth. She forced her eyes to remain open and unmoving...a light more dazzling than the sun. Her arms strained upward toward the window, her body vibrated, her breathing came in deep gasps — its brillance greater than anything that could be imagined and there it was, waiting, waiting, waiting, beyond the black curtain.

The grief that had clouded all of the nuns' eyes lessened as the days passed, and they gradually grew aware of the changes that had taken place in Joanna. She no longer was a girl. True, her bosom had not yet begun to grow; in stature she was still a child. But her way was different. Not that she was always serious, although her face often showed that she was deep in thought. Not that she wouldn't join with the others during the meal, laughing and joking. But her manner had become so deliberate when she spoke. There was no longer any hesitancy, and her gaze had grown steady, almost piercing, so that most found it difficult not to shift their eyes away. And instead of joining with the others during those moments devoted to play, she would smile and wave when asked, but continue with her task of work or study.

As the time passed, different nuns would remark about how much Joanna had changed. More often than not, she was the first one to arise in the morning and when the others arrived in the chapel, yawning and rubbing at their sleep-filled eyes, they frequently found her deeply engrossed in studying some volume by the flickering rush light. And she rarely asked them any questions now. When she had first arrived, she had left many of them exhausted with her questions. Now she gained her answers from the volumes. Or, she could be found with her lips moving in a whisper, yet this was not praying.

"She asks herself questions," Marla murmured to Wilma, after having stood for several moments in the passageway outside of Joanna's room. "She asks questions, then replies, 'I must find the answer — it is important that I learn the answer.' What sort of a child is this?"

"She is no longer a child." Wilma shook her head. "She has become wise — her father, a holy monk; her mother, dying to give her life. Rescued from her village when all the rest were slaughtered. Saving those soldiers from the burning pitch. How else should she be but wise?" She shook her head slowly. "She will soon be as wise as the abbess, then..." Her voice trailed off in a murmur.

Fall came, then winter, without the abbess asking Joanna what would be her choice. It might have been that the woman had forgotten her promise to ask the girl for her answer at the end of summer. That terrible week in the city of Engelheim had confused time. So much had happened, so much pain, now so many regrets, such self-incrimination. Or it might have been that the abbess perceived the

Joanna with whom she had spoken in the fields in the springtime before that tragic week in Engelheim, was no longer. The Joanna who stood before the reading stand, every feature of whose face attested to the depth of her concentration, the Joanna who walked with such a firm step, her lips pressed tight together, the Joanna whose eyes had grown so piercing, was a new being. During the seven days of Engelheim her cocoon of childhood had opened, releasing someone strange who, although encased in the body of a girl, was no child.

It was almost exactly a year to the day of her entrance into the convent that Joanna knocked on the door of the abbess' chamber. Her face showing a mixture of surprise and anger at this interruption, the abbess pulled back the bolt and opened the door in response to the knock. For several seconds they faced each other in the half light, Joanna holding the eyes of the woman without wavering. Then as if it had been a contest which Joanna had won, the abbess beckoned her in.

Books, scrolls and documents occupied half the chamber, and there was a massive table spread with fresh sheepskins covered with writing; one skin only partially filled, the ink not yet dry. Motioning toward the sheepskins, the abbess said, "Some thoughts I have about St. Paul. There are certain things he said with which I take exception."

"That women cannot be priests!" Joanna offered, in a brittle voice.

"He never spoke to Jesus. Not once did he lay eyes on Him, yet again and again he speaks for our Savior," the abbess said, then hesitated, her eyes darting for a moment to the door. "Why should we not be priests? Why should this murderer of St. Stephen deny to such as we the priesthood?" Her voice was almost a hiss. They stood for several moments looking at one another."

"I will be a priest," Joanna's voice was steady. "That is what I came to tell you, Mother Brita. You asked for my choice, remember?"

The abbess nodded.

"But, holy mother, there is more than the choice of betrothal to a man as his wife or to Christ as a nun; more than just those two choices you offered me. I will be a priest!"

"What bishop will ordain a woman?" The abbess frowned as she asked the question.

"I will become a man. I was a man at the walls of Engelheim. All of us were men. I was given a man's spurs by the knight. To the soldiers of Engelheim my name is John. Why not to others?"

"But, Joanna, you are a woman. Within a year you will have the body of a woman — "

"I will bind my bosom. I will shave my pate. I will learn to roughen my voice. I will coarsen my cheeks by rubbing them with sand and soot. I will be a monk, as my father was. I will study in the university, then gain priesthood from the bishop. Even if I must go to Rome and petition the pope, I will be a priest. That is my choice, Mother Brita."

"The university...go to Rome and petition the pope... In all the eight hundred years since our Savior's death, there has never been a child such as you, Joanna." The abbess hesitated, smoothed away an invisible wrinkle in her robe, then continued. "Out there," she pointed to the window through which could be seen a sliver of the gray winter sky, "out there, you may not survive. You saw how it was, the cruelty, the violence, the death. One as sensitive as you, my Joanna... Stay with us in the convent. Here you can study. Here you will have time to talk, to share. When I am old, you will be the abbess, dear Joanna." The abbess eased down on her stool next to the table. She began to stroke the sheets of sheepskin with the tips of her fingers. "This is a cruel world, even for nobles and kings. Since the death of the Great Charles, each year the darkness grows greater. He struck a light, did our noble King Charles; it flickered for its little moment, then with his death was extinguished. Even Rome has grown savage, even Rome — The cardinals and bishops are scarcely more than heathens. If St. Peter were alive he would burn the throne given his name." The abbess softened her voice to a whisper. "He would burn the throne and drive them all from the cathedrals and palaces as did Jesus from the temple courtyard — there have been those who sat upon the papal throne whose lives have been an abomination." She examined the face of the girl. Her eyes took in the serious, firm-set mouth, the slight frown, so strange for a child scarcely in her thirteenth year, and those steady eyes as unwavering as her own once had been.

"This world is dark, Joanna, and each day grows darker. If there is to be preserved so much as a single ray of light, it will be here within these walls. Stay with us, child. I give you my promise that when you are grown you will be the abbess. Stay with us."

"There is a light beyond the black curtain of the sky, Mother Brita." Joanna's voice had a strange hollow sound. "I must reach this light. It calls to me. I know it is dark out there, holy mother. But if I reach this light..." The abbess took in a deep breath, let it out with a sigh, then nodded.

"If you become a priest, Joanna, and then they find that you are not a man, they will kill you. Are you prepared to hide your woman-ness for the rest of your life?"

"Hide it? Yes, Mother Brita. I will conceal my sex from the world, but I will never forget what I am. Every breath I breathe will be the breath of a woman, every thought. I will not forget."

The abbess turned back to the table and toyed with the sheet on which she had been writing. "Come to my room each afternoon, Joanna, and I will try to share with you what I have learned from my years of study. I will prepare you in every way that I can for the university. Then, if you have not changed your mind, you can leave at the end of the summer. If you have not changed your mind."

III

AACHEN

*T*he leaves of the linden trees that grew alongside the convent had just begun to turn yellow the day Joanna started her journey. She had announced her intentions that morning at prayers, and within moments had been surrounded by nuns shaking their heads, warning her of the dangers, a few taking firm hold of her arms as if to physically prevent her departure. It took a series of sharp orders from the abbess before they let her alone.

Marla and Wilma were stunned. They looked at the abbess with pleading in their eyes. Marla murmured again and again, "She is too young, too young," while Wilma made unsuccessful efforts to force back the sobs that rose from her chest.

Both women, by their special right as her friend and protector, followed Joanna to her room and again begged her to reconsider. As she had once been comforted by them, Joanna now became the comforter, hugging them, whispering special words into their ears, stroking their hands and cheeks. Wilma managed to bring her emotions under control, but Marla grew so upset she had to leave.

"You are determined, Joanna?" Wilma tried to force her voice to sound steady. Joanna inclined her head. "Then I will accompany you." Joanna started to shake her head. "With your permission, little sister, or without it, I will go along. As God is my witness, I swear you will not travel through these forests alone."

Joanna stared at the woman. The lines on her face had never been sharper. Both of her hands were knotted into fists. An image of those hands holding an armed crossbow rose, for a moment, into Joanna's mind. "Why should you leave this place that you love, my sister?" She rested her hand on the woman's arm — the muscles were knotted and as hard as oak. "I must go, but there is no need for you to."

"As you are determined, Joanna, so I am determined. Not the abbess, not the bishop, not the pope himself will prevent me from going with you!"

The waiting nuns had formed two lines in the courtyard just inside the outer gate with the abbess standing away from the others. As Joanna walked slowly through their ranks in her monk's robe, she stared carefully at each face as if to etch the features into her mind. "May Christ take care of you, my child," one murmured. "May the Blessed Virgin watch over you always," whispered another. "Come back to us, Joanna, come back to us," they called after her as she moved toward the gate. Then just before she passed through the gate the abbess embraced her.

"Find the light, Joanna," the woman whispered in a voice so soft no one else could hear. "Find this light, God knows the world can use it, my beautiful, loving child." She showered her cheeks with kisses. "When you have had enough of the world, come back to us. We will be waiting for you, Joanna. I will be waiting."

Just before they entered the woods, Joanna turned and looked back at the convent. The abbess still stood at the gate; other nuns could be seen inside the courtyard on their knees, praying. She raised her eyes to the narrow window of her room, the room in which she had found a greater peace than any she had ever known: those quiet times deep in thought and meditation, lying on her bed staring up at the star-filled sky. She felt a heaviness inside as if hands pulled down on her muscles and bones. She found it difficult to breathe. Why had she left that place in which she had known such happiness? What sort of life faced her, dressed in the clothes of a man, traveling through brigand-infested forests, to cities filled with hate and with violence? No one would think the worse of her if she changed her mind and again took up the life of a nun. Hadn't she been promised that when a woman she would be made abbess? She glanced at Wilma who was staring intently at her face, then turned her eyes back to the convent, to the window of her room. She could not be certain but wasn't that a face staring back at her from the window? Two large eyes, reddened by weeping. Was it Marla she saw? Or the sallow features of the face of the woman she would someday be if she went back to the convent?

Fighting against those hands that pulled on her muscles and bones, she turned away and entered the forest. Wilma followed, her crossbow, armed with a steel-tipped shaft, ready in her hand.

The girl and her hatchet-faced woman companion were fated to be tested as to the firmness of their resolve at once. There is a force, some say, that imposes such tests. Why else should there have been four sturdy beggars, each armed with a heavy cudgel, waiting for them deep in these woods? Travellers came and went daily through this forest which stood between the convent and the city of Engelheim. So close to the city, so frequently travelled, it was judged to be safe. Soldiers from the city were known to patrol its pathways from time to time. Yet this day, four ragged men who lived by their cunning and the strength of their arms were waiting to intercept them.

Halfway through the forest, their path detoured around a great oak tree that hid what lay ahead. Just as Joanna was about to step over its gnarled roots, which rose from the ground in a twisting pattern, the snapping of a twig caused her to stop. There were wolves in these woods, although they were only known to attack when starving in the depths of winter, and this was still early autumn. But there were also wild dogs, driven from the city and grown savage as they hunted hares and other creatures in packs. These dogs were not above turning on human beings on occasion. Joanna glanced back at Wilma who held her crossbow aimed directly ahead, a second shaft ready in her hand. She too had heard the twig snap. With her eyes focused forward on the oak tree, Joanna took several careful steps backward as she unsheathed the short sword with which she was armed.

Standing side by side, Joanna and Wilma waited. A minute passed; then, without any attempt to hide their footfalls, four men stepped out from behind the far side of the great oak tree.

Although no bigger than other men, to Joanna these men appeared huge. And they were as dirty as the least washed man of her village. Even their lips were stained. The nails of their hands were ragged and black as the hoofs of a wild boar. Their faces showed the unmistakable features of the peasant — sloping forehead, broad nose, elongated ears, lower jaw heavy and thrust forward, their eyes small and placed close together. These could have been men from the village north of her village gone savage, men whose huts had been burned by brigands or soldiers, now homeless, desperate and dangerous.

Joanna and Wilma stared at the men. They were poorly armed. Cudgels were their only weapons. Yet they were four. And their strength showed in the slope of their shoulders. Their half-open mouths were like the mouths of foxes closing in on a trapped hare.

The men stared back at the two monks, one scarcely half grown, the other nothing but gristle and bone.

"We are Benedictine monks," Wilma's voice was guttural and

could easily have been taken for that of a man. "We travel under protection of the Church to do Christ's work. Let us pass."

The beggars took several steps forward, but stopped as Wilma steadied her crossbow. "As Christ is my witness, two of you will die before you take another step. Although a monk, I know enough of the use of this crossbow, I promise, to pierce two through the throat and then give a sufficient account of myself to the other two with my sword. Which two will die first?" As Wilma spoke Joanna tightened her grip on her sword, braced her body, and prepared to rush forward and thrust the weapon upward with all her strength.

The oldest beggar whose face was twisted to one side by a dark purple scar, grinned. His teeth were either missing or broken off at their roots. His tongue was swollen and as he grinned it forced itself partially out between his lips. "We will not harm you, holy monks." The man's voice cracked as if he were unused to speaking. "We are thirsty and only beg for a single copper coin with which to drink your health." He started to take a step forward, but froze as Wilma shifted her crossbow so that it pointed directly at him. Making a sound that was something like a laugh, he wagged his head from side to side. "No, no, holy father, you have nothing to fear from us. We believe in Christ — see." He made the sign of the cross on his chest. The other three also crossed themselves. "Would you deny thirsty men who are parched for the littlest drop of mead, holy fathers?" The man stretched out his hand. "What sort of charity is this, threatening homeless men who have lost their families with your weapons? Are you priests or soldiers?"

With her crossbow still aimed at the man, Wilma eased her other hand inside her tunic and extracted two copper coins. She held them up so that the men could see them. Then with a sudden sweep of her arm, tossed both coins deep into the thicket. The four men gasped, hesitated a moment, then one started for the thicket, and his movement set the other three into motion. Cursing and screaming at each other, kicking, jabbing with their elbows, they fought their way into the thicket. The moment they were out of sight, Wilma and Joanna started running in the direction of the city and only stopped their flight when they emerged from the woods into the broad field which lead up to its walls.

Gasping and coughing from their exertion, they rested, glancing from time to time back at the woods. Both had suffered scratches on their hands and faces from whipping branches.

"After you had brought down two with your crossbow, Wilma, would we have been able to defend against the other two with our swords?" Joanna leaned her head against Wilma's shoulder. For the moment she felt small and helpless.

"Had they attacked, I would have been able to fell only one. Perhaps I might have pierced another with my sword, but I doubt it would have been a mortal wound. Then they would have taken us and killed us, and, if they found we were women, debauched us," Wilma answered.

"I was prepared to rush at them with my sword." Joanna listened to herself speak — the words sounded weak.

"They would have broken your head with their cudgels before you could have reached them." The woman stroked the girl's head, trying to steady her hand. "For women like us, brashness and bravery will serve very little purpose. If we are to stay alive, it will be from cunning and skill. That, and the grace of God." She allowed her hand to rest on the girl's head. "Without God's divine protection, we would have been slaughtered in the forest." Wilma's face took on a puzzled expression. Scarcely realizing what she did, she fingered the hairs on her chin in the manner of a man. "Or it may have been a test, Joanna. Perhaps those men were sent to test our resolution...or was it a warning; a warning of what is to come? If such a thing can happen in the safe forest of Engelheim, what may we expect in the other forests..." She stared back toward the place where the pathway emerged from the woods.

As they sat together in the field, resting, the warmth of the sun soothing their bruises and easing their aching muscles, the girl who had been badly shaken by the experience gradually grew stronger, while the woman shrank down into herself as waves of uncertainty and apprehension rolled over her. Sensing what was happening, Joanna put her arms around Wilma's shoulders and rocked her gently back and forth as if she were a child. "You showed such courage, Wilma; made such a brave show I believed that we would be able to take them in a fight. You made them believe!"

"But, if what I tried had not worked — if they had seen through my cunning — the dogs and the wolves now would be fighting each other for our flesh. How are two women travelling alone to survive when, less than an hour into their journey, such a thing happens as just took place in the forest? It was a warning, Joanna. We must return to the convent!"

"A warning, Wilma? Or proof that the Blessed Virgin watches over us? You yourself said that without God's protection we would not have had a chance. You yourself said that this might have been a test." Wilma unwrapped the girl's arms from her shoulders and stretched out on the grass.

"How are we to know? How are we to know?" Wilma murmured. "A proof, or a warning. Which?"

"I know!" Joanna's voice rang with certainty. "I know. In here I know." She crossed her hands against her chest. She hesitated, took in a deep breath, then went on. "I am the child of a holy monk. My sainted mother died that I might be born." As she spoke, her eyes opened wide and began to stare through the woman. "Have you not heard these things, Wilma?" The girl's breathing grew more rapid. "Why did I survive when so many others were slaughtered in the village? Why did the priest take me? Why did I choose the cross, not the doll? I wanted that doll, but my hand grasped the cross. Why all these things, Wilma!" Her voice rose and words spilled out, one tumbling against the other. "The enemy force was turned away from the walls of Engelheim. Had the knight and the lieutenants been killed by the boiling pitch, there would have been no one left in command. It was I who saved them from the boiling pitch, Wilma. My hands, my hands guided by a greater force, Wilma, the same force that caused them to grasp the cross. And that great light which lies beyond the curtain of the sky — I know it is there — waits for me. No, Wilma, how could what happened in the forest have been a warning? Not with everything else that has happened. It was a proof of our strength, a proof that we are under divine protection. Why else should such a thing have happened in those woods, if not to tell us that nothing can hurt us." She gripped Wilma's shoulder. Her hands had such strength the woman winced. "Those four beggars were not men!" The fingers of the girl's hand dug in. "They were holy angels sent down by God with His message." Her eyes shifted wildly from side to side. She let go of the woman's shoulder and clapped her hands together. "Can't you see it, Wilma? It is all a part of a plan."

Overwhelmed by a surge of emotion, Wilma embraced the girl and hugged her tightly. "You are a strange child, Joanna. I do not know what to make of what you are saying. Yet your life declares that you have been under divine protection. Perhaps the walls of Engelheim would have fallen..." She held the girl in a vise-like grip as she felt waves of excitement rising inside of her. "Perhaps that is why I went to the convent, why I left Aachen where my father was a merchant, and traveled to this convent — so that I would be here when you came." Tears of joy filled the woman's eyes. "I defied my father to come to the convent. Ugly as I am, I could have been married. There were many in my city who would have gladly married me, the daughter of a rich merchant. But I knew my life must be in a convent in the service of Christ...yes, had they been desperate beggars they would have attacked us. It was not my cunning. It was not luck. As you said, Joanna, they must have been sent to give us a message. As you said, it is all a part of a plan."

They lay together in the field, locked in each other's arms, each feeling the breath of the other on her cheeks. The lowing of cattle could be heard in the distance, along with the rustle and scratch of insects. No longer concerned about who might emerge from the dark forest, they lay together, their eyes closed against the sun's rays.

Joanna drifted into the space between waking and sleeping. Her body had grown light, as if filled with air. Not even in her room in the convent, lying on her bed covered by the blanket of woolly sheepskin had she felt such peace. It all lay out there, everything. Waiting. Anything was possible.

So light had her body grown it felt as if the slightest wind could have sent her tumbling into the sky. Her breath flowed in and out effortlessly. She raised her hands until they were framed by the blue of the sky — small and delicately formed, yet strong. Hands that had done their share of hard work. But they were unmistakably the hands of a child. Who would take them seriously? Deep in her mind the image of Rolf's hand formed. Thick, broad palms covered with calluses tough as dried bull hide, fingers with such strength they could crack a walnut as easily as her fingers could crush a ripe blackberry. Then the gray hands of the priest took the place of those of Rolf. Long thin fingers with ridged, brown nails that curved over the tips like a hawk's talons, hands that were always cold, yet hands that also could crush. What work would her hands do? What writings would they leave behind? She had read and studied the works of the ancient Romans: Pliny, Ovid, Quintillian. Would the writings of her hands live when she was gone? Would these hands which could never be as strong as those of a man leave their mark on the world? All of Europe felt the power of the hands of the Great Charles. Unable to read or write more than his name, he had formed an empire, founded monasteries, gathered into libraries the wisdom of the ancients, created new laws. If the illiterate Charlemagne could do such a thing, why not one with a mind like hers, one whose life already declared her destiny?

"I will suck their learning from their brains," she softly murmured. "I will master Greek and Hebrew. I will read all the volumes in the libraries of the universities..."

Her murmurs, although soft, stirred Wilma into wakefulness. Her mix of thoughts and dreams had taken her to Aachen, to the heavy-timbered house in which she had been born. Was her merchant father who wore his sable robe summer and winter still alive? And her mother? Then she remembered that wheezing, bent woman with a face harsher than her own was gone, had died the year she left to join the nuns. How could she have forgotten this? Her own mother. How strange. The woman sighed deeply. *I will visit her grave,* she determined. *I will see if my father is still alive — if dead, I will say the mass for him.*

A gnat buzzed close to her ear and she roughly brushed it away. "In what direction will we travel, Joanna?" She rested her head in her hands. 'There is a great cathedral at Aachen, the city of my birth. This cathedral, built by the Great Charles, dwarfs the church of Engelheim as the bull dwarfs the lamb." Joanna leaned closer to the her. "The body of Charlemagne lies in a crypt within this cathedral." Joanna's eyes began to glisten. "When he was alive, the wisest men not only of Christendom but of the East came to this place, brought gifts of books writ in all the great languages. If you are to see the world and learn its many ways, what better place to visit than this city?"

"In what direction is Aachen?" Joanna asked, excitement showing in her face.

"To the west, my little sister. A month's careful journey to the west."

"The land of the Ingels lies to the west." Joanna's voice rang with pleasure. "We will go to Aachen. We will see the cathedral, spend time with the monks and the other learned ones. And you can visit your home, Wilma." she laughed in delight. "Then we will travel to the land of the Ingels where my father and mother were born. To the famous universities of that place." She clapped her hands together. "There is so much to learn. So much to do."

Word of the arrival of two monks from the east was brought to the Bishop of Aachen as he worked in his study. Merchants came and went all the time. Visiting barons and knights with their retainers were a common sight. But two monks worn from weeks of travel, one as fair and finely formed as a woman, the other reported to be as ugly as the gargoyles carved into the stonework of the cathedral, and from the east — this was no occurrence of routine importance.

"They say the younger one's face could be taken for a Grecian bust if it were of marble, not flesh, Your Eminence," the priest's secretary reported to the bishop. "They ask permission to study our volumes, to be allowed to sit with us and listen during learned disputations." The bishop stared, unblinking, at his secretary, his tiny eyes resembling buttons of pale blue glass set in the folds of his wrinkled face.

"From the east...or from Rome, sent here to spy upon us?" muttered the bishop. The secretary sucked in his breath. "When have you heard of monks journeying west? If they leave their monastery it is always south to Rome, never west. And the younger one with his fine features...perhaps of noble birth! A cardinal's bastard? The son of a duke?" The bishop drummed his fingers on the table. "I have enemies in Rome. There are those who would be glad to gain damaging information of the Bishop of Aachen." He forced himself out of his seat onto his crippled legs, holding the table for support.

"From the east!" he snorted. "They expect me to believe a thing like this? We must be careful." He nodded his head rapidly. "We must not reveal we know who they are. Treat them as we treat other travellers. Make them welcome, but no more than, say, priests from the district would be welcome." He paused and rapidly licked his lips. "Yet we must be certain to put on a good face. Have all the masses said properly — perhaps extra masses, and I myself will conduct disputations." He paused, took in a deep breath and set his jaw. "Offer them hospitality in the cathedral. In a monk's cell. Simple food, but enough. And at all times one of my servants must be near enough so we know of their actions; if possible, to hear what they say. Are my orders clear?"

The priest nodded. "Forgive me, Your Eminence, for not seeing through their ruse."

"That is why I am the bishop. It is my duty to see clearly into all things. Now, send for them and have them brought into my presence. At the west chapel. I will perform evening mass. Have enough candles lit. I do not want them to take back word to Rome that I scrimp."

The appearance of the bishop's bailiff in his flame-red gown at the inn where they had arrived earlier that afternoon made Joanna and Wilma uneasy. He entered the low-ceilinged room, his crooked staff of office in his hand, followed by half a score of armed retainers. The innkeeper blanched white and trembled. His fat, surly wife who never troubled herself for any traveller, threw her apron over her head. The several servants stood frozen. The other guests cowered down in their seats, trying to make themselves look as inconspicuous as possible.

Then when the bailiff flanked by his men approached the table where they sat, Joanna and Wilma began to be afraid.

Booming out in his full voice, a voice used for reading the bishop's proclamations in the city square, he ordered the two monks to come with him, then sent the landlord scurrying for their few belongings. The bailiff's face was as florid as his gown, his mouth curled down permanently in contempt. Wilma and Joanna gripped hands, their bodies tense. But when he declared that they were to be guests of the bishop, that they were to be in his presence this very evening, they both had to fight back their tears as waves of relief swept through them.

Scores of the curious could be seen at their windows as the small procession marched through the narrow streets in the direction of the cathedral. The crooked staff of office, pointed forward, cleared a path through the crowded streets as cleanly as if it had been a razor-sharp scythe. If anything, the streets of Aachen were dirtier than those of Engelheim, and although somewhat wider, they were as dark because the sloping roofs of the buildings were so constructed that those on both sides of the street almost touched. Yet, despite the dirt and darkness of the streets, and despite the stench and din, which brought back sharp memories of Engelheim, Joanna did not experience a moment of distress. As she marched along, she thought how foolish she had been, being frightened at the appearance of the bailiff. How could she have allowed herself to forget who she was, the protection under which she travelled? How very foolish of her. Such a thing would never happen again. For was not the bailiff's appearance another proof? Two road-stained travellers, their garments frayed, and here they were, guests of the powerful Bishop of Aachen, to be taken directly into his presence. She smiled as she strode along, making certain her gestures and movements were those of a man.

But the moment she stepped out of the darkened streets into the great square where the cathedral stood, the fear which she had judged so foolish again returned. Never in her wildest imaginings had she dreamed there could be a structure of this size and of such magnificence. Its spires appeared to touch the sky. The late afternoon sun was reflected in a thousand places from its masonry. Decorations were everywhere: masks, crosses, scrollwork; and the colors of the windows were like scores of trapped rainbows. Inside, beyond the wide-open doors, there appeared to be more flickering candle flames than the stars of the sky. "God's palace!" she exclaimed, and Wilma nodded. The crowd clustered before the doors gave way at the approach of the bailiff, bowing and pulling at their forelocks as he passed by.

As great as had been Joanna's awe at first viewing the cathedral, it was multiplied many times once inside. She looked up. The arched ceiling, higher than the tallest tree in the forest, was held up by great marble columns. Sounds echoed throughout the huge chamber. She could hear the murmur of prayer, yet could not be certain from where it came. Everywhere there were flickering candles, oil lamps set high on posts; everywhere crosses, statues of stone and wood, some of the Christ, several of His Mother, others she did not recognize. Hundreds stood or knelt within this vast chamber. The light of the setting sun made her head reel. Then they were at the west chapel, separated from the rest of the cathedral by a grillwork of bronze.

Standing before an altar crowded with gold and silver candlesticks, decorated with cloths of silk dyed crimson and purple, his back to the mass of kneeling men and women who filled this moderate space, was a man dressed as Joanna had imagined only princes and kings dressed — cloak stitched with gold thread, red, blue and yellow jewels formed into patterns. On his head he wore a tall crown made of three crosses joined together by a filigree of silver and strips of white fur. Yet this crown, for all its size, could not hide the fact that the man conducting the mass was scarcely taller than she.

She knelt alongside a group of men dressed in the furs of merchants and they, having noted that she entered the chapel in the company of the bishop's bailiff, quickly made room for her, crowding against one another.

Although her face was set in an expression of deep concentration so that those who glanced in her direction judged her to be absorbed in prayer, in fact, Joanna's eyes and attention darted around the ornate chamber. All who were there hearing the mass were finely dressed. In contrast to these men and women with their jewels, silks and furs, she and Wilma looked like beggars in their stained travel-worn garments. She found herself hugging her arms against her chest to hide the frayed ends of her sleeves, and forced herself to uncross her arms. She glanced at Wilma. Although kneeling, the woman had taken an almost defiant stance, with her elbows jutting out, guaranteeing her an extra portion of space. And although her eyes were fixed on the ground, she held her head high, kept her shoulders squared, and her jaw thrust forward. Her father had been a merchant of this city as rich and powerful as any one of them. She lived a life of poverty by choice, not of necessity. During the response, while most mumbled, her voice boomed out with such force that eyes turned for a moment in her direction.

When the mass was over, with unmistakable gestures of disrespect, the bailiff waved the lesser merchants and minor officials together with their wives out of the chapel. The two score who remained were the rulers of Aachen. Only these were granted the privilege of easy access to the bishop. Only these, together with the highest church officers, were allowed to be present when the bishop granted an audience.

Leaning heavily on his secretary for support, the bishop hobbled the few paces from the altar to his throne. Once there he easily pulled his body up into his seat with his powerful arms.

Joanna stared at the man's face. It was as wrinkled as a dried apple. So deep were the wrinkles that when his lips were together it was difficult to see where his mouth began or ended. His nose resembled a lump of brownish moss. Yet the most startling thing about the man's face was his eyes — tiny, but of such a transparent blue they could have been taken for glass beads. An image of old Clari with her pouch of colored beads appeared for a moment in Joanna's mind.

"I understand that you are of our Benedictine brothers who live to the east." The bishop pointed in their direction with a hand which drooped from its wrist. "From the district of Engelheim, is it not?"

Joanna and Wilma inclined their heads.

"We are pleased to extend our hospitality. It is a rare occurrence to receive visitors from the far side of the Rhine. Those few who have been brought into our presence were, if my memory serves me, merchants..." The bishop's secretary whispered for a moment in his ear. "Also, several knights. But never in our episcopy have those who have taken orders risked the river, the forests, and the mountains to visit this city. Although when the Great Charles had Aachen as his capital, I am certain it was different. But the Great Charles is dead these twenty-five years..." The bishop paused, as he picked at his lower lip for several moments. "One would expect monks who are prepared to risk dangerous journeys to travel south. To visit our Holy Father, the Bishop of Rome, and kneel in his presence and receive his blessing." The bishop broke off and stared at them.

"We only stay in Aachen a little time," Wilma said in a roughened voice. "My brother in Christ, John," she rested her hand gently on Joanna's shoulder, "is the son of an English monk. His mother, a holy woman, was also of that race. They did Christ's work amongst the Saxon heathens, during which work, John was born; his birth at the cost of the holy woman's life. We travel to the land of the Ingels to seek out those of the blood of brother John. To do honor to his father and mother in the place where they were born. To visit the

great centers of learning and to kneel at the sacred grave of Venerable
Bede of blessed memory."

"So you stopped here in Aachen for only a day or two." The
bishop pursed his lips. "I had heard you were here to study our many
volumes. To join in our disputations. To listen to the lectures of our
learned scholars."

"We are here, Your Eminence, to study, with your permission,
your volumes." Joanna started to rise from her kneeling position,
checked herself, and remained kneeling on one knee. "I have the
Latin, but lack Hebrew and Greek. If I may be permitted to remain
here until I have mastered those two languages — if we may be permitted to stay until the spring — " Joanna's statement was interrupted by a roar of laughter from the assemblage.

The bishop raised his hand, ordering silence. "Why do you
laugh?" He forced his voice into mock seriousness. "Less than half a
year may be sufficient time for this pretty monk to gain a mastery of
Greek and Hebrew. Have you not noted his high forehead which
declares his intelligence? Did you not hear what his fine-featured companion said about the holiness of his birth?"

The bishop was interrupted by a second roar of laughter greater
than the first.

"It is well-known that they grow such fine scholars in those
'peaceful' lands to the east that several months of study should be sufficient for that lovely lad to gain proficiency in languages which it
takes our dullards five and more years to master."

Joanna felt the blood rushing to her face, but she forced herself
not to lower her head. Then, without fully realizing what she did, she
got to her feet, threw back her shoulders, crossed her arms over her
chest and stared directly at the bishop. The bailiff took several steps in
her direction, but was waved back as the bishop glanced uneasily at
his secretary. This show of defiance was proof his earlier suspicions
were justified.

"There are only two kinds who can master those ancient languages in the several months between fall and spring!" A voice
boomed out from just beyond the bronze latticework which separated
the chapel from the rest of the cathedral. From the expressions of all
who were gathered, it could be seen that this was a voice with which
they were familiar. The bishop's shoulders twitched a little and he
glanced again at his secretary, then shifted his eyes to the entrance as
a short but powerfully built man dressed in ermine walked in.
Everyone made way for this newcomer. The bishop, smiling and nodding, beckoned the man close and, almost as if by magic, a chair ap-

peared next to his throne. The newcomer, whose staff, crested with a globe and golden eagle, declared him to be count of the palace and second in rank only to the bishop, ponderously took his seat.

"Of the two kinds that can so easily learn these languages," the count of the palace continued, his eyes traveling slowly around the chamber, "are first those of the holiness of such as the sainted Alcuin who instructed the Great Charlemagne — their holiness gives to them a genuis not granted to other men." He fastened his eyes on Joanna. "The other kind who can so easily master languages — so that there is no one they cannot understand, no one with whom they cannot converse — the others make their home in the realm of Satan!"

Although the throne on which he sat declared the bishop to be of higher rank than the count of the castle, from the way the bishop deferred to the man, from his uneasy glances and the forced sound of his voice, it was apparent that the greater power lay in the hands of the one in ermine, under whose direct command were the soldiers of the garrison.

"He is little more than a child." The bishop pointed at Joanna. "When I was of this age, I too was given to making rash statements. We will be pleased with his progress if he has memorized the alphabet and is able to pick out a few words by spring."

With a rough, coughing sound that was not a cough, the count silenced the bishop. His thick lips twisted into a sneer. "Was it a rash statement, boy?" he asked Joanna. "Was it only the bragging of a lad whose virgin face has never known the caress of a razor?" He let out a harsh laugh. "I thought you who had taken orders were not given to lying and bragging like street urchins." A number of the merchants added their laughter to that of the count.

Wilma tried to catch Joanna's eye. If she confessed to having exaggerated a little there would be more laughter, but that would be the end of it. But if she persisted... Wilma made a soft sound in her throat as she tried to draw the other's attention.

For a moment Joanna felt a tightening in her chest. The air tingled in her nostrils as it had during violent lightning storms. It was the odor of danger. She hesitated, then, remembering who she was, allowed her mouth to speak.

"I know nothing of *your* street urchins," she answered the count. An uneasy sound spread through the assemblage. "If given instruction, I will gain enough Hebrew and Greek by the end of winter. And for you to suggest that the son of a holy monk and the saintly woman who traveled with him amongst the heathens might be from Satan's realm is a cruel insult to their memories."

A shocked gasp rose from the assemblage. The count's face turned a deep purple, as throbbing veins showed in his forehead. He turned to his lieutenant and started to give the order that Joanna be seized, when Wilma got up to her feet and took a step in his drection.

"We are holy men!" Her voice rattled and hissed. "We stand in the chapel of the cathedral in the presence of the bishop. Who are you to order such as we be seized?"

The bishop gripped the arms of his throne tightly trying to force his body not to tremble. "They are here in our presence by our express order." He nodded at the count of the palace and tried to smile, shrugging his shoulders as he spoke. "And this is the cathedral, your honor, and they are monks."

"Or minions of Satan!" the count interrupted in a roar. "Either that one with a face of a gargoyle and that one with the features of an angel are the two holiest men in all of Christendom and they have freely placed their lives at risk, or they have been sent here from the Dark Kingdom to insinuate themselves amongst us." Bubbles of saliva formed in the corners of his mouth. "We must put them to the test."

The bishop hesitated, glanced quickly around the room, then nodded.

"If you are holy men, then prove it by showing us a miracle, or as I know that Christ died for us, I'll have your ugly head at the end of a pike before the world grows a day older." The count stabbed a finger in the direction of Wilma. "You," he shifted his finger toward Joanna, "I will give you as a plaything to my soldiers. Many of them have developed an appetite for boys and one as pretty as you..." He let out a wet, ugly sound. He shifted back to Wilma. "A miracle to prove to us who you are so that we may pay you proper respect, or..." He made a cutting motion around his neck.

Wilma's face had drained of color and her eyes bulged. Her heart beat with such force she thought it must burst out of her chest. Although her eyes were fixed on the count of the palace, she could scarcely see him. Everything else was dark. All the others gathered in the chapel were masked in darkness. *Holy Mary, Mother of God, help me,* the words pounded in her brain. Then her mouth opened and words came out.

"Holy Mary, Mother of God, let me perform a miracle in your name." Everyone in the chapel watched the woman intently. The bishop and the count leaned forward in their seats. "Holy Mary, Mother of God...Holy Mary, Mother of God..." No one moved, most scarcely breathed. "A miracle. Give me the strength to perform a miracle."

Wilma's mind raced. She glanced for a moment at Joanna who stared at her, her mouth partially opened, her eyes glazed.

"Holy Mother of God, grant me the power to transform my body into that of a woman so that in my corporal being I can reflect Your glory. Let me be turned into a woman for all the time I am here in Aachen."

The count's eyes opened wide, and his lips parted. The bishop was unable to control his tremble. All the onlookers stiffened. Then Wilma drew her shoulders back and thrust her chest forward. As if they were a single person, everyone sucked in their breath — there was a swelling of the monk's chest beneath his tunic. Then with a wild gesture she tore open her tunic, tore open the shirt beneath and revealed small but well-formed breasts.

The merchants and officers of the city, as if caught by a great wind, pushed backwards. Several of their women swooned. The count, without realizing what he did, raised an arm in defense. The bishop cowered on his throne.

"Must I now bring down a thunderbolt and destroy your castle as further proof?" Wilma roared at the count.

"Enough proof! Enough proof! Enough proof!" The bishop waved both arms frantically.

Her breasts still exposed, Wilma took a step in the count's direction. The officers who flanked him shrank backwards, their lips blue, their teeth chattering. "Have I provided sufficient proof for you, your honor?" She advanced another step toward the count. His eyes blinked rapidly as if burned with smoke.

"Proof enough! Proof enough, holy man." He formed the cross with his two arms,then kissed the place where they joined again and again.

Holding her torn tunic open, with a great show of deliberation, Wilma slowly turned so that all could clearly see her bosom. Then she moved back and took her place alongside Joanna. As she closed her tunic and adjusted her rope belt, she addressed the assemblage. "What I have just done in the name of our sacred mother Mary, whose blessed Son bled and died for us, is as nothing compared to what this lad, if challenged, can do." She laid her hand carefully on Joanna's shoulder. "The son of a holy monk doing Christ's work, whose mother suffered agony and death to give him birth. Untainted as the new-fallen snow. His mind filled with only the purest of thoughts. His life dedicated since the age of ten to the service of our Lord. He has but to raise his hand..." Wilma raised her hand, and they all cowered, many gasping and gibbering in fear. "Is it still your intention, honorable count, to give him as a plaything to your soldiers?"

The count vigorously shook his head.

"Yet if this still be your intention, John my little brother in Christ need only scoop up a handful of earth and cast it to the wind to bring such a plague to your soldiers and to the inhabitants of Aachen that those who live a hundred years from now will speak of this year as the time of the great death."

There was silence after Wilma's words. Both the bishop and the count stared at the two monks, their faces reflecting their fear and confusion. Then the count forced himself to his feet and took several steps in their direction. "I knew all along you were holy men," he said rapidly. "When I entered the chapel, I felt a heat as if a great fire blazed. My words were only so that you could prove your holiness to these others." He made a wide, sweeping gesture with his arm. "So that they could pay you sufficient respect, make proper obeisance." His loose lips tried to smile. "The moment I set eyes on you, I could see the golden light that surrounds your head, could see in the features of little brother John perfect holiness."

The chapel filled with exclamations. "Yes, there is golden light that surrounds their heads...See how perfect are his features...It is as if there is a roaring fire...I knew at once they were holy..."

During these exclamations the bishop whispered to his secretary, "They are from Rome, it is certain they are from Rome. The older one I am certain is of royal blood, a duke, or a prince with his face disguised into ugliness." The secretary vigorously nodded. "They may carry with them a message from the Holy Father..."

"That you are to be a cardinal, Your Eminence?" the secretary offered. "Perhaps they come with the authority of the Pope to see if everything is as it should be, and then declare your elevation to a prince of the church."

"No, no. Do not say such a thing. I am not worthy of that honor. More likely they were sent here to spy. Sent by my enemies, yet..." The bishop hesitated. "Yet the Holy Father knows of my loyalty, of my many years of devoted service." He forced a cough. "But it is more likely they are here as spies." He glanced at them again. "Whichever is the case, we must be careful."

The secretary gravely nodded, his eyes on Joanna and Wilma standing quietly amidst the tumult in the chapel.

In all of Aachen only those who had lost the power of hearing or who were possessed by demons had not heard of the miracle by sunrise the next morning. It was on everyone's lips. As it passed from one to the other, bits were added to it: The monk's breasts had grown from two to three. His face had changed for a moment into a perfect likeness of the Virgin. He had given birth to a lamb whose wool was of silver, there in front of the entire assemblage. A fountain flowing with wine had appeared from which all had drunk. Gold coins had fallen like droplets of rain. Those in the audience who suffered from coughs, ulcers, and gout were instantly cured. And the old men and women declared that if the two holy monks remained in Aachen the city would regain the great prosperity it had known in the days when Charlemagne made it his capital.

Gifts of wool cloth, baskets of freshly baked bread, and crocks of mead and beer were left at the entrance of the cathedral for the two monks. Crowds that at times numbered as many as a thousand gathered in the open square before the cathedral to catch a glimpse, if possible, of the two holy men. Cripples and women carrying deformed children begged entrance to receive a touch from the monks that must instantly cure. But while the city spoke and thought of little else, Joanna and Wilma sat in the chamber to which they had been assigned, their arms wrapped tightly around one another.

"If the abbess could have seen you, Wilma," Joanna laughed, then kissed the woman several times on the cheek.

"Be careful, little sister," Wilma touched a finger to her lips. "They may try to listen."

"Give me a miracle." In a softened voice Joanna mimicked the count of the palace. "Or I'll have your head at the end of a pike." "Did you see their eyes, Wilma? Did you see the way they trembled?" Her body shook with laughter and tears filled her eyes.

"I thought the count would be taken with apoplexy and I would be guilty of his death." Wilma joined in the laughter. "If the bishop didn't soil himself when I opened my tunic, I will gladly pay a penance of a hundred Paternosters."

"Oh, you are a wicked woman, Wilma, deceiving a bishop, a count, and all those noble men and women. A woman deceiving a bishop who has gained his authority from the Pope!"

"But there were several moments, my little sister," Wilma's voice took on a serious note, "several moments when I would not have given the smallest part of a copper grochen for my chances of living another day. The thought of you being given over to the soldiers of the garrison..." She closed her eyes tight and shook her head. "For several moments it was as if a cold knife had pierced my chest." She hesitated, took in a full breath, and faced Joanna. "But was it wise to declare that you would master Hebrew and Greek before spring? And then when challenged by the count, to insist? You took a great risk, Joanna."

"Risk?" Joanna shrugged. "I will master Hebrew and Greek by the end of winter. Would you have had me tell that vile man that I was like one of his street urchins? Would you have had me crawl up to him and kiss his foot?"

"But the risk, Joanna."

"What risk? We serve the Mother of God. We are under divine protection. Have we not had sufficient proof?" She rested the palm of her hand against Wilma's cheek.

"What if I had not been able to think clearly, if I had not thought of doing what I did?"

"Then we would have had a miracle," Joanna smiled. "Perhaps the thunderbolt you mentioned, or some other thing."

"Oh, Joanna, Joanna, you are a strange child. Was there ever a child such as you?"

"And you are not strange, Wilma? A man who changes herself into a woman and then shamelessly displays her breasts? Threatening a count who commands a garrison of soldiers? Defying a bishop? And was it a nice thing to threaten all those high-born people with a plague? Are you Moses?" She took hold of the woman's hand. "Yet Moses was a stammerer and I have never heard anyone declare themselves as clearly as you. And you call me strange!"

Their hands joined together, the two monks continued to sit side by side, from time to time laughing and whispering.

"They appear to have no concerns," the servant assigned to keep them under observation reported to the bishop. "They are more light-hearted than any monks I have ever seen, and appear to be as close as father and son."

"Did you overhear any of their conversation?" the bishop asked.

The servant frowned. "I think I heard the older one use the word risk — I cannot be certain. For the rest, they kept their voices too soft. But they laughed a lot, Your Eminence. I cannot remember ever hearing such laughter in this cathedral."

"I am uneasy with their laughter." The bishop turned to his secretary. "What does it mean?" He drummed his fingers on his desk. "And the word 'risk'. Whose risk? What risk?" The man's face appeared to have grown more deeply wrinkled and his breathing was labored. "I am too old for risks. At my age, what is needed is quiet and comfort and sufficient time for study and prayer. I do not like that word 'risk'. Are they preparing some sort of test?" He looked hard at his secretary. The man, through long experience with the bishop, knowing what was required of him, kept his face fixed in a serious expression but did not answer. "My health cannot stand tests!" The bishop brought his fist down on his desk. "It is trial enough when the count of the palace swaggers into my chapel and challenges two emissaries from Rome — almost certainly of royal blood."

"And schooled in black magic, Your Eminence," the secretary chose his words carefully. "When the older one called for his miracle, it was not to be changed into a woman, but only to have the body of a woman. His ugly face was not changed by a single bump or scraggly whisker. And, Your Eminence, he showed only breasts." The bishop listened intently. "Those who have mastered the practice of magic, I have heard, find it no great feat to produce breasts at will. After all, a man already has paps. But to alter his manly parts or his features, that would truly take a miracle."

"Black magic," the bishop shuddered. "I would have rather it had been a miracle." The bishop picked at his lower lip for a few seconds. "Then they may not be from Rome?"

"From Rome, certainly. As Your Eminence said. I have heard it said there are cardinals in that city, more than a few, who will employ magic for their purposes — and who are not above schooling tonsured monks in the use of magic. I have heard some can talk to ravens and in this way transmit messages from a distance."

"Messages! They will send messages to Rome! We have a plague of ravens here in Aachen."

"But, Your Eminence, if the messages are all favorable, if they tell of our hospitality, if they declare Your Eminence's piety, if they attest to the excellence of the scholars of this cathedral — if such messages are transmitted, by the end of winter you may receive an invitation to come to Rome for your cardinal's cap."

"It is a long and difficult journey...with my infirmity of the bowels..." The bishop sighed. "But if I am called, I must go."

"And once in Rome, Your Eminence, no need to hurry back. A year of rest and contemplation in the city of the blessed St. Peter would be no more than your due. And if during this time a need should arise to elect a new pope..."

The bishop waved his secretary silent. "You allow your imagination to run away with you." A slight smile softened his lips. "But a year in Rome sharing holy thoughts with my revered colleagues would be no more than my due. A year spent in that warmer climate away from this accursed damp and cold might add to my span another five years." The bishop pulled his fur robe more tightly around his shoulders.

"Yes, the messages carried by their ravens must be favorable," the bishop continued. "That angel-faced boy declares he will master Greek and Hebrew. Perhaps that is a test to determine the worth of our scholars." The bishop patted his soft belly. "Well, we have no need to be ashamed of our scholars. The quality of learning has not lessened here in Aachen since the days of the Great Charles. I doubt if there is a greater scholar of ancient languages in all of Christendom than our venerable Sigbert. Even in his blindness, I would match him against any scholar with vision as keen as a hawk." The bishop chuckled, causing rolls of flesh on his neck to flap up and down. "Our Sigbert has stored in his memory more volumes than are contained in many monasteries." The bishop patted his belly again. "When I go to Rome I will take him with me."

"He will amaze them," the secretary offered. The bishop vigorously nodded.

"I will assign Sigbert to be the boy's tutor." The bishop continued to nod his head. "An arrogant one, that John. Declaring he will master both languages by the end of the winter."

"But he would not back down before the threats of the count," the secretary laughed. "Did you hear him say, 'your street urchins' to the count? Did you see the count's face at that?"

"We will do all in our power to assist the boy in fulfilling his declaration." The bishop squeezed his hands together. "Then we will arrange for a test by our most learned men — invite everyone to attend this test." The bishop's face now was so wreathed in smiles that his eyes were reduced to tiny slits. "And if the boy's arrogance is justified — and we will spare no effort to insure that it is — then when he has proved his mastery we will arrange for a document to be prepared, addressed to the count, making reference to his street urchins and other suitable matters; and we will have this document nailed to the door of the cathedral during the night. But we will neglect to append a signature."

"When he hears of this document he will be struck down with the apoplexy," the secretary added gleefully. "And, Your Eminence, would it not be wise to have several copies of this document prepared to be carried direct to the count by these same street urchins?"

"That a priest should offer such a suggestion," the bishop made a clucking sound. "For this suggestion, you must do a penance of a score of Paternosters." The secretary nodded. "But so that your throat should not grow too dry while you say this penance, I will order a flask of my best wine sent up to your room."

Matins over — for the first time in memory, the bishop had appeared to lead this mass — Joanna was hunched over the finely carved reading table in her room studying the *Mystagogical Catechesis of Cyril of Jerusalem*, contained in a large, worn volume of the writings of the patristic fathers. She had selected this volume from the library, aware of the sounds of surprise and awe of the several librarians. Wilma had slipped away to make certain cautious inquiries about the fate of her father. Except for the occasional splash of rain against the small leaded window caused by shifts in the wind, it was silent. The great bronze doors leading into the sanctuary were closed against the public and would remain closed until noon. The monks and priests were closeted in their cells and rooms. If there were any sounds coming from the kitchen at the far end of the cathedral, these were deadened by thick stone walls. Even the hordes of rats that inhabited the great structure were silent — resting after a night of busy scratching and scurrying.

Joanna's eyes moved slowly from line to line, forcing the complicated thoughts into her brain, raising questions, exploring which questions she would later attempt to have answered. So absorbed in study and so deep her concentration, it was as if Cyril had stepped out of seven centuries of dust and spoken to her. Suddenly her concentration was exploded, her questions scattered by a heavy knock on her door.

She restrained herself from uttering some intemperate remark, taking several seconds to compose her features, and to check that her clothes were all in order. Then fighting off the irritation she felt, she went to open the door as the knock sounded again.

The man who stood in the hallway waiting was the tallest human being she had ever seen. To enter her room, he had to hunch down and even then his head came within a fraction of an inch of striking the lintel. His shoulders were broader by at least a hand's width than those of the knight who commanded the defenders of the wall at Engelheim. His chest was much deeper, as deep as a tame dancing bear she had once seen. His hands were more than twice the size of her own, with fingers and knuckles showing such strength that she was unable to control a shudder. Yet the man's face was not harsh. His mouth, jaw and nose, although large, were well formed and in proportion. But the strangest thing was his eyes. She glanced at them several times, but could not see their pupils, and although the lids were open, they constantly fluttered like those of a very young bird.

He took several steps forward, then abruptly stopped as his thigh struck against the edge of her writing desk. Then she understood about his eyes. "Are you the monk John?" the man asked. He spoke in the purest Latin and the modulation of his voice and its softness was in sharp contrast to his strength and size.

Joanna nodded, but then, realizing what she did, answered in careful Latin that she was John.

"I am Sigbert. The bishop sent me to be your tutor. You are the one who declared you will be the master of Hebrew and Greek in less than half a year?" Joanna made an affirmative sound. "You do not know any words of these languages as yet?" Joanna indicated that she did not. "Then you are either the greatest ass or the most remarkable genius in all of Christendom. We will soon determine which."

With that, Sigbert began intoning words in Hebrew and Greek with their Latin equivalent. He spoke slowly, repeating each set three times. After something over a score of sets, he paused and nodded at Joanna. She took a deep breath, cleared her throat, and without hesitation repeated the sets exactly as given.

Sigbert made a noise deep in his chest and, still standing in the middle of the room, intoned another series of sets. When he paused, just as before, Joanna repeated them back without hesitation, and without being asked, repeated the first series of sets again.

"Let me embrace you, John," said the man, and he opened his massive arms wide. Joanna remained where she was. "As God is my witness I will embrace you, brother John. Step forward this instant."

As if she had lost the ability to resist, Joanna allowed herself to be embraced although she made not the slightest show of response.

"When I heard about your declaration in the chapel, I laughed." Sigbert released Joanna. "My affection for the count of the castle is very little. But his use of the expression 'street urchin' might have been my own if I had been present to hear your arrogant declaration, brother John." The man groped around until he found a stool, then sat down. "And you are arrogant. Although you have just given me more than sufficient proof of your skills, you are an arrogant one. For those who have taken orders, it is best to wear the cloak of humility, no matter if your thoughts are otherwise."

"Humility is the cloak of doubters." The words leapt from Joanna's lips before she was able to control them.

"Then doubt, brother John. When you are of a sufficient age and have gained sufficient rank, you may on occasion reveal your certainty. But until that time, you risk more than you gain by not showing humility." The man paused and ran the fingers of his hand through his thick hair. "And have you considered, brother John, that arrogance may be no less a cloak of doubt than humility?" Joanna caught her breath. The works of the patristic fathers which she had been reading rang with a certainty that was more than certainty; rang with arrogance. She stared at Sigbert. Did he understand the full implications of what he had just said? Thoughts spun through her mind. Had there ever been declarations more arrogant than those of Paul in his letters to the newly formed Christian communities? Was his arrogance a mask for his doubt?

"I will learn to be humble, if you will teach me," said Joanna.

Sigbert exploded into laughter, bringing his hand down on his thigh with force enough to bring a fully armored man to his knees.

"You have found me out, little brother John. Any lessons in humility you would get from me would prove to be about as effective as a course of instruction in good manners from the count of the palace. We will stick to that which I know." The man let out another explosion of laughter.

Had Wilma not entered the room shortly before noon, Sigbert and Joanna might have missed the mid-day meal. In his wildest imagining, the man had never pictured a pupil with the ability of Joanna. She had already acquired a vocabulary of over a hundred words in both Hebrew and Greek, and was beginning to use them in phrases. As for Joanna, she had never experienced a tutor with the intensity and self-confidence of the venerable Sigbert. Both lost track of time. Both ignored whatever signals of hunger that came from their stomachs. Both lost their awareness that a world existed outside this room. And both were unable to control expressions of annoyance and sounds of irritation when Wilma entered the room.

"I have been better received by strangers," Wilma said in a choked voice, after Sigbert left. "The way you looked at me, Joanna, as if I were a toad." Joanna blushed and hung her head. But when Wilma asked about the huge man, Joanna was unable to contain her excitement — her eyes glistened and her breathing quickened.

"He is the wisest man in the world, Wilma! The things he taught me went into my mind with such ease! He is blind, Wilma, but I am certain he must have read every volume ever written."

"Every volume, Joanna?" Wilma hesitated, then drew the girl close to her. "His assignment may be more than just a tutor, little sister. Those who are blind can often find out things hidden from those who have perfect vision. Learn what you can from the man, but be careful. Remember he is in the employ of the bishop. Be careful, dearest Joanna. If our true identity is discovered...." She was only partially successful in controlling a shudder.

As he had been ordered, Sigbert reported to the bishop each afternoon. Wanting to be certain, his first few reports were cautious. The young monk certainly had ability. Was an alert pupil. Things were progressing well. But then after the passage of a week, now certain of his pupil's extraordinary ability and fired with excitement, the man was unable to restrain himself any longer.

"I will risk my chance of salvation, Your Eminence, if he is not another Alcuin!" Sigbert stood before the bishop and his secretary. "He sucks knowledge from my brain as dried moss sucks up water. Scarcely are the words out of my mouth when he gives them back to me in a way that proves his understanding. After a morning with that John my mind is so exhausted I am forced to sleep half the afternoon. One week and he knows as much of the two ancient languages as others gain in three or four months."

"Then he will master them by the end of winter?" the bishop interrupted.

"More than master them, Your Eminence. Unless I am suffering from a softening of the brain so that I can no longer think clearly, this young monk by the name of John will be able to instruct others in these languages by the end of winter, will be able to enter into learned disputations in either language, if called upon. Never have I known a mind as quick as his. As I already said, Your Eminence, it leaves me exhausted."

"The count of the palace will be so pleased to hear about this," the secretary murmured softly to the bishop. "I would gladly do a penance of a thousand Paternosters just to see his face."

"The demands of our friendship require that I send him intelligence of John's progress," the bishop murmured back, taking care that Sigbert did not overhear him. "Had it not been for the count's interest in the boy, he might never have been granted as expert a course of instruction."

"The count will appreciate your generosity in assigning your most learned scholar as a tutor," the secretary murmured back. "If it pleases Your Eminence, I will visit him myself. Perhaps if bring him the present of a psalter..."

"He cannot read a word, not a word," the bishop gurgled. "When he makes his mark, his hand must be guided." The gurgles turned into suppressed squeals. "Yes, you must bring him a present of a psalter — one carefully illuminated and of sufficient worth." The bishop closed his eyes and allowed a smile to play on his lips.

Had his own chaplain not been present the count would have ripped the psalter into shreds after the bishop's secretary left. So great was his effort in controlling his hand, that purple veins stood out of his neck and the pulse in his temple grew visible. Flinging the psalter at the chaplain, he dismissed all his attendants except his lieutenant in such a voice that they stumbled over one another in their haste to get out of the hall.

He glared at the door through which the secretary had departed. "I swear on the grave of my father that the bishop will suffer for this mockery." The count's body shook with the force of his anger. "One blow of this fist and his skull would break open like a rotted pomegranate. That pile of stinking turds has lived long enough." The count waved his fist before the face of his lieutenant.

"I have a cousin who works in the storeroom of the cathedral, Your Honor. For a piece of gold I think I can convince him to slip a noose of pig gut around the bishop's neck while he sleeps."

"Murder the bishop?" The pulse in the count's temple grew stronger. "I would put my left hand into the fire and hold it there until it was burnt black if such a thing were possible."

"Give me your order and the bishop will be wearing another sort of collar before the world grows a day older."

"And when word reaches Rome, the Pope will order half the knights in the empire into Aachen who will then fit us with like collars. No, the bishop cannot be harmed — may he rot in hell for all of eternity. No, there is nothing we can do to that one." The count walked over to the window and stared in the direction of the cathedral. "Soldiers commanded by my father helped drag the stones that made its walls." He pointed toward the great structure, and the lieutenant who stood at his side nodded. "If he knew what sort of a man now sat on its throne he would not be able to rest peacefully in his grave. Sending a psalter to the count of the castle!" The count gripped the iron grill work guarding the window and with a powerful wrench pulled it partially free.

"If my cousin cannot serve Your Honor by visiting the bishop in his room, perhaps he can serve in some lesser fashion." The lieutenant paused for a moment. "Whose arrogant words gave rise to the events which led to this act of mockery?" he asked.

The count slowly turned his head until his eyes were focused directly on those of the lieutenant.

"Had it not been for that pretty boy and his companion with the face of a demon...." The lieutenant broke off as the count's lips pulled back, exposing the points of his teeth. "For a small piece of gold, my cousin will visit those monks and give them such presents that their faces will have turned black by morning."

"Not the older one! You heard him threaten to bring down a thunderbolt on this palace. He is too dangerous. But the young whelp, that arrogant pup would look well wearing your cousin's collar. And it would be a fair return for the psalter, although it is best if we do not acknowledge this gift." His face showing a faint semblance of a smile, the count reached into the wallet which hung at his hip, extracted a gold coin which he placed in the lieutenant's hand. Then, without another word, his eyes again focused in the direction of the cathedral, he dismissed the man.

Joanna struggled to settle down into sleep. Several times she had almost slipped away when a thought, phrased in Hebrew or Greek, dropped on her mind like a hot spark, jolting her awake. She had suffered this same difficulty in falling asleep each night for the entire week since the start of her instructions; yet each morning she awoke refreshed and alert, her eyes clear, her body relaxed and light. She tried to concentrate on Wilma's deep, even breathing. The woman had gone out each day in search of information about her family, but thus far had learned nothing. Afraid to be seen by anyone who might recognize her, she avoided the section of the city where she had once lived, confining her investigation to queries made of various merchants; questions to different parish priests; visits to several graveyards and a conversation with an old scribe whose task it was to record important events that took place in the city.

"Poor Wilma," Joanna silently formed the words with her lips. The woman's face had looked so troubled each time after she returned. And she had shown a certain uneasiness with Sigbert. Joanna wanted to tell the woman that she had no reason to be jealous of her tutor, that all she was interested in was the scholar's knowledge, that as for the rest of him she detested him as a man. She wanted to say these things, but somehow she could not. She could almost hear Wilma protesting that it was ridiculous to suggest that she might be jealous, that even to say such a thing was an insult.

"He is a man!" Joanna whispered softly, forcing a hiss of contempt into her voice. "Except for his knowledge, he is like all the others." But he was not like the other men she had known. Being blind made him different. Somehow, because he could not see her, she felt almost as safe with him as with a woman. Alone in her room with him, she did not have to take care that some chance action would reveal her sex. And his blindness allowed her to openly examine his face. Except for Rolf, and he only when he slept, Joanna had never openly studied a man's features. She liked Sigbert's almost square jaw, softened by a slight indentation in the chin. And those clouded eyes of his were so strange. Their shifting back and forth and the flutter of their lids made it appear that the man was weak and frightened. But then she would lower her eyes to his thick neck, to his shoulders knotted with muscle, to his huge hands and powerful fingers. Sampson could not have been more powerful. Wilma groaned in her sleep, made some sounds that were not quite words, then settled back into her deep regular breathing. Joanna settled herself down in her bed, folded her hands over her chest and allowed her lids to slowly close as fatigue began to ease her toward the dark curtain of sleep.

Outside the door of the room, pressed into the shadow of a shallow alcove, the lieutenant's cousin waited. His face and hands blackened with soot, a tight leather cap on his head, he had been standing there motionless for more than an hour. Twice he had tensed himself in preparation for entering the room, but the sounds of Joanna adjusting herself in her bed caused him to remain where he was. He had kissed his cousin's hand and fallen to his knees when offered the piece of gold. He and all his family stood in awe of this principle knight of the palace, and now to be given a piece of gold, enough to buy land for his sons, he would have gladly kissed the knight's feet in gratitude. A moment's work with a noose made of twisted pig gut, and he would be rich.

The man eased out of the alcove, then brought his ear close to the door. The deep, roughened sounds of the older one were just as they had been for the past hour. He could not hear breathing sounds from the younger one, but the boy no longer stirred in his bed, thus must be asleep. Adjusting his dagger so that its haft protruded from his tunic, holding the ready noose in one hand, he carefully pressed down on the wooden door handle with the other. There was a faint click as the latch pulled free. The man waited several seconds while he steadied his breathing, then slowly pushed the door open.

The sound of the latch being released caught Joanna just as she

was about to fall asleep. A rat, she vaguely thought, making no effort
to open her eyes. She began to slip again toward sleep when a movement of air coming from the direction of the door jerked her mind
awake.

Holding her body still, she opened her eyes. The indistinct
shadow of a man loomed in the doorway. Tensing her muscles and
holding her breath, she kept her eyes on the shadowy form as it approached. Then, just as he reached her bed, she let out a shriek, leapt
up, kicked at his face with all her strength, then uttering a second
shriek, leapt in the direction of Wilma who already was half out of her
bed, the knife she always kept by her side in her hand.

The man dropped the noose, pulled his dagger out and rushed at
Wilma as she came at him. The point of his weapon caught the muscle
of her shoulder, but as he was trying to escape out the door, her knife
sliced into his face, laying it open from hairline to jaw.

The shrieks and sounds of struggle brought several guards running to the room, but by the time they arrived the assassin was gone,
leaving behind a trail of blood. Within minutes, the entire cathedral
was awake and before the passage of an hour, the bishop had ordered
Wilma and Joanna into his presence.

Hastily dressed, his eyes still puffed with sleep, the bishop sat at
his desk, his secretary also showing signs of recent sleep standing on
one side, the archdeacon of the cathedral, a gaunt, dark-faced, scowling man, standing on the other, while lesser functionaries were arranged around the room. The captain of the cathedral guards presented the assassin's noose to the bishop. "We found it on the young
monk's bed." He gravely shook his head. "Only a miracle saved him
from being strangled." He carefully laid the noose on the bishop's
desk. "The older one received a nasty cut, Your Eminence, but he
gave as good as he got. There is a trail of blood leading down the
hallway, then out to the courtyard, but it is too dark to follow the trail
any further."

"An attempted assassination!" the bishop sputtered with rage.
"And of a monk, here in this cathedral!" He brought his fist down full
force on his desk. "This is a desecration. The assassin must be found.
All who are connected with this vile attempt to murder a servant of
Christ and in His most holy temple will be anathematized. Will be
brought to trial and then turned over to the public hangman for burning." He struggled to his feet, a foam of saliva showing on his lips, his
face the color of raw liver. "Even if those who are responsible for this
shameful desecration prove to be of high birth, as Christ is my witness, I swear they will suffer the extreme penalty just as if they were

common footpads or tavern cutpurses." He turned to his secretary for a moment and they exchanged a glance of understanding. "I want every servant of the cathedral examined for a fresh wound." He turned to the archdeacon. "I want these two monks guarded night and day." He flung a gesture in the direction of Joanna and Wilma. "They must be protected. When the guilty ones are brought to trial, we will need them as witnesses."

The archdeacon inclined his head, then ceremoniously cleared his throat. "Is it your belief that several are involved in this attempted assassination, Your Eminence? Only one was seen in the room."

"It is more than just a belief. I will not say any names. I will not make any accusations until I have sufficient proof. But as I know Christ died for us, I know that there was more than one involved." A fresh wave of rage swept over the man and he brought his fist down on his desk again. "I will not rest until the guilty have been brought to trial and punished."

Her face drained of color, her shoulder throbbing from the wound, Wilma was questioned again about the details of the attack and the nature of the wound she inflicted on the assassin. And the bishop muttered angrily when all the monk could say about the man was that he was of average size and that she believed it was his face that she wounded. Joanna could add nothing. Her memory of the shadowed form was confused and distorted. At the time he had appeared huge. She knew she had kicked at him, but could not tell where her foot connected. As she stood in the bishop's chamber, brightly lit with more than a score of rush lights, the incident felt like a dream, a nightmare from which she had been awakened, and about which she was now being questioned.

But when the archdeacon for some unexplained reason felt it necessary to test the noose to see if it fitted over her head and she felt the cold dampness of the twisted pig gut against her neck, the dreamlike quality of the incident evaporated, and Joanna felt a sinking sensation in her abdomen.

By early afternoon the assassin had been found. In obedience to the bishop's orders, all the servants of the cathedral were examined for wounds and questioned, and when it was discovered that one of the pantrymen was missing, the bishop's bailiff, accompanied by a dozen armed men, went to his home and found him hiding in the cellar under a pile of hay. The man's cheek had been laid open so that in one place his teeth could be seen. His neck and shoulder were covered with clots of blood and he was so weak that for most of the distance to the cathedral he had to be carried.

What sort of questions were asked of the man and the nature of his answers, no one could learn. He had been taken immediately to a subterranean cell by the bailiff and had been visited by the archdeacon and the bishop's secretary. But what was learned, and then quickly passed from mouth to mouth until the entire cathedral buzzed with this information, was the close kinship of the man to the count of the castle's lieutenant and principal knight. By late afternoon, a messenger had been dispatched by the bishop to travel south to Toulon to inform the papal legate what had happened.

Joanna and Wilma learned of the assassin's capture and of his relationship with the count's lieutenant from Sigbert. His face the color of chalk, his lips looking as if they were powdered with dust, the huge man shouldered through the armed guards in the hallway, bringing his finger to his lips as he carefully shut the door. Easing down on a stool he gestured to them to come close; then in a voice little more than a whisper, told them what had taken place.

"It was the count who ordered your death, my little brother." The man nodded his head as he spoke. "No one says his name, but everyone knows he must have been the one. You insulted his honor; and then the bishop for his own reasons made certain the count did not forget this insult. They hate each other. And now you are in even worse danger. Both of you. You are witnesses to this attempted assassination. You are the ones who will be called, together with the assassin, when the count and his lieutenant are brought to trial." Sigbert rubbed his hand over his eyes. "As I know there is a God in heaven, I know the count will spare no effort to have both of you put to death. Without you there can be no trial. And he has enough gold to hire an army of assassins." As the man spoke, Joanna's throat grew so tight she couldn't swallow and Wilma bit so deeply into her lip that the corners of her mouth were tinged red with blood. "I will stay here with you day and night — I will sleep on the floor. But unless you can escape...." Sigbert made a helpless gesture.

"The bishop will never permit it," Wilma's voice, although reduced almost to a whisper, cracked as she spoke. "They are both madmen. The bishop no less than the count. We have done nothing. Nothing." She stopped speaking as the throb in her shoulder rose up through her into her head.

When the bishop went down to the subterranean cell late that afternoon to question the captured assassin, he found the man dead, a crossbow shaft fired through the peep hole in the iron door neatly placed in his neck. The sight of the dead man aroused such a rage in the bishop that for a time he could not speak. Only after he was bled by his physician and forced to sniff spirits of nitre could his words be understood.

"He confessed being in the employ of the count?" the bishop asked the archdeacon in a croak.

"He said his commission was from the principle knight, his cousin, but in the name of the count," the archdeacon replied. "At first he said nothing but after the application of just a little torture, he freely confessed. His payment was a piece of gold with which he intended to purchase land for his sons..." The bishop waved the man silent.

"I will risk my chance of salvation if that crossbow shaft was not purchased with a like piece of gold from the same source," the bishop muttered. "He destroys the chief witness against him."

"It will be enough if the two monks testify to the attempted assassination, Your Eminence," the archdeacon said in a confident voice. "Alive or dead, everyone knows the man was related by blood to the count's lieutenant and we have recovered the piece of gold from his slut-wife. Where should a man like him who works for grochens get a coin of such value? All we need is for the monks to declare under oath that the man entered their chamber bent on assassination — the wound on the older one's shoulder is additional proof. A hundred will testify to the count's anger at brother John. Who in all of Aachen has not heard of brother John's declaration of 'your street urchins?' The count further condemns himself by this vile murder."

"Before he is given over to the public hangman to be burnt, I will have him tortured." The bishop spoke softly so that only those who were closest to him could hear. "I will have him tortured until he begs for death. By bringing violence into this cathedral the very authority of the Church is threatened."

"Yet the count has more than two gold coins in his wallet," the secretary, taking care that his words were not overheard, whispered into the bishop's ear. "If the two monks are not alive to testify, Your Eminence, we have no case."

The bishop turned to the bailiff and pointed a trembling finger at the midsection of the man. "I place the two monks in your charge. If any harm comes to them I will declare you excommunicate. One way or the other the hangman will have his work to do. Do I make my meaning clear?" The bailiff nodded. "Other than your own self, my secretary, or the archdeacon, no one is to enter their chamber."

"The blind scholar is with them now. I will order him instantly removed." The bailiff started to turn toward one of his men.

"He may remain." The bishop waved his hand. "No need to interfere with the course of instruction. But there are no other exceptions." He hesitated. "Even if a priest or a scribe comes saying he has permission, seize him. I will give no one permission. No one. Do you understand?" Again the bailiff nodded.

"As great as I believed your danger when we spoke this morning, I now believe it to be even greater." Sigbert spoke to Wilma and Joanna in a voice which he tried to force soft, but so great was his agitation that some of his words rang louder than he intended. He took in several deep breaths, laced his hands together until the fingers turned white, then continued. "The man who visited you last night now wears a crossbow shaft in his throat — shot as easily as if he had been standing in the midst of the public square. If I know anything, I know the count will find a way to kill both of you. He will never allow a trial to take place. Not if it costs him his entire fortune. And there are those who would behead their own mothers for a gold coin. Even some who live within the walls of this cathedral. Some who may have even taken orders." The faces of the woman and the girl drained of color as they listened to the man.

"But if we stay alive until the trial then we will be safe?" Wilma's voice was almost pleading.

"The count has brothers and sons and friends. Do you think they will allow those who caused his disgrace and death to remain alive!" The man's face showed deep lines in his forehead and around his eyes — it was almost as if an unseen hand pulled at his skin. "But you will not remain alive until the trial. It will take weeks, perhaps a month before the papal legate arrives. They will not let you remain alive. They will find a way."

"Then we must escape." Joanna spoke in a voice carefully drained of emotion. "I have no wish to die because of a quarrel between a bishop and a count. We will find a way to escape."

"But in the meantime, my little brother, we must exercise extreme caution." Sigbert unclasped his hands. "Do not eat or drink anything that does not come directly from these hands. Not so much as a crust of bread or a mouthful of water. With the score of soldiers they have guarding you out there in the hall, I am certain the first attempts to kill you will be with poison. But you must pretend to eat whatever you are given so as not to arouse any suspicion. If the count and his men discover that I am bringing you food, blind as I am, they will easily find a way so that what I carry is filled with poison. I will need several days to devise a method for your escape. In the meantime, let them think the poison they are feeding you (and there will be poison) is slowly working. Act as if you are unwell. Put a portion of the food into the rat holes so they have no doubts that you have eaten. At night moan and groan. If they believe their poison is working, they will not attempt another method."

After Sigbert left their chamber, Wilma and Joanna stared at one another for a long time without speaking. Outside, in the hallway, they could hear the muffled sounds of the soldiers: the creak of leather fittings, the clank of weapons and armor, coughs, throat clearings, occasional snatches of conversation. The last rays of autumn sun slanted through the narrow window forming patches of deep orange on the stone walls. From time to time, Wilma sighed. When she shifted her body, she groaned as the throb in her wounded shoulder worsened. Finally, drawing Joanna close to her with her good arm, trying to steady her voice, she said softly, "I cannot see any way for us to escape. If only I had not suggested that we come to Aachen, my little sister. If only I had resisted the hunger to learn the fate of my father. It was for my own selfish needs that I urged Aachen, and now we face certain death. And I still do not know any more about my father." Tears filled the woman's eyes then spilled out and ran down her cheeks.

Joanna carefully brushed the tears from the woman's cheeks. "You are a silly goose to blame yourself for what has happened. If I had been less arrogant...It has been a good lesson. But I know I am protected, that we are under divine protection. Before three days we will escape. Sigbert will find a way."

Following Sigbert's suggestion, they stuffed a portion of the food given to them by their guards down various rat holes, then during the night when awakened at different times by Sigbert, who insisted upon staying the night in their chamber, they groaned and moaned, although they both doubted that any attempt on them would be made so soon. But whatever doubts they may have had vanished in the morning when they awoke and saw two dead rats lying on the floor.

Joanna stared at the rodents with horror and fascination. Then she raised her eyes to Sigbert's face. The huge man, his back resting against the door, had allowed himself to fall asleep. Without his warning it might have been she and Wilma instead of those gray creatures with dried blood on their snouts. Joanna glanced at Wilma. The woman's face showed the same horror. She looked again at the dead creatures, at their scaly tails, their little paws clenched into fists, then she shifted her eyes back to the face of the sleeping man. Even sleep had not been able to smooth out the deep lines and creases in his forehead and around his eyes. His lips were slightly parted and, like a sleeping baby, a bubble formed from time to time. Joanna was unable to keep her eyes from glancing down at the man's swollen crotch showing between his wide-sprawled legs. She swallowed several times as she felt heat rise from her chest into her throat. This man was so different from the other men she had known. Was her father like this man, she wondered?

"If not for Sigbert, we would be dead," Wilma murmured, unable to turn her eyes away from the dead rodents. "He will find a way for us to escape. He will find a way..." Her voice trailed off.

Unable to control herself, not fully aware of her actions, Joanna jumped up, ran over to the man and threw her arms around his neck jerking him suddenly into wakefulness. A flood of tears poured from her eyes onto his cheeks. "Thank you. Thank you," she forced out between her sobs, then she showered his forehead, eyes, and lips with kisses.

When Sigbert learned the reason for this show of affection, he gently pushed Joanna away, then held out his hands for the dead creatures. "There is no time to lose," he muttered in a hoarse voice. "If they find you are not dead from their poison, after a few days they will use another method. A method against which we may not be able to defend." His fingers examined the stiffened bodies of the rodents. "If only I were not blind," he murmured. He let the two rats fall to the floor. "Yet if my eyes were like those of other men, I would not be allowed to remain here in this room with you — they would not allow me to come and go as I please with no more concern than they would have at the coming and going of a dog." He stopped speaking and Wilma and Joanna waited for him to continue. Several minutes passed. The man's breathing had grown deep and regular, and, except for the fact that his eyes were still open, he might have been taken for asleep. Then he asked, "How is this room furnished, brother John?" Joanna was startled. Her mind had begun to drift as she watched the breathing movements of his thick chest. "Tell me exactly. Everything."

"A table, two stools, a covered bucket for slops, two beds and, except for a cross carved of stone which hangs next to the window, nothing else."

"Bare as a room inhabited by monks should be," Sigbert murmured half to himself. "And the beds, brother John. What sort of bedding?"

"Bundles of straw, rushes, and a sheepskin covering."

"And the straw has not been changed since you have been here?" Sigbert asked.

"From its stink and from various little creatures that inhabit it, it has not been changed in six months," Wilma answered.

"Filled with bed bugs and lice, and you guests of the bishop." Sigbert shook his head. "I will complain to the bailiff at once."

That evening, when the blind man appeared in the hallway leading to the monk's room carrying a large sack of straw and rushes on his back, the soldiers on guard started laughing. They had heard the man's voice thundering at the bailiff about the disgraceful condition of the room, had heard the insults heaped on their commmander's head — never in the memory of any of them had the venerable Sigbert called another son of a whore. They had pounded one another's arms as the bailiff exploded in anger, telling the blind man if there was to be any new bedding he would have to fetch it himself.

Now, giving the huge man, whose black tunic was dusted with flakes of snow, a few friendly pats on the shoulder, they passed him into the monk's room. And when he left the room an hour later, carrying the same sack now filled with old straw and rushes, not wanting to play host to the lice and bed bugs that swarmed on the outside of the sack, they kept their distance. Not so much as a breath of suspicion crossed any of their minds, for when the door had opened, the soldiers could see both of the monks lying snuggly in bed under their thick sheepskin covers.

Only a man as powerful as Sigbert could have carried that sack with an appearance of so little effort. And as he approached the guards stationed at the rear entrance to the cathedral, he made a show of scratching with one hand, dislodging some of the insects he had so carefully placed in his hair. This caused the soldiers to recoil as, faces screwed up into expressions of disgust, they waved the blind man out into the night.

Walking slowly, concentrating all the power of his mind on the icy street whose every twist and obstacle he had carefully studied, Sigbert moved away from the cathedral. Once, hearing a familiar cough — a scribe returning from some errand — he announced with a laugh that he was transporting some ripe bedding, and the scribe without another sound hurried away. But the moment he reached a narrow alley used mostly by the populace for relieving themselves, holding one arm straight out, his back bent under the weight of the sack, he walked quickly into the darkness.

IV

THE CAVE

*O*nly the few minutes that it took a frantic messenger to race the short distance from the cathedral separated the explosion of activity in the castle, generated by bellowed orders from the count, from like activity set into motion by high-pitched shrieks from the bishop.

The bailiff entering the monks' room with their breakfast should have been suspicious when he found that the door was not barred, just as the guards should have been suspicious hours earlier when the blind man did not return to take up his vigil in their room. That the two monks were still in bed at this hour did not arouse the bailiff's suspicion as he placed their breakfast on the table. But they lay so still, their faces hidden under the sheepskins — had something happened to them?

The bailiff's scream of anguish could be heard halfway through the cathedral. As the soldiers rushed into the room, they found him holding onto the table for support, eyes bulging, struggling to catch his breath. Then when he was half helped, half carried into the presence of the bishop, who stripped him of his authority on the spot and ordered that he be imprisoned until the monks were found, the bailiff fainted, cutting his forehead as he fell and had to be carried unconscious from the room.

The first order issued by the bishop was for the cathedral to be sealed shut and then searched from the rafters supporting the highest steeple to the subterranean cells, cisterns, and catacombs.

The count's first order was for the formation of search parties to comb the city, groups of mounted men to search along the several roads leading away from Aachen.

By midday, the bishop publicly proclaimed a reward of a double handful of silver for the safe return of the two monks. The count also declared a reward, but his reward was in gold, was not publicly announced, and made no condition about the monks' safe return.

By late afternoon, the bishop was beginning to resign himself to the loss of the two monks. If they showed up later, there could always be a trial. And as the hours passed he allowed himself to consider the disadvantages of a trial. Having the count's brothers, sons, and cousins as enemies might prove to be a problem. But the count's distress grew greater with each passing hour. If the monks made good their escape and reached the papal legate or some other high church dignitary, he could be tried and condemned in absentia, and once condemned could be taken and put to death by anyone who wanted to curry favor with the Church.

The promise of silver from the cathedral, of gold from the palace, kept bands of armed men, carrying blazing torches, out in the streets and alleyways of Aachen late into the night. At different times, two bands would confront one another where the streets crossed, and, neither band willing to give way, they would clash, using their torches and staffs as weapons. Although no one was killed in these clashes, more than a dozen had their heads broken and several sheds and buildings were set afire. Only the appearance of the city watch, helmeted and carrying their swords unsheathed, who ordered every man back to his home under the penalty of death, prevented even more serious consequences.

While search parties combed every inch of the cathedral, probed the various subterranean passages of the city, peered into lofts and cellars, looked under mounds of hay, and even prodded into piles of manure with sticks; while bands of mounted men searched the highways beyond the walls of the city, then fanned out into the countryside, Joanna, Wilma and Sigbert were hidden in the one place no one thought to search.

From the moment his plans were laid, Sigbert knew that his blindness would prevent any rapid departure from the city, for they had no horses. Even if they had horses, they would have been unable to leave until morning when the gates were opened and by then it might have been too late. Their only chance of safety was to find a hiding place where even the most alert searcher would not think to look. Thus it was that Sigbert, after freeing the two monks from the sack and after catching his breath, led the way through a series of narrow alleys to a seldom-used passage leading down into the cellar of the palace. And it was in the great vault where casks of wine and mead were stored that they found a safe hiding place.

For four days they stayed hidden in the cellar, waiting for the search to slacken. On the several occasions when the steward came

down to draw pitchers of drink for the count's table, they crawled behind the wine casks, covered themselves with straw and lay motionless. But the steward never remained in the cellar longer than he had
to, for he was a nervous little man, and the place swarmed with rats.

Much of their time was devoted to study. At times it was almost
as if they were back in the room in the cathedral. When Sigbert and
Joanna spoke in Latin, Wilma occasionally joined in the conversation.
But when they employed Greek or Hebrew words, she would occupy
herself with other matters.

It was as Sigbert addressed Joanna in Hebrew, using the word
from the passage of Isaiah which speaks of the young woman who will
conceive, that Joanna realized he had discovered her secret. She
glanced at Wilma who was trying to repair a tear in her tunic with a
bone needle — the woman was unaware of what had happened. She
shifted her glance to Sigbert's face. Had he let slip this word by accident, or was it deliberate? The man's expression told nothing. She
continued with the Hebrew conversation as if the word had been without any special significance. But there was something about the man's
lips, as if he were concealing a smile. Something about the way the
corners of his mouth tightened a little.

"So you know our secret." Joanna shifted from Hebrew to Latin,
and Wilma's head jerked up from her work. "How long have you
known, my venerable tutor?" she continued, ignoring Wilma's frantic
expression.

Allowing his lips to settle into a grin, Sigbert cleared his throat
several times. "How long, little brother, or should I say, little sister?
How long have I known that you and your companion were of the
same sex as Christ's mother? From the first moment of the first day I
stepped into your room." He paused and gave his stomach a slow and
deliberate scratch. "Those whose eyes have sight are often blinded by
what they see. Not being able to see your monk's robes, your shaved
pates, the way you must exaggerate your walk, I knew at once you
were women. And that great miracle of yours — what is your real
name?" Wilma hesitated a moment, then told him: "That great
miracle of yours, Wilma, stuck in my craw the moment I heard of it.
Not that I deny miracles, but somehow yours seemed just too con-
venient. And you." He laid his hand on Joanna's shoulder. "Without
my eyes to fool me, how could I not have heard the girlish ring to your
voice despite all your efforts to roughen it? Even if you had been silent
I would have known. Somehow, I would have known. We who are
blind learn to sense certain things."

"He knew it all the time," Wilma muttered. "Yet he said nothing." She shook her head slowly.

"I am a scholar and a tutor, not an executioner. Had I breathed a word of what I knew, you might have been put to death."

Joanna took the man's hand and held it with both of hers. Wilma hesitated, then reached out and took the other.

By the fifth day after the monks' escape, all the search parties had been recalled. Even those most greedy for the rewards resigned themselves to the fact that the two holy men and the blind scholar somehow had made their way into the mountains where they could find shelter in the caves of hermits and never be discovered. So the extra guards had been withdrawn from the city gates and those few guards on duty scarcely noticed the charcoal burner, his face and hands stained grey-black, accompanied by his ugly wife and their ragged daughter as the three passed out the western gate and then turned off onto a pathway leading into the woods.

That day, Joanna and Wilma traveled as women, but when they emerged from the cattle shed in which they had found a little shelter during the cold night, they were again dressed as men — women traveling the forests and roads without armed protection risked too much danger.

"Another day's travel and we should be out of the district of Aachen," Wilma said as they crouched around a small fire during their midday rest.

"Out of the district, but not beyond the count's reach," Sigbert answered. "That one cares nothing for districts. Until we put a body of water between us and Aachen, we will not be safe. The count has long arms and many friends."

"The bishop also," Wilma added.

"Yes, the bishop. He was once my protector and friend..." Sigbert sighed.

Keeping to pathways in the forests, avoiding the main roads even when these were the more direct and would have saved them many miles, the three traveled in a westerly direction. Some nights they were forced to huddle together, sharing the warmth of their bodies, with leaves and twigs piled over them as their only protection from the weather. Those nights were painful, leaving them stiff with aching muscles, their insides quivering from the cold. But some nights when fortune was with them, they came upon farm houses that doubled as inns. These, without exception, were filthy, crawling with lice and vermin, providing no more than an armful of sour straw on the bare floor for beds. But at least they were warm, had a fire blazing in the hearth, and offered a cooked meal of sorts. When they entered these inns, except for a demand for payment of a copper grochen in advance by the drink-swollen landlord, they were scarcely noticed. Hunters, woodgatherers, or just wandering, masterless men, was the assessment of those who glanced at them as they entered the various smoke-blackened public rooms. They had discarded all appearance of clerics, wore daggers in their belts, their heads covered with strips of colored cloth in the manner of men who owe allegiance to no master. Joanna had blackened her teeth, drawn a scar on one cheek with charcoal and red ochre, wore a patch over one eye so that despite her slight build, her appearance was fierce. Wilma, by the use of charcoal, bits of wool pasted to her cheeks and chin, had heightened her masculine features. Sigbert's size alone was sufficient to give him a fierce appearance, and he was careful to keep his eyes hooded to hide the fact that he was blind. Wilma and Joanna had perfected a method of walking close to the man to guide him, yet without revealing what they were doing.

Knowing the ways of landlords in inns such as these, Sigbert arranged that one of them should always remain awake. And it was during their third week of travel, while he was on guard, that a landlord and his wife, armed with heavy clubs, approached them on tiptoe. Believing all three of their guests asleep (their eyes were closed and had been closed for over an hour) the two had signaled one another. Sigbert, alert as only a blind man can be alert, waited till they were close, till he could hear their breathing, could smell their stink, then he leapt up and cracked their heads together, knocking the landlord senseless and stunning the landlady, but not enough to prevent her from screaming. Within moments, the landlord's two lumbering sons appeared, quickly followed by several swollen-eyed servants armed with staffs.

Although the three of them managed to escape, it was not without injury. The wound in Wilma's shoulder had been reopened, Sigbert's nose bled and his hand was cut. Joanna showed a lump on her jaw almost the size of the fist that had struck her, and her left arm was numb from a blow to her shoulder.

Out in the winter night, a fierce north wind brought in gusts of snow, their bodies throbbed from their injuries and their spirits were severely depressed. They struggled through the night, but as the minutes passed they realized they might fail to survive until morning. Just when they seemed at the point of sinking into the snow forever, Joanna saw a point of light flickering from within a cave partially hidden by a thicket of thorny bushes.

She started to rush forward, but was stopped by Sigbert's iron grip. "What if there are brigands in that cave, Joanna?" he whispered.

"But I am so cold..." the girl chattered. "My arm is numb — I can't go on."

Wilma gripped Sigbert's arm. "If there is only one or two, even three, we can take the cave from them." The woman's words came in quick gasps. "If we move carefully the wind will hide our sounds. If we surprise them... Better to fight for that warm cave than freeze to death out here."

"Fight brigands! A girl. A woman. A blind man. With only daggers and clubs for weapons." Sigbert snorted.

"They may not be brigands," Joanna forced her words through her chattering teeth. "There may be a holy man to give us shelter. Or a cow-herd." The man shrugged, then nodded.

Hunched down, their weapons in their hands, they approached the cave, Wilma leading, Joanna in the rear. They paused at half a dozen paces from its entrance. Then they rushed in.

They were greeted, as if they had been expected, by a creature who although recognizable as human was so unkempt and smoke-stained that it was impossible to determine its sex or age. The creature laughed and clapped its hands as they entered the cave, then threw them several pieces of burnt meat as if they were dogs coming in from the hunt. Wilma quickly whispered to Sigbert a description of the creature and how they had been greeted. And Sigbert, his club held tightly in his hand, his ears alert for any sound, stepped forward.

"We are lost and cold and need shelter," he addressed the creature. "We can pay..." His words were interrupted by a shriek of laughter. "Just one night," he continued. "We will leave as soon as it is morning."

"Just one night?" The creature spoke in a voice that was almost a cackle. "Only one night with poor Sofia, when she would gladly have you stay a hundred?"

Sigbert slowly lowered the club and his arm relaxed.

"Every night Sofia prepares for visitors." She gestured toward the chunks of roasted meat. "And now when visitors come they can only stay one night." Tears filled the woman's eyes and her body began to sway from side to side.

Joanna felt her strength draining away and allowed herself to sink down to the floor of the cave. "The little girl is so tired and see the swelling on her jaw." Wilma stiffened. The woman knew Joanna's sex. "And you, my lady," the woman turned to Wilma, "your shoulder is bleeding. You must rest. Come close to the fire."

"You know we are women?" Wilma said carefully. "Despite our dress..."

"Sofia knows. You cannot fool Sofia. And Sofia knows that one is blind." She gestured toward Sigbert. "And she knows all three of you are holy ones." Sigbert sucked in his breath. "That is why Sofia lives here in this cave alone. Because she knows too much. Because she can see things no others can." She started laughing and clapping her hands. "But now Sofia has guests. Three holy ones come to visit her. Now she does not need to be alone."

Wilma eased herself down to the floor of the cave next to Joanna and sighed, but Sigbert remained standing. Giggling and making clucking sounds in her throat, Sofia stirred the fire and tossed a handful of grey powder onto it which caused a spout of red flame.

"What else do you know, Sofia?" Sigbert addressed the woman.

"That you are frightened. That you are learned. That, although you have wisdom, you are not wise. Not like that one will some day be." She pointed at Joanna, who was almost asleep. "Sofia knows the depth of your affection for the child." She nodded toward Wilma. "Sofia knows how brave you have been." She clapped her hands, bounced up and down, and started to giggle. "For Sofia everything is so clear."

Trying to keep his voice under control, Sigbert asked the woman what else she knew.

"How frightened all soldiers are," she answered. "How much the knights fear although boldly dressed in their armor. Sofia knows of the doubts of priests..." Her voice faded away, as she ran her crooked fingers through her hair in a desperate gesture. "But these are not important things. Sofia knows of the mystery of the sea. The magic of the circles that join all to all. Sofia can hear the whisper of stones, the cries of trees, the silver sound made by the orbs of heaven. And there are times when Sofia stares into the ashes after the fire is gone, she knows what will be."

"Are you a witch?" Sigbert asked.

"Those who drove me from my village called me a witch. Those who dragged me before the priest and would have had me burned called me a witch. But I am no witch. Just a woman whose husband and six children were taken so that now she is alone. Just a woman who in her loneliness learned to listen. To listen to herself and to others. And to see. To see with such a terrible clarity that there were times she fought the urge to thrust burning coals into her eyes, but even as she struggled against this temptation, she knew that even blind, she could see.'' She raised her hands as if to clap them together, then let them fall back to her lap.

"You are no witch," Sigbert said softly.

Except for an occasional tired flicker of flame, the fire in the fire pit had been reduced to a pile of dull red embers when Joanna opened her eyes. Although her jaw still ached and the numbness in her arm was only partially gone, her sleep had been so deep that she felt refreshed and, for the first time in several weeks, she felt safe. The cave was warm. On one side of her lay Wilma, an occasional soft moan interrupting her deep, familiar breathing. On the other side Sigbert sprawled, his huge body and outstretched arms and legs occupying at least a quarter of the cave's sandy floor. His deep, regular breathing sounds were as soothing as the murmur of the river north of her village once had been. Joanna stared at the rough, smoke-blackened roof of the cave. In the dim light shapes of savage creatures formed, moved, then dissolved with new and even more savage shapes appearing. Joanna closed her eyes as she tried to recapture the safe feeling she had experienced upon awakening: it was all cruel, all savage, all dangerous, everything. There was no safety. At any moment... She reopened her eyes. The cave was bare, except for one side of the fire pit where there lay a heap — of refuse and ash? But then the heap moved, twisted itself into the shape of a human being. Sofia somehow had been erased from her mind while she slept. The creature crawled in her direction. Joanna froze, her breath catching in her throat. Then she remembered and allowed herself to breathe again.

Bringing a crooked finger to her lips, then shaking her head a single time, the old woman gestured for Joanna to follow her out of the cave. Joanna hesitated several moments, but then as if drawn by invisible ropes, she rose up, eased past Wilma's sleeping form, and stepped out into the frosty night.

Bathed in the light of the full moon, everything was a silvery white. Even the old woman standing ankle deep in the fresh snow, her head thrown back, her arms outstretched, glistened.

"Look, child, look," Sofia pointed upwards.

Joanna looked up at the ringed moon.

"It is God's night eye," Sofia murmured. A crow lifted off of the high branches of a tall tree, scattering handfuls of snowflakes into the air. It rose toward the moon, then for a moment was completely framed in the silver orb. Sofia clapped her hands, but made no sound. "He gives us a gift, child, a precious gift," she said softly. Then expos-

ing her toothless gums in a silent laugh, she beckoned Joanna to follow her.

With hands so careful that scarcely a thimbleful of snow was disturbed, Sofia parted the branches of a gnarled dwarfed tree that
guarded one side of a dell scarcely half a dozen paces in width. Because of the close protection of trees and bushes, the ground was free
of snow. Almost exactly in the center of the dell, intent upon its search
for grubs and other favored morsels, a badger dug to the roots of the
grasses with its strong quick paws. The old woman watched the busy
creature — her fixed eyes and trembling lips revealing the depth of her
fascination. The badger's coat was so soft and rich, its movements so
certain. Joanna was caught up in the fascination. "Another gift,"
Sofia breathed into her ear. "There are so many gifts, so many gifts."

Scarcely realizing what she did, Joanna took the old woman's
hand as they headed back to the cave, and Wilma, who was startled
into wakefulness by their sounds, was at first surprised, then puzzled
as she saw Joanna and the old crone enter the cave together, hand in
hand.

"She admits that the priest declared she is a witch, as did all those
who lived in her village," Wilma whispered softly into Sigbert's ear as
she watched Joanna and the old woman sitting at the far end of the
cave as they intently watched a spider building its web. "How can you
be so certain she is not a witch?" Wilma fought against feelings of anger. "You cannot see the creature. Ugly as I am, compared to that
one, I could be taken for a noted beauty. And she has captured Joanna's fascination. I doubt if her body has known the blessings of water
in more than a year — her hair looks more like the snakes of the
Medusa, so thickened and roped with filth that at any moment I expect them to hiss and writhe. Yet, despite all of this, our Joanna, who
has learned to worship cleanliness, presses up against her, takes her
hand, does not recoil when the creature's breath is upon her, and she
scarcely gives either one of us a moment of her attention."

Sigbert licked his lips and made a rumbling sound in his chest.
For him the old woman's appearance was of little importance. But of
great importance was the warmth and comparative safety of this cave.
For the first time since leaving Aachen he had allowed himself to relax
his vigilance; for the first time in weeks he did not feel burdened down.
Yet there were witches, evil ones. And if this strange creature who
lived alone in a cave was in fact a witch, what a prize one like Joanna
would be. A mind as sharp as any in Christendom, a determination

not unlike that of St. Paul or St. John who was cousin to Jesus. Any witch would employ all her evil spells and vile incantations to claim a prize as valuable as Joanna.

"We will rest here another day, sister Wilma," Sigbert sighed. "Another day will restore at least a portion of our energy. As you say, she may be a witch. Too great a risk..." He sighed again. "But if she is not a witch, if as she says she is only a forlorn old woman who has lost her husband and six children, who was driven from her village because of her clarity of vision..."

"If you could see the creature, Sigbert," Wilma said softly, bringing her lips so close to the man's ear he could feel her breath. "Hideous. If you could see her, you would insist that we quit this cave at once, not wait until tomorrow. You must trust my eyes."

"Your eyes...yes. Another day, and we will continue our journey," Sigbert mumbled. He leaned in the direction of Joanna and the old woman, concentrating so that he might hear what they were saying. Wilma nodded, as if in response to a question she had asked herself, then she too leaned in their direction.

"You have been to Aachen?" said Sofia. Joanna nodded yes. "Then you have seen the great cathedral." Joanna nodded again. "I too — so many years ago, when the Great Charles was still alive. Yet that cathedral with all its magnificence, that cathedral, although the work of ten thousand pairs of hands, of scores of the finest artisans, is of no finer construction than the web of this single spider." The old woman reached out a careful hand and using the tip of her finger vibrated the web. "See the pattern, my child. See how each thread is exactly in its place. Made by a creature half the size of the tip of my smallest finger, yet so perfect."

Joanna gazed at the web and made a soft sound in her chest — the words of the old woman filled her like warm milk.

"This web is a proof of God, Joanna." Sofia softened her voice so that Sigbert and Wilma had to strain to hear. "A spider formed such a web in the dead branch of a tree which stood before the hut in which I used to live." There was a bubbly, almost a girlish quality to the old woman's voice. "I awoke and saw that web shimmering in the sunlight and it being Sunday I carefully broke off the branch and carried it to church to show the priest. 'Is this not a proof of God, is this not his handiwork'? I asked him as I held up the branch with its delicately woven web." The old woman paused for several moments, then continued in a flat voice. "He ordered me from the church. He declared that I desecrated God's place with a piece of refuse. Those who were gathered that Sunday laughed at me and mocked me. The branch was snatched from me and ground underfoot amidst hoots and catcalls. Yet all the words of the priest were not truth. The thick volume of inscribed velum in its doeskin binding from which he read was not truth. But the web..."

"And the crow that flew up into the moon," Joanna interrupted. "And the badger digging amongst the roots of the grasses in the dell."

"Yes, yes. You understand. All of those things. There are so many truths. Everywhere."

The sun had not yet risen when Wilma gently shook Joanna to wakefulness the next morning. Bringing her forefinger to her lips, she motioned for the girl to follow her outside the cave where Sigbert waited with their few possessions. Her mind still thick with sleep, Joanna yawned, stretched, then, scarcely aware of what she was doing, started to follow Wilma and Sigbert as they headed toward the pathway leading out of the woods. She had taken perhaps a score of paces, was just passing the great tree from which the crow had risen, when she came to an abrupt stop.

Wilma and Sigbert took another half dozen steps before they realized she no longer followed. Glancing backwards with irritation, Wilma made a quick gesture for Joanna to come on, but she shook her head. They stared at one another, their breaths smoking in the frosty air. Then Wilma said, "Standing motionless in this severe weather will give you the ague, Joanna."

"It is warm in the cave," Joanna answered.

"In the cave you will come down with the contagion; in all my years I never saw a more loathsome, filthy creature."

"She is stained with smoke. When I lived with Gerberta in our hut, my skin was not much lighter."

"But her hair, Joanna, like snakes and lizards."

"What reason has she for combing her hair?"

"Her hands are like claws," said Wilma, her voice rising in agitation. "Like the clawed hands of a witch. And the blackness of her skin is more than smoke stains. It is filth. Years of unwashed filth."

"Filth?" Joanna shrugged. "Several buckets of steamy water and a handful of fine sand... If she has a reason to be clean in time she will bathe. But her mind, Wilma. Her words. She sees things, knows things. In her mind there is so much wisdom, so much for me to learn."

Sigbert, who had stood motionless and silent during this exchange, began rubbing his hands together. "I am your tutor." He tried to mask the hollow sound in his voice by forcing its tone deep. "You have not yet mastered Hebrew and Greek. And there are many other things I have stored within my mind. Volumes."

"Yes, I have not yet mastered Hebrew and Greek," Joanna spoke in a flattened, almost lifeless voice. "And I know how much is stored in your mind, my venerable tutor." The girl began to tremble. "And I am hungry for your storehouse of learning, for the Hebrew and Greek I must yet master. But that which is contained in the mind of that one," she gestured toward the cave, "is more than volumes, more than learning." A gust of wind powdered her face with snow swept from the branches of the tree, bits clinging to her hair and eyebrows. "I must stay with Sofia for a certain time."

"How long?" asked Wilma in a tight voice.

"Until I have learned what I need to learn."

"Strange child," Wilma murmured. "Was there ever a child like you, Joanna? Would you separate from Wilma who has protected you and loved you as a mother; would you separate from Sigbert after all he has done?"

"Why must we separate?" Joanna stretched out her arms in their direction. "I want you to stay with me. There is no reason for us to separate."

"But if it is our determination to go on," Wilma said slowly and evenly.

"I will remain," said Joanna.

"If we insist that you accompany us?"

"I will defy you. As much as I love you; as much as I love both of you, I will defy you!"

"If we should take you by the hand," Sigbert joined in.

"I will manage to escape." Tears formed in Joanna's eyes. "Do not force me to escape. Do not force me to defy you. Stay with me. Please."

"Then we have no choice." Sigbert shrugged and took a step in Joanna's direction. "Since she will not willingly accompany us and it is almost a certainty that if we force her she will escape, and since I would rather cut off my right arm than abandon her, then we must stay with her in that overripe cave until she is ready to leave." He turned to Wilma. "I say we, when I should only speak for myself."

"You speak for me also," Wilma sighed. "Satan and all his minions could not force me to abandon this child. Yet to remain in the cave with that witch," she shuddered, "and as you say it is ripe, Sigbert. Yet with the application of a sufficient quantity of boiling water..." Joanna did not wait for the woman to finish as she rushed forward to embrace her.

When they reentered the cave they found the old woman huddled next to the fire pit, moaning and rocking back and forth, traces of tears showing on her withered cheeks. But as soon as they were inside, her head snapped up with the quick motion of a bird, her eyes brightened and she clapped her hands. Joanna hesitated, then breaking away from Wilma and Sigbert, rushed across the floor of the cave and embraced the old woman.

The days that followed flowed effortlessly and almost imperceptibly one into the other. Wilma, muttering, assumed the role of housekeeper and soon the cave was as clean as her room in the convent, although to be sure the slovenliness of the old woman and her foul odor remained an obstacle to Wilma's passion for order. Sigbert devoted a portion of each morning to instructing Joanna. Then for the rest of the day he lounged about, carving delicate figures from bits of wood, allowing himself the luxury of leisure for the first time in his life.

After the mid-day meal was eaten, Joanna turned her entire attention to Sofia and the two, more often than not, remained involved with one another until dark. For the first few days Wilma choked back her resentment as she watched Joanna kneel beside the old woman, almost touching. But by the end of the first week her resentment dissolved, and she felt a sort of peace as she heard their murmurs and watched their bodies, each responding to the other's almost imperceptible motions as if they were engaged in a delicate naiad-like dance.

For the first week, most of what Sofia shared with Joanna related to her observations of various woodland creatures. She spoke of how the mother deer taught her child to gain safety by remaining motionless. "The splashes of sunlight and the bits of shadow blend exactly with the dappled fawn, Joanna," Sofia's eyes sparkled with excitement. "I have sat half the afternoon not thirty paces from a motionless fawn and never saw the creature until, signaled by its mother, it sprang up and bounced across the field. As I sat I saw a wolf pass not ten steps distant, yet that hungry hunter with all his sharp vision, with all of his skill, like me, had no awareness of its presence." She told of how a robin built its nest. "I watched the bird examining the tree just to the left of this cave, Joanna. It hopped along a branch, flew up in the air, landed back on the branch, then hopped along it again. It had to find just the right place — protected from the wind, yet not too close to the trunk of the tree where a wild cat or some other hungry creature could scramble up and get at the nest. Hers had to be a slender branch, safe from climbing animals yet one that would not sway too much in a storm. And, Joanna, that robin chose exactly the right place. I watched it build its nest of twigs which it then lined with moss and milkweed down. Later I climbed up to where I could see the speckled blue eggs that lay in that nest. Each day I climbed up until there were baby birds with open beaks crying with all the strength in their little beings for their mother to feed them good things to eat. And how that robin worked to feed her children!" Sofia clapped her hands and bounced up and down. "No matter how many grubs, grasshoppers and worms she fed them, it was never enough. Seeing those fledglings grow until at last they left their nest was among the most joyous experiences of my life." A film formed in the woman's eyes. "None of my fledglings ever left their nest — all died," she murmured. Then she told of the time she saw two sleek brown otters play. How they chased each other in wild abandon, then finding a place where they could slide down into the brook, slid again and again, clapping their front paws together as they splashed into the water. "I wanted so much to join them, Joanna." Sofia's breathing had grown rapid. "Such freedom. Yet had I approached, they would have hidden. So my delight was to watch. To watch and to feel here inside my chest their excitement and their happiness."

After each story Joanna would ask questions. And each time these questions, some of which were answered by Sofia, some of which she herself answered, would lead away from the habits of forest creatures to the way of human beings. The stillness of the baby deer took them to certain holy men and women who remained motionless for days at a time as their beings reached out in an attempt to embrace the Supreme Being. The robin building her nest led them to such awesome ones as Alexander and Caesar and the Great Charlemagne, each of whom had built mighty empires, yet each of whose empires in time crumbled. The sporting otters took them to excited discussions of the lives of mistrels and strolling jugglers, of itinerant friars and masterless men of no gainful occupation, even to such as magicians and black monks who celebrate the mass at midnight.

Her resentment gone, there were times when the murmur of their conversation drew Wilma into an almost trance-like state as she reclined on the sandy floor of the cave during the long afternoons. But after the passage of several weeks, often when Wilma would settle down prepared to be soothed by the murmur, there was silence instead. At first these periods of silence only lasted a few minutes. But gradually they grew longer until hours would pass without either the old woman or the girl making a sound. Yet by their upright postures, by the set of their shoulders and backs, they showed that they were awake and alert. Several times Wilma was about to ask Sigbert what he made of this strange behavior, but then restrained herself — the man had turned so much into himself, was grown so silent except during the hour or two in the morning devoted to instruction. Yet in the softness of his features, in his languid movements, she could see that he was experiencing contentment, a lifetime of pressure and tension relieved. The fear that always hangs over the blind man like an invisible but choking miasma had dissolved here in the safety of this warm close cave. He of course was aware of the long periods of strange silence shared by Joanna and the old woman yet showed no concern; so why should I? thought Wilma. Thus when she was moved to share her uneasiness with the blind man, she restrained herself.

A single event interrupted the even flow of time as the days of the winter glided past. It was the sixth week. A temporary thaw caused most of the snow to melt and the nearby brook, which had been locked in ice since mid-Autumn, now flowed. Wilma had awakened earlier than was her wont and after automatically checking on Joanna, who lay curled next to her in deep sleep, and after rearranging Sigbert's blanket which he had thrown off during the night, she turned her attention toward the corner of the cave where the old woman slept. For several moments she couldn't be sure — the corner was cluttered with Sofia's belongings. But as her eyes adjusted to the dimness, she could see that the old woman was gone. At first this did not seem to be of significance. She must have stepped outside to relieve herself or for some like purpose. But as time passed and the old woman did not return, Wilma grew uneasy. "I will count slowly to a thousand and then if she has not come back, I will wake Sigbert," she decided. She started to count, and as the numbers formed on her lips, her thoughts turned to Sofia. Because of the creature's foul odor, she had always carefully maintained a certain distance between them. Yet, little by little, during the course of the weeks, despite all her filth and her unkempt condition, the old woman had become a part of her life. Wilma sighed deeply and continued counting. In a way, the four of them formed a sort of family, her thinking went on. They lived together, ate together, each was constantly aware of the other. "Who else if not these three is my family?" she asked herself, still counting. "Sofia is what she is, as I am what I am — and Joanna loves her." She forced her lips to continue to count, although her uneasiness had grown so great her hands were cold and trembled. "What if something happened to her — if she went out to relieve herself and was taken by a wild animal?" She felt a stab of shame at having always maintained that distance between herself and the old woman. "I will embrace her when she returns," she decided. "I will tell her of my gratitude for all of her hospitality to us." She continued to count. But when she reached seven hundred, overwhelmed by her uneasiness, she awoke Sigbert. And although she tried to keep her voice soft, her agitation had harshened it and Joanna also awoke.

Their faces drained of color, their mouths dry, struggling to control their emotions, they waited for the first light of morning to start their search. Only the iron grip of Sigbert on her arm prevented Joanna from rushing out into the darkness. "She may be lying out there with a broken leg," she cried as she struggled helplessly against the man's strength. But then, realizing all too well the reasons for his restraint, she hunched back down on the floor and waited for sunrise.

But the eastern horizon was still dark when the bark curtain guarding the entrance to the cave was thrust aside and Sofia entered. All three involuntarily sighed as the tension poured out of their bodies. Then Wilma, acting upon her determination, stood up, forced herself to take the several steps and embraced the old woman. For the first several seconds she held her breath, then angry at herself, breathed in deeply — there was no foul odor. She breathed in a second time. Only a delicate aroma of bark and herbs. She broke away from the woman and cast several armfuls of sticks onto the glowing embers in the fire pit. In moments the cave was lit with leaping flames; Sofia had scrubbed away the grime of years in the nearby stream until her skin was pink. She had washed her clothing which still dripped from the sleeves and hem. She had cut and combed her hair and her fingernails were as clean and carefully pared as those of any nun.

Scarcely aware of what she was doing, Wilma, in a full voice, told Sigbert of this transformation and as she spoke Sofia laughed and clapped her hands.

"What reason was there for me to care for my appearance," Sofia said as she leaned close to the fire pit, rubbing her chilled hands together. "There was no one to whom I mattered. No one would even know if I sickened and died. Why bother with my appearance? After being driven from my village I attempted other places, but each time was driven off with kicks and threats." She paused as she pressed her warmed hands against her cheeks. "I allowed myself to grow dirty, laughed at my reflection in the pond which had become scarcely human because...because in this way I defied them." She turned her head for a moment toward the entrance of the cave, then turned back to the fire. "And almost from the first moment Joanna didn't care. As

she sat close and listened to my words, as she took my hand whose
filth and blackened nails would make anyone else shudder, there was
awakened within me a portion which had long been asleep." The old
woman picked up a stick and stirred the fire, causing a cone of sparks
to rise through the air. "And even though I repelled you," she motioned toward Wilma and Sigbert, "even though the sight and smell of
me was disgusting to you, you stayed here as my guests. And, gentle
lady, learned man, Sofia knew from moment to moment exactly how
you felt. At first I reveled in your uneasiness. Then it became a test.
Would you be able to see the human soul hidden within? 'If they want
me, they must search through this bundle of filthy rags,' I determined.
And I took every occasion to breathe upon you, to come close when
you would have preferred me to remain on the far side of the cave. You
thought me unaware." She laughed softly. "Unaware? Sofia, who can
see with such clarity that her brain burns as if afire. And, gentle lady,
I knew how much you resented the many hours Joanna spent with me,
the neglect you felt." Wilma felt her face burn with embarrassment.
"I knew how you felt, gentle lady, and at first enjoyed every moment
of it. But in time... But in time..." Sofia stirred the fire again. "I tested
you; I had no right, yet I tested you. But now I am ashamed. All the
anger I had for them I placed on you. Ten hundred nights I waited in
this cave for someone to enter, so that I could make him suffer the
horror of my appearance. I knew what I did, gentle lady, learned man,
dearest Joanna; I knew exactly what I did. As I knew what I was
doing as I did everything in my power to seduce you away from your
companions, Joanna, by sharing with you that which you hungered
for." She paused for several moments, then continued. "Perhaps I
should be sorry for what I did." She shrugged. "But I am not. I did
what I did because I was who I was. I had been deeply hurt and was
filled with anger. But now that is all over. Because of you that is all
over." She laughed and bounced up and down like a little child.
"Everything is new. Each day, with the rising sun, the world is born
again." She sprang up, rushed to the cave's entrance and pulled back
the curtain, allowing the sunlight to flood in. "And this day I am reborn! See how clean I am. I rubbed my skin with sand and herbs for
hours; oh, how the cold water stung. But who said it is easy to be
born?" With that she rushed back across the cave, grabbed Joanna's
hands and started to dance. They danced, encouraged by the laughs
and fingersnaps of Wilma and Sigbert until, overcome by exhaustion,
they collapsed to the floor of the cave.

"The old Sofia is dead," Sofia said between gasps. "If you find
her carcass, throw it to the foxes, but I doubt they will touch it — so

dirty." She held up both her hands and examined them carefully in the slanting shaft of sunlight. "I wonder what work these hands will do?" She turned them over in the sunlight; the skin covering their knuckles was almost transparent, showing gnarled bones and thick black veins that told of their years of endless work.

Joanna stared at the woman's hands as she bathed them in the sunlight. Her own hands, resting in the darkness of her lap, felt cold. She lifted them into the sunlight. Their fine bones and delicate, tapering fingers were in stark contrast to the hands of the old woman. Held there in the morning sunlight, they looked as if they were encased in gloves made of fine-spun threads of gold.

"What will these hands do, Sofia?" Joanna asked in a soft voice.

The old woman allowed Joanna's hands to rest in hers as she carefully examined their texture and shape. "Writings of the most profound wisdom will flow from these hands. These hands will, in time, comfort thousands." She turned the hands over and traced the lines in their pink palms with a careful finger. "These hands will rule, Joanna."

Wilma and Sigbert who were listening intently caught their breaths.

"They will rule with such compassion, countless men and women will worship them. These hands will hold the spade that digs the grave, my child." The woman's voice cracked as she spoke. Suddenly her eyes opened wide as her face drained of color. With a rough gesture she thrust Joanna's hands out of the sunlight, muttering something about the foolishness of listening to the words of an old woman whose mind had become twisted from living too long alone in a cave.

"What else do you see in my hands, Sofia?" Joanna lifted them back into the sunlight and held them steady. "I am no child."

With a sudden movement, Sofia leapt up, grabbed Joanna by her arms, forcing her up, and began to dance as before. "So serious. This child is so serious. Sofia suffers a moment of indigestion and this silly child believes she has seen some terrible secret." Joanna tried to break away from the old woman, but could not and was forced to join in the dance.

"If all the mysteries were revealed, what would be the use of living?" Sofia sang and increased the vigor of her dance.

Submitting to the woman's strength, Joanna allowed herself to be led in the dance, but there was no luster in her eyes, no smile on her lips, and her movements were awkward and leaden.

Spring and then summer found Joanna, Wilma and Sigbert still living in the cave with Sofia. Sometimes they talked about continuing their travels. But the days flowed by so smoothly and there was no urgent reason to move on. So the seasons passed until it was early autumn. The girl who had entered the cave in the dead of winter had ripened into a woman.

She stood before a pool of water hidden by a tangle of gnarled trees and thorny bushes where she went several times a week to bathe. The air was still and the pool, with only the faintest of shimmers, reflected her woman's body. She stared at the reflection — somehow she had failed to record in the remembering portion of her mind the changes which had taken place during the course of the passing months. The woman reflected from the still pond seemed strange and unfamiliar to her. So many of her thoughts had been directed toward that time when she would be a woman. Yet now that it had happened, it felt unreal. She searched in the reflection for the remnants of the girl, for the slender, almost boyish creature with which she was so familiar. But except for certain features of the face, the girl was gone.

She slid into the sun-warmed water and allowed herself to float. She stared upward — she had never seen the sky such a perfect blue. She kept her eyes open without blinking and the blue filled with what appeared to be thousands of shimmering creatures formed of fine silver threads. She listened, and their delicate beating wings formed a sound like that of distant chimes. Or was it the sound of the waters of the pool she heard? Hidden away in the dark recesses of her mind was that day when Sofia read her future in her hands. But now in the thick sunlight of early autumn, floating effortlessly in these waters, the old woman's words gradually returned. What could a woman's hands rule? Would she become an abbess like Mother Brita? But an abbess, at most, only ruled half a hundred and Sofia had spoken of thousands. Then Joanna remembered her declaration that she would become a priest. Strange how that had slipped from her mind. She ran her fingertips along her thighs and hips, then cupped her hands over her breasts. Was her determination to become a priest only the foolish fancy of a child? Why travel any further; she had seen enough, learned enough? Why not return to the peace of the convent? Mother Brita had promised that in time she would be abbess. What foolishness it would be for her to deny her womanliness and seek ordination as a priest. Yet there was that prediction of Sofia.

As she emerged from the pool, a sharp gust of wind from the east caused her to shudder. Then she froze as the image of the weather-beaten hut in which she had been born formed at the edge of the thicket. It was so real — the sticks she had torn away to make the crosses were still missing. And there, a few paces distant, her mother's grave. She opened her arms. She would embrace that green mound which had once offered her such comfort. She ran forward. But the mound was gone and the hut dissolved into nothingness, leaving only thorny bushes and gnarled trees. Yet there were things she must ask her mother. Things she could never gain from Sofia or from Wilma or from Sigbert. Only from her mother.

"I must go away for a time and be alone," Joanna said with her eyes fixed on the fire after the evening meal was over. "There are things I can only learn when I am alone." Sofia began to nod her head.

"Alone, Joanna?" Wilma asked.

"Yes, alone. What I seek I can never find if in the company of another."

"A girl of your age alone in these forests, in these hills!" Sigbert's voice rumbled in his chest. "There are men in these forests as savage as wild dogs; men who would willingly face an eternity in hell for the chance at a virgin maid such as you, my little Joanna."

"Not so little, my venerable tutor. If the cloud could lift from your eyes, you would see that I have become a woman."

"A woman, Joanna!" Wilma said with a laugh. "You have years yet before you become a woman. And no more of this foolishness about going off alone."

"I am fourteen years of age, Wilma. Many are married, with a child at their breast at my age. And I am determined to go into the forest alone. Do you believe that the divine protection under which I have lived all these years would desert me now, dear foolish Wilma?"

"There are men so savage they will risk the very thunderbolts of heaven to get at you, Joanna!" Sigbert burst out.

"I will take that chance — I must be alone. I need the silence as the wanderer in the stony desert needs a well of cool water."

As Joanna spoke, Sofia rocked back and forth, muttering softly to herself. Then, in the silence that followed Joanna's declaration, her mutters turned into words.

"She seeks the lonely place, away from all others, that she may meet herself face to face. She seeks the place of the roaring silence that she may hear herself. Only alone beyond words, which always are lies, can one find union."

Except for the soft hiss of the glowing embers in the firepit, there was no sound after Sofia stopped speaking. Although the night was warm, the air felt cold inside the cave. Then from some place deep in the forest came the howl of a wolf and the tears she had been restraining flowed from Wilma's eyes.

The sun had not yet risen, although the eastern sky was filled with streamers of pale crimson light when Joanna, carrying a few possessions wrapped in a blanket, slipped out of the cave. But she had scarcely crossed the clearing when Wilma, whom she had believed asleep, sat bolt upright. She shook Sigbert awake, digging her nails into his shoulder when he tried to roll over and go back to sleep.

"She has left!"

As if her words were a spark landing on the back of his neck, he leapt to his feet.

"We cannot let her go! I have this feeling here," he brought his hand against his chest in a hard slap, "I have this terrible feeling that some horror is about to descend."

"We cannot stop her, Sigbert," Wilma said. "When that one is determined..." She shook her head. "But, as Christ is my witness, I will not allow her to go alone!"

Sigbert groped out and took her by the hand.

"I will wait a few more minutes, then follow her. If anyone dares lay hands on that precious child..." She squeezed Sigbert's hand with all of her considerable strength. "I will take a sword and a knife. God will grant me the strength of ten if needs be. As I know His only begotten Son died for our sins, I know He will give me this strength."

"If only I had eyes..." Sigbert groaned as he gripped his forehead with his free hand.

"Wait for us, Sigbert. We will return — a week, no more than two. I will protect her. I promise you we will return."

Taking care not to step on any fallen branches, moving with the grace of a woodland deer, Wilma followed Joanna, never more than several hundred paces to the rear. At night, when Joanna slept, Wilma moved in close, often less than two score paces separating them. On occasion she would crawl up on her hands and knees to take a furtive peep at the sleeping face, then force herself to retreat the necessary distance.

The fourth day they came to a hill almost bare of vegetation at his summit. And there, among a clutter of great boulders that might have been cast on that lonely place by the hand of some huge being in the days when giants walked the earth, Joanna settled down for her experience of stillness and meditation.

At times, when sharp gusts of wind shuddered and bent the few scrawny bushes that clung to that exposed place, when it whipped Joanna's hair and tugged at her flimsy clothing, Wilma struggled to restrain herself from rushing up the short distance that separated them and throwing her arms around the shivering girl. At other times when the sun shone down in its full majesty, the woman would gaze from her place of vantage at how the golden light made Joanna glow as if she were filled with fire. Then in the dancing air, her form would change so that at times she was almost unrecognizable. Once, after a extended period of staring, Wilma blinked to clear her vision, and the form sitting on the crest of the hill was that of the statue of the Madonna that graced the church she had attended as a girl. Wilma caught her breath, and whispered the words of the Hail Mary. But then the form was again that of Joanna, golden Joanna whose face showed such peace.

During the course of the first day of her meditation, those who had touched her life returned to whisper their greetings to Joanna. The children of her village with whom she had played. The village women who had cared for her, who had shared their gossip and their secrets. The men of her village. Coarse men, yet so fearful; so burdened by their years of grinding toil. Were there any traces of her village or had time and weather obliterated it all? Then there was Gerberta and Magda, poor frightened Magda. Some day she would seek out Gerberta and tell her how much love she had for her. And it would be good to hug Magda and to whisper together as they had early mornings before Gerberta was awake. Then came the sisters of the convent, Mother Brita's face still showing traces of her once striking beauty. There was Marla, who had taken her that first day from the priest. All those gentle, loving women. She could hear their silver voices calling her to return to the safe quiet of the convent. Calling her to join with them in their simple tasks, in their prayer, in their laughter at dinner time. Was her room with its narrow window through which she had so often stared at the pointed stars waiting for her return? Or was it now home to another? So many had touched her life. There was the bishop and the count of the palace. And Sigbert, giant Sigbert, standing a head taller than other men, yet so gentle and so vulnerable because of the cloud placed over his eyes. And Sofia that strange, wonderful creature. Joanna smiled as she thought of the way the woman laughed and clapped her hands. Now so clean, with nails as pink as those of a day-old baby. Then her thoughts turned to Wil-

ma. How was it possible that she had once viewed the woman as ugly?
The very faces of the angels that stood in the great cathedral of
Aachen were not as beautiful to her.

But after the first day of her meditation, Joanna was no longer
visited by any of those who had touched her life. Now disconnected
thoughts, like bits of dry leaf swirled by the wind, passed through her
mind. Some of these thoughts were sharp like thorns and they stung.
But then as she reached out to these thoughts, trying to connect them,
to understand them, like old leaves, they disintegrated into powder.

By the end of the second day, she felt the beginning of a great
rage — hot coals tamped down into the corners of her brain, heating
the bones of her skull. During sleep this rage grew until she awoke
shouting and cursing. Words she was unaware she knew spat from her
lips. She tried to wrestle a great boulder, tried to dislodge it, to force it
from the place where it had rested for centuries, to roll it down the hill
so that its mass would crash into the trees below, tearing them,
wounding them.

"Why can't I be like other young women?" she shouted at the
morning sky.

Then the sun started laughing and the roar of its laughter forced
her down to her knees, caused her to crouch, her head hunched between her shoulders on that stony open place.

"Live the life of a priest? I live the life of a priest, denying my
womanhood, spending my years in musty, darkened churches
amongst bloodless men? No!" she jerked her head up and defied the
sun. "With my brain, with my gift of words and with my womanliness," she stroked her breasts, "with these gifts I will find a prince
who will take me for his princess." She started to laugh. "As Sofia
said, I will rule. These hands will rule." She raised her hands to the
sun. "I will rule as did the wives of Roman Emperors." Her laughter
grew so strong it shook her body. "I will go to the land of Ingels, to the
place of my father's birth, and there I will find a prince. When this
prince sees me, when he hears me speak, he will want me as his wife."
She would wear gowns of silken cloth edged with patterns of silver
thread; gowns that would display her womanly figure to its full advantage. And she would wear a crown whose burnished metal would defy
the radiance of the sun. From all corners of the earth people would
come to her and she would listen to their supplications, would grant
their requests when they were just, would sternly rebuke them when
she must. When travellers came from distant lands she would offer
them hospitality for a season so that she could learn their strange languages. The wisest men in the world would hear of her respect for

learning and cross the mountains and the seas to visit her. For these venerable ones she would leave her finely carved throne and greet them as equals, taking their hands as a declaration of respect. All those marvelous minds gathered in her palace, all that adoration... Joanna's eyes fluttered, closed, and her lips formed into a smile.

"She has had a vision," Wilma formed the words with her lips as she watched Joanna's face, haloed by the rays of the sun. "She has gained an understanding." She made the sign of the cross. "She has put aside all thoughts of worldly matters, has dedicated her life to Christ Jesus." The woman's lip movements turned to whispers. "How I ache to embrace her, to tell her how dear she is to me. But I must restrain myself. Must not reveal my presence."

Joanna rose to her feet, the smile still on her lips. "Sigbert will know how I may meet a prince," she murmured. "He will devise a plan so that the prince hears of me and comes to me and I will pretend I do not know he is a prince; will treat him no differently than any other. This will make him want me!"

She started down the hill but had not taken a dozen steps when she abruptly stopped, crossed her arms tightly over her chest, and turned her face upwards. "I promise to be a good princess," she said softly to the sky. "I promise always to be both kind and fair." She hesitated several moments, then continued. "I will make a much better princess than a priest. Besides, did not St. Paul declare a woman may not be a priest!" She waited several moments as if listening for a reply, then, taking in a deep breath, continued down the hill.

Although it had taken Joanna four days to travel from the cave to the place of her meditation, her return was accomplished in just under two. Her feet seemed to scarcely touch the ground as she crossed the fields and other open spaces. In the woods she moved with the quickness and ease of a young fox. It took all of Wilma's energy to keep up with her. At times she gasped so hard for breath she was certain the girl would hear her. But Joanna was so filled with her own thoughts that nothing short of a thunderclap would have penetrated her ears.

It was early afternoon of the second day of travel away from the hill that she reached the vicinity of the cave. She had not realized she was so close, had expected to travel at least another half day, when, skirting around a cluster of trees and bushes which looked familiar, she entered the little dell where the badger had so busily scratched for food that moonlit winter night. Glancing up at the position of the sun, Joanna decided that Sofia and Sigbert must have already taken the mid-day meal, and were probably resting.

"I will surprise them," she murmured. "I will move as carefully as a stalking ferret, then burst in on them."

Joanna approached the cave, then hesitated several seconds before entering the small clearing that led to its entrance. There were no sounds. She suppressed a giggle — they were asleep. Her surprise would be complete.

She raced across the open space, scarcely noticing that the cave entrance was not covered by the bark curtain. She rushed inside, shouting their names, and for the first few moments the contrast between the darkness of the cave and the brightness outside did not allow her to see. But then she became aware of the scene before her.

In one corner a mass that had once been Sigbert huddled, its arms and legs twisted in an awkward position, its head missing. Swarms of ants and beetles filled the scores of open wounds. On the other side of the cave lay Sofia, her wide-spread legs tied to stakes driven into the sandy floor. Her torn groin also swarmed with ants and beetles. There were no other wounds on the woman's body, but her open mouth and staring eyes which did not blink as insects scurried in and out declared that she was just as dead as the headless man.

Joanna stared at the carnage, not understanding. They had heard her coming, were playing a joke on her. This was not real. Could not be real. But then she saw the fire pit and the charred head. A terrible scream filled the cave. A scream more piercing than any she had ever heard. It was she who screamed, but it was as if the rock of the cave, the sandy floor, the deep earth below the floor leading down to hell had screamed.

Then Wilma burst into the cave. Joanna felt the powerful hand of the woman gripping her arm. She felt herself being dragged out, out into the sunlight toward the woods with a terrible urgency. Several times her legs buckled under her, but still the hand dragged her. Her body was whipped by branches, cut by thorns. Across the dell, then deeper and deeper into the woods. When she tried to struggle free, the woman's fingernails dug into her flesh with such force that she would have screamed if she had the breath. Deeper and deeper into the woods with no chance for her to rest, the woman now a frenzied monster dragging her further and further from that cave.

"We will rest until the moon rises, Joanna, then go on." Wilma spoke in a lifeless voice, as they huddled at the base of an ancient tree, their arms wrapped tightly around each other. "They may still be in these woods, Joanna." The girl inclined her head, understanding all too well who 'they' were.

Trying to organize the numbness and confusion into coherent thoughts, Joanna opened her mouth several times, but no words would come. If she could only close her eyes and sleep. She allowed the lids to flutter down, but forced them open as crawling ants and beetles, fat from their feast, filled her eyes. "Why...Why such things?" Her words tasted of rusted metal. "Why does God allow..." Her voice trailed off. Had these several years been a dream, she wondered. Was she still with Gerberta, fleeing her village — her silent village with that large, snow-covered mound just beyond, out in the field.

"Why does God!" The strange, harsh voice startled Joanna; it was not Gerberta's voice. The years had not been a dream. "There is no God." Wilma's voice grated like two coarse stones rubbed together.

"No God?"

"No God, my child. Nothing. We swim in a black sea filled with monsters. But I will not let you drown. Wilma will fight against these monsters until her last gasp of breath."

"Shouldn't we have buried them, Wilma?"

"What difference if they be buried or if they lie for all eternity in that cave? There is no God. There is no chance of resurrection. And, Joanna, there is no Hell, only here. Let them rot in the cave; it makes no difference. It is all meaningless, emptiness. Except for each minute that we are alive. Nothing else has any meaning."

"Nothing else." Unseen fingers moved Joanna's lips, forced her tongue and throat to form words. Why did she speak when all she wanted was to sink back into numbed silence?

"From this moment I am no more nun." Wilma started to form the cross with her forefingers, then pulled her hands apart and spat. "I will lay with any man who will have me. I will deposit my dung in the chancel of the church if I have the chance. I will fling handfuls into the face of the pretend Messiah, who if He be truly God's Son should be torn from His cross and trampled for allowing such things to be." Flecks of saliva clung to the woman's lips, and foam filled the corners of her mouth. "Instead of praise, each morning and each evening I will curse God's name for the deception to which I gave my life for so many years." Then, thrusting her hand under her tunic, Wilma brought out a tarnished silver cross suspended from a fine chain. With a sudden, violent movement she jerked the cross, breaking the chain and, with a wide sweep of her arm, threw it into the woods.

Her eyes glazed with fatigue, their lids now leaden, Joanna stared at the place in the forest where the cross had fallen. Would a flame spring up and set fire to the rotted wood and dead leaves that lay everywhere? she wondered. Then her thoughts shifted to the smoldering firepit in the cave, but before the image of what lay in that pit could form, she forced her thoughts back with a shudder. Overcome with fatigue, rubbing at her eyes, she started to stretch out on the soft forest floor — the darkness of sleep, like the safe arms of Gerberta when she was a little girl, drew her. But another pair of arms roughly jerked her to her feet.

"No sleep," Wilma hissed. "We will put another half day's journey between us and this place." Then, seeing Joanna's hollow eyes and the way she trembled in the thin rays of the dying moon the woman pulled her close. "I have sworn to protect you, my little sister. If I allow you to sleep now, it may be that sleep from which there is no awakening. This very moment they may be silently approaching, their hands fouled with blood, their jowls dripping with foam. When we are safe, Joanna, you can sleep long and deep with your head cradled in my lap. When we are safe."

Although sleep had been promised after another half day's travel, they traveled almost twice that distance before Wilma judged it safe. For hours, they had struggled through tangles of bushes where there was no path, scrambled up hills, crossed rapid streams by means of fallen trees and slippery rocks — both had scores of scratches on their hands and faces. But finally Wilma sank to her knees in the midst of a wide field whose tall autumn grasses provided complete concealment. She pulled Joanna down beside her, and bringing a finger to her lips in the sign of silence, listened intently for over a minute. Other than the faint scurrying sounds of insects and the slight rustle of the grasses stirred from time to time by a soft breeze, there was no sound.

"Sleep now, Joanna," Wilma murmured, cradling the girl in her arms. "Here we are safe. Even if they followed us through the woods, in this field, hidden in these high grasses, they will not find us."

Joanna closed her eyes as a sound escaped her lips that was both a sigh and a whimper. She allowed herself to be cradled and comforted, allowed the safe sharp sweat smell of the woman to envelope her. It was so familiar, a thousand times in the hut with Gerberta... Yet she could not sleep. It was as if sprigs of stinging nettle were being drawn along her arms and legs. They found their way to her face, to her eyes, forcing their lids open against the burning.

"It was I that brought this terrible calamity, Wilma," Joanna said slowly, measuring each word. "I determined to turn away from the Church, not to dedicate my life to the service of our Creator. It was

this betrayal," again the whimper-sigh, "this betrayal of my holy purpose, this determination to seek the secular life that brought about
their destruction. I was hurrying back to the cave to beg Sigbert to tell
me how I might meet a prince. The daughter of a holy monk whose
mother died to give her life, one so favored by the Almighty now seeking a prince so that she might rule as a princess. How should there not
have been a tragedy?"

"They were killed by a band of brigands or, more likely, a company of peasants inflamed by the words of their priest. Had you been
there in the cave, Joanna, had we been there, we would have died in a
like manner. You must not blame yourself for what happened, little
sister. Only be thankful that you were not there."

"Brigands?" Joanna shrugged. "Brigands or peasants or soldiers
or even sturdy beggars drawn to that cave because of my evil determination. Had I taken them by the hand and led them to the cave, I
would be no more guilty. This was a punishment." Joanna began to
tremble and sob.

"You do not have such power, Joanna." Wilma stroked the girl's
forehead.

"I do not have the power, but the Almighty was displeased with
me and their deaths were my punishment."

"The Almighty." Wilma made an unpleasant sound in her nose.
"An Almighty who would do such a thing is a demon! But there is no
Almighty. There is nothing, Joanna. Nothing!" Wilma raised her
voice almost to a shout. But it was as if Joanna had not heard the
woman.

"I swear on the head of my father, the holy monk; I swear on my
mother's grave; I swear on my life that I will never again let such
thoughts enter my mind — I will drive them away! If they come I will
whip my legs with sticks till they bleed. I will beat myself till the
thoughts are gone. My life from this moment until I draw my last
breath will be dedicated to the Church. God, hear me: I swear to serve
You in every possible way. If a prince should appear asking for my
hand, I will drive him away with sticks and curses. I serve only You,
and Christ, Your Son. My thoughts are only for You. Only for You."
Joanna's body began to shake violently. Her teeth chattered.

Wilma held her tightly as she tried to warm her with her body.
Then gradually the trembling and chattering ceased as the girl's
breathing grew regular and deep.

Her eyes burning from lack of sleep, Wilma continued to stare
down at Joanna. The last remnants of the old moon cast barely
enough light for her to distinguish the girl's features. The high fore-

head, so much like that of the noble abbess, was deeply furrowed; there were lines around the eyes; the lips moved as though in speech. "She has seen too much," Wilma whispered. "Scarcely more than a child and she has seen a lifetime of this world's horrors. Any more and she will be robbed of her youth — will be as withered as I am withered. Her beauty gone."

Wilma leaned closer to the sleeping girl. "Blaming yourself for their deaths. You poor, sensitive child. The chance of death, of violence, of cruelty is everywhere, always. The air reeks of death. The screams of the tortured and maimed rise up from every quarter of this land. Animals who call themselves men, inflamed by their blood lust, stalk one another — attack, butcher, maraud. And you take the blame for one of these chance happenings upon yourself, dearest sister." Wilma's head began to slowly shake. "I who once so fervently believed now have nothing. It is all an insane joke schemed and carried out by demons." She raised her face and tried to focus her swimming eyes on the sliver of moon. "I am left with nothing!" Her voice grew strident. "Nothing except a single orphan child whose reason will crack if exposed to any more cruel buffets. Will You drive this child insane?" She raised a clenched fist, then let if fall back into her lap. "Why do I waste my breath. There is no one to hear. Nothing."

With a sigh that racked her body, she stretched out on the ground next to Joanna. Then, positioning her body so that it would protect the girl from the wind, she murmured softly to the sleeping form, "For as long as I have life, Joanna, whatever emotion I am capable of will be for you. Whatever love. Whatever belief..." The murmur faded and, except for faint scratching sounds of the busy insects, there was silence.

Maintaining their disguise as men, taking care that their faces were stained with bark and earth to hide any trace of womanliness, their breasts bound so tight their chests ached, Joanna and Wilma journeyed south. A few muttered words when they awoke in the field determined their direction. In the south there would be warmth. To the west, in the land of the Ingles, they would find damp and cold. That far to the south, then to the east, lay the city of Athens, the one place in all of Christendom where there still existed a great center of learning, where the darkness that had followed the death of the Great Charles had not yet reached. Finding hospitality in the huts of various holy hermits because of their knowledge of Latin, they obtained sufficient nourishment to keep themselves from starving. Their clothing was so patched and frayed, their appearance so unkempt, they did not dare approach the priests in the occasional towns and cities they passed. Once, when they ventured too close to a walled city — the promise of an easy day's travel along a cleared road having tempted them from the forest — a band of the city's inhabitants set upon them with sticks, driving them back into the forest, leaving both of them bloody and bruised, their garments in even worse repair.

As they travelled, for Joanna the horror of the cave gradually receded, replaced by softened images of Sigbert and Sofia who at times walked with her and talked with her. And in time, Joanna in some mysterious fashion of her own, converted Sofia into the person of her dead mother, Sigbert into a sort of divine lover.

By the time they had reached the warm country of the south which bordered on the great Mediterranean Sea, Joanna was no longer able to make a separation between the Sofia and Sigbert of her imagination and the woman and man as they once were. When she offered prayers for the soul of her mother, as she often did before falling asleep, she used the name Sofia. And Sigbert had become the one to whom she had once been betrothed, the one who if fate had granted him a few more years of life, she would have taken as her husband. Yet she never revealed any of this to Wilma. Whenever the woman made reference to the dead ones, Joanna would shake her head and wave her silent. After several of these attempts, Wilma, believing this subject to be too painful, carefully avoided mentioning either of them again.

V

MARSEILLES

*I*t was late winter when they finally came in sight of the great port city of Marseilles. Yet the air was warm and, except for a chill during the first hours of the morning, Wilma and Joanna were comfortable enough in their threadbare, tattered clothing. They stood on a slight rise and gazed out beyond the bustling city with its many docks filled with ships to the shimmering sea, to where the water joined the sky in the far distance. As they gazed, they felt a tightening in the throat and a quickening of breath; it was the first time they had ever seen such a vast expanse of water.

Then their attention was gradually drawn back to the city. It was difficult to determine where Marseilles ended or began, for surrounding the city were scores of markets and groups of brightly colored tents into which men by the ones and twos entered for a time, then left, but only men. There were crowds gathered around jugglers, storytellers and singers. Threading through these were trains of loaded donkeys led by fierce-looking men dressed in long striped robes, armed knights and soldiers on horseback and heavy wagons pulled by pairs of yoked oxen filled to the overflowing with wood, straw or hay.

A shift of wind brought to their nostrils the aroma of roasting meat. Their hands began to tremble and they swallowed again and again. It had been weeks since they had tasted anything other than moldy dried cheese, sour porridge, and rock-hard bread. Joanna started toward the city, but hadn't taken dozen steps when she was stopped by Wilma gripping her hard on the shoulder.

"If we try to enter the city dressed in these rags, they will attack us with sticks. Have you forgotten?" Wilma made a motion with her head to the rear. "It was more than a week before the ache went out of my bones from that beating." She kept her grip on the other's shoulder.

"Then we must bow our heads and enter the city as beggars, Wilma. Once inside we may find a priest or monk who will listen to us."

"These rags are not even fit for beggars, Joanna. The urchins will throw rocks at us; they will set their dogs on us."

Joanna shaded her eyes and tried to make out the details of a group gathered around several men dressed in brightly colored clothes. It was too far for her to hear any sounds, but she could see their exaggerated movements, the way the spectators laughed, stamped their feet, and clapped their hands. "Our rags may be unfit for beggars, Wilma, but if we declare ourselves to be players."

"Players, Joanna! I am a nun, a sister..." she broke off and clapped a hand over her mouth. Then in a soft voice said, "For a moment, I forgot."

"If we tie colored ribbons to these rags, wave pig bladders attached to sticks, no one will question that we are players. Then if we perform they may throw us a few copper coins, enough to gain a taste of that meat, Wilma!" Joanna's eyes sparkled with excitement. "See how they gather around those jugglers. We can play the story of Jacob when he deceived Isaac. Christ and Satan in the Desert. David and Goliath. We know those stories." Suddenly Joanna's face drained of excitement and her shoulders sagged. "But we have no colored ribbons to brighten these rags, no pig bladders, and no means to purchase them."

Wilma's eyebrows drew together and she stared hard at Joanna. "Players? Jacob and Isaac, Christ and Satan? Yet in the convent there were times as we read from the Scriptures we would pretend. I once was Joseph warning Pharoah; once was Peter doubting Christ — " her voice trailed off and she sighed.

"But without ribbons and other things," Joanna's voice broke.

"If we must have ribbons, Joanna." Wilma rummaged inside her tattered garments. "Just before we left the convent the abbess gave me this to keep for you. She said it was yours." Wilma opened her hand.

"My father's silver coin!" Joanna sucked in her breath. "It is the coin he gave Gerberta." She reached out and carefully took the coin, then held it so that the rays of the sun fell on its gleaming surface. "My father, the holy monk, still cares for his daughter," she murmured.

Their garments made less severe by garlands of vines and leaves with which they had decorated themselves, Joanna and Wilma cautiously approached the tent of a Jewish cloth merchant. Dancing and making wild gestures with their arms, with broad grins fixed on their faces, they had approached the city and, after making a group of cart drivers laugh with their antics, they had found out about the merchant Jew. Joanna hesitated. She had heard stories about Jews: how they mixed the blood of Christian virgins into the batter of their unleavened bread, how at times they would roast and eat an unwary Christian. But Wilma, whose father traded with Jews, who had played with Jewish children when she was a child, reassured her.

"Although terrible things are said about Jews, many of those who say these things are the very same ones who worship Christ, himself a Jew; who study the words of Paul, a Jew; who speak reverentially of the Hebrew prophets, all ancestors to the Jews who live today.

"Christ? The Hebrew prophets?" Joanna's face took on a bewildered expression. "I never realized, I never was told that Jews were descended from the same nation as the prophets, as Christ."

The tent flap opened and the merchant emerged as they approached. Although of average size, his shoulders were exceptionally broad and this breadth was accentuated by his rich cloak of red fox skins. A bristling fur cap partially covered his bald and perspiring head. This cap, at first glance, appeared to be an extension of his grizzled side whiskers and beard. His nose was hooked, even more so than Wilma's, his eyes were deep-set and black, creating an appearance of fierceness, yet his lips were delicately formed and sensitive. Making a deliberate show of the thick, elaborately carved cudgel he held in one hand, the merchant gestured for them to stop while they were still a half a dozen paces distant. But when Joanna opened her hand and displayed the silver coin, he motioned them closer.

"How do I know the coin is not stolen?" The merchant's eyes remained riveted on the piece of silver as Joanna told him of their needs.

"It is mine," Joanna replied, with some heat. "It belongs to my father."

"So you say," shrugged the merchant. "But if it should prove to be stolen; if its rightful owner should come and claim it, then I have parted with my merchandise and have nothing to show for it." He frowned fiercely. "To protect myself, to protect my family that depends on me, I must charge you triple." He cleared his throat. "Taking a silver coin from two of such an appearance as you is a great risk. It is my soft heart which prevents me from charging you quadruple."

"Why do you keep on saying the coin is stolen!" Joanna struggled to control her anger. "I told you my father..." she hesitated, caught the merchant's eyes which she held for several moments, then continued her sentence in Hebrew.

The man's mouth fell open and he gasped. For several seconds his lips moved, forming the same words Joanna had used — testing their authenticity. then, flinging his cudgel aside, he threw his arms around Joanna and embraced her.

"You are one of us and, may God split my tongue, I ask triple." Tears flowed from the merchant's eyes. "In this land of Jew haters, a Jew declares he does not trust a fellow Jew!" The merchant's head rolled from side to side. He tightened his embrace so that Joanna did not have breath enough to clarify the misunderstanding.

"This fine young man of a devout Jewish family of Aachen was orphaned a year ago, Excellency," said Wilma nodding deferentially to the merchant. "A band of drunken murderers attacked his home while he was in school and I and several companions who knew and revered his parents managed to smuggle him out of the city and I have been with him ever since." Wilma made a show of wiping her eyes. "And look at us, Excellency, at our condition."

The merchant cleared his throat, but did not appear to be displeased at being addressed in this fashion. Then he released Joanna and with studied deliberation smoothed down and ordered his fur cloak.

As soon as she was released Joanna turned to Wilma, her face flaming, her eyes glaring. But the woman avoided her eyes as her hands made small futile adjustments to her ragged garments. "What he says, what he just said," Joanna turned back to the merchant, gesturing with one hand in Wilma's direction, "what you have just heard..."

"No need to say anything more, my co-religionist. It must be too painful, too painful."

"He is brave, very brave, that one." Wilma pointed at Joanna. "He never complains. He bears his suffering with true resignation."

"It was the will of God..." the merchant fumbled. "I do not know your name."

"We gave him the name John as a protection." Wilma's face showed not a trace of anything other than seriousness. "His true name is Joshua but it is best if we continue to call him John."

The merchant nodded gravely.

"The ribbons," Joanna forced the words between her clenched jaws, holding out the coin again to the merchant as her eyes darted angrily in Wilma's direction.

"Put your coin away, Joshua... What was your father's name?"

"Also Joshua," Wilma offered.

"Put your coin away, Joshua ben Joshua. It was your father's gift to you — a rare and beautiful coin. You must keep it as a remembrance of your father." The merchant sniffed, then swallowed hard. "I will trust you for the few bits of cloth you require. If a Jew cannot trust a fellow Jew here in this land where we Jews are so reviled..." He did not finish his statement.

Their rags now decorated with colored ribbons, their bellies much restored by a meal of roast mutton provided by the merchant, their heads crowned with leather caps to which streamers and tassels were attached, each carrying an inflated pig bladder affixed to a stick in one hand, a rattle in the other, Joanna and Wilma passed through the gates of Marseilles just after sunset.

The city teemed with people. It was some sort of local celebration, with huge bonfires blazing in the open spaces. The two shouldered their way through the crowds without speaking. After they left the merchant's tent Joanna had turned angrily on Wilma. But instead of replying, the older woman had shrugged and grinned. Muttering unpleasant words such as "liar" and "deceiver," Joanna had jerked away when Wilma tried to take her hand. And as they maneuvered through the throngs of celebrating people, Joanna muttered under her breath, "With a dozen words she has turned me into a Jew. She cares nothing for truth, that one." But when Wilma again tried to take her hand, she did not pull away.

As they moved toward the center of the city, the press of the people grew greater until they were swept along by the masses struggling to enter the great public square. Bonfires were everywhere in the square — at least a score. On a raised platform, illuminated by blazing torches whose flames with every shift of the wind came dangerously close to the strings of pennants and banners, jugglers performed. Fountains of colored balls rose into the air from their quick hands, the balls catching the light of the blazing torches as they rose and fell, each blending into the other so that at times they appeared to be streams of liquid gold. Then the jugglers began tossing short swords into the air and at one another. The two women watched in fascination, their eyes opened unnaturally wide — how those sharp swords did not cut and pierce, they could not understand. They pressed closer. The jugglers formed two pyramids, each composed of six men and the two men who stood at the apex threw blazing brands back and forth at one another. At this the crowd shouted and cheered, showering the platform with small copper coins, loaves of hard-baked bread, strings of onions, and even several good firm cheeses wrapped in straw. As the jugglers broke their pyramids to collect these coins and the other things, they waved at the crowd to encourage them to contribute more.

A portion of the crowd was beginning to shift in the direction of a group of singers gathered at the far end of square when a huge lout of a lad, his face a mass of sores and pimples, his hands the size of hams, shouted in a voice that could be matched by a lion, "Look, players! Look, players!" His ham-hands gestured wildly in Joanna's and Wilma's direction.

As if they were dolls fashioned from bits of bark, the two were lifted up by scores of hands and passed over the heads of the crowd until they reached the platform. The jugglers quickly gave way and within moments Joanna and Wilma stood alone on the illuminated wooden square with hundreds of upturned faces, mouths opened in shouts and laughs, focused in their direction. Not knowing what else to do, Joanna started chasing Wilma around the platform, swinging the pig bladder wildly over her head. Wilma ran with awkward, exaggerated movements, leaping up and down, waving both arms frantically, and screaming in feigned terror; Joanna, now also running with exaggerated, jerky movements, pounded Wilma with the bladder whenever she could. The crowd roared and a sprinkling of copper coins landed on the platform.

"David and Goliath!" demanded the lion-voiced lout who had first identified them. "David and Goliath!" he demanded again, and the crowd took up his cry.

At that, Joanna crouched down on one corner of the platform trying to catch her breath while Wilma, still gasping from her exertions, walked slowly around the platform, bring her foot down with a loud stamp at each step. Contorting her face into the ugliest expression possible, her teeth bared, she approached the edge of the platform, making threatening gestures with her hands as she forced a harsh roar from the deep of her chest. The crowd howled with laughter. She stomped across the platform, gestured and roared at the crowd on the other side. More howls of laughter from the crowd. Then, standing in the middle of the platform, Wilma made defiant movements, slashing at the air with the stick and its attached pig bladder. Then she jumped up and down, bringing her weight full force so that the boards groaned. The crowd pressed so close the platform was walled solid on all four sides with heads and torsos.

Wilma's grimaces, roars, and gestures went on for several minutes undisturbed. But finally Joanna rose from her crouch and, hunched down, began to slowly circle the woman. Cries of: "David," "It is David," "It is the shepherd" came from the crowd. Joanna continued to circle and for the first minute or two Wilma pretended not to see her. This caused waves of hysterical laughter to sweep through the hundreds who were assembled. But then Goliath saw the circling

David, who, because she was hunched down, appeared to be only half the other's size, and started to scream threats, insults, and challenges. The frenzy of the crowd grew so great that the pressure against the platform made it creak and tremble — several urchins who tried to mount the platform were jerked off and hurled unceremoniously to the rear. Joanna-David, answered the threats and taunts of the giant with laughter and insulting gestures. This caused Goliath to grow even more excited, his insults and threats more vicious. Then Joanna removed her tasseled hat and with a wide sweeping gesture whirled it around her head several times, then let fly, striking Wilma on the breastbone. As if the leather hat had been an iron-tipped shaft shot with the full force of a crossbow directly at her heart, Wilma fell to the platform, her arms and legs twitching, gurgling sounds coming from her throat. Joanna quickly moved in upon her fallen victim, picked up that one's stick, lifted it high in the air, then brought it down in such a fashion it appeared to strike the fallen giant's neck. The end of the stick broke and the pig bladder bounced across the platform toward the mass of straining, clutching hands.

Copper coins and foodstuffs showered down. Wilma and Joanna managed to secure some of this, but much was pilfered by the dozens of ragged urchins who swarmed over the platform.

Dripping with perspiration, so exhausted they could scarcely speak, trying to hold onto the food and coins they had secured, Joanna and Wilma struggled with the little energy they had left to escape the crowd that pressed in on all sides. Wilma's legs buckled and only by clutching at Joanna was she able to stay on her feet. But the weight of the woman grew too great and Joanna felt herself about to fall. With the last bit of energy left to her, she fought to stay erect, fought to keep the weight of the other from pulling her to the ground among those hundreds of stamping, moving feet.

Suddenly, she felt an arm as hard as oak around her shoulders, a hand whose fingers gripped like hawk's talons seizing her arm; she felt herself again secure on her feet, being propelled forward with Wilma still clinging to her for support.

Only when they were well within one of the narrow, twisting streets that led away from the great square was Joanna able to turn her head and confirm the identity of the person who had rescued her. It was the merchant Jew, of course. Who else in this seething city cared if two strolling players fell beneath the feet of a mob and were trampled to death?

"You make a fine King David, Joshua ben Joshua," the merchant laughed. "But the story came close to ending in a manner different from the Scriptures." He released Joanna and began smoothing down the ruffled fur of his cloak. In the semi-darkness of the street the broad-shouldered man reminded Joanna of a bear she had seen grooming itself in the woods near her village.

"Swine!" he said, staring in the direction from which they had come. Yellows and reds in strange, distorted shapes from the bonfires in the great square played on the walls of the houses at the far end of the street. "You give them an entertainment as fine as anything ever seen here in this city, and the next minute they try to trample you to death. Worse than swine."

As if an offer of hospitality had been made and accepted, the merchant led the way through the narrow streets until they reached a house constructed of heavy timbers, set apart from the other houses, and guarded by a high wall topped with sharpened wooden sticks. They approached the narrow, iron-work gate behind which a huge dog crouched, silent yet tense and ready. The merchant suddenly stopped and faced Joanna and Wilma, then brought his hand to his forehead in a sharp slap. "I have the manners of a sheepgelder. Forgive me. I did not give you my name. And here you are about to enter my home. Welcome to the home of Solomon ben David." He made a deep bow. With that, he whistled at the dog who wagged his tail frantically as soft, almost human cries came from its gaping mouth. The dog bounded after them as they made their way along the short path that led to the house, licking, in an indiscriminate fashion, the hands of Wilma, Joanna and its master.

A single knock from the merchant's huge fist, and the door swung open, revealing a blaze of light from scores of lamps and candles, and, framed in this light, was the fattest woman Joanna had ever seen. She appeared to be as broad as she was tall, with a head attached to her shoulders without the benefit of a neck. The woman's face resembled nothing so much as a mass of dough prepared for baking bread, shaped, for a lark, into a caricature of a head. Her hands, which emerged in some mysterious fashion from the mass of her body, twitched and wriggled with delight as she greeted her husband, causing the jewels set into the rings which encircled all five fingers of each hand to flash and sparkle.

"Miriam, my beautiful wife!" The merchant introduced the woman with an expansive gesture of both arms. And from the expression on his face and from his tone of voice, it was obvious that in his eyes she was beautiful.

The introduction over, the merchant told his wife how he came to be acquainted with these two ragged players and, as he explained, the

woman kept nodding her head, each nod causing ripples to travel up
and down her bloated body. "A fellow Jew gives a splendid performance of King David." The merchant threw back his head and let out
a loud laugh. "Such a David has not been seen since the days when
the Kingdoms of Israel and Judea were one. How could a Solomon
whose father was also a David not insist that this David come to his
house as a guest?" The woman tried to laugh, but it came out as more
of a wheeze. "And since I had so much pleasure from watching that
Goliath lose his head at the hands of David, how could I not invite him
also as a guest?"

Their skins still tingling and still short of breath from the almost
scalding water in which they had bathed, Joanna and Wilma were led
into the main room of the merchant's house in which some fifteen
people were seated around a large table covered by surely a score of
steaming, smoking dishes. Space was made for them at the far end of
the table and then after the intoning of several Hebrew blessings, they
were served with food whose taste and aroma were unequaled by anything either had ever eaten before. Only when both of them were gasping, so stuffed they were unable to swallow another morsel, did the
merchant and his wife cease ordering their servants to heap more and
more upon their plates. Yet they were not the only ones gasping by the
end of the meal. Except for a thin, dry, wrinkled old man wrapped
from head to foot in white-and-black striped cloth, who had partaken
of only a few sparse bites and who had not been urged on by the host
and hostess, all the guests gasped, their faces a deep, mottled red, with
beads of perspiration showing on their foreheads.

"Now that we have filled our bellies, are you not going to introduce your two guests, Solomon ben David?" the wrinkled old man addressed the merchant. Several times during the course of the meal
both Joanna and Wilma had noticed the man staring in their direction
but had avoided meeting his eyes.

"To have introduced them before partaking of this meal would
have been a declaration that only friends, never strangers, share in the
hospitality of Solomon ben David," said the merchant. To this the old
wrinkled man gravely nodded. "The younger one is of our blood and
comes to us from the city of Aachen." The merchant inclined his head
in Joanna's direction. "The other is a gentile, although a loyal friend
and companion to our co-religionist." The merchant nodded at Wilma, but in a less ceremonious fashion.

"The younger with his blue eyes, fair skin, and finely made features is one of us?" The old wrinkled man's voice rumbled as he spoke. "And the other one, with his hooked nose and dark skin, is a gentile?" The old man shook his head. He cleared his throat and pulled his striped cloak more tightly around his shoulders although the room was sufficiently warm. "I have heard that certain Jews from the north view those of us who live here in the south as being easily gulled. Is it that your two guests have switched identities, Solomon ben David, so that we may provide substance for their mirth? Of all human emotions, I regard mirth with least favor."

"I am satisfied that each is what he claims to be, Rabbi," the merchant answered deferentially. "But since I do not have even a hundredth part of your wisdom. If you have any doubt..." The merchant shrugged and motioned with his head in Wilma and Joanna's direction.

At that, the old rabbi turned toward Joanna, his unwavering eyes burning into her eyes which she refused to shift away, and addressed her in sonorous Hebrew. The ancient language flowed from the old man's lips effortlessly — none of the slight hesitations and occasional slurs of Sigbert when he spoke the language.

The prophets Amos and Jeremiah must have spoken in just such a fashion, Joanna thought as she listened to the wizened man. Then, imitating his cadence and tone, she answered in a Hebrew purer than any she had ever spoken. It was as if each of her words was a gentle hand, stroking the old man's cheeks and brow, for, as she spoke, his features softened, tight lines around his eyes and at the corners of his mouth were ironed out, and his eyes grew lustrous as they filled with moisture.

"Was there ever a sound more beautiful than the language of our fathers, my dearest son?" The rabbi placed his hands for several moments on Joanna's head. "Forgive me for doubting — an old man's failing. In the name of all the Jews of Marseilles, I welcome you and your gentile companion. Such a beautiful Hebrew! Such a beautiful Hebrew!"

The rabbi having fallen silent, the other guests questioned Joanna about her plans for the future and, on learning that it was her intention to travel to Athens, various ones, the rabbi and the merchant included, urged her to reconsider and remain in their midst.

"Athens is a decadent place, a place where unnatural practices are encouraged among young men," the merchant declared as his wife clucked her agreement.

"The Jews of this city would be strengthened by the addition of one such as Joshua ben Joshua," the old rabbi intoned.

Others declared against Athens as they warned about the danger
of pirates and slavers that faced those who ventured the length of the
Mediterranean. Aware that any further mention of her plans to travel
to Athens would only alienate her from these important repre-
sentatives of the community gathered in the room, Joanna nodded
gravely at these warnings.

"Because of you I am a Jew, for better or for worse, as long as we are
in Marseilles," Joanna said softly as soon as they were in the privacy
of their room. Wilma winked broadly and allowed herself a chuckle.
"If Mother Brita ever learned of this deceit..."

"She urged that we deceive as to our sex when we marched into
Engelheim," Wilma laughed. "If it is all right to deceive as to one's
sex, why not as to one's religion? Besides, since I am no more a Christian, I am of half a mind to declare myself a Jew."

Joanna sucked in her breath. "You would never do such a thing,
Wilma! Do you forget that they were the ones who crucified our
Lord?" To this Wilma turned her face partially away and shrugged.

Each avoided speaking to the other, avoided even making
momentary eye contact as they prepared for bed. But once under the
coarse blankets of the straw-filled bed they shared, both, as if tickled
with a feather, at the same moment burst into laughter.

"Oh, Wilma, you should have seen yourself jumping around on
that platform, making those hideous faces and horrible sounds,"
Joanna gasped through her laughter.

"And you, Joanna," gurgled Wilma, "spouting your Hebrew —
little King David invited to join this tribe of Jews — the old man
could scarcely restrain himself from weeping. Several of them must be
making plans, this very minute, to introduce such a fair-faced scholar
to their marriageable daughters."

Joanna nestled up to the woman. "Wilma, what a strange and
wonderful Providence has led us to this place — so much risk, so
many dangers, yet here we are together, safe in this warm bed." She
nestled closer. "Did you hear what the merchant said — the best King
David he has ever seen," she murmured. "Next time we will employ
several of the urchins to help us gather the coins. With practice our
performance can only grow better. In time we will earn enough for
our passage to Athens..." Snores from the older woman put an end to
her murmurs.

Her heart beating so that it felt as if it would leap from her chest,
her breath coming in short gasps, Joanna was wrenched from her

sleep by shouts reverberating through the house. At first she could not remember where she was. For so many weeks, they had slept in gullies, under haystacks, in rude huts, or out in the open that the close darkness of the room felt alien and unfamiliar. But then a snort from Wilma, as she was forced into wakefulness, swept away Joanna's momentary confusion.

The merchant, his face a dead pale, his chest heaving, met them on the landing as they emerged from their room. Throwing up his arms in a helpless gesture, he croaked, "My wife is dying — I have sent a servant for the physician but she will be dead before he arrives." Then as if overcome by a wave of dizziness, he clutched at the wall.

Not needing any further permission other than that implied by this statement, Joanna, followed closely by Wilma, rushed past the man and entered his bedroom.

Sprawled on the bed like some giant fish, the merchant's wife lay flapping, her mouth gaping wide, her eyes bulging, her skin each moment turning a deeper blue. Other than a high-pitched whistle, such as that made by a single reed, issuing from her open mouth, the woman was unable to make a sound.

Forcing down a feeling of revulsion, Joanna bent over the dying woman and brought her mouth in contact with hers. Several times, as a girl in her village, she had seen old Clari blow the breath of life into mouths of newborn infants. She herself had attempted to restore a baby pig which had fallen into the river. The same desperate feeling she had known kneeling over the drowned creature on the bank of the river half her lifetime ago, again overwhelmed Joanna.

In moments the initial sense of revulsion was gone, now all that mattered was that her breath should fill the chest of this dying creature. Again and again she breathed into the woman's mouth.

The merchant, crazed with grief, reeled into the room, saw Joanna with her mouth pressed against the mouth of his wife and with a shriek attacked her, flailing at her exposed back with his fists. It took the combined efforts of Wilma and the merchant's servants to pull the powerful man away. He struggled desperately for several seconds but then, suddenly understanding what was being done, burst into tears and tore at his hair and beard.

Gasping for beath, her shoulders and back aching from the beating, Joanna lifted her head for several seconds. A wave of dizziness caused her eyes to lose their focus — she could hear the sound of the river. If she hesitated the little creature that had fallen into the water would die. Its life was in her hands. So, taking in a deep breath, her eyes still swimming with dizziness, she again pressed her mouth against the gaping mouth of the woman.

"Not only has he brought to us the gift of Hebrew, but also his skill as a physician," The old rabbi, who was also the chief physician, addressed Joanna after he completed his treatment of the merchant's wife. He had entered the room as Joanna still breathed into the woman's mouth, had watched with wonder showing in his face, and had only taken over with his treatment when the last traces of bluish color in the woman's skin were gone.

"I have never seen such a thing done before." The old man's eyes traveled around the room as his long, delicately formed fingers stroked his beard. "Yet what would be more appropriate for one who struggles for breath — offering the breath of life."

As if his body was racked with a convulsion, the merchant suddenly threw himself at Joanna's feet. "You have restored my wife to me!" he choked. Tears gushed from his eyes and he pressed his face for several seconds against the tile floor. "Sharing your very breath with the one I love best in all this world, yet in my madness I struck at you. Can you ever forgive me?"

Joanna reached out and tried to raise the merchant to his feet. But he struggled against this and brought his face again to the tile floor. "For as long as you are in Marseilles — a month, a year, twenty years — you and your companion are the guests of Solomon ben David. My home is your home, to enter and leave at any hour of the day or night as you please. You will sit at my table on my left hand with the choicest portion being yours. Even if you should honor my house for twenty years, may God grant it, I will still be in your debt for the priceless gift you have restored to me this night."

The old rabbi bowed in Joanna's direction. "And the least return I can make to you for my learning the art of the breath of life is to share with you those few skills I have as a physician. I have prayed for one such as you to appear before my time here on earth came to an end. I have trained several physicians, but God knows more are needed — so much sickness, so much death. Will you allow me to share with you those few things I know, Joshua ben Joshua?"

To this offer, in a barely audible voice, as tears filled her eyes, Joanna answered yes.

By early afternoon of the next day all of the several hundred families that comprised the Jewish community of Marseilles had heard about the fair young Jew from the north whose blue eyes and regular features must cause the hearts of any maiden or widow to skip a beat. All during the afternoon and well into the evening, families dressed in their Sabbath best, as many as half a dozen at a time, visited the merchant's house to feast their eyes on the young scholar, to listen, with delight, to his flowing, nearly perfect Hebrew, to shake their heads in wonder as the merchant recounted over and over the remarkable events of the previous night. The following day the visits continued, the merchant neglecting his business so that he might personally act as host. Only when the last of the families had made their call did he return to his tent outside the walls of the city.

As soon as the ceremonial visits were over, the rabbi-physician, making good his promise, sent an armed servant to guide the youth from Aachen each day through the narrow, twisting, often dangerous streets of the city to his house. There, Joanna would watch the old man as one sufferer after another in an unending number presented themselves with a bewildering variety of complaints. The physician's hands moving with a deftness and certainty surprising in one of his advanced age would probe, cut, bind and plaster almost as if they had minds of their own while the old man, in a sing-song voice, detailed what he was doing, the nature of the disease or injury, and what the probable prognosis would be. Since most of those who presented themselves were non-Jews, it was easy to carry on this monologue without distress to his patients by the use of Hebrew. When the patients were Jews, the physician said nothing.

For the first few days, Joanna just watched. But as the days of her apprenticeship grew into weeks, she gradually fell into the routine of assisting the old physician in his setting and binding, handing him his instruments for cutting and probing as needed, at times even performing simple procedures herself under his direction.

Although originally it had been their intention to continue to perform as players in order to raise the passage money to Athens, several months passed with neither Joanna nor Wilma making any reference to this plan. But finally Joanna, sensing Wilma's growing restlessness, suggested that it was time they performed again.

Without mentioning anything to the merchant, to his wife, or to the physician, accompanied by a half dozen urchins they had recruited from the neighborhood, their clothing bedecked with colored ribbons, the two made their way toward the large square where a festival honoring a local saint was being held.

The crowd gave way as the little procession entered the square and this time Joanna and Wilma needed no urging to mount the platform which was decorated with leafy boughs, crosses, and a large effigy of the saint. This being no occasion to perform anything as violent as the confrontation between David and Goliath, they had settled upon the still very popular account of the relationship between Pope Leo III and the Great Charles.

Gaining a nod of permission from a ragged monk who stood to one side of the platform, with a reverential bow toward the effigy of the saint, Joanna lifted the tall miter from the saint's head and placed it on her own. Then, crossing her arms over her chest, she moved to the center of the platform. A hush fell over the crowd. Hundreds of faces with eyes glazed from drink and hours of excitement strained upwards. It grew so still that it was as if the waiting hundreds had stopped breathing. Then Wilma stepped forward.

"The citizens of Rome, debauched and steeped in venery, had fallen into such evil ways that even the Vicar of Christ was no longer safe in the city of St. Peter." She intoned in a forced voice this tale she had heard so many times, since childhood, from wandering storytellers. "Thus it was that Pope Leo III, a good and saintly man, was set upon by a howling mob as he walked the streets deep in contemplation." Her voice took on the rhythmic quality that had held her in an almost trance-like fascination when, as a child, she had listened to the tale. Responding to the rhythm of these words, Joanna moved slowly around the platform, her arms still crossed over her chest, her eyes turned heavenward. "Driven by Satan's minions, members of that mob drew forth their knives and came upon that innocent and defenseless man." Joanna stopped and threw out her arms as if to defend herself. "It was their intention to blind the Pope's eyes and cut out his tongue and to this end they slashed again and again at Christ's envoy here on earth." Joanna reeled from side to side, whirling around, ducking, flailing her arms, as gasps and cries came from the audience. "Alone and undefended amongst an armed mob of hundreds, yet their bodkins could not reach his eyes, could not enter his mouth and pierce his tongue." Joanna's gyrations and flailings grew more frantic. Moans of anguish escaped her lips. "Even armed hundreds are no match for a single righteous one, for such a one is protected by God's own archangels. Although their knives rent his forehead and cheeks, spilling pope Leo's holy, precious blood, they could not blind him, could not strike him dumb." Joanna clutched at her face, fell to her knees, then rocked backwards and forwards as shudders convulsed her body. "It was then that the Great Charles, having learned of this disgrace, set forth with a mighty army of knights and barons to rescue the Apostolic See. Charlemagne alone of all the great rulers of the earth declared an intention to restore the

Mother Church. With great pomp, armor so burnished it dazzled in the sun, pennants and banner flying, the Great Charles entered the city of Rome and came up to the Pope...'' Wilma marched slowly around the platform, her stiffened arms moving in a military fashion. She stopped at each of the four corners, searched in all directions, then moved on until finally, almost as if by chance, her eyes rested on the kneeling form of the battered Pope. A wild cheer rose from the audience as she approached the kneeling figure and then with gestures of obeisance assisted the Pontiff to his feet. "For this noble and selfless service, the Pope bestowed upon Charlemagne the titles of Emperor and Augustus." With an exaggerated show of ceremony, Joanna placed both of her hands on Wilma's head, ignoring the older woman's gestures of protest. "Again and again the Great Charles declared that he had not come to Rome to gain such honors, only to restore the Church." The action was frozen as Wilma went on in her forced voice: "But Pope Leo insisted that of all the kings of the world, no one was more deserving of these titles. And so it was that Charlemagne became Emperor." Wilma lowered herself to her knees, covered her face with her hands as Joanna formed a crown of a leafy bough and placed it carefully on the bowed head. This act set off a thunderous cheer from the crowd, scores tossing their caps into the air, and then coins began to rain upon the platform.

While the urchins they employed scurried about to pick up these coins — the crowned emperor still kneeling — Joanna, her head high, her shoulders thrown back, walked to the edge of the platform and with wide, sweeping motions of her hands, blessed the crowd. This produced a fresh rain of coins, together with a number of food offerings placed at the Pontiff's feet. Then, beckoning the Great Charles and the urchins to follow, after making a lordly gesture which caused the crowd to separate and form a passageway out of the square, Joanna descended from the platform in the most regal of fashions, waved aside those few uncouth ones that dared to obstruct her passage for so much as a moment, and processed out of the square, her anointed hands bestowing blessings on both sides until the very last moment.

His usually sallow face now blotched with scarlet, his physician's staff gripped in his white-knuckled fist, flecks of saliva showing on his lips and in his beard, the rabbi-physician confronted Joanna and Wilma as they entered the merchant's house. The merchant, his thick brows drawn together in a troubled frown, his bald head gleaming with perspiration, stood to one side. Several other prominent members of the Jewish community were present, each showing a like troubled expression.

"You have been welcomed into the bosom of Marseilles' Jewry — I have shared what few skills I have with you as I would with a son — yet you do such a thing." The physician pointed his staff, which he could not prevent from shaking, at Joanna. "All the gentile people of consequence who live in this city are aware that you have been honored by the Jewish community, that you are the guest of Solomon ben David, that you are apprenticed as a physician. How they must laugh and mock us as they gain intelligence of that vile and disgraceful performance you offered to that drunken rabble." The old man struggled with his emotions, then after several seconds brought himself back under control. "You insult this community by your actions. You bring disgrace upon yourself; upon your dead father who I understand was a good and pious Jew." Joanna felt her face burning and she struggled with her eyes which wanted to turn away. "The gentile one I cannot fault." The old man made a perfunctory gesture in the direction of Wilma. " But you, a scholar whose command of Hebrew is scarcely equalled by any in this city; but you... And for what? A handful of copper coins."

"If you had needed money, Joshua," the merchant reached out his hand toward Joanna, "I must blame myself for not offering it to you for whatever needs you may have. For the gift you restored to me, all of my cash would not be a sufficient reward."

"It was to enable us to purchase a passage to Athens," Joanna said slowly, her mouth having become uncomfortably dry. "We did not intend to bring disgrace..."

"Did not intend! Did not intend!" the old man interrupted. "Are you a lout? A fool? It would be disgrace enough for a Jew honored by this community to exhibit himself in any fashion before such a rabble. But a Jew who declares he is Pope; who blesses with his hands, who makes the sign of the cross..." A fit of coughing interrupted the physician.

"And what is this nonsense about Athens?" the old man went on in a strained voice, struggling for breath. "Did we not tell you of the abominations which take place in that city where men lay with men? Have you not been offered a home and a profession here in Marseilles? In time, a wife with a sufficient dowry would have been found for you. A stranger from the north given such an opportunity, yet you continue to talk about Athens!"

Choosing her words carefully, struggling against an uneasiness that rose up from the deeper portions of her chest, Joanna started speaking. "I, we, did not intend to offend. We are grateful for all the hospitality given to us. But at no time did we declare a determination to settle permanently here in Marseilles. If you assumed otherwise, I am sorry, and I regret that I did not restate my intentions in such a manner that there could be no mistaking them. I, we, have a great hunger to visit Athens, to experience the remnants of an ancient civilization, to steep ourselves in the learning for which that city is so renowned."

Sputtering with anger, the old rabbi shook his staff at Joanna. "Assumed otherwise! Words! You did not say, but your actions said. A hundred young men would give themselves over, as Jacob did to Laban for three weeks of years, to learn what I have taught you. Taught you without making any demands, young Joshua. But there was an understanding! By your manner, by your acceptance of my teachings, there was an understanding."

Joanna hesitated then slowly shook her head.

"You Absalom!" hissed the old rabbi. "Do not forget what happened to that one when he betrayed King David."

With a sudden movement the rabbi turned to the merchant. "Is he still your guest, that one? Will you continue to have him and his gentile cohort here in your house after his bringing us such a disgrace, after he continues to defy his elders with his intention to visit the city of abomination?" The merchant lowered his eyes, licked his lips several times, and finally shook his head.

It took Joanna and Wilma several days to recover from the shock of their removal from the clean, comfortable house of the merchant to the squalid, rat and lice-infested quarters in one of the poorest sections of the city. Although expelled from the Jewish community, no respectable Christian would shelter a known Jew; thus they were forced to seek habitation among some of the most disreputable elements of the city — jugglers, montebanks, beggars and thieves. At Joanna's insistence they left behind the clothing they had been given and were once again dressed in rags.

"This is what comes of assuming a false identity." Joanna pointed toward a bed bug she had just killed. "I knew nothing good would come of it," her voice rang with accusation.

"We are no worse off than we were before we entered the city, my sister," Wilma said in a lazy fashion. "In fact, we have already found part of our passage money. Two or three performances and we will have enough. And, dearest Joanna, with your quick mind you must be well on your way to becoming a physician. Perhaps when we get to Athens you will declare yourself one." She grinned and winked.

"You are without a conscience, Wilma," Joanna muttered with feigned severity. "Set myself up as a physician..." She frowned and chewed on her lower lip for several seconds. "Yet I have mastered a number of treatments. Perhaps with a little more experience..."

"Oh, Joanna, Joanna," laughed Wilma, "in the long, sad history of this world has there ever been two women who have had such adventures as we?" She picked up the dead bed bug and flicked it against the wall. "And with a mind such as yours, with your boundless determination, our adventures are far from over. What next, my little Joanna? What next?"

The next day, their spirits fully restored, the two women recruited several assistants from those who lived in that same tumbledown building and, after affixing their ribbons and gathering certain props, they again headed for the great square.

Rather than a single, lengthy performance, they had decided upon a series of short incidents of Christ's ministry. This would encourage the crowd to shower coins several times instead of only once. The first was to be Christ's baptism by St. John. Then Christ healing the leper. Finally, Christ struggling up the hill to Golgotha under the whips of the Roman soldiers. They had considered doing the beheading of John the Baptist. But having already done the beheading of Goliath, both agreed this might be less pleasing to the crowd.

Only a few score loungers were scattered throughout the great square as they entered it. In one corner a hawker of baked meats of an indeterminable origin was trying to persuade several grime-encrusted footsoldiers whose clothing was mostly patches to make a purchase. On the platform, four or five mangy, half-starved dogs were worrying a bitch, even more mangy, who slowly circled the platform, snapping ineffectually from time to time at her tormenters. And no less than two dozen pigs moved around the square at will, foraging in the many piles of refuse.

Joanna and Wilma hesitated just after entering the square. Had they come alone, they might have decided to return another time — something about the place made them uneasy; perhaps it was the foraging pigs sucking and grunting. But they had promised the four retainers they had recruited a share in the profits and these were no street urchins that might be easily bought off for a copper grochen or two, but hulking men with years of fear and anger etched deeply into their faces. So signalling the men to follow, holding themselves proudly despite their uneasiness, they marched forward, Joanna beating on a drum she had fashioned from a small wine cask, Wilma trilling on a reed pipe.

As if a signal had gone out into the narrow, twisting streets, Joanna and Wilma's appearance in the great square caused an inpouring of people from all directions. By the time they had mounted the platform and encouraged the dogs to continue their activities elsewhere, the square was half-filled. By the time they swept the platform clean of the dogs' befoulings and arranged their few props, the square was almost filled with more arriving by the moment.

Their preparations made, Joanna, wearing a crown, which appeared to be of thorns, moved to the center of the platform and raised both arms high. But instead of silencing the crowd this gesture set off a wave of hisses and catcalls. She glanced uneasily at Wilma who answered with a slight shrug. Then Joanna took several steps forward, raised her arms again, and this time there was a lessening of noise, yet an undercurrent of sound continued, a sound much like that of a nest of hornets stirred into anger by a stick.

"Having gained intelligence that my most holy and deeply revered cousin John was immersing those who came to him in the waters of the river, I begged leave from my father Joseph and left the carpenter's bench where we worked together and started in his direction." Joanna's words rang with authority and, although high-pitched, could be heard by all except those just entering the square.

The hornets' sound grew less.

"There at the river I saw a multitude gathered around my saintly cousin, those not in the water kneeling on the bank of the river, offering praise to the Eternal Father, as the saintly John poured handfuls of water over the heads of the grateful sinners."

Wilma moved to the edge of the platform and made dipping motions with her hand.

"Determined to kneel in those cool waters, to have these waters poured upon my head, I moved forward..."

"You! How dare you pretend to be Our Lord!" shouted a cowled monk who had elbowed his way through the crowd up to the platform. "Your kind killed our Blessed Savior. Now you mock Him!"

The hornet sound rose from the crowd. Joanna forced herself to remain where she was, forced her features to retain the appearance of calm. But Wilma backed away from the edge of the platform, easing in Joanna's direction.

"Christ-killers! Christ-killers!" a haggard, toothless woman, whose pendulous breasts showed through her torn garments, started shouting. Others took up the cry.

"How does a Jew dare to appear before Christians?" The hawker of roast meats waved an iron skewer in the air. "They crucified our Lord. They should be crucified!"

The hornet sound rose to a roar. A horse turd arched through the air and struck Wilma on the chest, then a shower of turds, rotted fruit and other refuse descended on the platform. Then came a shower of stones, several striking the two woman as they huddled in the middle of the platform, their arms wrapped around their faces for protection. More stones were hurled, together with a storm of refuse, and the crowd took up the cry of, "Crucify them! Crucify them!"

Shocked into numbness by this sudden violence, badly bruised by the stones and half blinded and half suffocated by the rain of refuse, neither Joanna nor Wilma offered any resistance as they felt powerful hands pulling them off the platform. Alone in the midst of that savage mob, both had given themselves up for dead.

But instead of suffering that terrible fate the crowd demanded, they were dragged out of the square into a side street. There, when Wilma tried to thank the half a dozen heavily armed men who had rescued them, she was cuffed into silence by their captain who declared they would be executed soon enough for their heresy. But at the bishop's pleasure.

Shrieks that could not have been any less than that of those damned eternally to Satan's realm rose up from half a hundred throats as Joanna and Wilma were tossed in among the tortured creatures imprisoned in the bishop's dungeon. The stone floor on which they sprawled was covered with a thick slime whose odor was so powerful both women gasped and had to fight for breath. Until their eyes adjusted to the faint light in this subterranean vault, they could not see. But all around they could hear cackles and shrieks, could feel the cold slime which by now partially covered them, and were forced to breathe a stench worse than any rotting carcass, worse than the fumes of burning sulphur. But gradually, as minutes passed, they were able to make out the shapes of their fellow prisoners.

Some were in such advanced stages of decay it was impossible to determine if they were men or women. Others lay still — dead, unconscious or sleeping, there was no way of knowing. Those more recently imprisoned cowered against the walls, fearing, for some inexplicable reason, the two newcomers. It was from these cowering ones that the tortured sounds came. The long-time inhabitants stayed silent, their motions slow like those of the strange creatures that live deep within caves. Rats, from time to time, scurried across the floor of the dungeon eager for the rich feast to be found in this place, yet wary, for if caught they would be instantly eaten. So wary were these rats they would not approach those prisoners who had died until several days had passed and there was unmistakable evidence of their death.

Their limbs shaking uncontrollably, their bodies throbbing from their injuries, Wilma and Joanna sat in the middle of the dungeon back to back, offering each other a measure of support. All the spaces along the wall were taken by the other prisoners, with several of the most recently arrived also out in the middle of the floor waiting for a space to be released by the death of its owner.

"You wondered what our next adventure would be." Joanna struggled to inject a note of lightness into her voice, but it cracked as a sob shook her body.

"It is all my fault," Wilma groaned shaking her head. "I swore to protect you, yet I have brought you to this. May God forgive me." She made the sign of the cross, the first time she had done so since that day Sigbert and Sofia had been butchered by the peasants. Again she made the sign of the cross as she whispered, "Forgive me. Please forgive me. Punish me, if You must, but have mercy on this innocent creature." She formed her forefingers into the cross and brought them to her lips. "What ever possessed me to deny You... I have been in the clutches of Satan."

Words came to Joanna's lips as she listened to the whispers of the woman, but she forced them back down.

"Take me, Sweet Jesus. Take me this very minute. But let her live. Only I am to blame. Only I."

"Wilma, Wilma, do you forget that I am under Divine protection?" This time Joanna's voice did not crack. "Was not our rescue from that mob a proof? They would have crucified us right there on that platform. Yet here we are, alive and in possession of all of our senses. It may be that our imprisonment is a test — of our faith. Yes, that is what it is. I am certain of it, Wilma. It is a test."

One of the creatures detached itself from the wall and crawled in their direction. They both stiffened as they watched its approach. Wilma reached inside her tunic for her knife, but the creature stopped several paces from them and held out its arm to which, where its hand should be, was attached a mass of rotting flesh. The creature crawled another pace closer.

"No, Wilma." Joanna grabbed the woman's arm as she pulled out her knife. "He needs help. Can't you see. He has come to us for help."

Wilma turned her eyes away from the man with a shudder, then nodded.

Kneeling before the man, his diseased arm resting in her lap, Joanna carefully cut away the rotting flesh with Wilma's knife. From time to time, tiny cries escaped the man's mouth, but he held his arm steady until Joanna finished the dissection and bound up the stump with several of the ribbons still attached to her garments. Then with his good hand the man reached into his rags and extracted a small withered apple which he handed to Joanna. Without a word he crawled back to his space against the wall.

Then, one by one, until she was overcome by exhaustion, other prisoners came to her for treatment. Finally, when she had to sleep, a space was made for her and Wilma against the wall.

When she awoke, other prisoners were patiently waiting for her services as a physician. All of their ribbons now gone, bits of cloth that had been carefully hidden by the prisoners were brought forth. This time Wilma assisted Joanna.

It was toward the end of the third day of their imprisonment — they had lost all sense of time and it felt much longer — all of their fellow prisoners had been given whatever treatment was possible, and several had returned for fresh bandaging; when the iron door of the dungeon swung open and half a dozen heavily armed masked men carrying blazing torches came in. The leader pointed to Joanna and Wilma and the men without a word seized them and rushed them out, slamming the heavy door behind them.

At first, the two women, whose eyes were dazzled by the blazing torches, were terrified, but then as they mounted the stone steps leading up from the dungeon, as they saw the warden of the dungeon lying bound and gagged on the landing, they realized what was happening.

In the street outside horses waited. Then they were galloping toward the wall of the city.

The next hour was a mass of confusion. Pulled from the backs of the horses, the two women were half dragged, half carried through a dark passageway that led under the wall of the city to a cove. Tossed into a skiff and covered with mats, they were rowed out to where a ship was moored. Finally, like sacks of grain they were carried aboard the ship. It was only then that the leader of the armed men removed his mask and revealed himself to be the merchant, Solomon ben David.

"This ship sails for Athens." The man's voice was harsh. "Your passage is paid. I owe you this — for my wife. You were fools, but I could not let you remain in that place." He gestured in the direction from which they had come. "Fools! Mad men! But one must pay one's debts, even to fools and mad men." He hesitated several moments. "May the God of our fathers protect you." He nodded at Joanna. "And may He also protect your gentile." He made a quick head motion toward Wilma. "But should you ever return to this city," he took a step toward Joanna so his breath was upon her, "should either one of you ever again be seen within the walls of this city, a punishment will be inflicted upon you from which, I give you my solemn word, you will never recover." With that the merchant and the other armed men, still masked, descended the rope ladder into the skiff and started for shore.

VI

SICILY

T he fishermen on the ancient quay fronting the city of Palermo looked up from the nets they were repairing as the two travel-soiled monks passed slowly by. Several of the fishermen furtively crossed themselves, then sighed and shook their heads as they returned to their work. "I will wager a prime day's catch that the soldiers of the caliph will have them both in chains before sunset," a squat, broad-shouldered man whose skin was burnt almost black muttered to the other fishermen who shrugged in response. "How the captain of that ship allowed them to disembark, I do not understand." He turned his head for several moments toward the ship at the end of the quay which was taking on fresh water and supplies.

"And the archdeacon will suffer because of them, and the priests," said a younger man. "Look, the younger one wears his cross openly." The younger man's features showed a pained expression as he bit his lower lip.

"I doubt the archdeacon or any of the priests know of these two monks, but, as you say, my son, they will suffer some punishment. The caliph will use any excuse to shame them."

"Perhaps we should warn them." The younger man made a quick gesture in the direction of the two monks who were mounting the stone stairway to the road that led into the city. The older man made an angry sound in his chest as he forcefully shook his head. "But they must not know, father, else they would not be dressed as monks and have the cross so visible."

"If they do not know, they will learn soon enough. If they do not know, they are fools to have ventured into this part of Sicily without first gaining information about conditions. But I doubt they do not know — it has been years since the Saracens first invaded."

"Then the two monks must have come here to be martyred — to

die for Christ," the younger man's voice broke.

"If the caliph believes they were invited to Palermo by the archdeacon or by some of the priests, there will be more than two martyrs." The older man tried to force his voice gruff, but it too broke.

Panting from their exertion and from the heat, Joanna and Wilma rested after completing the climb up to the roadway.

"Those fishermen," Joanna pointed in the direction of the quay, "they turned their eyes away from us after a single glance and appeared to be afraid, Wilma." The older woman shrugged. "We do not even know what place this is. Perhaps we should have waited..."

"Waited until they had us sold into slavery, Joanna!" Wilma interrupted. "You heard the captain and the pilot talking — it was you that understood their bastard Greek — about selling us to the slave merchants when they reached Malta. You are always speaking about the Divine protection under which we travel. Well, it was this protection, my sister, which made that scum on the ship numb themselves with wine, so we could escape." A wave of dizziness caused the woman to close her eyes and grip the rock on which they were sitting for support. "If we do not take advantage of Divine protection when it is offered, my little sister," Wilma went on in a softened voice, "if we fail to recognize this protection when it is offered..." Joanna nodded her understanding. "And, my dearest Joanna," Wilma sighed, "another few days of sailing on that tossing ship, vomiting out my guts, surrounded by hostile men, I doubt I should have survived." Joanna took hold of the woman's hand, which had grown so thin that every bone showed through the skin.

"We will find a priest or a monk who will take us in," Joanna said as she helped Wilma to her feet. "We will stay here for a little time, gain some knowledge of the inhabitants, then continue on to Athens. Perhaps we can find some better clothes. Our robes are so soiled from the filth on that ship." She forced a laugh. "Perhaps that is why we are here, so that we would not arrive in Athens wearing rags again." With that they started in the direction of the city, Wilma, still short of breath, leaning on Joanna for support.

Although the road along which they travelled was in good repair, they met no one and the several huts they passed appeared to be deserted. Exhausted after less than an hour of travel, they rested at a marble fountain carved in the likeness of a ram — the city still several leagues distant.

Joanna examined the carvings on the fountain, shading her eyes and squinting as she tried to make out their fine detail. "The lettering on this fountain is in Greek, Wilma." She began tracing the carving with the tip of her finger.

"We are in Greece?" Wilma lifted her face from her hands and looked at Joanna with a bewildered expression.

"Not Greece, the city of Palermo, Wilma. We are at the ancient city of Palermo in Sicily!"

"Palermo, Joanna! Palermo. May the Virgin protect us." The sound of Wilma's voice caused Joanna's face to drain of color.

"Is there something the matter, Wilma?"

"Something the matter? Something the matter! We are in the land of the Saracens. Just about the time you were born, my poor Joanna, they started their conquest of this island. It has been five or six years since they captured Palermo — the western half of this island is now in their hands. But how could you know of this?" Suddenly Wilma glanced around, fear showing in her face. "No wonder those fishermen looked at us the way they did. Two monks, one wearing the cross, entering this land now ruled by the followers of that infidel Mahamat. We would have been better off staying with the ship, taking our chances of escaping when we reached Malta." Without asking permission, she took hold of the thong suspending Joanna's cross and was just about to cut it when her hand was frozen by the sound of approaching horses' hoofs.

Looking wildly about for a place to hide, her knife in her one hand, her other hand clutching at Joanna, Wilma struggled to her feet. But before they had a chance to move, half a dozen armed riders, their faces covered with black cloths, were upon them.

Muttering the words of the Hail Mary, Wilma started sinking to her knees, but before she could reach the ground, she was jerked onto the back of one of the horses by a pair of powerful hands. A second pair of hands plucked Joanna up as if she were a half-filled sack of wheat. Less than ten seconds had passed altogether before the horsemen with their two prisoners were thundering up the road in the direction of the city.

Scarcely able to breathe from the way she lay across the back of the galloping horse, blinded by the clouds of dust kicked up from the roadway, Joanna struggled to control the terror that threatened to overwhelm her.

She tried to relieve the pressure on her abdomen by twisting, but a hand that felt like a stone slab kept her pinioned. The cross Wilma had been unable to cut away pressed deep into her bound breasts, sending stabs of pain through her chest and shoulders. "Get rid of the cross," flashed through her brain; "tear it off before the Saracens see it." She tried to force her hand between her chest and the sweating, undulating shoulder of the horse. Her hand would only go part way and she tried to twist against the horseman's stone hand to give it entrance. Inch by inch, her fingers, bruised by the pressure, partially numbed, crept closer to the cross. Then she could feel the wood of the cross — the abbess holding out the tray on which lay the dark cross with its silver fittings and the gaily decorated doll — her hand tried to find the knot holding the cross to its thong — the doll so lovely, so gaily clothed, more perfectly made than any she had ever seen; the cross dark and cold — the nails on her fingers broke as she struggled with the knot — holding the cross in her hands, the gathered nuns murmuring while the doll turned into ashes on the glowing embers of the fire.

With a wrench, she pulled her hand away from the cross, pulled her hand out of the space between her chest and the horse's shoulder. "Saracens, or even eaters of human flesh, I still wear my cross," she gasped. With a powerful twist of her body, she wrenched herself partially from the stone hand and started slipping from the horse down toward its pounding hoofs. Gripping the muscles of her shoulder with such power it felt as if they were being torn loose, the hand dragged her back up as she tried to force through her dust-choked throat: "I will wear this cross, if it should cost me my life."

The pounding horse and the stone slab hand pressed the breath out of her chest so that she felt herself sinking into blackness. Then the horse was reigned to a stop and she was being handed down, down to waiting hands that were hard and rough. Half-dragged, half-carried, she was taken out of the sunlight into the dark. She knew it was dark, although she could not see, her eyes were so gummed with dust. The dark place grew cooler as they descended — she could feel the worn stone steps under her feet. Then the shock of cold water thrown into her face. More cold water, forcing her to choke and gasp. And then she could see again, breathe again. No more hands dragging her, holding her. She felt for her cross. It was still there. She forced her shoulders back, pulled herself tall as she blinked against the grit still in her eyes, restraining her hands from rubbing them — frightened children rub their eyes.

Something lay on the floor next to her. She could feel its presence. Then, her eyes almost cleared, she glanced down. A shudder racked her body. It was Wilma. She clenched her teeth, trying to fight off fresh waves of dizziness. They had killed the woman, would soon kill her, but she would show no weakness, would not allow herself to swoon. Then Wilma stirred, uttered a long groan, and slowly and painfully forced herself first to her knees, then to her feet. As Joanna had restrained her hands from rubbing her eyes, she now restrained them from offering assistance to Wilma. She would not sully any of Wilma's dignity before those gathered in this chamber. More than a score surrounded them, all robed, all armed. Yet here in this place, none still wore black cloths to conceal their faces.

"Who are you?" One of the robed men, whose hair was almost white, took several steps in her direction.

"We are monks of the Benedictine order, by name, John and William," Joanna replied. Then her mouth fell open as she realized the question had been asked in Latin and she had, without thinking, answered it in the same language.

"Benedictine monks..." The white-haired man made a whistling sound in his throat. "Benedictine monks in robes with the tonsure, wearing a cross, on this half of Sicily." A film of moisture showed in his eyes which he tried to blink away.

"You are not Saracens?" Joanna asked. In their long robes with their curved swords, their swarthy faces and hooked noses, they looked so strange, so fierce. Were they trying to trap her?

"Saracens! You ask the archdeacon, the priests, and the deacons of Palermo if they are Saracens?" The white-haired man's voice, although strong and resonant, was gentle. "How could you know?" he said half to himself.

"You are religious," Wilma addressed the man in a voice that was reduced to a hoarse whisper. "Then why..." she made a despairing motion with her dirt-stained hands, "why did you arrest us and carry us here in such a fashion?" Despite all of her efforts tears showed in her eyes. Two of the younger robed men, responding to a glance from the white-haired man, detached themselves from the others and brought a bench for Wilma and Joanna to sit on; then they brought each of them a gourd filled with cold water to drink. "From the way you took us, and the manner you carried us — flung over the backs of your horses, then, choking in the dust, with pebbles kicked up from your horses' hoofs striking our faces — " Wilma broke off and slowly lifted the gourd to her lips.

"Better to have suffered a temporary distress than to have received the more permanent treatment you would have certainly had if the soldiers of the caliph had taken you." The white-haired man stroked his strong, jutting chin with his fingertips, then reached out the same hand and laid it for a moment on Wilma's head. "How many years since I have seen the tonsure on one of us..." Murmurs from the other robed men mixed with his words.

"When I heard from one of my people that two monks had disembarked from a ship out of Marseilles, two tonsured monks in robes, one wearing the cross, I will confess that my first reaction was rage." The man furrowed his brow and turned his face partially away so that his heavily hooked nose and prominent chin were silhouetted in the torchlight of the low-ceilinged subterrranean chamber. "Yes, my brothers in Christ," he continued, "my first emotion was rage, not concern with your safety. If the caliph of this city learned of your presence, were my thoughts, he would use this as an excuse to wreak a vengeance on us." He turned his head back so that he again faced Wilma and Joanna directly. "The church is in chains here on this portion of the island of Sicily. Here the followers of that cursed infidel Mahamat grind the servants of Christ under their heels."

"We did not know what place this was — we escaped our ship because we learned that the captain planned to sell us to slave merchants when the ship reached Malta," Joanna addressed the white-haired man. "They all were drunk on wine, so we escaped. We travel to Athens."

"As brother John said," Wilma joined in, "we did not know what land this is, and if our presence should be cause of a calamity..." She broke off.

"There will be no calamity, dearest brother. We secured you in time. And, dearest brother, although rage was my first emotion — rage that came from fear of what might happen to the remnants of the Church if the caliph found out that his orders against the tonsure, the wearing of the cross, the use of religious vestments had been violated — as I, as we," the white-haired man made a sweeping gesture which included the other robed men, "as we mobilized our forces to secure your persons, our concern was also in saving you from the torture and death you would have surely received at the hands of the caliph. Even if you were madmen or fools — and how should we view two who stride brazenly, dressed as you are, into this land ruled by infidels — even if you proved to be the greatest fools in all the world, you were still of our cloth." With that, the white-haired man removed his robe, revealing his silken vestments stitched with gold and silver thread. All the others then took off their robes — all wore vestments, but less ornate than that of the white-haired man.

"I am the archdeacon. My name is Antonius." Then, one by one, in a ceremonious fashion, he introduced the priests and the deacons to Joanna and Wilma.

Although several of the deacons were young, the priests were all older men, with deep wrinkles, missing teeth, and liver-spotting on their hands.

Noting the puzzled expressions on Joanna and Wilma's faces, the archdeacon answered their unasked question. "The bishop is forbidden to ordain any new priests. This prohibition by the caliph is enforced on pain of death. The bishop lives as a virtual prisoner of the caliph. I rule as best I can in his stead." The archdeacon sighed deeply. "I can raise worthy ones to the diaconate but have no authority to ordain priests. In a few more years..." He made a slight gesture toward the priests, bit his lower lip, and shook his head. "Are you priests?" he asked Joanna and Wilma.

"Brothers, not priests," Wilma answered.

"You travel to Athens. Do you go to that place to study for the priesthood?" the archdeacon asked.

"I do not seek the priesthood," Wilma answered. "I am not worthy and this head of mine could never contain sufficient learning." She half smiled. "But Brother John mastered Greek and Hebrew under the guidance of the venerable Sigbert of Aachen, you must have heard of that one. Brother John, who has labored over the works of the Patristic Fathers, who has gained the skills of a physician under the chief physician of Marseilles, will be a priest in time. If it is God's wish, even more than a priest."

"You are a physician, Brother John?" The archdeacon turned to Joanna using a halting Greek.

Joanna answered in a flowing Greek, offering details about the method of her instruction, but saying nothing of how she came to be chosen by the rabbi-physician as his student.

"We have in our midst, by God's favor, a remarkable scholar," the archdeacon addressed the priests and deacons in a vulgarized Latin. "And he is a physician."

"Not yet a physician, Your Reverence," Joanna interrupted. "I have gained some few skills but there is still much I must learn."

"And he is modest, as becomes a cleric and a true scholar," the archdeacon continued. "Perhaps his arrival in our midst is an omen that the years of oppression we have known are coming to an end."

"May it be as you say, Your Reverence," the oldest priest, a toothless, sunken-cheeked man, said in a quavering voice. "To see the tonsure again," he pointed his trembling hand in the direction of Joanna and Wilma, "to hear about tutors and scholars and to listen to that one's flawless Latin... may it be as you suggest, Antonius, an omen that portends a change."

"You wish to travel to Athens to study." The archdeacon turned his attention back to the two monks. "As you are our brothers in Christ, we will help you as best we can. But it will take time and careful preparation. There are informers everywhere." He frowned. "We will have to wait for the arrival of a friendly ship, one whose captain we can trust. That may not happen for weeks or months. Few Christian ships come to these shores since the conquest of the Saracens. Those ships that do come, like the one on which you arrived, more often than not are carrying contraband or engaged in the slave trade."

Joanna listened intently to the man's words. Behind his promise to help she sensed there was something he wanted. She glanced at Wilma who appeared to be wrapped in her own thoughts.

"Are there are any tasks we can do until the ship arrives?" Joanna offered.

"You are our guests," the archdeacon quickly replied. "But for the time you must spend here with us, there are certain things..." He swallowed hard. "The faces and names of all of us are well known." He indicated the deacons and the priests that were ranged around the chamber, serious, attentive expressions of their faces. "If any one of us should absent himself from this city for as little as a single day, his absence will be noted. We are under strict orders to remain within this district. Yet there are deacons, monks, and priests in the interior with whom it is essential we communicate. Some are isolated in the mountains, watching the peasants who live in their districts each day growing more and more heathen. They despair. They hunger for a communication from the bishop, yearn for the sound of Latin, for the holy language from which they can gain much needed inspiration. Some are sick and may never recover without the services of a physician." The archdeacon paused, then with studied movements made the sign of the cross. "You are God-sent, brother John, brother William. If you allow us, we will dress you as peasants, as goatherds. We will shave your heads to hide the tonsure. If asked, you can say your heads were shaved because of the itch. Dressed as goatherds, your faces unknown to any of the caliph's spies or soldiers, you can come and go and not be noticed. Can we beg you for this service for the time you are our guests, brother John, brother William?"

"Our lives are dedicated to the service of Christ and His Holy Church," Joanna answered. "To allow us to serve the Church in this fashion — to minister to the needs of your priests and deacons — is a great gift." Wilma nodded at Joanna's words. "Perhaps that is the reason we are here," Joanna said softly.

"You are God-sent. Your services will be of inestimable value." The archdeacon reached out his hand to the two seated monks and drew them to their feet. "But first you must meet the bishop. Despite the orders of the caliph, nothing is done in this diocese without his knowledge and express permission."

Dressed in rags even worse than those they had worn when they entered Marseilles, their heads shaved and covered with caps of raw goatskin, their faces and hands stained a dark brown, Joanna and Wilma followed the youngest of the deacons at a distance of a dozen paces through the gate and into the city of Palermo. As they had been instructed, they kept their eyes riveted on the ground, their heads bowed, their arms crossed over their chests. They hugged the walls whenever a soldier or any other in authority passed, bowing low in reverence. Only in the most furtive of fashions did either of them glance at the buildings, statues and other structures they passed.

Here and there were traces of what had once been a center of a great civilization. Several of the ancient buildings still stood, with an occasional statue or fountain much defaced and weatherbeaten, but for the rest, the city was in a pitiful condition. Its stone streets, the craft of Grecian and Roman artisans and engineers, were now pitted and potholed and choked with refuse so that in places they were virtually impassable to any vehicle, and difficult to traverse by any but the most skilled horsemen. They passed a church whose timbers and stonework showed evidences of a fire. The entrance to this structure was befouled with garbage and the excrement of animals. From the interior of the church there belched forth such a stench that for several moments it sickened Joanna and Wilma who had grown used to stenches. It was as if all the Saracen soldiers of the city used this place as their latrine.

A mounted Saracen whose rank must have been that of a knight rode past. The deacon who led them fell to his knees, pressed his face into the filth of the roadway, and grovelled until the hoofbeats could no longer be heard. Joanna and Wilma, responding to the actions of their guide and to the fierce appearance of the mounted man, whose curved sword gleamed in the reflection of the sun, also grovelled, but they did not press their faces into the filth of the roadway.

As they passed a house decorated with blue pennants on which were embroidered stars and crescents a basin of slops was poured down on the head of the deacon. Shouts in a strange language and laughter followed the dumping of these slops. Joanna and Wilma braced themselves, but the inhabitants had no interest in a pair of dirty, ragged goatherds.

Sickened by what had just happened, fighting the urge to pick up several of the loose stones of the roadway and hurl them at the laughing, mocking, mustached faces showing in the windows of the building, Joanna kept her eyes on the young deacon who made no effort to clean away the foul matter that soiled his garments. It was as if he were unaware of what had happened. Almost as if in response to Joanna's thoughts, Wilma muttered, "This sort of thing must happen to them daily." Her face showed a pained expression. "I never thought to see Christ's Holy Church in such a condition. And I, I denied His Church, declared for a time against the vows I had taken. Can I ever be forgiven?"

They reached the compound where the caliph lived, and the deacon, after indicating a gate in the rear leading to the garden, disappeared into a side street. The gate was guarded by a fat, sleepy-eyed soldier whose hairy, louse-infested belly was exposed to the sun through his open tunic. Other than giving a grunt, the soldier scarcely noticed the two goatherds as they passed through the gate. He concentrated on the long, slow scratches he gave his swollen belly.

Two men were waiting inside the garden. They stood in the shadows and for the first moments after passing through the gate Joanna and Wilma did not see them. But then a movement in the shadows attracted their attention. Fear that they had been lured into this place to be killed caused Wilma to reach inside her garments for her knife. But then from the shadows came Latin words, and the knife was replaced in its sheath.

They followed the men to an open space next to the wall that was closely guarded by a tangle of thorny bushes. There, the two men turned to greet them, the older one offering his hand, the younger bowing deeply. Both were dressed in the stained, coarse garments worn by the poorest class of artisans and the calluses and broken nails of their hands declared that their garments were not disguises. Joanna raised her eyes to their faces. The older man, slender of build and slightly above average height, had a high forehead and fine features. Although it was evident that he was no longer young, perhaps already into his seventh decade, this appearance of age did not come from any wrinkles in his face or a whitening of his hair, for his face was as smooth as any youth's and his hair was thick and black; yet there was something about his features that marked him as one who had lived a long time. The younger man was well above average height, with broad shoulders, deep chest, and thickly corded muscles. Joanna caught his eyes for a moment, then turned her eyes away. There was something familiar about his face. His expression, his features, stirred a portion of her memory. But then her attention was drawn back to the older man who started to address them.

"Brother William, Brother John, you are welcome — more than welcome." He inclined his head a fraction. "My archdeacon informs me you are willing to undertake certain tasks desperately needed here in our diocese."

"You are the bishop?" Wilma asked, surprise showing in her face.

"I am the bishop." The man tried to smile, but the smile would not come. "Forbidden to say mass in public, ordered under pain of death not to ordain any priests, denied the use of my vestments..." He fingered the frayed edges of his garments. "Prohibited even the suggestion of the tonsure. Yet I am still the bishop."

"Forgive..." Wilma fell to her knees and took the man's hand, "forgive my question, Your Eminence." The bishop placed his hand for a moment on Wilma's head, then with a show of kindness raised her to her feet.

"You are a physician, trained in Marseilles?"

"Not I, Your Eminence, not I. This one." Wilma turned toward Joanna.

"So young!" The bishop was unable to hide the surprise in his voice. "My archdeacon did not make it clear — he was so filled with excitement." He stared at Joanna for several seconds, making no effort to conceal his examination of her features. "So young, so young, yet we must put our trust in you," he murmured. Then in a louder voice, "And there will be danger." Joanna nodded. "If the infidels who hold this half of the island should learn that you travel as our emissary, it would mean death for both of you." He hesitated. "And for me — for the bishop." Then, as if stricken with sudden pain, the man's features tightened and he rapidly shook his head. "I cannot stay with you any longer. The caliph and his captains constantly check on me, and expect to see me working in the garden. If they do not see me, they will grow suspicious." With that, the bishop introduced the younger man.

"Brother Marcos is my secretary. He will tell you of the places you must visit, will repeat the messages to be delivered until you have committed them to memory. When he speaks, it is with our voice."

"Now I must return to my tasks in the garden, brother William, brother John. Go with God, and with the bishop's blessing." With that, he placed his hands on their heads, whispered the ancient words, and was gone.

For the rest of the day, until the lengthening shadows of evening cast the little clearing next to the wall into darkness, the bishop's secretary instructed Joanna and Wilma as to the location of the various clerics they would visit, repeating the bishop's message several times until Joanna had everything perfectly committed to memory. As she listened to this handsome young man's words, glancing from time to time at his face, which showed such a serious expression, her feeling that something about him was familiar grew stronger. But it was not until they both had passed out of the side gate, still guarded by the sleepy, scratching soldier, that Joanna realized what it was about the man that was so familiar.

She gripped Wilma's arm excitedly. "Except for his eyes, he reminds me of Sigbert!"

"Except for his eyes! What! Whose?"

"Brother Marcos of course." Joanna tightened her grip on the woman's arm. "Not as tall or as broad in the shoulders as Sigbert. It is more in the way he carries himself. And, Wilma, his nose and mouth and the cleft in his chin — it is Sigbert." Tears filled her eyes.

"Sigbert..." Wilma said softly. "Poor Sigbert, may God rest his soul. The time we spent in the cave seems so long ago." She leaned against a broken marble column that once was a part of a Roman temple. "I am growing weary, Joanna. Those weeks on the ship — my bones feel old. Yet we must carry the bishop's messages, must serve the Church. There is no choice." A deep sigh escaped the woman. "Joanna, you say the bishop's secretary has Sigbert's features? I did not notice. Perhaps so."

Supplied by the archdeacon with several small silver coins which they secreted in their garments, each carrying a wallet filled with onions, bread and cheese, and each gripping a stout cudgel carved from dense wood, Joanna and Wilma passed out of the gates of Palermo just after they were opened at sunrise. The road they took was the same one they had traveled from the quay. They passed the side road leading to the subterranean room to which they had been taken by the thundering horses the day before. Only the day before? That short time had been so crowded. In less than twenty hours, they had evolved from helpless prisoners, expecting to be put to death, to emissaries of the bishop, emissaries doing work of great importance for the Church.

They walked slowly, Joanna deliberately slowing her pace because Wilma's breathing was so labored, her eyes so hollow. They reached the portion of the road where the stone steps led down to the quay. Below them, the size of beetles, the fishermen were still repairing their nets. But the ship from Marseilles was gone. Wilma found a cool place in the shadows to rest while Joanna stared out to sea. How long would it take them to reach Athens? she wondered. Would they ever reach that famed city? Even if not discovered to be emissaries of the bishop, traveling into the interior of this island would be dangerous. They did not have to be warned of bandits. The wild and mountainous nature of the country guaranteed there would be bands of lawless men.

Her thoughts shifted. Images of Sigbert came into her mind, and the meeting with Brother Marcos. Here were two men who were not like the harelipped widow's son, his eyes inflamed, panting, his soot-black hands reaching up under her shift. She forced that scene back into the dark recesses of her mind. She awakened Wilma and they continued on their way, knowing they still had far to go that day to find safety from the Saracens.

Resting frequently, seeking shady places to sleep during the hottest portion of the afternoon, Joanna and Wilma followed the road for five days as it led inland. Often they would walk for hours without seeing another human being. Then a cluster of poorly built huts whose inhabitants scowled and made threatening gestures warning them to keep their distance. Once a company of armed Saracens thundered past on lathered horses from whose gaping mouths hung ropes of saliva, and it was as if both of them were invisible or at most vermin beneath notice, for none of the riders so much as glanced in their direction and had they not scurried off the road, they would have been pelted with stones from the flying hoofs, if not run down.

Mid-morning of the fifth day, they reached a narrow road leading up into the mountains and marked by the remnants of a shrine whose stonework had been worn smooth by hundreds of years of exposure to sun and wind. Two days travel along this road would bring them to a village high in the mountains where several monks still lived in a sort of monastery in defiance of the caliph's edicts. There were messages for these monks from the bishop, together with an order for one of their number to lead them to an even more remote village where it was rumored that the local priest still held public mass and performed all the other sacraments. This priest, it was said, suffered from deep, suppurating ulcers of the legs and was badly in need of the services of a physician. Then, even further in the interior, there would be other villages, other priests or deacons.

They rested in the shadow of the ancient shrine, but they found little relief as waves of heated air danced off the granite of the mountains and rolled down on them. Except for their breaths struggling in and out their chests, there was no sound, not even the whine of insects. Minute by minute, the heat grew greater.

"I never knew there could be such heat," croaked Wilma. "In my father's house and later in the convent during the cold and damp days of winter I dreamed of a land where the sun shone hot, but now I would crawl on my knees a hundred leagues to exchange this heat for the worst of that cold and damp."

Joanna wet a cloth with water from her flask, then placed it over Wilma's eyes as the woman sighed.

"Two days travel and we will be in the monks' village, away from the Saracens, out of danger. There we can bathe and rest for a time," Joanna said softly.

"Two days travel." Wilma tried to suppress a groan. "I feel my age in my bones, dearest sister. I have almost forty years. Many are dead before they reach this age, Joanna. My mother — "

"You will live to a great age, Wilma. No less than another twenty years." Joanna pressed her index finger against Wilma's lips as the woman tried to declare that at most she had another four or five years. "Have you forgotten, I am a physician?" Joanna forced a laugh. "You suffer a temporary indisposition. Twenty more years, did I say? More likely you will survive the full three score and ten promised in the Scriptures." To this Wilma shook her head.

"I will be satisfied if I survive long enough to see you safely to Athens. In Athens, where learning is still revered, you will be safe; you will no longer need me as your companion."

"But if I should then travel to Rome to kneel before Christ's Vicar here on earth; if I should travel to that place, who will be my companion if you are gone?"

Smiling at the younger woman, Wilma said softly, "I will try to stay alive, dearest sister. I will try with all the strength God has given me to be with you when you enter the Eternal City."

Suddenly she started laughing — for the first few moments it was forced, but then it turned into full laughter which shook her body. "In the midst of the most desolate land anywhere on earth, facing we know not what dangers, not knowing if we will be alive this time next week, there is mournful talk whether poor Wilma will accompany poor Joanna when she travels to Rome years hence. Were there ever two such silly geese as we!" Wilma clapped her hands together and Joanna joined in the laughter.

Exhausted from their hours of travel along that narrow, twisting road leading up into the mountains, neither woman had enough breath left for speech as they settled down for the night on a ledge of ground partially hidden behind a great boulder. The sun had just set and the mountains were bathed with streaks of blood-red light. Below the valley boiled with the orange and crimson substance of the sun, the shrine where they had rested erupted with tongues of flame. In the silence of the mountains there was a roar that filled Joanna's ears. She focused her eyes on a high crag that looked as if it dripped blood. There was a face. She rubbed her eyes, looked again. It was gone. In the little light which remained, she examined all the crags and outcroppings carefully. There were no more faces. Yet there had been that one, or was it a trick of her vision?

Then it was dark and with the dark came a moaning wind and cold that troubled their sleep. Then again morning with the sun coming down on them like a fist. No more faces, although Joanna's eyes kept darting in every direction despite the glare. No more faces, yet she felt a presence as if eyes were following their slow upward progress. But she said nothing to Wilma, as she had said nothing about that single glimpse of a face.

Mid-morning of their third day of climbing into the mountains, the road skirted a deep precipice, then turned inland between two high crags. One minute they were among the scattered boulders and sharp flints of the mountains, the next minute they were entering a small, partially cultivated valley, in the midst of which stood a village of half a hundred mudbrick huts.

They shaded their eyes and carefully examined the valley. On the far side of the village several men were working in a terraced field, whose rich green was in contrast to the strips of brown, sun-scorched grassland that bordered it. Even from this distance they could see that the men wore long robes with hoods covering their heads, despite the heat.

They started down the road into the valley and had not taken a hundred steps when a herd of goats, bleating, their bronze bells tinkling, surrounded them and began nuzzling and rubbing against their legs. An unexpected wave of emotion caused Joanna to drop to her knees and embrace and stroke the bleating creatures that pressed against her. Tears from a place deep in her memory flowed out into Wilma's eyes as she watched Joanna, then she too dropped to her knees.

A strange, guttural, animal-like sound caused both women to look up. A creature — dwarf or malformed child — made the sounds from its gaping, twisted mouth. Its fear-filled bulging eyes darted from side to side. It waved a stick in their direction, although as they started to rise, the creature ran backward a score of paces and partially hid behind a thorny bush. Despite all their entreaties and their exaggerated gestures of friendship, which included an offer of a large onion, the goatherd would not leave the protection of the bush where he continued to make the guttural sounds and wave his stick at them.

Except for the goatherd, they met no one for the remaining half a league they traveled to the village, although they paused at a hollow where a cook fire still burned under a clay pot filled with a bubbling, extremely pungent fluid.

"They are hiding," Joanna said in a softened voice, as they examined the abandoned fire and bubbling pot. Wilma nodded. "They must have heard the cries of the goatherd — taken us for Saracen soldiers or bandits."

At that Wilma started laughing. Then she leaned over the bubbling pot and took a deep sniff. "Those who live in this place have no need to fear soldiers or bandits. A plate of this will drive off even the fiercest." She rubbed at her tearing eyes with her sleeve. "Have you ever smelled such a vile stuff?"

Joanna leaned over the pot, took a cautious sniff, then making an unpleasant face, rapidly shook her head.

They walked the remaining distance to the village, their hands gripping their knives beneath their tunics. Once there, they hesitated for several minutes, searching the single, dusty street for any movements, listening for any sound. Except for the flap of window cloths in the wind and the shudder of bushes, there was no movement.

They glanced uneasily at one another. At any moment, scores might erupt from those silent huts. When the villagers realized there were only two, saw that all their trepidation had been caused by a pair of ragged goatherds, not a detachment of soldiers or a company of bandits, might not their fear suddenly turn into rage? They took several steps into the deserted street, then halted and again listened. Now from the huts they could hear soft sounds.

Wilma shook her head and motioned for them to retreat; Joanna nodded, and they were both just about to back out of the village when a powerfully built man with unnaturally long arms emerged from a hut partway down the street. His teeth bared in the manner of a dog guarding his master's house, his eyes narrowed into slits, hunched over in the posture of a wrestler so that his knuckles almost touched the ground, the man stared at them. Then in a guttural language that was not Latin, yet contained enough Latin so that he could be understood, he ordered them to leave the village. The sound of this man's voice brought faces to the doors of the other huts — all the faces were of men, swarthy-skinned, hooked-nosed with prominent cheekbones, all scowling and showing their teeth.

Forcing herself to stand tall, Joanna took a single step in the man's direction and stated that they had come to this village to confer with the monks that lived here.

"No monks!" the man snarled at Joanna. Hissing, growling sounds came from the more than two score other men who had emerged from their huts and lined both sides of the street.

"When we entered this valley," Joanna gestured to the rear, "we saw monks working in the fields on the far side of this village."

"No monks!" The man reached one of his long arms inside the door of his hut and brought out a thick club studded with iron spikes.

"We are Christians — we are monks who carry important messages for the monks who live in this village." Joanna took another step in the man's direction, and Wilma who had held back at first, joined her.

"No Christians in this village." The man raised his club. "We all pray to the God of Mahamat in this village." Affirmative grunts came from the two score other men. "No Christians, no monks in this village. Go away!" The man advanced several paces in their direction and a number of the other men stepped away from their huts and joined him.

Joanna looked at Wilma, caught her eyes for a moment, took a deep breath, then in a full voice, started intoning the Te Deum. After several seconds, as soon as the shock of surprise wore off, Wilma, also in a full voice, joined in. The sound of the ancient litany rolled through the village, causing some of the men to tremble and the leader of the village to hesitate as he glanced from one to another of the villagers as if seeking advice as to what he should do next. Throwing their heads back, sucking in great lungfuls of air, the two women increased the volume of their chant until it could be heard echoing through the valley. Then from a hut at the far end of the village, a hut somewhat larger than the others, a file of seven men emerged, dressed in brown robes which reached the ground, cowls covering their heads.

The men of the village gave way as the robed ones approached. Then the huts erupted and disgorged women and children until the street was choked with villagers.

Stopping a half a dozen paces from Joanna and Wilma, who still chanted in full voice, the leader of the robed men drew back his cowl, exposing a deeply wrinkled, tear-stained face. At this, the two women broke off their chanting.

"How many years has it been since I heard the blessed words of the Te Deum?" the wrinkled old man said in broken Latin. "We are monks." He turned his head for a moment toward the six other men, then turned back to the two women. "We are monks whose lives are sworn to serve the Lord Jesus Christ. Yet we have forgotten so many of the words." Fresh tears showed in the old man's eyes. "No priest, no psalter, not so much as a single page of the Holy Scriptures here in this valley — so long we have stayed here away from all the others, we have forgotten." The old man covered his face with his hands and wept openly. Sounds of weeping came from the other monks, although they kept their faces hidden within their cowls.

"When the soldiers of the infidel Mahamat came to this valley, we hid our robes." Sobs choked the old man and for more than a minute he struggled, then continued in a halting fashion. "While those soldiers were in this valley, we denied the Christ, said the name of their god Allah. We laughed when they laughed. We gave them presents. We were afraid and although we put on our robes again, we are ashamed. Yet we are still Christians." The old man took the remaining few steps that separated him from Joanna and Wilma, fell to his knees and then showered their feet with kisses. The other monks came up and also fell to their knees, groveling in the roadway, their faces pressed into the dust.

It took several minutes and much earnest entreaty before Joanna and Wilma were able to get the monks back on their feet. Then as they accompanied them through the village, again and again, one or another of the robed men would snatch up their hands and cover them with kisses. The villagers, as they passed, bowed and murmured words neither Joanna nor Wilma understood.

In the monks' hut, a foul-smelling, poorly illuminated structure scarcely large enough for the seven who lived in it, now, choked with the addition of the two visitors and several leading members of the village, Joanna and Wilma were offered pitchers of milk, wedges of a fresh, rich cheese, chunks of coarse yet tasty bread, and plates of stew whose overpowering odor declared them to be the same substance they had discovered bubbling over the abandoned fire. Not wishing to insult their hosts, they both tasted of this stew. If anything, the taste was more distressing than its odor. It was as if live coals had been placed in their mouths. Their lips and tongues felt as if they had swollen to several times their normal size. They struggled for breath, perspiration broke out on their foreheads, and tears streamed from their eyes. Yet the monks and the leading villagers who joined in this feast gobbled great mouthfuls, nodding and smacking their lips, al-

though they too showed beads of perspiration upon their foreheads
and tears in their eyes.

After they had recovered from the stew both Joanna and Wilma
attempted to relate the details of who they were and the nature of the
messages they carried, but with a show of much politeness and
deference, they were waved into silence with more milk, bread and
cheese being offered them — their reaction to the stew had been
noted, and no more of this fiery substance was pressed upon them.
Only when the feast was over and each had been presented with a
finely made jacket of embroidered kid-skin were they able to convey
the messages from the bishop.

As they told of the bishop's concern with the welfare of the
monks, as they related details of the bishop's virtual imprisonment by
the caliph, the monks and the leading villagers wept.

"We thought the Church dead on this island — that we were the
only ones left — it has been so many years." The old monk clasped
and unclasped his hands as he struggled for the correct words through
his sobs.

"Only ones left?" Joanna's face showed a puzzled expression.
"The bishop told us you would lead us to a priest who lived in another
village three days' journey to the east. That there were other
priests..."

"Three days' journey to the east." The old monk sadly shook his
head. "He was buried in a pit by the Saracens more than five years
ago. Only his head was left above ground and the beetles and ants ate
at it until his eyes and flesh were gone."

Joanna shuddered as the image of Sigbert's head lying in the
firepit, of the beetles and ants crawling in and out of Sofia's torn groin
flashed through her mind.

"You shudder, most revered brother John." The old man nodded
at Joanna. "And well you should. The old priest's screams were heard
for two days before the end came. Other priests, other holy men of
these mountains were put into the pit by those who follow Mahamat.
There are no more priests, no more holy men." Joanna started to protest, but the old man raised his hand. "We are not holy men. Had we
been holy, we would have suffered the pit. But we hid our robes. We
laughed and sang with the soldiers when they visited this village. We
said the name of their god. We are not holy — we are an abomination
and will suffer the torments of hell for all eternity."

"But when the bishop learns what has happened — how the soldiers came, how they treated the priests and the others — when the
bishop hears from us all that has happened, he will grant you forgive-

ness."

"Even the forgiveness of the bishop is not enough, not enough."

"But if the bishop should write a message to the pope, to Christ's vicar in Rome; if the pope should grant you forgiveness..." Joanna's face took on a flush. "Would not the forgiveness of the pope be enough?"

"Yes, the pope. Yes, that would be enough for he is Christ's representative here on earth. Then we would be in God's grace again."

The old monk paused then went on, "But you say you are physicians. In this village we suffer terribly from sores." He pulled up the sleeve of his robe and exposed a number of scab-encrusted lesions. At a nod, other monks exposed their arms as did the several villagers. All showed the same angry-looking scab-encrusted lesions.

Ordering them all out of the dark hut into the street, Joanna began examining these lesions. She had seen like lesions on several children treated by the rabbi-physician. He had washed the sores with a mixture of nitre and water, then had picked away the scab with the point of a lancet, informing her, as he worked, that only if exposed to the air would they heal.

Using some of the nitre they carried with them, employing the point of her knife as a lancet, her hands gentle yet certain, she started treating the lesions. As Joanna worked, Wilma told the monks and the villagers about how strong the Church still was in other places in Europe. She detailed the size and magnificence of the cathedral at Aachen, spoke about the thousands of nuns, monks and priests who were distributed among the hundreds of convents, monasteries and churches in more than a score of kingdoms. And her account of the vitality of the Church in the rest of Europe served to restore the monks. Faces that had been lifeless were now filled with animation. Previously downcast eyes were lifted and glistened. And they showered her with questions:

How often was the mass performed each day? What sort of vestments were worn by the bishop? How were the priests and monks treated by the soldiers and knights? Then they wanted to know about the missionaries who traveled among the heathens, about the holy hermits who lived in caves. These questions Wilma answered as best she could while Joanna concentrated on her treatments.

During a pause in the questioning, Joanna looked up for a moment and asked the senior monk if he or one of the other monks would accompany them as a guide while they continued their travels to the west, as they searched in the various valleys for any remnants of Christians that might be left. At this, the animation went out of the man's face, his eyes grew lifeless, and a like thing happened to the other monks. Then mumbling something incomprehensible, he retreated into the hut, quickly followed by the other monks.

After she had recovered from the shocks of the monks' abrupt withdrawal, Joanna asked the man who had first confronted them when they entered the village, "Will you or one of your villagers come with us as a guide?" Twisting his face, which had once showed such fierceness, into a foolish expression, the man shrugged and pulled on his lower lip as he backed away until he had reentered his hut. The several other men, whose faces Joanna's questioning eyes fell upon, retreated in like fashion into their huts. After a long stare at the huts into which the men had retreated, she turned to the scab-encrusted lesions of the several score women and children who had stayed in the background while the men of the village had been treated.

She worked for several minutes, but then a series of sounds that were not quite words drew her attention. It was the dwarf goatherd they had met upon first entering the valley — she had thought he was a child, had scarcely glanced at his face. Pointing first at himself, then in the direction leading out of the village, the goatherd continued to make these sounds, his wizened face twisting and tightening as he struggled to make himself understood.

"He wants to be our guide," Joanna said as she gained an understanding of his meaning. The little man laughed and bounced up and down in a manner reminiscent of Sofia.

"You know the way through these mountains?" Wilma asked the man. As an answer the goatherd started bleating and then put fingers on both sides of his head to simulate horns.

"He tells us that he has followed the goats through the mountains — that he knows the mountains." Joanna interpreted the man's sounds and actions, which he affirmed by a series of body gyrations while a chirping laughter issued from his gaping mouth.

Joanna's eyes darted to Wilma, then back to the little man. "We are grateful for your offer and we accept. What is your name?"

Screwing his face into an attempt at a serious expression, the man formed the word: "Nicco."

"That is a friendly name." Joanna smiled at the little man. "You know many things about these mountains, do you not, Nicco?" At this, the goatherd grinned so broadly his eyes were lost in the folds of his face. "You have discovered hidden springs of water and secret caves for shelter?" Still grinning, Nicco inclined his head. "We are fortunate to have you as our guide."

"Fortunate." Wilma echoed, but her voice contained a questioning sound.

As the last traces of daylight seeped out of the valley, Joanna finished her work. As soon as the treatment was completed, each had disappeared into his or her hut without so much as a nod of appreciation. With darkness, the village street was left deserted except for the goatherd and then, after a wild series of gestures he too disappeared. Muttering about the strange behavior of the monks and villagers, the two women found a shed used for sheltering goats at the edge of the village where they settled down for the night.

"It may be best for us to return to Palermo, Joanna," Wilma murmured as she wrapped her sheepskin covering around her shoulders against the night's cold. "To continue inland may be without purpose if, as the old monk said, all the priests are slaughtered." She hesitated. "Without purpose, and dangerous."

"How much can we trust those frightened monks?" Joanna reached out and took Wilma's hand. "My heart aches, Wilma, for what the Church has suffered on this island, for what has happened to these monks and to so many others." She sighed. "Who can blame them for being what they are? But for us to turn back with the bishop's messages undelivered, without our seeing for ourselves..." She tightened her grip on Wilma's hand. "And even if all the priests were slaughtered, there still may be deacons, holy hermits, and others whose lives are dedicated to Christ who will rejoice to hear that the Church in this diocese is not dead." She released Wilma's hand, crossed her arms under her head, and stared upward through the loose thatch to the star-choked sky. "If there are no holy men left or if those we find have forgotten their religion, as have the monks of this village, there may be a few peasants who still declare themselves Christians. These we can nourish with our words." She paused again for the space of a dozen slow deep breaths as she stared unblinking at the sky. "And if there are no more Christians in these lost villages," she went on, "then I will tell whoever we encounter of 'The Good News' as did my father to the heathens of the East."

"If the Saracens should hear of this!" Wilma said in a tight voice. "Even the bishop, under pain of death, is forbidden to say mass. Even the bishop."

"Christ died for us and He was the Son of God. If there is a need, cannot we whose lives are not worth a thousandth of His do as much for Him?"

"They will put us in the pit, Joanna." Wilma's voice sounded dry and old.

"Then I will sing praises to Christ — give thanks for serving Him in this way as long as I still have breath."

Several minutes passed in silence. Joanna's thoughts drifted as she slipped toward sleep. Just as she was about to be enveloped by the dark curtain she heard Wilma whisper the words, "So be it."

A stick half again as tall as himself tightly held in his hand, blowing notes every few seconds on a reed whistle which the dozen goats he drove seemed to understand, the dwarf goatherd led the way out of the far end of the valley.

None of the villagers had emerged from their huts as Joanna and Wilma made their simple preparations for departure just before sunrise, although from the murmurs, and other sounds, it was apparent that all the village was awake. The old monk appeared for a moment at the door of his hut, his lips parted as if he were about to speak, but then his features tightened and he withdrew into the shadows.

Moving with an ease and a grace that neither Joanna nor Wilma would have thought possible in so deformed a creature, the goatherd led them through the pass, then along the edge of the mountain on a path scarcely more than two spans in width. As sure-footed as his goats, he led them with no appearance of concern for the sheer dropoff and the jumble of sharp, broken rocks waiting far below. While Joanna and Wilma hugged the cliff, their hands constantly searching for outcroppings or exposed roots to hold onto, Nicco leapt easily over obstructions, his feet coming, from time to time, so close to the edge that handfuls of pebbles were dislodged and showered down the side of the mountain.

It took them three days of difficult and exhausting travel to reach the next village to the east. They were able to see the huts long before they reached them. Unlike the other village this one did not lie hidden in a valley, but was formed in tiers on a long gradual slope of a mountain. From a distance the slope where the village lay looked like a crescent of polished jade, with the village itself a series of dark lines etched into its center.

As had been the case with the first village, this one also showed no signs of life as they approached its outskirts. Its huts were in poor repair, several with roofs fallen in. They entered the short street that separated the first two tiers of houses, but this time no leader emerged from one of the huts to warn them back. Only a skulking dog, half starved and showing bared fangs, snarled at them. Then, still snarling, the dog retreated into a gully. Separating from Nicco, who let his goats out into a shallow basin covered with lush grass, Joanna and Wilma entered the street dividing the next two tiers of houses. They hadn't taken a dozen steps when a stooped, wrinkled, red-eyed woman emerged from the darkness of one of the huts. She looked at them, blinking in the light, her mouth making the chewing motions often seen in those who have no teeth. Then she gestured them closer and, when they were close, brought her face to within inches of theirs.

"You are not Saracens — I did not think you were. Saracens do not travel on foot, are not accompanied by goats. You are Christians?" Joanna and Wilma nodded. "They are Christians!" The woman raised her voice. Several other women of like age and condition appeared at the doors of their huts. "If you came to steal, we have nothing left." The woman shrugged. "Look for yourselves."

"We did not come to steal," Joanna said gently. "We were sent by the bishop to bring certain messages to your priest." The word "priest" sent a shudder through the woman's body. "We have learned of his fate," Joanna went on. "But we came to see if we could be of use to others. We are Christian monks."

"Christian monks?" The woman's lips started to tremble. "Do not let the Saracens know this. If they learn you are Christian monks and have been in this village..." She covered her eyes with her work-swollen hands. Then she said in a barely audible voice, "If they learn you have been here, they will come again."

"We heard how they put your priest into a pit."

"Our priest — so long ago," the woman interrupted Joanna. "They came again. Three years after the priest, they came again." Then a flood of word mixed with dry sobs burst from the woman.

She told them how after the priest's death, a young deacon who had kept hidden during the Saracen raid, took over his functions. Although terrified of their return, the villagers, under the loving guidance of this deacon, continued with their Christian practices. She told them that after the passage of a year, believing themselves safe, the villagers erected a shrine to their martyred priest. But then the Saracens raided again. This time all the men of the village suffered the pit. All the children and younger women were taken as slaves. The score of older women, after being repeatedly raped and beaten, were left in their broken huts with the warning that the followers of Mahamat would again return.

"It would have been better had they put us in the pit with our men," muttered a second woman who had come up. This woman's face was a mass of scars. "The village is dead. We are its corpses. We have no men." The woman's voice broke for a moment. "Our children have been taken — we are dead."

"Bandits came to this village just before the season of Christ's birth." The first woman started speaking again. "They rode through the streets, looked inside the huts, then left. Not even the bandits will have any part of us. Very soon, may God grant it, we will lie alongside our men." The other women slowly nodded.

All of Joanna's offers to minister to them — most of the women's eyelids were swollen and granular, many showed deep, angry ulcers on their arms and legs — were refused, although several attempted smiles of appreciation. But they begged for the blessings of the two monks, each in turn kneeling before Joanna and Wilma, murmuring softly as they felt the hands placed on their heads, heard the ancient holy words.

Then Nicco was alongside them with his goats. The little man understood what had happened. He divided his flock of goats. Half he tethered to the various huts, the other half, without so much as a backward glance, he started driving out of the village to the east.

Joanna and Wilma watched the little man until he reached a portion of the slope where the grass ended and the flints and rocks of the mountain began. Then, after looking long and deep into the eyes of the two women with whom they had conversed, they turned and followed the goatherd.

A day's travel away from the village, as they were taking their noonday meal in a shallow gully where the goats could find a few clumps of brownish grass on which to browse, a sound or perhaps it was the movement of a shadow caused them to look up. On both sides of the gully were ranged more than a score of armed men wearing garments of stitched goatskin from which the hair had not been removed. They were heavily bearded, with the exposed portions of their faces burnt almost black. Their hooked noses, thin-lipped mouths and closely set, squinting eyes gave them a merciless appearance.

The word "Saracens" escaped Wilma's lips as she hunched down and pressed her chin into her chest. Nicco rolled himself into a sort of a ball among his goats and lay still, his head wrapped tightly in his arms. But Joanna continued to stare up at the armed men, her eyes traveling from face to face.

With a start she recognized one. Her eyes had not played tricks upon her. Then the man leapt down into the gully, a short, broad-bladed sword in one hand, a whip of plaited horsehair in the other. She tensed and clenched her jaw for the expected sword thrust. The man was standing directly over her. She could smell the odor of the unsheathed blade, the stink of the goatskin, the stench of sweat. Her eyes were riveted on the blade, waiting for its sudden forward movement. She forced them away from the blade to the man's face. She felt herself rising, the tensed muscles of her calves and thighs pushing her upward.

"You are not afraid of bandits?" the man exploded in laughter. The other men on both sides of the gully joined in his laughter. "Everyone is afraid of bandits." With a flick of his wrist he caused his whip to tear away the edge of Joanna's sleeve, yet it did not touch her skin. "Have you not heard that bandits cut off the balls of pretty boys like you?" The point of the sword was less than the width of a finger from her crotch and it moved in a tiny circle. "Cut off your balls and bugger you til your guts hang out." The other men increased their laughter. "But for this one," the sword point deftly flicked the cap from Wilma's head, "for this one with the face of a pig's abortion, no buggery. This one we hang by his heels until his eyes burst from his head."

A wave of uncontrollable anger so intense it drove away her fear brought Wilma to her feet. At this, the bandit with a quick motion rammed the haft of his sword into her midsection, sending the woman sprawling as she choked and gasped.

A bandit, dressed the same as the others, yet whose manner declared he was of higher rank, descended into the gully. "We have had our little amusement." This man's voice was harsh and its sound caused all the laughter to cease. "But now to more serious things. We have need of a physician. You will come with us now and those other two will also or we will do those things to you that were promised by my son." The first man made a playful thrust at Joanna's midsection, the point of his sword just cutting into her jerkin but not reaching her skin.

"We are Christian monks." Still gasping, Wilma forced herself to her knees and addressed the man who had just spoken. "We serve Christ and His Holy Church."

"Some of our women are Christians," the man shrugged. "If they have need of your words, they may have them. But you join us to treat our wounds, to salve our sores. Anything else you do is of no importance. But should you try to escape," his lips curled back in a vicious grin, "we will do to you what they did to your Christ."

It was a journey of two days on the backs of their sure-footed ponies to the main encampment of the bandits. Several times during the course of the journey, without provocation, one or another bandit would roughly handle Nicco or taunt Wilma about her ugliness. Each time Joanna angrily approached the bandit leader, demanding better treatment for her friends. And each time, after making muttered threats and staring at her in his evil fashion, the leader ordered the rough handling and taunting stopped. By the time they reached the encampment, it was generally understood that as long as Joanna provided them with her services as physician, her companions would be left undisturbed.

The encampment, which consisted of over a hundred tents and lean-to's, was widely scattered over a rock-strewn plateau, guarded on three sides by towering cliffs with only a single, narrow, easily defended path leading in. Sounds that might have been taken for bird calls echoed across the plateau as the party approached, and they were met by a company of at least two score heavily armed men who escorted them in amidst a wild chorus of shouts and cheers.

To Joanna's eyes, the encampment appeared to be a mass of seething confusion. Dozens of half-naked children ran about wildly. Well over half a hundred young women, captured from various villages, stirred cook-fires or moved about. Those who did not show swollen abdomens cradled or suckled newly born infants. Scattered groups of half-grown boys trained with wooden swords or practiced at straw targets with short bows made of horn. Sheep, goats, and donkeys wandered about aimlessly, browsing on the thorny bushes or searching between the boulders for remnants of dry grass. Only after Joanna grew used to this strange scene did she realize that there were at least some elements of order in this confusion: ranged around the periphery of the encampment stood a number of armed sentinels; the horses were all carefully staked out and supplied with hay and sufficient water, and the older women worked in groups grinding grain, scraping skins, or repairing torn garments.

As the mounted party entered the encampment, the children swarmed in, pulling at the legs of the horsemen, shouting and laughing as they begged for gifts. And the men emptied their wallets of presents they had collected or fashioned — polished stones of unusual colors, roots and burls of an odd shape, tiny figures laboriously carved of bits of bone, rings and bracelets made of horsehair, and a scattering of old, worn coins of little value. The children squealed as the gifts were showered upon them, yet they did not struggle with one another, rather those who secured the most, without hesitation, shared their prizes with those who had been less fortunate.

After the children had received all their gifts, young women —
those who were pregnant or carried nursing babies — crowded in.
They also begged for gifts and were given bolts of cloth and shiny copper birds and flowers for their hair, these also fashioned by the men.
The young women pressed in close to their men as they rode through
the camp constantly staring at the three strangers with expressions of
wonder on their faces.

The half-grown boys did not approach the mounted band, but
they did temporarily suspend their training. And when the band
passed the places where they were gathered, they raised their weapons
in salute.

The older women continued with their tasks as the men passed
although they clacked their tongues against the roofs of their mouths,
whistled, and shouted guttural greetings that were more sounds than
words.

Joanna struggled to keep her face impassive, to hold herself erect
on the back of the pony, to appear indifferent to the strange sights,
shouts, and confusion. Wilma also sat erect, but she was unable to restrain herself from biting her lip and from balling her hands into tight
fists. Nicco, who sat on the same pony behind Wilma, hugged the
woman tightly around the waist, pressed his face into her back so he
could not see, and softly moaned. Even after they had dismounted, the
little man attempted to keep his face pressed against Wilma's back,
his arms around her waist, and when pulled away from her by one of
the men, he sank to the ground and rolled himself into a tight ball like
a hedgehog, and lay motionless without making a sound.

Although the place where the three dismounted was not closed in
by any sort of fence or wall, was not even defined as separate from the
rest of the encampment by a circle of rope or other device, they could
not have been more securely imprisoned had they been placed in a
dungeon, for all around them half-grown boys were stationed each
armed with a heavy wooden sword and a short steel dagger; each
showing a serious, almost grim expression on his face, all with their
eyes fixed, unmoving and rarely blinking, on their charges.

Joanna looked around at the ring of unsmiling faces — the oldest
could not have been much more than eleven years of age, the youngest
scarcely seven. Yet these were not children to be treated lightly. Not
even with the youngest was there so much as a trace of anything playful. Once, when she took several steps in the direction of the one who
appeared to be the oldest, a sound like that made by a dog disturbed
while eating warned her back into the center of the circle.

"I never thought of bandits having wives and children, living in a village of their own," Wilma murmured as Joanna squatted back down beside her. "Whenever I thought about bandits, they were men, grown men who lived like savages. But here we are, surrounded by bandit children." She attempted a laugh which came out more like a dry cough. Then she sighed. "How shall we ever escape from this place?"

"Escape?" Joanna assumed a thoughtful expression. "With their knowledge of these mountains, with their ponies, we would not get half a league before we were retaken."

It was just after the moon had risen that the leader of the band who had captured them came for Joanna. Wilma, who had also started to rise, was ordered back and when she tried to protest and made as if to defy the man's order, the circle of half-grown boys closed in until they formed a tight wall around her.

"Your friend will not be harmed this time," the man said gruffly to Joanna, and in a voice loud enough to be heard by Wilma. "But he must learn to obey. All who live in this camp obey. Next time he will be beaten." The man looked into Joanna's face, whose features were silvered by the moonlight. "Even I must obey the orders of the chief who is my father. And when I become chief, I must obey, as he obeys, the ways of our fathers." Finally, he nodded, made a harsh sound in his throat, and ordered Joanna to follow him.

He led her to a compound at the far end of the encampment, separated from the general clutter of tents and lean-to's by a wall of skins stretched between upright posts. This compound was closely guarded by men who carried swords of steel, and was brightly illuminated by at least half a hundred blazing torches. In the center of the compound, on a sort of low platform made of several dozen sheepskins, lay an old man whose chest heaved with every breath, whose jaw hung open, and whose eyes stared but appeared not to see. Kneeling on one side of the old man was the one who had first taunted Joanna when they were captured. On the other side knelt a shapeless, deeply wrinkled woman from whom moans arose from time to time.

"Our chief Salvatore — my father." The one who accompanied Joanna bowed toward the old man. "I too am Salvatore, as is my son." He nodded at the kneeling man. "My father caught an arrow in his shoulder. He has suffered a score of days with this arrow whose point broke off and is lodged between the bones. Each day his wound causes him to grow weaker." The man laid his hand on Joanna's shoulder, his fingers gripping muscles but not so they caused her any pain. "You are a physician. Cure my father, our chief."

Turning to face the man so that his hand fell away from her

shoulder, Joanna answered, "I cure no one. I offer treatments, but only by God's mercy are there cures." She hesitated then said, "From the appearance of your father, he may be beyond God's mercy." An ugly sound came from the man and this sound was picked up by the circle of men. "The arrow point has been in his shoulder too long — the flesh may be moribund. His eyes are open, but he does not see. He may be beyond God's help."

"If the chief, my father, should not survive, the blame will be yours, physician. If he lives, I will consider again your God."

Drawing in a deep breath, Joanna sank to her knees, folded her hands together while her lips moved silently for more than a minute. Then she crossed herself, stood up, and approached the unconscious man.

She worked until the moon hung directly overhead. For the first few minutes, cutting into the swollen, discolored flesh to allow the puss to escape, Joanna whispered the name of Christ again and again. But as she probed deeper into the wound, her mind gradually shifted until all of her thoughts were on the hands of the rabbi-physician: she could see his skillful fingers separating the strands of muscle, his lancet carefully avoiding tendons and blood vessels; and her hands became those of the physician. When she finally turned away from the wounded man, who had started moaning, the broken arrow point lay in the palm of her bloody hand. This was taken by the chief's son, who placed it on a piece of silk and then, one by one, the armed men came up to look at it.

Joanna turned back to the moaning man, whose eyelids were beginning to flutter, and bathed his temples with water, poured a quantity of new wine into the open wound, then, after sprinkling it with nitre, bound it with several silken cloths she had been given.

Her treatment done, she remained with the unconscious chief until the first light of morning showed on the horizon. From time to time, when her eyes started to close, she forced herself awake by pinching her cheeks, then fought sleep by repeating the Lord's name over and over.

It was as if with the coming of light the chief's life had been restored to him. For, as the crest of the mountain to the east grew bright, his eyes opened and he called for water in a rusty voice.

For the next three days Joanna treated a seemingly endless stream of men, women and children for wounds, sores, ulcers, rotted teeth and a variety of other conditions. Four times each day she was called by the chief's grandson, known as young Salvatore, to minister to his grandfather.

The evening visit to the chief on the second day found the man breathing in a labored fashion, his eyes dull and wandering. Uneasy, Joanna reopened the wound and let out a quantity of foul-smelling puss. By the next morning his eyes were clear and his breathing was less labored. And that evening, when Joanna arrived, she found the chief sitting up and going at a joint of roast mutton with his few teeth.

The chief's son greeted her with a respectful nod and a place was made for her next to the chief. "My father, our chief, eats like a starved wolf," he said with a rough laugh.

"Old Salvatore still has one or two years left," the old chief croaked, spraying bits of meat from his mouth.

"You will outlive the youngest boy of this village, my father. You will live to bury every one of us." At this the chief slapped his thigh and laughed, spraying out the remaining bits of meat.

"You shame every one of us with your strength," young Salvatore called out. "Only the strongest man in the world could have survived as did you, my grandfather."

"Another hand of weeks," the chief opened and closed his hands, "another hand of weeks — no more than two hands — and I will lead this band on such a raid that our women and children will shout our names all night, so many will be their presents." He slapped his thigh again. "And we will gain fresh women. My loins ache for one showing the first little buds of womanhood."

"You will yet lead this band on a hundred raids," the chief's son shouted. "You will lead raids with soldiers who are not yet born."

"If not a hundred more raids, my son, at least another score." The chief took a quick bite from the joint of meat. "Only a score." He spoke less loudly between chews. "I have no desire to lead raids whose soldiers are not yet born. Such raids are for my son and, when it shall be the proper time, for my grandson."

"My son tells me you will take no credit for curing me of my wound." The chief turned his attention to Joanna. Their eyes met and Joanna inclined her head. "Great shame would be cast upon me, physician, if the one who preserved this old and worthless life did not receive fine presents. For that one, I have a spirited young pony." The chief clapped his hands and a half-grown boy led a carefully groomed, bright-eyed, prancing pony into the compound. "For the one whose skills delayed my son from becoming chief for another year or two, there is also a piece of gold." The chief reached inside his tunic and brought out the largest coin Joanna had ever seen. It filled the palm of the man's hand. "And for that one, there is also a fine sword." He clapped his hands again and another boy came up carrying a sword in a jeweled scabbard. The armed men standing about sucked in their breaths. "Since you were the one who cured me, physician, these presents are yours — it was your hands that treated me." Again their eyes met. The chief's mouth twisted into a strange grin. "Take these presents, physician. You have earned them."

"They are fine presents." Joanna hesitated, not sure how to address the man. "I have never seen finer presents, Your Honor." She remembered how pleased the merchant Jew had been when addressed in this fashion. "But these presents are not mine. I did not cure you. I treated your wounds with these hands, but the cure was in the hands of God and Christ His Son."

"God! Christ!" The chief spat out. "Yes, now I remember, you are a Christian monk — one of those ball-less ones who deny their manhood." Curls of anger showed at the corners of the chief's mouth and his tiny, close-set eyes narrowed. "You will take these presents, Christian monk. You have cured me, and I will discharge my debt!" Joanna fought to control her limbs from trembling.

"I did not cure you, Your Honor. I cannot accept your gifts." She tried to roughen her voice, but it cracked like a young boy's.

In a rage, the chief struggled to his feet, using young Salvatore for support. "Take him away! He insults your chief." Half a dozen hands reached out for Joanna and she was dragged the entire distance from the chief's compound to the place where Wilma and Nicco stayed, under close guard. As she was dragged, she was kicked several times, her shoulders, back and legs were badly bruised by stones; then, as she was tossed at Wilma's feet, one of the soldiers brought down his whip hard across her chest, causing her such agony in her bound bosom that it was several minutes before she could catch her breath.

Just as the moon cleared the top of the mountain, Joanna was stirred roughly from her sleep. She had been asleep less than an hour and was confused and groggy at this sudden awakening. Her body throbbed and ached from all the rough treatment. Although the hands of the two soldiers who awoke her were not gentle, she suffered no further abuse as they led her toward the chief's compound.

As they entered the brightly lit area, the first thing Joanna saw was the high-spirited pony she had been offered as a gift, and next to the pony, lying on silken cloth, the sword and the golden coin. Although she struggled to control herself, she could feel her scalp tighten and her stomach start to churn.

"You see, physician, your rudeness is forgiven," the chief called out as Joanna approached. "Here are your fine gifts, waiting for you. Take them."

Then it was as if the churning stomach had filled with fire. As if the words of the chief were sparks which set her blood aflame she roared, "No!" at the chief. "I spit on your gifts." She spat on the silken cloth and all who were gathered in that compound gasped. "You insult the Lord God who saved your miserable, sin-stained life by offering me these gifts." The words erupted from her mouth. Several men started in her direction, but the chief waved them back.

"So you do have balls, physician." The chief laughed. "Puny as you are, with sticks for arms — I doubt if the least woman of this village is not stronger than you — you have the balls of a man. I had not expected to find such a thing in a Christian monk. Since you have proved your balls, and since you treated me — see, I did not say cured — you are now one of us and will be given the respect due a soldier." With that, the chief ordered Joanna to sit at his left hand and for the rest of the night she fought against sleep as the bandits feasted and different ones recounted past heroic exploits.

When she finally returned to Wilma and Nicco, she found the ring of armed boys had disappeared and that a fine tent whose floor was covered with sheepskins had been erected for their use.

It was exactly four weeks from the time they had entered the encampment — the moon was in the same phase it had been the night Joanna worked on the unconscious chief — that Joanna, accompanied by Wilma, was again ordered into the chief's presence. All of his vigor had been restored. He showed not the slightest trace of his near brush with death. He strode back and forth across the compound. Despite his vigor, the man's face reflected signs of deep distress and as soon as she saw him, Joanna knew this was to be no social visit.

"Physician," the chief ordered her to come close, "again I have need of your services."

Joanna inclined her head.

"The wife of young Salvatore, my grandson, lies in that tent." He pointed toward a large tent on the far side of the compound. "It is her time to give birth, but the infant will not come. She has struggled three nights and three days within that tent. The old women attend her, but their skills are not enough. She will die, the child of my grandson will be lost — he may be a boy! Flesh of my flesh!" The chief glared at Joanna as he waited for her response.

"I am a physician," Joanna spoke slowly, choosing her words

carefully. "I was trained by the chief physician of the Jews of Marseilles." The chief made an impatient sound, but did not interrupt. "I was taught how to treat breaks and wounds, was instructed as to fevers, sickness of the bowels, faints, and vomits. I can cut for stone and can pull teeth, but I have no training in the skills of a midwife." Her face grew tight and troubled. "I was trained by a Jew, a rabbi. For Jews, birth is unclean, is only for the hands of women. I know nothing of the mysteries of birth. Nothing."

"As Brother John said, his training excluded everything concerning birth," Wilma spoke out in a full voice. The chief's face darkened and an ugly sound rose from his chest at this interruption. "Hear me, honorable chief." Wilma took several steps toward the man. "I am no physician. But my mother was a noted midwife. The noblest families of Aachen called upon her for her services. And as a youth, I accompanied her and her assisted her in more than a score of difficult cases."

"The unborn infant of your grandson's wife may, in his vigor, have twisted himself into a strange position." Wilma drew her hands across her abdomen from one hip to another. "With God's help, I may be able to release your grandson's son."

"Son," the chief murmured the word, then motioned Wilma toward the tent.

Shouts rang through the bandits' encampment, great fires were lit, and an almost deafening din exploded as the men beat the hafts of their swords against their bucklers at the news that the wife of the chief's grandson had been delivered of a male child.

Her hands and arms blood-stained, her face dripping with perspiration, Wilma had emerged from the tent carrying the newborn, squalling child. When it could be seen that its genitals were those of a male, the old chief had let out a shriek, leapt into the air, then ran around the compound pounding the shoulders and backs of his soldiers as he continued to shriek like a man totally bereft of his reason. Finally, having calmed down a little, he had taken the infant from Wilma, declaring that now she too was a soldier. Then, holding the dripping, squalling infant in such a way that its genitals could be clearly seen, he had marched through the entire encampment.

With Joanna and Wilma sitting at his left hand, with the still unwashed infant lying on a lambskin between his feet, with his son and grandson at his right hand and his deeply wrinkled wife kneeling directly behind, the chief received the declarations of loyalty to himself and to those of his blood from each of his soldiers in turn. One by one, the men came up, knelt, declared their loyalty, pressed their lips to the foot of the infant, and left a suitable gift.

After the last soldier had made his obeisance, the chief ordered a male goat brought up which, with a single stroke of his sword, he decapitated in such a way that the creature's blood spurted on the infant.

"What name shall this child of my blood be given?" he asked in a booming voice. All the soldiers in a single voice answered: Salvatore. "Then it shall be Salvatore!" The chief laid his hands on the head of the infant, who appeared to be wallowing in the warm blood of the goat. "Not only Sicily, but all of Italy will one day know of the deeds of this Salvatore."

The chief rubbed the goat's blood over the infant's hands and feet until they were completely covered.

"When he is grown, this Salvatore will be so fierce that in comparison I will be remembered as a woman." Shouts of "No! No!" came from the gathered soldiers. The chief grinned and made a half-hearted attempt to quiet the soldiers.

"This child, my grandson, will be brave," the chief's son stepped out into the middle of the circle, "but if he proves to be half as brave as our chief, my father, all of Sicily, and yes, all of Italy will tremble at his name." The soldiers cheered, whistled, and clapped. "Half as brave as my father and even the Arabs who live along the coast of Africa will hear his name." He turned and faced the chief. "How many raids have you led, my father? How many wounds have you suffered? How many heads have you sent rolling with those hands of yours? How many women have felt the thrust of your great weapon? Only a scholar like one of these monks could know the number." Then one of the older soldiers stood up and in a voice that was almost a shout started to give an account of one of the raids led by the chief.

He spoke of the great size of the village — more than two hundred huts. He described the difficulty of this village's location, the fierce defense put up by its men, the terrible heat they had suffered which caused several of their men's brains to boil in their skulls. As he spoke, the eyes of all the soldiers glistened, and they grunted and nodded their heads.

"Is he not a great man, our chief?" the chief's son loudly asked Joanna and Wilma after the old soldier had completed his account of the raid. Without waiting for answer, he went on, "You are men, despite your monkish robes, you are men and as men do you not hunger for a taste of battle? My father, the chief, has declared you have balls, but would you not like to prove your balls in a raid such as that led by my father?"

"The chief, your father, is a brave man, a very brave man," Joanna spoke out in a strong voice which she automatically roughened. "But we have no need to prove our balls in battle. We have already fought." A questioning murmur rose up from the listening soldiers and the chief leaned in her direction. "And ours was not a raid on a mountain village of two hundred huts, but a full-scale battle against an army of soldiers who once served the Great Charles." With that Joanna stood up, moved to the center of the circle, and started to give an account of how a band of monks assisted in the defense of the walls of the city of Engelheim. Except for the true sex of the monks and except for her heroic role with the cauldron of boiling pitch, she recounted all of the events in order and in minute detail.

The chief appeared to be shrunken into himself by the time Joanna had finished.

"But you gained no booty from your battle, Christian monk," the chief's son hissed at Joanna, drops of saliva spraying from his mouth. "You raped no women, carried off no young girls." He hesitated a moment. "And hiding behind those walls you proved very little of your manhood." Wilma, who had been listening intently, her eyes fixed on the face of the chief's son, let out a raucous laugh and rose to her feet.

"We gained no booty as you gained in your raids on little villages." Wilma spoke in a voice that contained an edge of contempt. "We raped no one, true, carried off no one, but ours was a battle against an army. More than half a thousand fighting men, no less than two hundred mounted, many heavily armored. Ours was a fight against some of the most savage soldiers in all Europe."

The chief groaned and covered his eyes with his hands.

"And as for proving manhood," Wilma's face was livid, her hands shook and her voice cracked, "as for proving manhood," she turned toward Joanna who tried to signal her with her eyes, "as for a proof of manhood, this one, still a half-grown boy, at great risk to his own life, saved the lives of the knight in command, his lieutenant, and several others." With that, Wilma, gesturing wildly with her hands, described how Joanna pushed the cauldron of boiling pitch over the wall just as the rope suspending it broke.

The face of the chief's son had drained of color and his lips twitched. "Do you say these things to shame my father, the chief — to shame his soldiers?" The man's voice, although hollow, contained an edge of viciousness.

"I have no wish to shame anyone. Even if this were my intention, I could not shame a man of known bravery such as your chief." Wilma held the eyes of the chief's son with her own. "I only defend the bravery of my brother in Christ, John. I only defend the bravery of my other brothers in Christ who fought to save the city of Engelheim, nine of whom gave up their lives in this fight."

"He does not shame the chief of this band," the chief declared in an old man's voice. "He does not shame my soldiers." He looked up and allowed his eyes to travel around the circle of watching men. "But we are shamed. And this shame cuts into my heart like a knife. All that brave talk of raiding villages defended only by a handful of poorly armed, frightened men. Yes, we are feared in these mountains. But by whom are we feared? By lice-infested, stinking peasants. By old, toothless women. By demented goatherds such as that twisted creature you brought with you."

The chief's eyes were now on Wilma. "But have we ever fought a battle against soldiers?" The chief struggled to his feet. "Have we ever risked an attack against a walled city?"

He shifted his eyes to his son. "You heap words of praise upon your father. Your words, like the thick wine made from honey, sweeten my mouth while dulling my mind." He shook his head slowly. "With such words I dulled the mind of my father. And he his father. And each, because of these words, died, believing himself the bravest of men. But I will not go to my death so believing. What I have heard from the lips of these two Christian monks has cleared my mind. We pretend to be soldiers, but we are only bandits who have never faced a battle with equals."

The chief gestured for the sleeping infant to be removed and a groan came from the ring of men. "I will not shame this infant who will be your chief with these womanish tales. And lest he be weakened by my feeble deeds, by those false accounts of my bravery, I order that he never be brought into my presence again."

Anguished groans came from the ring of soldiers and the chief's grandson approached, his two hands clenched together, crying "No! No!"

As an answer, the chief felled his grandson with a powerful and perfectly placed kick to his midsection. "I am still the chief!" he roared.

"But if you could yet fight such a battle," Joanna addressed the chief, bracing herself for the blow that might come.

The chief's eyes narrowed and his muscles tensed.

"If you could speak of such a battle to your grandson's son, would you not then order him into your presence?" They stared at each other in the flickering torch light.

"How should I fight such a battle?" The chief's words came slowly and dangerously.

"Palermo!" Joanna spat out.

They continued to look at each other, neither one speaking for a time. Then the chief said, with a slight hesitation in his voice, "We are men of the mountains. Not one of us has ever been to this city of Palermo. We know nothing of Palermo except that it is a Sicilian city inhabited by thousands."

"You know nothing of Palermo." Joanna's eyes bored into those of the chief. "Yet the Saracens of Africa know this city, know it as a place where they take their pleasure, know its once proud streets where Sicilian men now are forced to cower, forced to grovel and press their faces in the dust when their haughty Saracen masters ride by. And, my chief, the Saracens know the Sicilian women of Palermo, whose bellies they have filled with their seed."

Except for the rustle of embers as they settled in the dying fire there was no sound for several long moments after Joanna stopped speaking. Then from the tent where the newborn infant had been taken there came a lusty cry.

"Palermo!" The chief said the word as if his mouth were filled with bitter, wormy fruit. "The bellies of our Sicilian women swollen with their seed..."

"And the bishop of Palermo, the bishop, my chief, a Sicilian, now serves the Saracen caliph as his servant." Joanna continued to hold the eyes of the chief without wavering. "You are not Christian, but would you have the highest ranked Sicilian churchman serve an African? An African, who by his every word, every gesture, mocks the men of Sicily? So little is his regard for whatever manhood there is left in this land that only a handful of soldiers guard the gates of the city, while the rest feast, take their pleasure with the women, and lie about at their ease."

"You have seen this with your own eyes, monk?" the chief asked.

"Also with my eyes," Wilma said as she moved forward and took her place alongside Joanna. "They have grown so confident, they declare that one of their men is more than a match for twenty of ours." Wilma forced her voice to ring with the sound of truth.

"I will shave my beard, put on a skirt, and be a woman if my soldiers are not more than a match for those Saracens!" shouted the chief's son.

"If you want to battle soldiers, my chief, they await you at Palermo," Joanna spoke in a taunting voice.

The chief's face went pale and his hands shook in anger.

"And if you want the son of your grandson to hear tales other than those of raids against poorly defended mountain villages, an attack upon Palermo, a battle against the Saracens, the liberation of the enslaved Sicilians, the freeing of the bishop by a band of non-Christians — all of these things will supply sufficient tales of true bravery for the son of your grandson."

"We are no more than three hundred soldiers." From the sound of the chief's voice all who listened were aware of the struggle going on within the man.

"And the Saracens can muster at least a thousand." Joanna answered the unspoken question in an icy voice.

"But, if as you say, they are grown overconfident, and we approach the city in small bands under the cover of night..."

"Then we will have the advantage of surprise," the chief's son interrupted, excitement ringing in his voice.

"But three hundred against a thousand!" The chief fought to hold onto the remnant of caution that was about to be swept away.

"Not three hundred, my chief," Joanna said each word slowly and clearly. "More than twice that number. We will send a message to the bishop that we are coming, and he will do what needs to be done so that when we storm the gates, we will have allies within."

When Joanna had finished, the chief's son opened his mouth as if to speak but was waved silent by his father. Then minutes passed with everyone's eyes riveted on the chief. Joanna reached out and touched Wilma's hand. It was as cold and as hard as stone.

A fresh wind signaling the coming of morning stirred the stunted bushes. "We go to Palermo," the chief muttered. "Our manhood demands we avenge the insults of the Saracens. The son of my grandson, those soldiers yet unborn, will mock us if we do nothing. As the monk says, although we are not Christians, we are Sicilians. If the women of Palermo are to be filled with seed, let it be the seed of their own kind, not the vile pollution of those Africans. And if we free that holy man, your bishop, we will gain much good fortune." The chief screwed up his face until his eyes were almost invisible among his wrinkles. "If we win this battle against the Saracens and take Palermo, we will become Christians. Tell this to your God, monk. Tell your God that Salvatore, chief of this band, swears on the head of his dead father that if granted victory, not only will all the soldiers of this band become Christians, but everyone to the least woman also, and we will raise crosses and altars to His honor wherever we travel in these mountains. Tell your God this, brother John, and if He is as powerful as all you Christians claim, we can be certain of our victory."

Had any one of the score of Saracen soldiers guarding the east wall of the city of Palermo turned his eyes toward the sloping plain leading down from the hills, he might have noted, in the middle distance, a caravan of merchants robed from head to foot guiding a string of heavily burdened ponies. Yet had this caravan been noted, it would have aroused no more than a passing interest. The past several hours had seen a movement of no less than a dozen such caravans. Those who thought about it at all put it down to the harvest season. But not a single pair of Saracen eyes was turned in the direction of the hills this time. Rather, the soldiers on duty concentrated all their attention on the thick-thighed, large-breasted women re-entering the city after their morning's work in the vineyards or among the olive trees. Yet there were eyes within the city that noted this caravan, eyes that carefully counted the number of robed men and laden ponies as they had counted the numbers in the earlier caravans.

The sun had scarcely risen that morning the bandit chief had announced his decision to attack Palermo, when Joanna, breathless from running, approached Nicco who was grazing his goats on a mountain slope above the encampment.

"You are to be a soldier in the service of Christ, Nicco!" Joanna had gasped.

The little man shrugged, grinned, then started pulling on the lobes of his ears.

"A message must be sent to the bishop of Palermo. Because," Joanna hesitated, "because of your size, you will not be stopped, will not be searched. There are times when a little man can serve Christ and His church where the fiercest giant of a soldier would fail."

"Christ?" Nicco said the name in his guttural voice.

"You do not know Christ?" Joanna let out her breath in a sigh. She stared at the little man whose face reddened under her scrutiny. "Then will you do this thing for me? Take the risk of a soldier?"

Without a moment's hesitation Nicco nodded, yes.

Resting only when exhaustion made his body tremble, his feet to lose their sure footing; sleeping only when he must and then in snatches of an hour at the most, Nicco had made his way through the mountains carrying the parchment he had been given, arriving in Palermo a full two days in advance of the others. Unnoticed, except for a dry horse turd casually lobbed at his head by a Saracen soldier, he had passed through the gates, found his way to the garden of the caliph, and delivered the parchment directly into the hands of the bishop whose appearance Joanna had carefully described to him.

By the next day every loyal Christian within Palermo had known the contents of that parchment and weapons which had been carefully hidden under floor boards, at the bottom of unused wells, beneath piles of manure, weapons rusted and dulled by disuse, were carried hidden beneath cloaks to certain safe houses just within the city walls where eager hands restored them and made them ready for use.

Had the Saracens entertained the slightest suspicion that the security of their captured city was about to be threatened, a single scout sent out under the cover of night could have confirmed that suspicion, for protected only by a stand of trees scarcely a half hour's easy walk from the city, those innocent-appearing caravans had joined together and were camped in a tight circle without fires and with weapons at the ready. But there was no suspicion among the more than one thousand Saracens who controlled the city of Palermo. Why should there have been? Their conquest of this portion of the island had been complete. For the past several years their control had been absolute. There was even talk in the caliph's court of extending the boundaries of the conquest in the direction of Messina. Other than the occasional Sicilian man driven by taunts to attack some Saracen soldier with stones or a dagger, and such ones were quickly dispatched, their heads displayed on pikes as a warning to others — other than these occasional acts of desperation, the Saracens felt themselves as secure as they would be in their homes on the far side of the Mediterranean.

At sunrise several of the score of soldiers assigned to guard the east wall started to open the gates. An unusually large crowd of peasants had gathered in the square waiting for the gates to open, perhaps as many as four hundred, twice the normal number, and this should have caused suspicion. But the Saracen soldiers were dulled from the wine they had drunk — in their African villages this substance was forbidden. And they should have been suspicious when almost half the number who streamed out through the gates made their way singly and in twos and threes in the direction of the copse of trees rather than toward the vineyards and places where the olives were grown. But who paid attention to unwashed Sicilians, their hair and garments crawling with lice, their sandles befouled with the excrement of cows? Yet had the officer commanding the platoon of Saracens been with his men rather than enjoying a ripe twelve year old maiden he had purchased from her crippled mother for a small silver coin, he might have been, if not suspicious, at least concerned at the large number of beggars and loungers congregated in the open space just inside the gates.

Had not the bandit chief chanced to seek privacy behind a tree to relieve himself and thus be only a few paces away from one of his soldiers stationed as a sentinel, the first Christian who entered that stand of trees would have certainly been split from crown to crotch, for the sentry had his sword already upraised when the chief, with a quick movement, was able to catch the man by his wrist.

Joanna felt her cheeks grow hot, her mouth grow thick, as the chief led in this man whom she recognized as brother Marcos, the bishop's secretary. She could only nod when he greeted her. And it took an effort for her to concentrate on the meaning of brother Marcos' words as he detailed to the bandit soldiers the preparations that had been made.

"Just as the sun reaches a place so that a stake driven into the ground casts no shadow, half a hundred of our number will start a diversion in the square before the caliph's palace." Brother Marcos spoke slowly and carefully, checking the straining faces of the soldiers pressed close around him to make sure his words were understood. "When this diversion begins, your men and my men, their weapons hidden under their clothing, start toward the city." He looked at the chief who nodded. "If the diversion is sufficient, with God's help and with the help of our disguises, we may get close to the gates before the Saracens are alerted. As soon as they give the alarm, we rush the gate. But only then." He glanced again at the chief. "Until the moment of alarm, we move like merchants — deliberately, not too quickly."

"As this Christian says," the chief addressed his men. "This city of Palermo is no mountain village to be recklessly stormed. These African soldiers, who defend the city, are no collection of frightened peasants who will run and hide as soon as they see the glint of a drawn weapon. It is no insult to your manhood, my soldiers, to approach this great city with caution. That we risk their greater numbers is sufficient proof of our manhood. To attack as we attack mountain villages with shouts and clashing weapons, would not be a sign of bravery but the actions of fools." The chief glared at certain men who had sought and gained a reputation for reckless bravery. "Once inside the walls of that city where we can confront them man to man..." The old chief's lips parted in a vicious grin. He turned to Joanna. "I will pull out my eye and place it in your hand, little monk, if for each of my soldiers who dies, there are not three Saracens with their guts spilled on the ground." The chief raised his hand and made a plucking motion at his eye.

"And those women of Palermo who mourn for their Saracen lovers whom we have slain," the chief swung around and faced his men, "those of us who are left will have the task of comforting these women. And in all of Sicily are there any men who know more of the art of giving a woman comfort than do the soldiers of Salvatore?"

"Four or five women for each of us; you lay a heavy burden on us, my father, my chief," the chief's son joined in. "The battle with the Saracens will be less of a task than that which faces your poor soldiers after it is won."

A roar of laughter swept through the ranks of the men.

"And because I am son of the chief and thus must set an example of service to my men, ten will be the number of mourning women I will comfort." He hesitated for a long moment, then sighed, "It is a heavy burden to be the chief's son." Again, there was a roar of laughter.

Even had the sun been less dazzling, even had their attention not been drawn towards the center of the city by the sounds of shouts rising in the still air, mixed with the harsh clash of weapons, the Saracen soldiers stationed along the east wall and at the gate would have scarcely granted more than a cursory glance at the small groups of robed merchants, leading their horses, and slowly straggling towards the city. Perhaps one of the soldiers might have hesitated an extra second as he noted the horses these merchants led were, without exception, unburdened. But merchants not only sold goods, they bought them, and there was wine and olive oil for sale in Palermo, to say nothing of the fine jewelry fashioned by local artisans from seashells and silver. But not a single soldier turned for a quick glance at the sloping plain. The shouts from the center of the city and the weapon clashes had grown louder, drawing their entire attention as they strained to see, as they readied their own weapons in case they should be called on for assistance.

The merchants were halfway across the plain, now in bands of a dozen or more, yet their approach was still not noticed.

The jaws of many of the bandit soldiers ached from clenching their teeth, their muscles were knotted hard as they forced themselves to walk slowly despite the open gate lying directly ahead. At this pace, it would yet take another seven or eight minutes before they reached the gate; had they mounted and let out their horses, they could be through that gate in no more than three.

Another minute passed, and still they had not been noticed. By now they were formed into bands of more than a score. Was it possible that they would enter the city with no opposition?

Another minute passed. The bandits now were formed into half a dozen bands of fifty each with the Christian soldiers, none of whom had horses, grouped on each flank. But then with a crash, one of the soldiers on the wall brought his unsheathed sword against his buckler as he shouted a warning. The alarm was taken up by other Saracen soldiers, and the half a dozen stationed at the gate started to swing it closed. It was then that the loungers and beggars revealed who they were as they cut down the Saracen soldiers and swung the heavy gate back open.

The alarm bell began to ring, its sound carrying into the city, but the soldiers who poured from their garrison at a run were unable to reach the gate in time to prevent the bandits, now mounted, from flooding through.

Ranged in a semicircle in the square, most of them still mounted, the bandits met the Saracen soldiers as they streamed in on foot from the narrow streets. And it was as the chief had declared it would be. Three Saracens died for each of his men. In places the blood ran so deep it reached the fetlocks of their horses. The Christian soldiers, who were unmounted and thus entered the city after the bandits, cleared the remnants of Saracens from the wall, but their loss was man for man.

Not an hour had passed before most of the eastern portion of the city, almost up to the central square, had been secured by the bandits and Christians, with heavy barricades in place in the various narrow streets to prevent any Saracen incursion.

The disturbance before the caliph's palace having been quelled with all the Christians who had participated in it killed, the caliph organized his remaining soldiers, some seven hundred, into several moderate size defensive bands to guard against any further enemy advance, with the main units mounted and directed out of the western gates with orders to circle the city and attack the invaders from the east. But by the time this main body of Saracen soldiers was in place several hundred paces from the eastern gate, it was already sunset, and too late to launch an attack.

Crouched behind the parapet of the wall, Joanna and Wilma stared out at the African soldiers. "Here on this wall," Joanna said taking Wilma's hand "all the years, shrink away and it is as if we are on the walls of Engelheim. Does it always have to happen this way? Saracens or the soldiers of the Great Charles, Palermo or Engelheim in the end they are just men with their bellies ripped open. All the same." She knotted her hands tightly together as a sound that was almost a moan escaped her lips. "It was I who brought them to this. Fight for the glory of Christ and His holy Church. Yet the smell of their blood, the blood of all of them, is the same. Perhaps we have traveled enough, Wilma, seen enough. If we live through this, it may be time for us to turn north, to return to the convent, to our sisters who love us."

"Back to the cold and damp of Germany, Joanna," said Wilma with a forced laugh. "My aching bones cry out against it. Besides, you promised that we would see the glories of Athens, would listen to the learned theologians gathered in that place." She drew Joanna close. "And Athens, sun-warmed Athens is so much nearer than Engelheim. And then there is Rome."

"Yes, Rome," Joanna whispered. "But in time, Wilma, if we are granted sufficient years, we will return to the convent, to its quiet, its safety. We will return to our sisters," she sighed deeply, "will take off this men's clothing and be women again."

Whatever response Wilma was about to make to this was lost as the bishop, who had arrived in this sector by means of subterranean passageways, called to them to come down.

Dressed for the first time in years in his robes, his jeweled mitre on his head, his crooked staff gripped firmly in his hand, the bishop waited for them. He was flanked on one side by the archdeacon and Marcos, on the other by the grinning bandit chief and his son. Handing the staff to his secretary, the bishop embraced each of the monks in turn. Then, ordering them both to kneel, he cut away a portion of their hair with a jeweled knife, declaring them both deacons. And then he anointed Joanna's forehead with holy oil and placed both hands on her bowed head, ordaining her a priest.

"You have done Christ's work this day," the bishop addressed the two kneeling monks. "Even if we should be defeated by the Saracens tomorrow, the victory won today will inspire all of Christendom to continue the struggle against the infidel Africans.

"And how should the Church express its gratitude to you," he turned to the chief and his son. "Not even Christians, yet more than fifty of your number have died this day in the name of the Savior." He reached out a hand to each of the men, and each took the proffered hand, bringing it to his lips. At this the assembled bandit soldiers shouted, clapped, and stamped their feet. But at a signal from their chief, they fell silent.

"The sons of the sons of soldiers yet unborn will tell their children stories of this day," the chief, in a booming voice, addressed his men. "Never in the long and brave history of this island have there been soldiers such as you. Not the Athenians, not even the Romans who once held this island could match their manhood with yours, my soldiers. And at sunrise, we will have the chance to fight again!" The soldiers resumed their cheering and clapping until they were again silenced by the chief. "I swore that if the Christian God, Christ, granted us a victory, allowed us to prove what manner of men we are, we would all become Christians." He turned to the bishop, "Will you make us Christians?" As an answer, the bishop gestured the bandits down to their knees.

Ordering Joanna and the several other priests to join with him, the bishop went from kneeling man to kneeling man baptizing from a helmet filled with water, each priest in turn laying hands, for a brief moment, on the newly baptized head.

Later, separated by some half a hundred paces from the other groups of Christians, the bishop, Marcos, the archdeacon, Wilma and Joanna gathered around a large blazing fire. Except for the bishop, for whom a stool had been provided, they sat crosslegged on the ground.

"What was done today adds to the glory of Christ and will be remembered for all time," the bishop stated in a measured voice. "And those heathen souls brought into His Holy Church this night must bring to the angels and archangels great joy. He paused for a moment. "For what you have done, Father John," he nodded toward Joanna, "and for what you have also done, brother William," the bishop reached out and touched Wilma lightly on the shoulder, "as lawful bishop in direct line of succession from St. Peter, I declare yours will be a place in heaven with not so much as a single day in purgation." The bishop made the sign of the cross over both women.

"And with his youth what other marvelous deeds will Father John yet perform for our Mother Church?" the archdeacon added.

"Yes. Other deeds..." the bishop said softly. He covered his eyes with his hands for several moments, then slowly nodded his head. "But if he remains here in Palermo there will be no further deeds. He, along with the rest of us, will be in the presence of The Father within a day, two days at the most." The bishop's secretary made a questioning sound. "Yes, my dearest Marcos. It will be no more than two days before we gain our judgement."

"But we won a great victory, Your Eminence," the archdeacon broke in.

"Yes, a great victory. But we are prisoners of our victory." All eyes were focussed on his face. "They will hammer their way in. They will assault the walls again and again. We are outnumbered almost three to one and they have the advantage of maneuverability. One day, no more than two, and we will be overrun." He was unable to control his eyes which filled with tears. "Overrun and if fortunate, slaughtered on the spot. If not..."

"Then we are to be martyrs for the Church," Marcos said resolutely.

"Yes, martyrs," said the bishop. "But for you, Brother Marcos, not yet. And Father John will have his chance to do all those marvelous deeds. As will you, Brother William." He nodded toward Wilma, his lips forming a wry smile.

"Marcos, my loyal friend, you will lead these two through the various passageways you know beneath the city; tomorrow, at the height of the Saracen attack, you will make your escape. There are certain fishermen, you know who I mean. They will sail you around the island to Syracuse. The archdeacon of Syracuse will arrange for your passage to Athens. I will provided you with certain writings to guarantee his cooperation."

"Not me, Your Eminence. You must go with them." Marcos shifted part way around, kneeling before the bishop. "Let me stay. Your life is too precious. Let it be you who guides them through the passageways."

The bishop laid his hands gently on the muscular shoulder of the kneeling man as he shook his head. "I am the bishop of Palermo, not of any other place. Whatever fate the Christians of this city suffer, I will suffer with them."

Marcos took hold of the hand and brought it to his lips as the bishop went on.

"Tomorrow we fight for the glory of Christ. If we give a sufficient account of ourselves, perhaps the Saracens will think twice before attempting other Sicilian cities."

"And then there is always the chance of a miracle," the archdeacon joined in, his voice driving like drumbeats from the deep of his chest. "The righteous although few in numbers can, with the grace of God, be as strong as legions."

"Yes a miracle," the bishop intoned. "If it be His will. But we prepare for death." With that the bishop drew Joanna aside and gave her an urgent message to be publicly delivered to Bishop Nikitas, the bishop of Athens.

The next morning, Joanna said farewell to the bishop and kissed his hand with reverence, knowing in her heart that his prediction of a slaughter by the Saracens would be true. Already the screams of the Christian defenders on the walls could be heard throughout the city as wave after wave of Saracens warriors mounted the scaling ladders they had constructed during the night. The limited weaponry of the defenders was no match for this onslaught.

As the gates of the city collapsed under the pounding of a huge tree used as a battering ram by the Africans, the bishop ordered the three travelers to leave at once. The life of every Christian in Palermo was now in danger.

Quickly Marcos led them through the narrow streets to a blacksmith's shop under whose floorboards was hidden the entrance to the subterranean passageway. Then he led them to a cave well beyond the western wall of the city where fishermen waited for them, having provisioned their largest boat for the journey out of Palermo.

VII

ATHENS

*T*he arrival in Greece of Joanna, Wilma and Marcos could not have been at a more fortuitous time. Immediately on disembarking from their boat at the port of Corinth and beginning their walk into Athens, they became aware of a celebration in progress.

The road was crowded as far as the eye could see with men and women bedecked in ribbons, many wearing tunics of carefully tooled leather, all moving in the same direction toward the city of Athens. Here and there in this festive throng a bearded man dressed in the long black robe of the cleric walked with measured steps, holding high above his head either a crucifix or an icon of one of the saints. From the side roads winding out toward the hilly countryside, new arrivals pressed into this throng. These, without exception, crowded around the nearest cleric kissing the hem and sleeves of his robe and begging to be allowed to kiss the crucifix or icon.

Joanna and Wilma had no way of knowing the reason for this celebration, but Marcos, who had served as an emissary of the bishop of Palermo to Nikitas, Bishop of Athens, ten years earlier, had some suspicion. When he had been in Athens not an icon was to be found in any one of the scores of churches in that city — churches which had contained hundreds of exquisitely painted portraits of the saints before the rule of Theophilus. Not only had this emperor, in his half mad religious zeal, ordered an end to this image worship, but many of the holy men who made their living by producing these icons had their hands cut off; those holy men more fortunate, together with many hundreds who worshipped their icons, were merely banished to remote corners of the country. Marcos' suspicion was confirmed when, after questioning several clerics who did not deign to answer, one cadaverous-looking priest whose beard swarmed with lice muttered: "The tyrant is dead. Theodora, his blessed wife, now rules in his place."

"These people worship pictures of their saints as other Christians worship relics," Marcos explained to Joanna, as they stood together watching the people streaming by.

Joanna swallowed and nodded, but said nothing. She found it difficult, almost impossible, to exchange even the simplest of words with this man, yet stole glances at him constantly when his eyes were turned in another direction. During all the days and weeks they traveled together, first to Syracuse, then on to Greece, Marcos had grown used to her ways, putting it down to the shyness a younger man often exhibits towards one older and more experienced. Yet there had been moments of puzzlement. The young priest had shown no shyness with the bishop and certainly must have taken an aggressive posture with the bandits in Sicily. But, Marcos recalled, there had been several older men of a certain worldly bearing in whose presence he too had once been shy.

"They carry their saints' pictures back to Athens," he went on. "The entire population of that city will probably turn out in celebration." Then Marcos explained in detail the history of the dead emperor, together with bits of earlier Grecian history, some of which Joanna already knew, yet gave not the slightest hint of knowing.

The three travelers camped that night in an olive grove, together with a group of merchants. At first the merchants showed a certain annoyance at their presence, but when Marcos informed them that he was the secretary to the bishop of Palermo, his two companions a priest and a deacon, they crowded in close offering choice portions of their food and flasks of their best wine.

With the death of Theophilus, the empress Theodora had recalled all the banished clerics to Athens and, following her example, a wave of love for all the servants of Christ swept through the country. Hermits, encrusted with filth who had remained hidden in their caves for years, came forth to the wild embrace of peasants, who, a month earlier, would have stoned them back into their caves. Monks who would have risked broken limbs had they dared appear from behind the walls of their monasteries while the emperor was still alive now were received with all their lice and unwashed stink into the noblest of homes. Had the three travelers been bearded in the manner of the Greeks, instead of clean-shaven, the gifts from these merchants might very well have been silk, perfumed balm, even pieces of silver jewelry instead of just food and wine.

But whatever niggardliness the merchants had shown was more

than compensated for the next day by a contingent of deacons of the bishop's court who had gained intelligence of their approach and came out from the city to greet them.

The fingers of both hands, not excluding the thumbs, displaying ornate rings set with sparkling jewels, their plain black, ankle length robes set off by heavy crucifixes fashioned of silver, gold, and mother-of-pearl, their heads adorned with caps of carefully brushed otter fur, the five deacons parted the crowd with their staffs, bowing low before the three travelers, which caused murmurs of surprise from many of the onlookers. For the garments of the three were travel-stained, their hands and faces begrimed from the dust of the road, and they were not bearded, and thus could not be of much consequence. But then when the deacons greeted the three as their brothers in Christ, when they knelt for the priestly blessing which Joanna supplied, and when they presented the three with their costly gifts, scores in that milling crowd sank to their knees and made obeisance. And then when the three, proceeded by the deacons, started into the city, hundreds formed ranks and followed.

The streets of the city were choked with celebrants, but these gave way to the holy procession as it made its way to the bishop's palace at the foot of the Acropolis.

"Do you remember how it was in Aachen when the bailiff of the bishop came for us and led us through the streets?" Joanna brought her lips close to Wilma's ear. Wilma smiled and nodded. "But this...I never imagined there could be so many people and such buildings." She raised her eyes to the ancient Acropolis that lay directly ahead.

"It is beyond belief," Wilma forced the words through a short-ness of breath. "Aachen, Marseilles, and Palermo taken together do not equal half of this. If deacons are dressed in such costly stuff, what will be the appearance of their bishop?" At this Joanna was unable to restrain an excited laugh.

As if an invisible scythe had swept their ranks, the hundreds who had followed them through the city fell away as they entered the grounds of the bishop's palace. Then as they walked along a path formed of crushed marble in the direction of the palace, Joanna experienced that same uneasiness she had known in Aachen as they left the narrow, twisting streets and approached the cathedral. But this uneasiness was swept away the moment they passed through the doors of the palace and entered the great reception chamber.

The bishop was holding another of his lavish banquets to celebrate the return of the icons, to which various returning holy men were invited, and he sat on his dais smiling and nodding and offering his blessing to each group as they entered the great chamber. But as the three were led in by the deacons, who held their staffs aloft, the bishop arose from his cushioned throne, a thing he had not done for any other of the guests, and called out a greeting, waving his large, soft, milk-white hands for them to come close. The hundreds of other guests buzzed with curiosity. The three were led to a place just below the dais and only when they were seated did the bishop lower his bulk back down to the thick cushions of his throne.

Joanna openly stared up at Nikitas. In no way was her anticipation of the splendor of this man disappointed by what she saw. The bishop was huge. His weight must have been that of two ordinary men, and although of average height, his shoulders were broader than those of any blacksmith or soldier she had ever seen. From the jewel-encrusted mitre resting on his head to his slippers made of strips of ermine and strands of pearls, the bishop was a mass of glitter and color. There was not a single thing about him which did not speak of wealth, down to the gold knife he wore at his belt, used to cut the holy loaf. His face had been carefully colored, cheeks and lips, and his beard was plaited with silken ribbons; only his eyes, which he could not adorn were discolored and dull.

He looked at Joanna and allowed his loose lips to part in a weak smile. "You are the priest?" he said in a sort of a gasp, using a rusty Latin.

Joanna answered in Greek (much to the pleasure of the hundreds of guests who had quieted down to listen) stating that she had been ordained by the bishop of Palermo and giving her name.

"So young," the bishop responded, again in a gasp. "You are so young, my dearest John. Here in the East few are raised to the priesthood before they have thirty years. Most must wait even longer — until their hair is grey." His gasp turned into a titter that was picked up by others, for the bishop's hair was thick and black, showing no trace of grey.

"How does my friend the bishop of Palermo?" Nikitas asked. But before Joanna had a chance to answer, he said, "I understand he is forced to spend his days with that Saracen caliph. What a tribulation. If I were in his condition I would simply perish."

"He *spends* no more time with the caliph, Your Excellency," said Joanna in a voice which contained a fine edge of anger. "He is with Christ Jesus now, before the Throne of God. He has been martyred."

"Martyred!" Nikitas' soft hands fluttered in a helpless gesture. "Although I am certain it will make me ill, I must know how it happened."

At that Joanna proceeded to give an account of the attack of the bandits; the capture of a portion of the city; their mass conversion — all of the events up to their secret departure from the city. Yet nowhere in this account did she make mention of her role in these events. But the moment she had finished, before she had a chance to sit back down, Marcos got to his feet and with a forced throat-clearing sound, drew the attention of everyone.

"Father John has deliberately excluded certain matters from his narration." Marcos tried to steady his voice and control a tremble he felt struggling to take hold of his limbs. "He neglected to mention that it was he, together with our good Brother William, who convinced that company of bandits, who had ravaged mountain valleys for years, that it was their duty to free the city from its Saracen invaders. And his priesthood, which Your Eminence has remarked is unusual in one so young, was granted by the bishop of Palermo in recognition of services rendered to the Church."

"You are too modest, dearest friend John." The bishop waved his hand in Joanna's direction. "Come, sit beside me." He shifted his bulk and patted the cushion. "Sit here so I can give you proper honor in the presence of these many men I have invited from all over this country."

Her cheeks burning, her eyes under careful control so that they did not rest for a single moment on Marcos, Joanna rose from her seat and climbed the steps to the Bishop's dais. The bishop wrapped his soft, damp hand around hers and pulled her down beside him.

Joanna forced herself to resist the urge to withdraw her hand and instead concentrated her attention on the several hundred men who filled the large chamber before whom servants had just spread a great feast. Although she had no way of knowing it there were several among the hundreds present whose reputation for piety was well-known throughout the entire East. These Marcos quickly recognized from his time in Athens and later told Joanna about them in considerable detail.

Father Matthew was one of these sainted individuals. It was common knowledge that during the entire reign of Theophilus, he had lived in a remote cave keeping so strict a fast that live worms dropped from his lips. Wizened, scarcely taller than a child of ten, with tiny eyes deepset, yet gleaming like those of a ferret, he had apparently abandoned his fast and now was stuffing a startling quantity of baked fish and stewed fowl in his mouth. But with Athanasius there was no doubt as to that for which his piety was famous. Joanna remarked to herself as her eyes fell upon this blubbery individual, whose dewlaps hung like those of a certain breed of hunting hound, that the man's filthiness was even greater than that of Sofia when they first entered her cave. And it was obvious that he was over-ripe, for even the other unwashed holy men whose scent could not have been that of lilacs allowed a certain space between themselves and him. But those who revered the name Athanasius might have been disappointed this day, for he was gobbling up food at an alarming rate despite his reputation of never eating a cooked meal, because the fires of the cookhouse brought into his mind the inextinguishable flames of hell. Another who was allowed an extra span of space on either side and in front, and back, was Meletius, whose body was covered with suppurating ulcers. These ulcers were compared with those of Job's. Yet Meletius was of such an advanced degree of holiness that he refused to scratch himself with potsherds to gain relief as did the prophet and when, by chance, a louse or other inhabitant of his hair, beard, or rags fell off, he would carefully place it in one of his wounds to miss none of the pains of the flesh and in this way qualify himself for the glorious rewards of heaven. Unlike these hermits, yet one who had the obvious respect of most of the others, was Father Paphnutius, a man so involved with spiritual matters, who experienced the ecstatic so constantly that at times he would drink the oil of his lamp instead of water. But of all the hundreds who were gathered at this banquet, the hermit Nikon, whose eyes burned like live coals in his face, whose mouth was twisted into a perpetual sneer, and whose gnarled hands opened and closed constantly as if to strangle, caused Joanna the most uneasiness. It was almost as if she could feel twin jets of heat from his eyes; but those hands of his must be as cold as those of a corpse she thought. Nikon who had once succumbed to the sinful yearnings of his flesh and as punishment had shut himself in a charnel house for thirty years. There, in that house of the dead, he forced himself to sleep standing up like a horse and would only take nourishment from herbs that grew from soil in which the dead were buried.

Joanna's attention was drawn away from this collection of mostly filthy, haggard, wild-appearing men by the bishop who was closely examining her features, his hand even more firmly locked around her hand.

"There is wisdom in your face, young priest," he said in a full voice. "Oh yes, I see more than bravery. I see wisdom."

The clammy wetness of Bishop Nikitas' hands and something

about the way he looked at her were warnings to be on guard.

"You have traveled to so many places, have studied with one of Christendom's greatest scholars." (One of the deacons who had quizzed Marcos on the way to the palace had given the bishop a whispered history of Joanna.) "All of these holy men gathered here, I am certain, are eager for your opinion concerning the Eucharist. A matter which concerns us deeply. Do you believe the bread and wine are actually changed into the body and blood of our Saviour? Or is it your opinion that these are a symbol and image of the Divine Body?"

Joanna wondered why she was being tested. An image of the abbess holding out the platter on which lay the doll and cross rose for a moment in her mind. She furrowed her brow as if deep in thought and quickly glanced around. Most of the several hundred were leaning forward concentrating all their attention on her. Except for a few whispers, all was silent. *If I give the wrong answer,* she thought, *they may refuse me admittance to their learned circle. Yet if I refuse to answer I am discredited.* She turned her eyes to the bishop's bloated face. Her mind raced as she comprehended that, for some reason, he wished to discredit her. Then she calmed herself and slowly gave her answer.

"For a recently ordained priest to be asked a question by a great bishop such as you are, Your Reverence, is a high honor. Few priests are given this sort of recognition."

A wave of whispers passed through the audience, together with some suppressed laughter at this initial response.

"But now to your question. While the sun is in the sky, its heat and light are also upon the earth; and in this sense the body and blood of Christ may also be found in the bread and wine of communion."

Some of the men present were unable to suppress their laughter at this metaphorical answer which still did not commit the young priest to either position. The bishop, not quite certain as to the meaning of Joanna's answer, and uneasy at the laughter, let go of her hand, stroked his chin ponderously, then nodded.

"Yes. Yes, as you say. The bread and wine are indeed the crucified body of the Savior, and our stomach is its grave in which it is interred by the priest."

"And after this interment, the spirit rises as did Christ after the Crucifixion," Joanna added.

At this the several hundreds clapped, pounded the table, a number rising to wave their crucifixes.

The hermit, Nikon, one of the few who had not clapped or pounded, stood up and stepped forward, the crucifix he carried pointed at Joanna as if it were a weapon. "And, my young priest, who has gained such a store of wisdom, what is your opinion regarding Mary, the wife of Joseph? In your learned opinion is she to be called Mother of God?" Second only to the meaning of the Eucharist was this matter of Mary, Mother of god or Mary, merely Christ-bearer. Bishop Nikitas, along with many of his eastern colleagues, held to the position that the divine personage could not have a mother as do mortal men, that Mary was merely the receptacle in which Christ was placed by the Heavenly Father.

Joanna placed her forefinger on her lips, as if to say hush, then slowly drew the finger down until it rested on her chin in the manner of a scholar. "As I and you, venerable sir, and all gathered here were granted our gifts of life from the Heavenly Father without whom we would not be, thus it is we have but a single parent. This was confirmed by Christ when he commanded all believers to pray to the Father who dwells in heaven. Yet did not each of us call the one who carried us in her womb mother? What name other than mother could the infant Jesus have used as he nestled against Mary's bosom?"

"This young John would better be called Daniel, for he has the gift of calming raging lions," Father Paphnutius called out. "Perhaps it is that the Almighty has sent him here with his handsome face and wise words to help unify us."

"Unify us!" shouted the hermit Nikon, advancing several steps in the direction of Joanna, his crucifix still pointing. "Insult is my view. Insult and mock us with his honeyed words which give non-answers to questions upon which rests the fate of Christ's Holy Church."

Hoots and laughter greeted this angry declaration, with several who were near the monk reaching out and tugging at his garments for him to sit back down.

Nikon hesitated a moment, but then, seeing that the bishop did not join in these hoots and jeers, he whirled around and struck at the clutching hands with his heavy crucifix. But as those who had been struck came at him, the deacons, at a signal from the bishop, put an end to the melee.

"I am young and there is so much I do not know," Joanna addressed the glowering hermit in a respectful voice as soon as order had been restored. Nikon snorted in contempt. "And it may be that the manner of my answering your question was defective."

She was interrupted by shouts of "No! No!"

Raising her hand to silence the crowd she went on, "For this defect I offer the excuse of a mind that is preoccupied and troubled."

Having the full attention of the assemblage, she turned to the bishop. "How should my mind not be troubled, being in your pres-

ence now for several hours, yet having not delivered the message im-
parted to me by the bishop of Palermo."

Bishop Nikitas waved his soft hands, as if brushing at insects,
then reluctantly nodded."

"I was instructed to carry the plea of the enslaved Christians of
Palermo and of the other conquered portions of Sicily to Your
Eminence; to beg you to use all of your great influence to urge the
Holy Father in Rome to organize an army among the Christian na-
tions of Europe. To beg Your Eminence to travel to Rome and present
this plea in person. To inform the Holy Father that if the Saracens are
not turned back, in time Rome itself may fall to the Saracen infidels.
The Bishop of Palermo, who at this very moment, I am certain, rests
among the angels and archangels also instructed me to convey to Your
Eminence his deepest love and his blessing."

Bishop Nikitas cleared his throat while wiping away bits of food
that still clung to his loose lips. "It is terrible, terrible." He shuddered
and wrung his hands. "The vilest of the vile, those followers of
Mahamat." He picked up a leg of chicken and took a thoughtful bite.
"Yet my health would not stand a trip to Rome at this time. There are
nights when I get scarcely and hour's sleep. Perhaps, with the help of
God, in six months or a year...But before another day, I will write begging that our suffering brethren in Sicily be succored. And I will use
the strongest language." He thumped his fist containing the chicken
leg on his knee. "And I will make no attempt to sleep this night. I will
devote all the hours of darkness to offering prayers for the soul of my
revered brother in Christ." With that the bishop stood up, made a
sweeping motion which declared the banquet and audience at an end,
and strode ponderously out of the room, the layers of fat on his belly
and back quivering.

The bishop's audience chamber, grown malodorous from the hundred
of unwashed bodies, finally left behind them, Joanna and Wilma with
Marcos a dozen paces in the lead toiled along the winding proces-
sional path on the western portion of the Acropolis that led up to the
summit where the neglected ruins of the Parthenon lay washed by the
yellow light of the ringed full moon.

It had taken them almost an hour to escape from the chamber after the bishop left. Scores pressed in around them, shouting questions.
Hands reached out to touch them. There had been moments when the
press and stink were so great, Joanna found herself growing faint. And
Wilma actually sank to her knees, her face drained of color, and had

to be rescued by Marcos who cleared a space for her with shoves and sharp elbow thrusts. Yet this rough treatment did not diminish the enthusiasm of most of the monks and hermits. A number followed them out of the palace when they finally reached the door and almost certainly would have trailed after them had Father Paphnutius, whose authority was almost equal to that of the bishop, not ordered them to allow the three travelers a period of privacy.

"When that one covered with ulcers attempted to embrace me, I was almost certain I would lose my dinner," said Joanna with a shudder, as they climbed. "I would never have believed it possible to find such opulence and filth in the same room."

"I have heard it said that even the wealth of the Holy Father does not compare to that of the bishops of the East," Wilma offered in a weary voice. "Not only have the bishops accumulated wealth, but the priests also." She passed her hand slowly over her brow. "For everything their priests demand payment. Even the poorest peasants must bring a present if they need their services." This last was said in a whisper as Wilma struggled to catch her breath.

Joanna called out to Marcos that they would rest, that they would meet him at the summit. Then she took Wilma's hands and led her to a remnant of a fallen marble column and the woman allowed herself to be led as if a child.

Although scarred with letters, symbols, and other graffiti, this portion of a structure, built a millenium and a half earlier and doubtless destroyed by the Persians when they laid waste to the Acropolis, was a thing of beauty. But now it lay in the midst of what appeared to be a thousand years' accumulation of refuse. Broken pots, animal bones, decayed building bricks, charred wood, slag from copper smelting, and piles of manure covered the ground.

"Pericles must have once walked along this path and now this," Joanna said softly almost to herself. "Somehow I expected Athens to be different, not like the other cities. Can they not see the beauty," she said, making a gesture in the direction of the city below. Then she turned her eyes to the Parthenon. "Like the gates of heaven."

Wilma raised her head from her hands and stared in the same direction. "Like the gates of heaven," she repeated. "Now the light of faith burns more dimly each year. Soon the light will be extinguished altogether, Joanna. If these are the conditions in Athens, what hope for the rest of the earth?"

Joanna took the woman's hand and held it between both of hers. It was cold and felt lifeless. She rubbed the hand trying to bring life back to it. "We stay here until I have learned as much as I can and do what I must to gain a sufficient reputation. Then, if it be God's will, to Rome.'' She paused several seconds. "In Rome, with God's help, I will gain an audience with the Pope. I will fall to my knees and offer to serve him.''

"And as his servant you will also have his ear, my sweet Joanna.'' Wilma smiled, her eyes crinkling, a thing she had not done in a long while. "With all that has happened already, who is to say that such a thing is not possible.''

With that they started along the path again.

Marcos was waiting for them when they completed the climb to the Parthenon. He had mounted a broken marble column and stood like a golden statue in the moonlight. Joanna felt her heart speed up when she saw him, his head tilted back, his arms raised as if to touch the sky. In so many ways he was like Sigbert. Not in scholarship, for Marcos was no serious scholar. But in his appearance, in his proud manner. Yet had the two men stood side by side, there would have been differences. Of course, in the eyes. And Sigbert's hair had been flaxen while Marcos' was a coppery brown. Sigbert had been the more massive man with a deep cleft in his chin, while Marcos' lips were more delicately formed and his nostrils flared. Yet in Joanna's mind the two had become almost the same.

Marcos forced a laugh to cover his embarrassment at being caught in this pose, then jumped down.

They walked among the ruins together while Wilma, again short of breath, rested, her eyes fixed unblinking at the flickering lights of the city that lay below. As they walked, Marcos made a show of examining different portions of the temple. Joanna walked alongside of him, stopping when he stopped, examining what he examined, exercising great care that their hands or shoulders did not touch, yet never allowing more than a single span of separation between them.

On the far side of the Parthenon a dwarf shepherd sat in the midst of his flock, cracking nuts and talking earnestly to a broad-shouldered ram who kept nodding. The sound of sheep bells echoed in the still air. A film of moisture clouded Joanna's eyes as she watched the little man. There was so much about him that resembled Nicco. She started toward him and he leapt up and with a frightened look bounded down the hill, his flock bleating in terror, fanning out on both sides of him.

"Foolish fellow,'' said Marcos gently. "I have a portion of a loaf in my wallet I would have given him, had he allowed me to overhear what he was saying to that ram.''

"He thought we were going to trick or tease him,'' said Joanna.

"Nicco, the little goatherd who carried my message from the bandits' village to the bishop — you must have seen him — ran away like that one when we first saw him. Yet in time we became friends."

"The little fellow hesitated half the morning before entering the garden and approaching the bishop." Marcos smiled in remembrance. "I saw him slip past the guard and then crouch in the shadow of some bushes. His head would dart out for a moment then back into the shadows. The bishop laughed when he saw his little face with those wizened features appearing and disappearing. But finally he came up, his limbs shaking like a week-old kid, and delivered your message."

"And then?" Joanna asked. Marcos shrugged.

"When we looked up after reading what you had written, he was gone. That was the last I saw of him."

"Perhaps he gathered his goats and. returned to his village," Joanna said softly, the male roughness she had trained herself to use almost absent. "I hope the little man found his way safely home. After the Christian forces have driven the Saracens out of Sicily, I will visit that village again."

"Then you may have to reach the hundred and twenty years of Abraham when he fathered Isaac before you make that visit," Marcos growled, his eyes and mouth hardening. "That fat pig Nikitas who used to correspond with my bishop, who would send messages of undying fraternal love, will continue to find sufficient defect in his health each six months for the rest of his miserable life so that he cannot make the trip to Rome." The corners of the man's mouth were curled down, his eyes narrowed, and the skin across his cheekbones was pulled tight, robbing his face for the moment of its handsomeness. "If Nikitas, who declared himself a friend, will do nothing, we cannot expect any other of the powerful bishops to make a move."

"The Holy Father in Rome will force the bishops, will call upon the kings to send their armies," declared Joanna. "When he learns what has happened, when he receives the plea for help..."

"And who will tell him? Who will deliver that plea?" Marcos muttered. "Who will be able to force his way through that crowd of toadies, of sycophants that constantly surround him. You? Me?" His angry eyes fastened on those of Joanna for several long moments, and she struggled against the urge to turn her's away.

"It may be that in time with patience and with the help of some of those monks, the bishop can be convinced," Joanna tried to force a ring of hope into her voice. Marcos' face softened.

"If there is any man in all of Christendom who can convince the bishop, you are the man, John." He took hold of Joanna's hand and her body tensed. "If there is any hope of the Church surviving the onslaughts of those heathen followers of Mahamat, of surviving the corruption and greed of its bishops and cardinals, that hope lies in such as you and Brother William. For these several weeks we have been together, at least a score of times I have ached to tell you of my admiration and love."

Joanna felt her face burning at his words, words that she wanted to hear yet feared. Marcos went on talking. "But each time I came up to you, it seemed to me you wanted to be alone, away from me. But here in this ancient place it feels right that I should declare my affection and friendship."

Marcos hesitated and swallowed several times as he shifted awkwardly from foot to foot. "It may sound strange for one like me who is older by ten years to speak in this fashion to you who is scarcely more than a boy. But I wanted you to know that you have my loyalty, not only as a fellow servant of Christ and His Holy Church, but as a friend."

Unable to trust her voice, Joanna nodded, then allowed her free hand to grip the thick muscles of Marcos' arm for the briefest of moments.

They walked again, picking their way carefully through the rubble: chunks of marble, boulders, granite building blocks left in this place by the Persian invaders who ravaged the land nearly five hundred years before the birth of Christ.

Marcos knelt by the remnant of a statue, the lower torso and a portion of one thigh still showing the exquisite skill of the sculptor's chisel which had defined each bulging muscle, each sinew. "What is it about us that drives us, again and again, to reduce beauty into rubble? We cannot go on much longer this way — cruelty, destruction, loss of faith. Unless Christ again appears amongst us, this world must be consumed in fire." The pain he had locked inside him since their escape from Sicily could not be held back. "If you could have been in Palermo before the Saracens, my friend," he said bitterly. "A joyous city filled with joyful people." His voice softened. "You should have heard their voices as they sang the old songs. A hundred men, arms locked together, tears of remembrance staining their faces. And the young women dancing, their heads thrown back, laughing; adorned with brightly colored ribbons and combs of seashell and burnished copper."

Joanna overcame her hesitation and knelt down beside the man.

"I should have remained in Palermo. Should have stayed at the bishop's side and died with him.'' He bowed his head until his chin pressed against his chest.

"You were born in Palermo?" In all the time they had been together, this was the first question Joanna had directly asked him. "Your skin is so fair," she continued, "and your hair not like that of other Sicilians."

"I was brought as a slave." Marcos turned his face partially anything before." He paused.

There was something in Marcos' manner, in the tone of his voice, that revealed embarrassment, and this puzzled Joanna as she waited for him to go on.

"I was brought as a slave," Marcos turned his face partially away. "I was taken by a soldier, but I do not know from where. The bishop bought me and had me raised to be a singer of Schola and to perform other necessary tasks. But then he came to love me like a father. He taught me, and I became a man. He gave me my freedom, then the tonsure, and then the honor of being his personal secretary."

With a sudden almost angry movement, Marcos turned his face and looked directly at Joanna. "So you see, Father John, my lineage is of the very lowest. A slave."

"The very lowest, or perhaps the highest, Brother Marcos. The son of a count perhaps, a cardinal's bastard, the child of a great and noble family."

"You are kind. Generous and kind." Marcos smiled.

"I too never knew my parents. But I was not raised in a bishop's palace," Joanna said softly. "The first ten years of my life were spent in a peasant's hut." Then she told Marcos some details of her birth and her early years. As she spoke of the holy monk, her father, of her mother who died to give her life, of Gerberta, Magda, and Rolf, she had to struggle against the urge to reveal the truth that she was a woman. She wanted to blurt out the truth; it would be such a relief. But no, it was not safe. Marcos' bishop had made her a priest. He might be enraged learning that the one to who he owed allegiance had been gulled.

"You will find your father, my friend," said Marcos. "I am certain that when it is the proper time, you will be reunited with that holy monk." Excitement showed in Marcos' face. "And what a marvelous reunion that will be. How proud your father will be of his son, now a priest. Or it is possible by that time, you will be more than a priest, Father John. More than a priest!" He laced his hands together. "How proud he will be. What I would not give to be present at that reunion." He paused for several seconds, then slowly pulled his hands apart. "What I would not give if there were a father with whom I could be reunited. But I have no father."

"Except Christ," said Joanna.

"Except Christ."

As if they had reached an unspoken agreement, they separated, Marcos continuing to walk among the ruins of the Parthenon, while Joanna turned back to where they had left Wilma.

Her eyes staring at the lights of Athens down below, her body held rigid, Wilma still sat where she had been left. As Joanna approached and saw her motionless form silhouetted against the dark purple sky, the irrational thought that Wilma somehow had been turned into stone entered her mind.

"Wilma," she called out.

Wilma groaned as she turned her eyes away from the lights of the city.

"You were so still. I thought..."

"You thought I might be dead." She forced herself to her feet. "Not yet. These bones and muscles still have some strength left. But I could think of worse places to die than among these ruins. There is such a feeling of timelessness here. In this place it is as if all were still. Past, present, future, all one." She faced Joanna directly and put her hands on the shoulder of the younger woman. "If I should die, Joanna, while we are still here in Athens, I ask that you bring me to this place."

Joanna grasped Wilma's hands, then nodded slowly.

The moon shining through the scores of tiny panes of leaded glass their only illumination, the three entered the bishop's guest house where they were to be quartered. Although the door stood wide open and a portion of the sloping wooden roof had been raised for ventilation, the air inside the building was close and stank of unwashed bodies, mildew and garlic. More than a hundred of the guests who had attended the banquet were stretched out on narrow pallets, filling the building's single cavernous room.

As the three picked their way through this clutter of human beings, they unavoidably tripped over outstretched arms and legs and were greeted with angry mutters. Several monks sat up and spewed out streams of curses. The few still unoccupied pallets lay in the deepest, most airless and malodorous portion of the far end of the room. Had they not been weighed down by exhaustion, they would have returned outdoors to sleep despite the chill. But bone deep fatigue forced them down on those pallets, which it was almost certain, provided homes for lice and bedbugs.

Moments after their heads touched their pallets, Wilma and Marcos were deep asleep. But despite her exhaustion, which caused a slight tremor of her limbs and a pressure in her chest and throat, sleep eluded Joanna. Fragments of thoughts stabbed at her mind: Marcos kneeling before the broken statue...Sigbert entering their room in the cathedral of Aachen warning them of danger...Sofia staring in horror from her dead eyes in which insects swarmed...the bandit chief shouting and gesturing. She opened her eyes wide to the foul darkness and tried to clear her mind of these stinging thoughts. She concentrated on the soft moans and groans, snores and belly rumbles that arose from the sleeping men. These sounds, the malodorous, close air, the scurrying and crawling insects which inhabited her pallet, all of this took her back to the little hut, to that other pallet where she had nestled alongside Gerberta seeking out the warmest places in that woman's billowing body.

Her eyes grew heavy. She took in a deep breath and was about to slip off to sleep when a hand as cold and hard as a slab of stone gripped her mouth. A second hand sunk into the flesh of her upper arm, another hand on the other arm. Hands grasped her thighs. She tried to struggle but she could not move. She tried to bite the hand over her mouth to call out to Wilma and Marcos but the hand gripped tighter, gripped with such force that it felt as if her teeth would break. Soundlessly the three pairs of hands on her body wrapped her in a thick blanket. Then she was lifted and carried carefully to the door, disturbing few of the sleepers.

Out in the night, the voice belonging to the hand that gripped her mouth whispered, "Such a pretty fellow, you are, with your beardless cheeks and soft lips. Is all of you as soft and pretty, little priest? We have certain presents for you such as you will remember if you live a hundred years." Her captors began to laugh softly, and Joanna again tried to struggle, but was restrained by their tightening grips.

Kneeling bareheaded on the ground, deep in meditation as was his wont during the several hours before sunrise, whether at home in his mud-brick hut or on the ground of the bishop's palace, Father Paphnutius was startled by the sound of muffled laughter. There was something about the laughter and the faint impression of muffled groans that was ominous. Stifling a complaint from his chill-stiffened muscles, he forced himself to his feet and peered into the darkness. Moving forward slowly and carefully in the direction of the sounds, he saw three cowled figures silhouetted against the waning moon leaning over something wrapped in a blanket on the ground. Using extreme caution, he approached closer just in time to see Joanna being roughly unrolled from the blanket.

Roaring imprecations in a voice that had been trained to address multitudes, Father Paphnutius rushed forward, striking with all his considerable strength at the heads of the cowled man, kicking with an agility amazing for one of his advanced age at their loins. Then as he struggled with the three men trying to pull the cowls away from their faces, he shouted for help in his stentorian voice, calling for Brother Marcos and Brother William to help save the young priest.

The advantage of surprise now over, the three men united their efforts and brought the old man down to his knees and began beating him unmercifully about the head. But his shouts, joined by Joanna's cries, had alerted the men in the guest house, and a large group came rushing out to help drive off the kidnappers.

It was Brother Marcos who pursued them to the wall they were attempting to scale. Two reached safety, but he caught the last one with his club, delivering a heavy blow to the man's cloth-shrouded face, before he too reached the safety of the other side of the wall.

Still shaking with rage, Marcos returned to the others. "Two I could not reach, but one will never forget this night," he said patting his club.

"Did you see any of their faces?" asked Father Paphnutius as he spat out blood and a piece of broken tooth. Marcos shook his head. "But you struck one?"

"Full in the face. I will offer a penance of a thousand Hail Marys if I didn't break his nose."

"Good!" said Father Paphnutius. Then he glanced upwards for a moment and crossed himself. "I will make certain inquiries in the morning." He hesitated for several moments, then went on. "I am not unacquainted with the names of various monks who have gained a reputation for their taste for boys and young men. I will make my inquiries among them."

"To have attempted such a thing on the person of a priest, a saintly priest like Father John!" growled Marcos.

The several other monks who had assisted in the rescue nodded their agreement.

While this exchange was taking place, Wilma knelt by Joanna's side, seeking assurance that she was all right. Joanna whispered back that except for some soreness in her jaw from the gripping hand and some lightheadedness, she was unhurt. Then Wilma hissed, "If I had been awake when they came, I would have cut out their livers with my knife. I swear before God that this would have been the last night on earth for more than one of those..." She broke off as Marcos came up.

Trying to compose his features he bent down and offered his hand to Joanna. She took it tremblingly, allowing him to pull her to her feet while Wilma watched from her crouched position on the ground, a deep sigh escaping her lips.

Sunrise found Joanna, Wilma and Marcos trudging alongside Father Paphnutius on the road that led past the Acropolis to the hills which lay just beyond. The old man had insisted they be his guests, declaring that the young priest John would not be safe any place in the city.

Not yet fully recovered from the terror of the night, Joanna showed a certain heaviness as she moved. Her eyes remained on the ground, her feet dragged so that from time to time she stumbled and had to be supported by Wilma and Marcos. For the first hour they traveled she would not allow herself to think or even feel.

They passed several clusters of huts generating a wild chorus of bleating goats, barking and growling dogs, snorting and braying asses. With each mile, the appearance of the land worsened, rocks and thorny bushes replacing vines and olive trees. Even the huts began to be of poorer construction, the dogs more savage, the goats and asses showing their bones through tight-stretched skins.

They reached a narrow path that led off from the road to a hut whose condition was worse than any they had seen. There were no windows and what little light that managed to filter in came from chinks between some of the smoke-blackened mud bricks which formed its walls and from several places in the roof where tiles had been pried loose by the wind. Yet Joanna and Wilma, on entering, both expressed their gratitude to the old man, each taking one of his hands and bringing it to her lips.

"I did not realize it was so small; it has always been so unimportant to me," the old man said, crinkles of amusement forming around his eyes. "Two small for all of us. I will sleep in the goat shed — since my poor goat died it has stood unused and this is a terrible waste." He waved away their protests. "I would be dishonored if my guests lived more poorly than I, their host. Besides, my lungs will benefit from the fresh air, and I have a good sheep skin to keep me warm. My only regret is there will be so little room for you three."

Wilma and Joanna looked at one another, trying to hide their consternation. They would not long be able to keep their secret from Marcos if he slept and stayed with them in the hut. But he spoke up abruptly.

"My lungs will also benefit from the fresh air." With that he turned, and hunched out the low, narrow door. Then with a broad grin which momentarily erased twenty years from his face, after telling Joanna and Wilma if they had need of anything not to hesitate and call out for him, Father Paphnutius followed Marcos outside.

"It is so strange, Wilma," Joanna shook her head. "Men like those who tried to do that terrible thing to me, and men like Father Paphnutius."

"And like Marcos," Wilma added.

"Yes, like Marcos." Joanna felt the blood rushing to her cheeks and turned her face partially away.

"You need not hide your blushes from me, dearest sister." Wilma pulled Joanna close and pressed her cheek against hers. "If I had the sight of only one eye, I could not have failed to notice how you color every time you are in his presence. And you need not be ashamed of your love, Joanna. For those of our sex love is as natural as breathing."

"I am not ashamed," whispered Joanna. "But it is a thing he can never know, Wilma. His affection for me is that of a brother." She sighed. "If he ever discovered my deception he would despise me."

"You cannot know this, Joanna. It is possible if he knew who you are, his feelings would match yours." Wilma hesitated. "But you have gone too far for that," she said slowly. "You are a priest. A priest, Joanna!" An urgency entered her voice. "If discovered to be a woman...no, he must never know. No one must ever know. They would stone you to death in the manner of the Hebrews." A shudder passed through the woman's body. "What we have done may be madness. But now there is no turning back." She sank down to the floor of the hut and pulled Joanna down beside her. "Besides, my sweetest Joanna, my daughter, there is a destiny you must fulfill. Yours is no ordinary life. No, Marcos must never know. No one must ever know. Never forget this. Even when I am gone, never forget this no matter how lonely you may be."

Despite a continuing uneasiness at Father Paphnutius staying in a goat shed while they occupied his hut, Joanna and Wilma quickly settled down into a routine of daily living. Both hungered for peace after all that journeying, all those many dangers. And in this hut there was peace. The local peasants stood in awe of Father Paphnutius and brought him presents of fruit and cheese, yet were careful not to disturb him or his guests. And they discouraged, with vigor, any beggar or other wanderer who attempted to approach. Equal to the two women's gratitude for this peace was their appreciation of the quiet. Not since those months spent in the cave with Sofia and Sigbert had they known such quiet. Even the night birds sang their songs more softly; the shepherds calling to their flocks used muted voices. And it was satisfying to do such tasks as gathering sticks for firewood, drawing water from the well, baking wheaten cakes on stones heated in the fire pit, picking wild berries. As she had spent a portion of each day with Sofia when they lived in the cave, so Joanna now began to spend a like portion of time with Father Paphnutius while Wilma and Marcos took walks together or worked on improving the condition of the goat shed. But this daily routine had scarcely established itself — only a week had gone by — when a visit of half a dozen holy men led by Father Matthew interrupted it. The tiny man whose fasts had once been such that live worms dropped from his lips, now showed a rotund appearance, proof that his fasting was a thing of the past.

"We have come to pay our respects to the young priest who so confounded our bishop," Father Matthew called out as he approached the hut.

"And to express our distress at that unfortunate incident which took place," a cadaverous-looking monk with flaring hair-clotted nostrils joined in.

Trying to hide her annoyance at this interruption of her studies with Father Paphnutius, Joanna came out of the hut to greet this delegation. They crowded close and she was almost overwhelmed as the stink of their unwashed bodies and odor of their fetid breaths enveloped her. Her distress was relieved by Father Paphnutius who came out and invited them to share some fruit and cheese with him. Careful to position herself to the leeward of these holy men, Joanna squatted down to listen — they were, after all, members of the highly regarded fraternity of Athenian theologians.

"All of Athens is buzzing about your young priest," Father Matthew addressed Father Paphnutius between sucks on an orange. "Wherever clerics congregate there is much laughter about the bishop's discomfiture. To have a beardless priest, and one so young, expose Nikitas as a do-nothing and as a fool causes much delight." He tossed the empty orange aside and dug his filth-encrusted fingers into a soft, ripe cheese. "Your priest, Father Paphnutius, by his manner and his brilliance has gained many friends here in Greece."

"Many friends and also certain enemies," intoned the gaunt monk who had scarcely touched any food.

"Is the bishop his enemy?" asked Father Paphnutius.

The gaunt monk shook his head. "The bishop has enough trouble with the hundreds he offended during those bitter years when our icons were forbidden. He seeks no new enemies and was heard to remark that the young priest displayed uncommon erudition."

"It is, alas, true that your priest has, ah, certain enemies," Father Matthew joined in. "Nikon has publicly declared his dislike. That a priest should be without a beard he finds particularly offensive. And he detests being bested in an exchange such as took place in the bishop's palace. I know of no one who is as easily offended as Nikon or who will hold a grudge as long."

"Do you think he was one of those who attempted that abomination?" Father Paphnutius asked, a frown darkening his features. Father Matthew and several other of the monks shook their heads. "I did not think so. His has not been a taste for boys.

"But I understand that a certain friend of his suffered an accident just about the time of that abomination," said Father Matthew. "And this one has a taste for comely youths."

"Tryphon!" said Father Paphnutius, smacking his fist into his palm. "Always declaring his piety. Insisting that he never wore a clean shirt but always one cast off by another. But there are stories told about what went on between Tryphon and his abbot and other ones in his monastery."

"This accident of Tryphon's was to his face, I have heard it said," the gaunt monk offered.

"If it was Tryphon then Nikon must have had some sort of hand in it," Father Paphnutius muttered. "Without Nikon's permission that one would not so much as take a piss."

"To have those two as enemies," Father Matthew frowned and stroked his beard, further matting it with the cheese which adhered to his fingers, "it might be wise of your priest not to venture back into Athens. I would not put it past Tryphon to attempt another abomination, and this time make sufficient preparations to ensure his success. As for Nikon, there is no way of knowing what plans are germinating in his mind."

"Father John will enter Athens as often as he pleases!" shouted Marcos who had just come up and heard the latter portion of the conversation. "It is not this priest who must worry about his safety." Marcos placed his hand firmly on Joanna's shoulder. "But those whose names you just mentioned. I will go to this Tryphon and if he is the one I struck, I will recognize him. And then, and then for that attempted abomination..." Marcos picked up a thick stick which he broke in two with a sharp crack.

Father Paphnutius beckoned Marcos to come closer, then took him by the hand. "I am one who avoids violence, yet I can understand your anger. Loyalty to a friend is one of the greatest virtues. But, Brother Marcos, you must not let your anger and your loyalty drive you to acts of foolishness."

Marcos' jaw tightened and his face suffused with dark blood.

"Any attempt on Tryphon would be answered by retaliation from others of his order. They would pull you limb from limb." Marcos started to reply, but Father Paphnutius put up his hand. "And remember, my friend, you are a Sicilian, not a Greek. Even those who have little use for such as Tryphon will not side with a Sicilian against him."

His face a deep scarlet, his chest heaving with his quickened breathing, Marcos started to declare that to avenge what had been done to Father John he would gladly risk his life, but was interrupted by Joanna who came toward him. "No vengeance, Marcos, no vengeance. I have seen enough of savagery. And do you forget, my friend, that we are Christians? Our way is forgiveness, not revenge." The gathered monks made grunts of approval. "Promise me as a friend and as a Christian you will not attempt to harm Tryphon. Promise me." Joanna took hold of Marcos' broad hand and held it with both of hers.

"I cannot forgive that off scouring," Marcos said in a guttural voice. "Perhaps I am not enough of a Christian. But, since it is your wish, I will not attempt to harm him." He pulled his hand free. "But I will curse him and pray that upon his death he gains the punishment of Hell." At this, except for Father Paphnutius, the gathered monks made the same grunts of approval they had at Joanna's statement.

Her mind churning with the events of the day, Joanna lay awake that night, staring up into the darkness. Several times she had settled down and attempted to sleep but with no success.

"Are you troubled, Joanna!" Wilma whispered, startling Joanna who had thought her asleep.

"My mind is so full, Wilma," Joanna answered.

"Are you disturbed about what you heard about Tryphon?"

"No. And that is what is so strange. I truly forgive him. Not just words, but in my heart. I think I understand, for the first time, the true meaning of forgiveness. It must be in one's heart. I feel as if I am filled with warm milk, Wilma. As if this milk has washed away the pain of all those sad things: Sigbert, Sofia, what happened at the walls of Engelheim, at the walls of Palermo. I will never forget, I will carry those things with me for the rest of my life. I am certain of this. But the pain, like smoldering coals in my breast... Gone. Now filled with warm milk."

Joanna began weeping softly. But then the weeping turned into deep sighs as she pressed close to Wilma and gradually allowed herself to slip off into sleep.

For many minutes after Joanna's regular breathing declared she was asleep, Wilma gently stroked the girl's soft hair, biting own on her lower lip to prevent any sound of her own pain and anguish from escaping.

The next several months saw one or another group of monks in attendance at Father Paphnutius' hut. And Joanna's reputation increased as each succeeding contingent told others about her brilliance, her comprehension of canon law, her mastery of Latin and Greek. This, coupled with accounts of her success with the Sicilian bandits, her skills as physician, her heroism at the wall of Engelheim, caused her to grow larger than life in the minds of most of the religious community of Athens.

Several times during these months intelligence was received that Tryphon and Nikon were muttering unfriendly things about Joanna, but were not attempting to take any action. And most of the visiting monks loudly lodged complaints against bishop Nikitas, directing these to Joanna and Father Paphnutius as if they, somehow, had been elevated to the rank of ecclesiastical judges. There was resentment regarding his high style of living, his equivocation and his imperious manners. But much of the monks' antagonism was a reflection of their anger at the bishop's support of the emperor during those years when the icons were destroyed and the icon makers mutilated or banished.

It was inevitable that the glowing reports of Joanna would, in time, reach the bishop's ears, as it was also inevitable that he would hear about the complaints against him aired in her presence. Thus to nobody's surprise the bishop announced he would invite the young priest to a second audience in his palace. To this audience, which was to include a great banquet, he also invited all of the priests and many of the monks of Athens.

Fearing that the bishop might have certain unsavory plans regarding Joanna's person, if not the bishop then possibly Tryphon or Nikon, Marcos and Father Paphnutius organized a party of sturdy monks armed with clubs to accompany them to the bishop's palace. When Joanna tried to object, Wilma sharply ordered Joanna not to interfere, declaring that these preparations were necessary. Then in a softer voice, she revealed that she did not have the strength to go along and that she would be burdened with anxiety unless these precautions were taken. At this Joanna swallowed several times and wordlessly nodded.

As the contingent approached the palace, their numbers were augmented by at least half a hundred, as groups of ragged monks and blazing-eyed ascetics joined their ranks. Then upon entering the garden fronting the bishop's palace, various monks burst out singing Alleluia while others shouted Deus Adjuva!

The tumultuous entrance into the great hall by this band led by Father Paphnutius disrupted the proceedings that were in progress. Then when the score of armed monks began stamping their feet, waving their clubs in the air, and shouting threats to any who dared harm young Father John, the bishop, his face darkening, raised his bulk from his throne, his crook in one hand while the forefinger of the other hand pointed menacingly at the disruptors. This action of the bishop, served to restore partial order. But when the bishop, in his most severe voice, called out the name of each of the armed monks in turn, order was fully restored.

"I am shocked at the manner of your entrance, Father Paphnutius," the bishop, still standing, addressed the old priest after all the rest were seated. "Never has my episcopy been so insulted — entering my presence armed and shouting like a band of street ruffians."

"For the shouts and the disruptions I offer my most profound apologies, Your Eminence," said Father Paphnutius as he rose and faced the bishop. "For any insult to the majesty of your office I impose upon myself a penance of a thousand Pater Nosters. But for entering your presence armed with clubs," he paused and shifted his gaze to Nikon who sat directly to the right of the bishop, then shifted his gaze to the left to Tryphon whose nose had been considerably altered in its shape, "for taking the precaution of guarding young Father John after the abomination which was attempted on the very grounds of your palace, and while Father John was your guest, Your Eminence, for this I make no apology."

"Abomination?" said the bishop. "I know nothing of any abomination, Father Paphnutius." His jaw hung slack and his wattles shook. "If an abomination was attempted, Father John," he turned to Joanna, "why did you not immediately come to me? This is the first I have heard of it." With that he slowly lowered himself to his throne, his head shaking ponderously from side to side.

Joanna was about to offer a response when Father Paphnutius

leaned toward her and whispered that the bishop knew every detail about the attack, that he had been told about it within hours of its occurrence.

"I shall order an investigation," the bishop muttered. Then in a louder voice. "But it may be that you suffered from indigestion, Father John, and it all was part of a bad dream."

"Bad dream, Your Eminence," Joanna said in a tight voice as she quickly signaled Marcos, who was half out of his chair, to remain silent. "Perhaps so. It felt real at the time. My jaw and my limbs were sore for days, but that may have been caused by something I ate. I am content to regard whatever may have happened as the product of an indigestion-induced dream."

"Enough of dreaming," the bishop rumbled. "All of Athens resounds with praises for your wisdom and erudition, Father John." He smiled at Joanna, exposing large, discolored teeth. "And I hear accounts of acts of bravery that would do credit to any knight. Also that you are a physician." He sighed. "If you can cure me of the headache which is a cross I have borne for years..." He made a languid motion with his hand, bringing it to rest on his broad, shiny forehead.

"I am certain the reports you have heard have been exaggerated, Your Eminence." Joanna rose from her seat and took several steps in the bishop's direction. "As for your headache, I am confidant that there are scores if not hundreds of physicians here in Athens whose skills would put those few I have acquired to shame." She tried to meet the bishop's eyes but he kept them turned just a fraction away.

"The day I entered Athens I delivered a message from the Bishop of Palermo, Your Eminence," she continued. "Would it be presumptuous on my part to ask if you have taken any action regarding that martyred holy man. Have you written to Rome?"

"Presumptuous, he says." The bishop's bulk shook with controlled mirth. " 'Martyred holy man.' he says." The bishop allowed himself a slight laugh. "He does not know that the Bishop of Palermo, rather than gaining his justly earned rewards at the Throne of St. Peter, is yet alive and, I understand, enjoys good health."

"The bishop lives!"

"He lives. And my informants tell me in comfort, daily catering to the whims of the Saracen caliph."

" 'Catering to the whims!' I saw him in the caliph's garden, Your Eminence." Joanna's face was deeply flushed. "He was dressed in clothing that would shame a beggar. Your informants fill your ears with lies, Your Eminence. The Bishop of Palermo, if he is alive, and I pray to God that he may be, serves the caliph as a slave and is treated as a cruel master treats a dog."

"Perhaps so. Perhaps so," the bishop said wearily. "And I must give thanks to Christ Our Savior for having spared my episcopal brother." He leisurely made the sign of the cross.

"And what of the others, Your Eminence?" said Joanna. "Do you have information as to the fate of the bandit chief, of his son, of his grandson."

"Slaughtered by the Saracens. And the world is well rid of such scum."

"It grieves me to hear Your Eminence use the word scum to describe a company of brave men who attempted to liberate a once Christian town from the hands of infidel Saracens."

A shocked murmur ran through the assemblage.

"It grieves me to hear a Christian of your exalted rank insulting the memory of Christians. For every last man of that band was baptized by the hand of ordained priests under the supervision of the bishop, your episcopal brother."

"Christians, young Father John," the bishop laughed. "Christians, so very young Father John. They were a band of lawless brutes who, had they lived, would have just as quickly embraced the way of the vile Mahamat. Christendom is far better off without Christians such as those."

"With deep respect to your exalted office, Your Eminence, I must declare that I am surprised to hear such things," Joanna said in a louder, yet still controlled voice. "Has the abundant life and soft living of Greece caused certain of its renowned theologians to forget that the central purpose of Christian belief is to spread 'the good news' to those born to heathen ignorance? Have certain struggles regarding icons and the holy men who produced them caused those who should be in the forefront of Christian understanding to forget the declarations they made when raised to holy office?"

Loud murmurs filled the large chamber and Nikon, the muscles around his eyes twitching, leaned close to the bishop and whispered in his ear. The bishop nodded and Nikon rose to his feet.

"Do I detect in your mouthings, young priest, an accusation leveled at any present here today?" The monk's face held the cruel look of a hunting wolf and as he spoke his gnarled, black veined hands clenched and unclenched. "Accusations against those in authority made by full-grown men would be seriously considered, and then, when found false, would bring upon these men a fatal punishment. But for one on whose lips his mother's milk still clings, stripping, beating and casting out into the gutter is sufficient."

Marcos, his breath rattling in his throat, his club clenched in his hand, rose to his feet, but Joanna begged him with her eyes to restrain himself and after glaring at Nikon for several seconds, he sat back down.

"Do not think for a single moment, young John, that being a priest will offer you protection if you intend to make accusations," Nikon snarled. "As a bishop, no doubt in a moment of lightheadedness induced by fatigue, ordained you a priest, so another bishop can strip you and declare you excommunicate."

"Yes, excommunicate!" Tryphon echoed.

Turning away from Joanna to the assembled monks, Nikon said, "See how the youth stands there shamed by his own words. All those declarations I have heard regarding his brilliance, all those statements about his holiness, yet there he stands cleanshaven in the fashion of those young men who sell their bodies to soldiers and sailors."

A buzz ran through the assembly at this, with several who had previously shown by their expression support for Joanna now indicating doubt. All eyes were fixed on her now.

"If my memory serves me, learned monk," Joanna said with her lips pursed in an imitation of a smile, "does not St. Paul make mention in his writings something about hair grown too long? And I have heard some place that St. Peter also expressed concern about this same matter, or has my memory played me false?"

"Your memory is sharp enough. As is your tongue. The blessed Paul spoke about hair grown overly long." Nikon placed his hand on his roughly cropped head. "And it was about the plaiting and adorning of hair that St. Peter wrote."

The bishop, whose beard was carefully plaited and tied with ribbons and silver ornaments shifted uneasily and tried to hide his irritation.

"Everywhere I go in the streets of Athens, young priest, I hear men extolling the learning and wisdom of Father John. Thus I must assume you are at least familiar with the earlier books of the Scriptures." The monk licked his lips with the tip of his tongue and brought his bony hands together, winding the fingers one over the other. "For the old, lapse of memory is a curse," he continued. "And I am old, my young and sharp-memoried priest. But despite this loss of the power of my mind, I have not quite forgot that the lawgiver, Moses, declared in Leviticus that men shall not make baldness upon their heads, neither shall they shave off the corner of their beards."

Hoots and laughter swept through the assemblage as Nikon, his face showing a twisted caricature of a smile, sat back down. Several of the monks who were known to be close allies of the bishop stabbed their fingers in Joanna's direction, shouting at her to take her seat which she quickly did, her face crimson with embarrassment.

The bishop still smarting at Nikon's reference to adorned hair waved his slablike hands for silence and several of his deacons pounded their staffs on the wooden floor. "Beard or no beard," the bishop declared in a loud voice when silence had finally been restored, "this is a matter of individual preference as is the manner, uh, a man chooses to groom his hair. And if Father John yet does not have complete mastery of Scriptures, I am confident that in time he will have. And who is there to doubt his brilliance, he being so young." The bishop's face lapsed into a grin and he looked around the large chamber, nodding at various of his guests. Finally his eyes came to rest on Joanna. "All this talk has given me a headache. It worsens by the minute and I will toss and turn all night if I do not get relief this afternoon. And opium gives me cramps worse than the headache. If you are the physician they say you are, young priest, cure my headache. If you do this, I will love you like a brother."

Glancing first at Marcos who was still scowling, then at Father Paphnutius who inclined his head a fraction, Joanna rose quickly and went up to the bishop.

A profound silence had fallen over the assemblage.

Placing her hands on his temples, she stared into his bloodshot eyes. Then with a gentle circular movement, she massaged his temples, drawing his head forward until it rested on his folded arms. Her fingers never stopping their massaging movements, she eased her hands to the back of his head, working her fingers into the thick folds of flesh, then down to the nape of his neck, feeling for space between the spine and the skull as the rabbi-physician had taught her.

Grunts and soft moans came from the bishop as she worked and various monks in the audience exchanged glances with one another.

Sensing a relaxation in the muscles and calculating the moment to be exactly right, Joanna suddenly twisted his head, first to one side, then to the other, causing the vertebra to pop as they came together in their proper alignment.

Allowing her arms to fall to her side, Joanna stepped back a pace and waited.

All the hundreds who were gathered in that chamber now had their eyes fixed on the bishop. Slowly, very slowly, he raised his head from his folded arms, his mouth hanging partially open. He sighed and there was a stirring among the many monks. But it was not this sigh that caused this stirring rather his expression. Around the eyes there was a softening and the deep lines etched into his forehead were noticeably smoother.

Bringing his hand carefully to his head, the bishop declared in a wonder-filled voice, "It is gone. Completely gone."

At this, Joanna bowed low to the bishop, turned and marched out of the chamber, closely followed by Marcos and Father Paphnutius while the rest of the assemblage murmured their amazement to one another.

The three made their way quickly through the streets of Athens. Soon they were on the road leading past the Acropolis in the direction of home. For the first hour of travel they did not stop to rest and Father Paphnutius and Marcos kept nervously glancing backwards. Finally, at a grunt from Father Paphnutius who had grown winded, they stopped to rest at a stone well where each scooped up handfuls of the cool water.

Sufficiently refreshed, they were about to continue when a group of eight masked and armed men appeared around the bend of the road. Their appearance was so sudden and their approach so rapid that the three were unable to make any attempt at escape, although Marcos managed to unsheath his short sword and Father Paphnutius pulled out the knife he used for cutting meat, while Joanna, who was unarmed, snatched up a rock with each hand. The masked men formed a partial circle around the three who had backed against the stone well. "We only want the young priest," said one of the men as he reached for Joanna. But Marcos raised his sword, maneuvering at the same time so that his body partially protected her. "Give us this sorcerer priest and the two of you can go in peace." The man made a motion as if again reaching for Joanna, and Father Paphnutius shifted toward Marcos so that now Joanna was completely protected.

"We do not want to harm you," another of the masked men said in a voice which he had roughened to disguise.

"Stand aside, you two!" shouted the one who had first spoken. "Give up this sorcerer."

Menacing with his knife, Father Paphnutius roared back, "I am Paphnutius. A priest who is not unknown in this land of Greece. One who has stood in the presence of the Pope in Rome. Is it your intention to risk eternal damnation by spilling my blood?"

All of the masked men quickly shook their heads, several grunting no.

"If it is your intention to burn in hell until the end of time with boiling lead your drink, blazing sulphur your only food, attempt to seize this priest. For I swear on my life, which means little to me, that my blood will be shed if you make this attempt."

"My blood will not send you to perdition," Marcos spat out his words. "But as I know Christ died for us I know that more than one of you will die this day if you make that attempt." Rivulets of perspiration ran down his neck and cheeks and the muscles in his thighs vibrated with tension.

During this, Joanna's thoughts raced. If they disregarded these warnings and attempted to seize her, should she defend herself with the rocks? submit and chance a later escape? or to avoid a fate which certainly would include terrible cruelty, leap into the well and end it all in an instant?

"I, Father Paphnutius, order you to depart with your souls left intact!" The old man flung out his arms in the direction of the city. "Go!" And all is forgiven."

The masked men hesitated several moments, shifting uneasily from foot to foot as their eyes met through the slits in their masks. Then the one who had first spoken bowed low to Father Paphnutius and started back down the road with the others closely following.

Shaking off the weakness which had caused her arms and legs to feel like water-soaked logs, Wilma rushed down the path to meet the three. "I knew from the way you walked something had happened," she panted.

"If not for Father Paphnutius and for Marcos..." Joanna choked.

"For what took place back there, Father John, give thanks to the Almighty, not to men," Father Paphnutius said. With that he turned away, and continued up the path to the goat shed, followed by Marcos several moments later.

Other than several sips of wine with honey, Joanna did not touch the simple meal Wilma had prepared. Upon entering the hut, she wrapped herself in a blanket, despite the mildness of the evening, and hunched down beside the firepit, her eyes focused on the glowing embers. Short of breath from her exertion, Wilma crouched on the other side of the firepit and waited. Finally, in a voice that might have been of one three times her age, Joanna said, "They called me a sorcerer, Wilma. They wanted to kill me. What is there about me that would cause men to want to kill me? I can understand that attempt by Tryphon and his two companions. I can understand the action of men driven by their lust. But I have done nothing to justify my murder."

"It is not what you have done, Joanna," Wilma said carefully. "It is who you are. And being who you are, men fear what you may do."

"Who I am? What I may do? I don't understand."

"There is a power within you, Joanna. Something about you —
only a blind man could not see." She hesitated. "No, even one who is
blind will sense it as did Sigbert. Strong men, righteous men are
drawn to you, Joanna. But fearful men, particularly those who claim
righteousness but whose actions declare otherwise, fear you and want
to destroy you. Oh, not that you on occasion do not display a foolish
arrogance. No, my dearest Joanna, not that there still is not much of
the young girl in you. But at the core of you there is such a strength..."
Wilma took in a deep breath. "I know it is there. As I know your life
has a divine purpose. And today when those masked men came for
you, as Father Paphnutius said, it was the Lord God who protected
you."

"Or was what happened today a warning, Wilma? A warning
that I am getting above myself, that my being a priest is an abomination." Joanna took hold of the woman's hands and held them hard. "I
have a growing feeling that somewhere along the road I am traveling,
the divine protection will end — if I attempt to travel too far." Wilma
quickly shook her head. "Yes, each of us has a limit beyond which it is
death to venture. I know this, in my heart I know this. But to break off
too soon, not to fulfill one's life's purpose..." Joanna let go of Wilma's
hand, picked up a stick, and poked at the embers in the pit. "I will be
cautious and should there be another warning," the tip of the stick
burst into flames, illuminating the hut a little, "then I will change
direction. Perhaps even return to the convent. I will stay alert, Wilma,
so as to know when it is the proper time."

For the three full years after that attack on the road, Joanna never
ventured out of sight of the hut. Even during those times when she
needed total privacy, she found it by retreating to an abandoned
goat shed higher on the hill. And during these years an endless stream
of monks, priests and scholars visited her. Some came for only a brief
exchange, some remained for weeks.

For Joanna the time flowed by effortlessly and almost imperceptibly, as it had in the cave with Sofia. For Marcos there were times
when each day felt as if it contained a hundred hours. When this happened he would leave for a week or two, traveling the countryside or
revisiting Athens. During these absences, try as she might, Joanna
was unable to restrain her sighs and was unable to shake off an oppressive heaviness. For Wilma the days, weeks, and months of these
three years passed with increasing rapidity. She could feel their pas-

sage in her muscles and bones, in her growing fatigue and worsening difficulty in breathing. Although Father Paphnutius was at least twenty years older than Wilma, the passage of these three years left scarcely a trace. Each of his days was divided into time spent in meditation, time for study with Joanna and visitors, and time when he, like Joanna, sought privacy up on the hill.

By the end of the three years, what with the constant traffic of monks and scholars, a sort of informal university developed where they lived. Reports of what was happening regularly were brought to Bishop Nikitas, whose concern about the growing popularity of the young priest was constantly stimulated by warnings from Nikon and Tryphon, who viewed what was taking place as a threat to the power of the bishop and thus to themselves.

It was a week into the fourth year since they had been attacked on the road, and the wind had been gusting without letup since late afternoon, bringing masses of frigid air down from the north, despite it being still early autumn. Although Joanna kept poking and replenishing the fire, it was chilly inside the hut because a number of the mud and wattle patches had been torn from the structure by the gusts. Even though it was almost midnight, three hours past the time she usually went to sleep, Joanna kept the fire blazing because Wilma had been coughing and gasping since early evening. Marcos was away on one of his periodic excursions, or she might have asked him to replace the dislodged patches. Father Paphnutius, despite the wind, had climbed the hill for his hours of nightly meditation. Without two pairs of hands in a wind such as this, it would have been futile to attempt any repairs to the hut. She considered running the several hundred paces up the hill to ask for his help. But from the way Wilma kept coughing, from the way she was trembling — the sheepskin blanket was cast off again and again — Joanna decided it would be best to remain where she was.

A violent coughing spasm brought Joanna to her knees alongside Wilma's pallet. Droplets of blood-tinged saliva stained the woman's lips. Although her lids were partially opened, her eyes were glazed and unseeing. Joanna tried to arouse the woman to administer a potion made of wine, honey, and slippery elm, but other than a deep groan, she did not respond. Then Joanna took Wilma's cold hand and held it between both of hers, rubbing it vigorously and from time to time, bringing it to her lips.

"In the morning the wind will stop and the sun will come out and you will be warm, Wilma," Joanna whispered to the unconscious woman, her breath steaming in the frigid air. "I will carry you outside the hut and you can rest your head in my lap and I will tell you things that will make you laugh."

A shudder passed through Wilma's body and her breath started to rattle in her throat.

"Not yet, Wilma, please not yet. Stay with me a little longer. I need you...I need you so much."

The rattle faded and Wilma's eyes opened wide. They were no longer glazed and they stared at Joanna seeing, understanding. She tried to form words but they would not come, only bubbles of the crimson saliva. Then her lips softened until they formed a smile as her eyes, still fixed on Joanna's face, darkened for all eternity.

Joanna's skill as physician enabled her to recognize death when it came. Yet she continued to rub Wilma's hands and spoke to her again. "You are my second mother, Wilma. If my first mother had lived, I doubt if she could have been what you were to me." She carefully replaced the hands and adjusted the sheepskin blanket on the still form. "Have I ever told you how beautiful you are, Wilma? You think yourself ugly because those with eyes who can only see what lies on the surface have told you so. But you are beautiful. Beautiful as a princess or a queen." She dabbed at the red stains on the woman's lips with a bit of cloth, then carefully closed her eyes. "We have had so many good times together, Wilma. And so many adventures. But now it is time for you to rest. Rest, my dearest mother, and gain your reward which, if there is a merciful God, and I know there is, will be in heaven. Rest. Rest, beautiful Wilma. When it is time, we will again be together." With that Joanna stretched out alongside the woman, embracing her stiffening body with both arms.

Father Paphnutius found them lying together when he entered the hut in the morning, one a lifeless corpse, the other coughing violently, drenched with perspiration and scarcely able to speak. Other than accepting a sip of water, Joanna would not allow the old man to help her, whispering, between bouts of coughing, that she wanted to remain alone with her friend a few more hours.

When Father Paphnutius re-entered the hut in the early afternoon Joanna refused to release the corpse. Gasping and coughing, her glazed eyes shifting wildly from side to side, she ordered him out. But just before dark, when Marcos, who had returned from his wandering, accompanied the old priest, Joanna, too weak to resist, released her hold on Wilma.

"Bury Brother William at once, at once!" she gasped as they made ready to carry out the corpse. "Bury him as he is, in his garment. He was modest in life, so should he be allowed to be in death."

Marcos and Father Paphnutius gravely inclined their heads.

By the time they returned from burying Wilma and securing her grave with heavy rocks against wolves and marauding wild dogs, Joanna had lost the power of speech. Yet when Father Paphnutius tried to apply balm to her throat and chest she mustered sufficient strength to cross her arms in a protective gesture and shake her head.

"Even in extremis, monks of that order are private about their persons," Father Paphnutius whispered to Marcos.

"But if he grows any worse we may not be able to continue to respect his modesty," Marcos answered, his face deeply troubled.

"Yet if it is his wish to be modest, even if he worsens, do we have the right..." the old man's voice trailed off. He sighed deeply. "Perhaps by morning he will be much restored, may God grant it. I will devote all the hours of this night praying for his restoration."

"As will I." Marcos made the sign of the cross over Joanna. "As will I."

Despite their prayers, Joanna's condition worsened during the night. When they reentered the hut in the morning they were unable to rouse her. Marcos was all for taking heroic measures with the unconscious priest: stripping off his garments, applying balm, then rubbing his skin vigorously with a coarse cloth. But Father Paphnutius frowned and shook his head.

"Not to respect the privacy of Father John when he is unable to defend it would be a transgression, my friend." He looked directly into Marcos' eyes. "Too often different ones of us use the excuse: it is best for him, to justify doing that which is objectionable to the other. In all the months and years Father John has been here with us, he has carefully guarded his privacy — not once have I seen him without his full robe. I cannot even remember an occasion when I saw him with his head uncovered..."

"But if this modesty should cost him his life?" Marcos interrupted.

Still frowning, after several pulls at his beard Father Paphnutius said slowly, "If it should come to that, we may have to take necessary remedies. But let us wait a few more hours and see how he does."

Although she still could not be aroused after the passage of several hours, Joanna's condition had not perceptibly worsened. It was then that Father Paphnutius decided to take the young priest to the Daphnion monastery in Athens where he had many friends and where there would be better protection from the inclement weather. "As soon as he is safely there, I will seek out the hermit Aegidius," the old priest said to Marcos. "You have certainly heard of that one."

Marcos shook his head.

"You are from Sicily, I forgot. Aegidius is one of our most holy men. Hundreds have been cured of terrible maladies by merely stepping for a moment in his shadow. On those rare occasions when he walks the streets of Athens, I have seen men contend with one another for a moment in his shadow, as dogs will struggle for scraps fallen from a butcher's block." With that, Father Paphnutius directed several young monks who had just arrived to construct a litter and after arming themselves with knives, clubs and other weapons, they started for Athens, chanting sacred songs along the way.

They had scarcely entered the city when word of this procession carrying the ailing young priest began to spread among the populace and their numbers were augmented first by dozens, then scores, and finally hundreds. By the time they reached the Daphnion monastery, more than a thousand had joined this procession with hundreds more rushing through the many, narrow streets in its direction. And all through that night and for most of the next day, hundreds of men and women milled about in the open space in front of the monastery offering prayers as they awaited word as to the condition of the young holy father.

The following day when the hermit Aegidius appeared in the company of Father Paphnutius, shouts arose from the crowd and both were lifted onto the shoulders of younger men and carried to the very door of the monastery.

While the crowds waited outside in the night praying for her recovery, Joanna lay on a straw pallet in a small windowless room raised to almost oven temperature by heated bricks which were constantly replenished. The monks of the monastery, after forcing down her throat a quantity of water in which certain barks had been soaked, almost causing her death from strangulation, then piled a half dozen sheepskins on her, securing them so that no matter how much she thrashed, they would not be dislodged.

Whether it was the prayers of the multitude, the treatment offered by the monks, or Joanna's own recuperative powers, by daybreak she had broken into a drenching sweat.

By the time Aegidius entered her chamber, she was on the way to recovery, although weak as a newborn thrush and scarcely able to

speak. Slowly, and with great deliberation, the hermit, in the presence
of the more than a dozen who had crowded into the chamber, moved
toward Joanna until his renowned shadow fell upon her. Her eyes fluttered open and there was a gasp from the assemblage. Father Paphnutius sank to his knees, quickly followed by Marcos and all the
others. Then they all crossed themselves as they gave thanks to Christ
Jesus for giving the hermit the power to perform this miraculous cure.
Through all of this the hermit triumphantly ginned.

Joanna's mind had cleared to a crystal clarity as a result of that
sweat. Fully realizing what was happening, and sensing what her role
should be, she blessed the hermit in the most feeble of voices, then after blessing the others, she gave thanks to the Lord God for allowing
this miracle. This so pleased Aegidius that he declared he would remain with the young priest until the restoration was complete. Word
of this reached the waiting crowd and was quickly transmitted
throughout the entire city, adding to Joanna's reputation, for the revered hermit had never before offered more than the curative power of
his shadow.

Desperate for some private moments in which to care for her person, Joanna, using her entire store of strength, rose from her pallet
early that afternoon and, assisted by the grinning hermit, entered the
common room of the monastery, declaring to all who were gathered
there that her cure was now complete. At this a great cheer went up,
the younger monks carrying the hermit out into the street on their
shoulders, while Joanna, after bowing and waving, retreated back to
the privacy of her chamber, whose door she then barred.

For the next ten days, despite a persistent weakness and nightly
recurring sweats, Joanna forced herself to attend the morning and evening prayers as proof that she was indeed recovering, thus insuring
that she would be left in privacy the rest of the time. When asked to
join the others for their single midday meal, she offered as an excuse
for refusing a need for a period of continuous prayer and contemplation as proof to the Almighty of her thankfulness for His lifesaving in-
tercession. And, indeed, many of her hours were devoted to prayer,
many to contemplation. Although again and again during these days
while her body mended, her thoughts turned to Wilma.

Several times in her delirium, as she was carried along the road to
Athens, she had engaged in disjointed conversation with Wilma.
Then, during the first night in the heated room, Wilma stood beside
her whispering comforting words and promising she would never
leave her. But with the coming of the drenching sweat and the return
of her clarity of thinking, she re-experienced that terrible feeling of

loneliness she had known years earlier when Gerberta left her with the priest. Never again would there be that closeness, that absolute trust, that understanding which transcended words. No more laughter, no more shared whispers. She tried to force herself to think about that moment some day in the future when they would be reunited in heaven, but this felt hollow. Wilma was no more and she missed her terribly.

During the second day of her stay in the chamber, in the midst of one of her periods of mourning, Joanna remembered what Wilma had said, as they sat partway up the Acropolis, their eyes fixed on the flickering lights of the city lying below: that she wanted this beautiful spot to be her final resting place.

"I promised Brother William that he would be buried on the Acropolis," Joanna said to Marcos as he entered her chamber late that afternoon. "He knew he would die here in Greece." Joanna blinked her eyes rapidly, trying to hold back tears that Marcos pretended not to notice. "It was such a little thing he asked. But now there is nothing that can be done."

Afraid that she would be unable to restrain her sobs Joanna, no longer able to speak, motioned Marcos out of the chamber. The door was scarcely shut when the sobs wrenched themselves from her chest and throat. Marcos hesitated on the other side of the door, listening.

Finally, with a determined nod toward the closed door, he left the monastery and headed north out of Athens in the direction of Father Paphnutius' hut.

Taking great care that his presence was undetected by Father Paphnutius, who had returned the day before and reoccupied his hut after more than three years in the goat shed, Marcos made his way up the hill to the place where Wilma had been buried.

Some of the earth near the grave showed evidences of wild animal activity, but the stones rolled on the grave had protected it thus far. A cloud obscured the three-quarter moon, casting the gravesite into darknness. Marcos sat down on one of the boulders to await its reappearance. For the several hours he had traveled the road from Athens his mind had been occupied continuously with the prospect of unearthing the body, then transporting it on a handcart to the Acropolis. He was almost certain he remembered the exact place where Brother William and Father John had stopped to rest while he continued on to the Parthenon. He would find a spot shaded by an olive or fig tree and after the body had been interred would add touches of decoration by transplanting succulents to border the grave site, and thorny bushes to cover the grave itself for protection. In addition, he would prepare a slate marker on which Brother William's name would be etched, together with a likeness of the cross, so that any who happened upon this grave would know it to be the resting place of a holy man.

The moon having reappeared and his energy fully restored by the few minutes of rest, Marcos set to work. Wrestling away the protecting boulders required a great effort, for he and Father Paphnutius had struggled together to place them on the grave. But one by one they were rolled aside. Digging away the recently turned loose earth required much less effort so that Marcos soon found himself chest deep in the grave with Brother William's hands and portions of his face exposed. At that moment the moon was again obscured by a cloud for which Marcos was grateful. The single glimpse of the twisted features having been quite enough. He worked on in the dark, quickly freeing the body. Then, propping it up, he climbed out of the grave, reached down, took firm hold of the tunic and pulled it out, tearing away portions of the frayed garment during the course of these exertions.

Panting and brushing dirt from his hair and face, Marcos waited for the moon to reappear before he continued with his work.

Finally, the cloud passed and the yellow light revealed that which had been concealed for so long through the tears in the garment.

Marcos leapt backward, tumbling over some of the boulders and almost falling into the grave. Not yet fully comprehending, his heart pounding so hard it felt as if it would explode in his chest his only thought was to tumble the corpse back in the grave and escape from that place. But then, little by little, as his mind calmed and his heart slowed down he began to understand. He forced himself up from where he lay and cautiously approached the corpse. Avoiding its twisted features which scarcely resembled those with which he had grown so familiar, he examined the rest: breasts, withered but unmistakably those of a woman, then the loins. Biting his lower lip so hard he could taste blood, Marcos sat down on a boulder and fixed his eyes on the torso of the corpse.

A gust of wind ruffled a portion of the torn garment. And it was as if this chance movement was a method used by the dead one to mock him. A cold rage for his having been treated like a buffoon gripped Marcos' heart and lungs. How they must have laughed at him. "What a simple fellow," they must have chuckled to one another. In the almost four years they had been together he had not gained even a suspicion of their true sex. In a hundred ways he had treated both of them as brothers, more than brothers. He had shared things about himself with them he would have never revealed, even if tortured, to a woman. How could they have betrayed his loyalty in such a fashion? "I, who showed my friendship in so many ways, yet you would not trust me," he hissed at the corpse. "They could have cut off both of my hands and I would not have revealed your secret." He kicked a clod of earth in the direction of the corpse. He raised his eyes to the three-quarter moon and watched as a ragged edge of a wandering cloud obscured a portion of its surface for several moments. He lowered his eyes to the corpse again. Yet how could they be certain I would not reveal their deception? he asked himself. The trusted secretary of a bishop, raised within the bosom of the Church, such a one, they must have believed, would rage if he learned that two women masquerading as monks, had gained elevation to the diaconate, one ordination as a priest. How should one raised as I was raised not be filled with righteous fury upon learning of a conspiracy which had demeaned my bishop? For their abomination any ecclesiastical court in Christendom would have condemned them to a slow and painful death.

He softly addressed the corpse, "Even though what you did was a terrible abomination, I would not have betrayed you; could not have betrayed Father John. We were friends." He reached his hands out toward the corpse, then let them fall. His eyes fluttered shut, and he allowed images of each to float through his mind. But soon the image of Brother William faded, leaving only that of Father John. He could see the young priest turning away from his glance. How on scores of occasions Father John had reddened at his approach. So many incidents of shyness, shyness from one who had brought a fierce band of bandits to the very walls of Palermo, who had faced up to Bishop Nikitas and to Nikon without flinching. How delicate he had appeared lying under the covering of sheepskin blankets when he had left him. How wan the face, its forehead covered with droplets of perspiration, lips usually of such a rosy hue now a pale blue. A rush of warmth filled his breast. *She is a woman* formed on his lips. Now he understood the intensity of his feelings that at different times had caused him concern. What a remarkable thing these two women had done. The risks they had taken. Their courage greater than most men.

He rose from the boulder and took the several steps to the corpse. "And everything you did, everything Father John did was not for self but for Christ and His Holy Church. How should this be an abomination," he murmured.

He knelt down and carefully rearranged Wilma's garments. Then he crossed her arms on her chest and with gentle movements brushed away the bits of earth clinging to her face. And then he carefully lifted the stiff form, placed it on the hand cart and, after covering it with fresh cut rushes, started in the direction of the Acropolis.

By the time Marcos returned to the monastery two days later, Joanna had grown uneasy at his absence. Despite the monks' concern for her welfare she felt like a stranger in this tight community of bearded men dressed in black with tall black hats on their heads which gave each an almost demonic appearance. When she heard the deep voice she knew so well asking if he might enter, Joanna took several seconds to compose herself then rose from her pallet to greet the man, fighting off an unexpected wave of dizziness.

Marcos' face was burnished from the wind, his hair windblown, and he stood so tall, so broad-shouldered. She ached for the comfort of his thick-muscled arms. But instead she indicated a wooden chest on which he might sit, then lay back down on the pallet, covering herself up to the chin with the sheepskin blanket.

Unable to find any words, which had been the case so often in his presence, Joanna glanced furtively at the man. Ordinarily Marcos stared directly at her and unless she was cautious their eyes would meet for a moment, but this time, his face was turned partially away as he studied with apparent interest the carefully fitted stones that formed the floor of the chamber. She glanced again. His face was still partially turned away and his interest now was directed toward the walls' construction. Joanna fixed her gaze directly on the man and now it was he who stole momentary glances, he whose face was deeply colored. Unable to endure the awkwardness of the situation any longer, Joanna said, "You visited Father Paphnutius?" Without waiting for an answer, she went on, "How is the holy priest?"

His eyes kept carefully on the floor, the finger of one hand tracing the fine space between the various stones, Marcos said, "I passed the priest's hut but did not see him, although as I passed I heard him giving thanks to God in a full voice." Joanna made a questioning sound and Marcos shifted so that now his face was turned completely away. "What you said about Brother William wanting to be buried on the Acropolis," his voice had softened and he slurred his words so that Joanna had to strain to hear. "Well, I thought what harm to grant this request."

"You took...you took Brother William's body to the Acropolis and buried him there?"

"I carried the body to the Acropolis. I buried it in the place you mentioned. The grave is marked with a slate on which I carved a cross and the name William." Marcos suddenly shifted and stared directly at Joanna. "But William is not her name, is it?"

Joanna sucked in her breath as she tried to control a shudder. "No," she whispered, "that was not her name. It was Wilma."

"And your name, Father John? Your name!" Marcos' eyebrows drew together in a frown.

"Joanna." Her mouth felt dry and her face burnt. "Joanna was the name given to me by the monk, my father, the name of my mother who died at my birth."

"How could I have not seen that you are a woman?" Marcos openly examined her features. "Now that I know, I can see it in your eyes, your mouth, the softness of your chin." He shook his head in wonder. "But it was not only I who was deceived. Everyone believes you are a man." He sought her eyes and she did not turn hers away. "Your voice, Father John, Joanna, what is your voice without its disguise."

"The voice of a woman," Joanna allowed it to flow naturally.

"The voice of a woman," Marcos softly repeated.

Several minutes passed without either one of them speaking. Finally Joanna broke the silence.

"You were angry when you discovered my deception." This was not a question, rather a simple statement. Marcos nodded. "I wanted to tell you, more than once the words were on my lips, I wanted so much to tell you but I was afraid to."

"Afraid that I would not understand, that I would be so angry I might betray you."

"You are the secretary to a bishop, Marcos, and you are a man."

"Yes, I was angry, Joanna. Joanna. It is strange to call you by this name. When I unearthed Brother William's...Wilma's corpse and saw...and saw certain things, and then knew you too must be a woman, I was filled with fury. At first I believed you had mocked me. But as my thoughts grew less heated, I understood." He hesitated, then went on. "Perhaps what you have done is an abomination. Yet your disguise allowed you to serve the Church in ways you could never have as a woman. And as I know that our Savior's mother was a woman, I know you will yet serve our church."

"I will serve for the rest of my life."

"Let God judge you, Joanna, if judgement there must be. Your secret is safe with me. More than safe. I will do everything in my power to protect you. But if your deception should ever become known..." He broke off and rubbed his hands over his perspiration-covered forehead. "If they," he made a vague gesture, "if they found out a woman had been ordained a priest." He sucked his breath. "They would destroy you. Even those who have declared their friendship would turn against you."

"Father Paphnutius?"

"Yes, even he. Even he." Marcos rubbed his hand over his forehead again. "Nikon and Tryphon, if they knew, would have you stoned to death."

"Stoned to death," Joanna echoed a whisper. "Wilma warned me against this. She warned me that even you, Marcos..."

"No! No! I swear...I would die for you, Joanna. My feelings for you...I would suffer a hundred tortures and never betray you. I have never felt toward anyone the way I feel toward you." He took Joanna's hand, held it for a moment, then as if it were a burning ember, let it go.

His voice now coming with great effort, his eyes again focused on the stone floor, Marcos went on, "How many times I asked myself, do I suffer from the same affliction of Tryphon and those others whose desires are for ones of their own sex? My feelings for you, Joanna, were so strong at times. How could I have such feelings for a man? I asked myself. How this tortured me. But now I understand. And what a relief is this understanding!" He paused as he attempted to control his rapid breathing. "If I could hope that in time you would feel a tenth part of what I feel for you — "

"A tenth part," Joanna's voice cracked. "Ten times a tenth part, Marcos. And then ten times that."

The man felt waves of heat sweep through his body such as he never experienced before.

"What are we to do?" Marcos' voice vibrated deep in his chest.

"We will love each other, Marcos. We will love each other with a pure love, as if brother and sister. I am still a priest."

"Yes, a priest," Marcos whispered.

More than an hour then passed with the only sounds deep sighs from one or the other. When the bell rang for noonday meal, Marcos slowly got to his feet and then after planting a single kiss on Joanna's forehead walked out of the chamber with the unsteady gait of an old man.

Although it had originally been Joanna's intention to leave the monastery and rejoin Father Paphnutius as soon as her strength had been completely restored, she found reasons to delay her departure, chief of which was its large library of rare books. And although her chief reason for continuing as the honored guest of the monastery was its books, she was not unresponsive to the constant stream of distinguished clerics who visited the monastery with the express purpose of discussing some obscure bit of theologia with the brilliant young German priest. Nor was she displeased by the crowds of Athenians who crowded around her whenever she ventured into the courtyard of the monastery, vying with one another to touch the hem of her robe or to kiss her hands, for her reputation as a healer was second only to that of the hermit Aegidius. She also gained satisfaction when she was called upon to exercise her physician's skills on various wellborn Athenians who were always seeking new ways of dealing with their multitudes of maladies, real and imagined. Yet there were times when Joanna yearned for the quiet of the country, for the clean air and the privacy nowhere to be found in the city of Athens. At these times she might have been willing to abandon all the attentions and advantages of the monastery had it not been for Marcos whose preference clearly lay in the hustle and bustle of the metropolis.

A year passed and Joanna's deepening involvement with the Athenian religious community was such that her yearnings for rejoining Father Paphnutius now rarely surfaced. And it is doubtful if the monks and priests who formed her ever-increasing entourage would have allowed her to quit the monastery even if it had been her intention. By the end of the second year in Athens, her authority had so increased that in all of Greece only the bishop himself held more power among the clerics. As the third year drew to its close, an increasing number of priests and monks were heard to declare that Nikitas had ruled long enough and was growing infirm and senile and should be replaced by a vigorous, young theologian such as Father John.

Although by the beginning of the fourth year of her residence in the monastery a majority of the religious community was declaredly in the camp of Father John, those who remained loyal to the bishop held considerable power and, despite their being a minority, were better organized and more fanatical in their determination. Nikon was clearly the leader of this group and as the schism widened between the anti and pro-Nikitas factions, he let it be widely known that the bishop held a growing suspicion that Father John, beneath his cloak of piety, was in fact a heretic.

Had it not been for the strength of the forces loyal to Joanna, the bishop, under the prodding of Nikon, would have ordered the priest to face an ecclesiastical trial. A dozen times he came within an ace of signing the condemnatory document prepared by the fanatical hermit but, remembering how unpopular he had been during the years of the banishment of the icons and how many of the icon worshippers were now resident in Athens, each time he withheld his signature. But finally realizing that unless he acted, before the passage of another half a year the young priest would be so powerful that even his bishop's mitre would prove no protection, Nikitas ordered a conclave of all the priests of Greece during which each priest would be examined as to the pureness of his piety and his loyalty to the Church.

Marcos burst into Joanna's chamber after he learned of the bishop's intentions, which had been announced by one of the deacons in the courtyard of the monastery. "That ancient tub of fat of a bishop is calling a conclave to test the piety of all the priests, Joanna," he shouted, his face blotched with anger. "But as I know Christ died for us, I know it is nothing more than an elaborate trap fashioned by Nikon to trap just one priest. And that one is you, Joanna." During the three years since his discovery of Joanna's identity, Marcos had transformed an ever-increasing passion for her into a loyalty whose intensity was such that each night in his prayers he begged God for the opportunity of laying down his life for the one he loved.

"Dearest Marcos," she took one of his hands between both of hers as she tried to calm him, "is it possible that you are mistaking shadows for demons?"

Marcos vigorously shook his head.

"To trap just one priest, I can not believe that the bishop would order every priest in Greece to his palace." She smiled at the man and felt her heart quicken as she did every time their eyes met. "When it is my turn to be questioned, I will be cautious with my answers," she went on. "I will choose my words carefully. And no matter how artfully provoked, I will not allow myself to be drawn into a disputation."

"No matter what you say, Nikon will twist your words against you, Joanna. Once inside his palace, the bishop can order you seized and thrown into his dungeon. Inside his palace with his deacons, his bailiffs, and his guards, it may not be possible for your friends to defend you. The bishop is afraid of you, Joanna. And he has reason to be. Do not go. Hide. Give your friends another six months and your position here in Greece will be such that the pope will be forced to declare you bishop. But if you fall into Nikitas' hands, if they ever imprison you in his dungeon — "

"But they must have a reason to imprison me, Marcos," Joanna interrupted. "And I will not provide them with that reason."

"They will find a way to trap you."

"If instead of a woman I were a man, Marcos, would you be as concerned?"

Marcos opened his mouth as if to answer, but instead, after making a vague gesture, he shuffled out of the chamber, muttering under his breath and shaking his head.

Although none of the monks of the monastery were priests, they had voted unanimously to accompany Father John and demand entrance to the palace despite the conclave being called only for priests. A score of the younger monks, after conferring with Marcos, had determined to fight their way into the palace should the bishop's guards deny them entrance. Had this taken place it is possible that segments of the Athenian citizenry would have become involved in this confrontation; that those loyal to the bishop then might have called upon the civil guards for assistance, and then the entire city might have become embroiled. But Aegidius the hermit decided to join the monks accompanying the popular young priest, and not even the most reckless of the bishop's guards dared to so much as question their right of entrance, knowing as they did that the revered hermit with a single gesture could call down an avalanche of citizens who would tear them limb from limb.

Bishop Nikitas masked his feelings with a grin and a wave of welcome the moment he saw that the hermit Aegidius was accompanying Father John. But Nikon — who had made arrangements for the hated priest to be instantly surrounded by a dozen of the bishop's guards — was unable to control his scowl as he saw the object of his hate safely secured in the midst of a half a hundred black-robed monks whose tall hats gave them such a fierce, almost frightening appearance. And he struggled against bearing his teeth in a snarl as he noticed that hanging from the belt of every monk was both a heavy cross and a knife used for carving meat.

As the contingent pushed its way through the several hundred milling priests, Nikon, unable to control himself, shouted, "What sort of an entrance is this into the bishop's presence, Father John? Only you, of all the many priests invited to this holy concave, come surrounded by armed retainers. Is it that you do not trust your bishop?"

"Armed retainers, friend Nikon?" growled Aegidius, pointing a dirt-encrusted long, bony finger. "Do you say that Aegidius, who serves only Christ, is a retainer?"

Nikon quickly shook his head.

"And these cloistered monks, friend Nikon, who have torn themselves away from their devotions to declare their love for their bishop, do you call these servants of Christ retainers?"

Nikon hunched down and chewed his lower lip.

"And so as not to tax the hospitality of the bishop, these good monks come supplied with their own cutlery. Is this a reason to accuse them of coming armed?"

Nikon's shoulders were up to his ears and a wordless mumble came from his chest.

"I cannot believe that you view the holy cross worn by these men as weapons, my brother in Christ." The hermit's voice rose. "If I heard any man refer to the cross in such a fashion, I doubt I could restrain my hand from hurling a rock at that one." With that Aegidius took a seat directly in front of the bishop's dais, gestured Joanna to sit next to him, then indicated that the rest of the monks should take their places on both sides, which they did by unceremoniously elbowing more than a score of priests out of the way.

Flapping his broad, soft, bejeweled hand as if to brush away whatever remnants of discontent that yet remained, Bishop Nikitas, after nodding at Aegidius who had fastened his bulging, unblinking eyes upon him, ordered the tests of priestly piety to begin.

One by one, as their names were shouted out by the bailiff, the priests came forward, many ashen-faced and trembling as memories of the icon persecution were stirred to the surface of their minds. In just such conclaves clerics had been summarily condemned to the amputation of both hands, to scourging through the city streets until their flesh hung in shreds from their backs, or if the judges were in a merciful mood, to banishment from Athens. One by one, the priests came forward, were asked questions by various deacons with an occasional question from the bishop and were then blessed and dismissed. Despite there being no condemnation and despite the nature of the questioning — in friendly voices with the questioners nodding and smiling — each priest approached the tribunal with some degree of trepidation, for even the most pious of priests have, if not behavior, at least thoughts they would prefer to keep secret.

During the questioning of the first score or so of priests, most of the others in the great chamber maintained a degree of decorum as they listened to the standard responses. But then as it all became routine the noise level grew until at times the bailiff had to pound his staff on the wooden floor as he attempted to restore order. But as the number who had been questioned and then dismissed grew greater and greater, the bailiff's success at restoring order grew less and less. Those who had successfully passed the test of piety swapped anecdotes, laughed uproariously, shared with one another pulls of wine from goat skin flasks, and offered shouted encouragement to those still awaiting their turn.

But when the bailiff called out: "Father John of the city of Engelheim!" within moments the shouts and laughter ceased, the goat skin flasks were corked and laid aside as every one of the several hundred pairs of eyes focused on Joanna.

She arose, stepped forward and positioned herself directly in front of the bishop. During these few moments Nikon signalled toward the door and was quickly joined by a tall man whose blond hair and fur cloak declared he came from a country far to the north. During the first several questions, which were routine in nature and were easily answered by Joanna, Nikon and the stranger earnestly engaged in whispered conversation. But then when the bishop asked in what way she guarded herself against the implantation of heretical thoughts by Satan or one of his minions, before Joanna had a chance to answer, Nikon leapt to his feet and shouted: "Guard against Satan, Your Eminence! This one welcomes that diabolical one." Uneasy murmurs rippled through the audience as the priests who were standing close to Joanna began to ease away. "For this so-called priest, the issue is not a chance heretical thought which even the most holy of us must at different times contend with. No, Your Eminence, with this clean-shaven man from Germany where this merchant also resides," he pointed at the blond stranger, "for John, or whatever his true name is, the question that needs be asked must deal with acts of witchcraft!" At this, a number of the monks of Joanna's monastery moved backward, darting glances at one another, while a dozen of the bishop's guards took up positions on both sides of her, as, at the same time three of the tallest guards surrounded Marcos, who had risen from his seat, pinioning his arms to his sides.

"Witchcraft, you say witchcraft, my brother in Christ?" The bishop shifted his bulk until he faced Nikon. "Such an accusation made without sufficient justification can lead to the condemnation of the accuser."

"I realize the seriousness of my accusations, Your Eminence," said Nikon in a thundering voice. "And should they prove frivolous, I will gladly pay the terrible penalty reserved for the practitioners of this black art." By now all of the monks who had accompanied Joanna had moved so far from her they were interspersed amongst the ranks of the priests. Only the hermit Aegidius remained where he was, but he appeared to be almost unaware of the proceedings as he sat closed-eyed with his chin pressed down against his chest.

Silently repeating the words of the Pater Noster as a method of keeping her emotions under control, Joanna continued to face the bishop with not so much as a single glance in Nikon's direction.

"The Lord God works in mysterious ways that are but poorly comprehended by mere mortals," Nikon went on. "And His hand is always sure and steady, never more so than when He protects His own Church against threats from the Fallen One. Thus it was no mere chance that this merchant from Germany, this honorable man from the city of Aachen, should have found his way to the city of Athens at this time." Nikon paused as he allowed his glance to move slowly around the great chamber, taking in the hundreds of intent expectant faces. "From the first moment I laid eyes on that one, Your Eminence," Nikon made a contemptuous hand motion in Joanna's direction, "from the very first moment that smooth-cheeked, soft featured creature entered this chamber more than seven years ago, I had my suspicions. But we are Christian, not pagan, thus we must keep suspicions, unless proven, to ourselves. And my suspicions have only increased as I followed the career of this so-called priest. How other than by the use of witchcraft did he so quickly gather his coterie of learned theologians of advanced years and he a youth whose mother's milk yet clings to his lips? How else other than by the casting of spells could he have converted Father Paphnutius, whose erudition and piety are well-known throughout the Christian world, to the condition of a toady? But today, Your Eminence, today it is God's will that my suspicions are confirmed." The hundreds in that large chamber stood silent. It was as if all held their breaths. "The name of this so-called priest and that of his deceased consort in witchcraft, William, are well known in the city of Aachen. Is that not so, honorable sir?" Nikon turned for a moment to the merchant who, after hearing a whispered translation from Greek to Latin from one of the deacons, inclined his head. "This John and that other one insinuated themselves into the presence of the bishop of that great city. And then in his presence and in the presence of all the notables who were gathered in the great cathedral, the other one displayed his witchcraft by turning himself into a woman and then back again to a man. So frightened were the townspeople and, alas, the bishop, fearing as they did that by use of some incantation the cathedral would be pulled down around their heads, they allowed the two to have their own way, even going so far as to grant them sumptuous quarters in the cathedral itself."

The bishop, whose attention had been riveted on Nikon, now turned to Joanna, making a series of clucking sounds such as those made by a patient mother to a misbehaving child.

"There is more, Your Eminence, much more," said Nikon in a feigned sorrowful voice. "In an attempt to gain the sympathy of the good fathers of the Aachen cathedral, this John accused one of the bishop's loyal servants of making an attempt against his life. So distraught was that poor man who enjoyed a well-deserved reputation for loyalty and obedience that in a fit of despondency, he committed the cardinal sin of suicide." Nikon sighed deeply. "More to be pitied than condemned, that one," he said in a stage whisper. Most of the gathered priests nodded their agreement. "Grieved at the loss of his faithful servant and troubled with suspicions about his two 'guests', the bishop ordered that they be confined to their room with a sufficient guard set to prevent their escape." Nikon broke off and engaged in a hurried whispered consultation with the German merchant. Then, taking several steps so that he stood alongside the bishop, directly facing Joanna, he went on. "When their closely guarded chamber was entered the following morning, they were gone! Only one door led into that chamber, Your Excellency, and that was barred from the outside. The windows were so narrow that only a ferret could have made egress, and then a sheer drop of more than a hundred feet." Nikon glared at Joanna. "Scores of honest men and women reported they had witnessed a pair of crows emerge from that window just after sunrise and then fly high over the city, disappearing into the haze of the morning to the south."

"Crows," the bishop muttered with a shudder.

"Black crows, Your Eminence. And this honorable merchant was one of those who saw that pair of crows and will so swear." Again there was a hurried translation of Greek to Latin and the merchant vigorously nodded. Then the merchant added that his father had been present when the other one turned himself into a woman and back again into a man. That he had come from the cathedral ashen faced and had taken to his bed with a fever as a result of this experience.

"Witchcraft! Vile witchcraft," the bishop said in a choked voice.

"Witchcraft?" said the hermit Aegidius who, up to that moment, appeared to be asleep. "An act no matter how unnatural it may be, does not establish witchcraft until the reasons for the act are determined. If they are diabolical, then, a just condemnation. But if it be shown that the act or acts were in the service of the Lord God..." The hermit broke off as he unwound his bony body, bringing himself to his feet. "If a sorcerer through the use of the blackest of arts caused the sun to stand still in the sky so that the ravaging of a Christian city might be completed by a horde of followers of the vile Mahamat, that would be witchcraft."

The bishop nodded slowly and made a sound in his chest which he hoped would convince the audience that he understood more than he did of what the hermit was getting at.

"Yet if a warrior in the service of the Almighty, so that he may complete his conquest for the just, causes the sun to pause for a time in the sky, is that witchcraft? When Joshua on the day his forces conquered the Amorites prayed that the sun stand still upon Gibeon and the sun so stood, giving the Israelites an extra hour of daylight; was that witchcraft?"

A buzz of murmurs and whispers filled the chamber while Aegidius took a sip of wine to relieve a dryness in his throat which caused his voice to crack.

"Had this young priest employed certain devices so that he might then consort with the Devil," the hermit continued, "that would be proof that the devices sprang from witchcraft. But is the Christian conversion of an entire village of heathen Sicilian bandits a matter which would gain for this John Satan's approval? And what of his attempt to free Palermo and its Christian bishop from the hands of the Saracens? Was that an act pleasing to the Devil? No, Your Eminence, despite Nikon's zeal, I hear no evidence of witchcraft. That transformation from man to woman of the deceased William could only have taken place with the assistance of the blessed Mother Mary who by this act affirmed to the theologians of Aachen that two strangers who had entered into their midst were holy ones. And then, realizing that these same two ones had been imprisoned and might well suffer some terrible fate, the Lord God ordered two of his archangels to carry them from their prison. Those were no crows your merchant saw, Nikon. Rather, the archangels Michael and Gabriel, doing the Lord's bidding so that this young priest and his revered companion could continue their service to Christ. Which they did, Nikon! Which they did, Your Eminence. Which Father John, whom I know to be amongst the most pious of men, whom I am honored to call brother and friend, still does." With that Aegidius placed his hands on Joanna's head and blessed her.

During the course of the hermit's speech, one by one, the monks of Joanna's monastery came forward, shoving aside the bishop's guards until, by the time the hermit offered his blessing, they formed a tight guard, each holding his cross aloft.

"We are grateful, holy hermit, for the clarity you have added to these proceedings," said the bishop after darting an angry glance at

Nikon. "It was my hope when I called this conclave that there would be just such offerings for the enrichment of my priests." Shifting his attention to Joanna, he went on. "My faith in your piety and dedication, my dearest brother in Christ, John, has been, if anything, further increased so that I, ah, feel impelled to demonstrate the depth of this faith and, yes, affection.

"How many hundreds of nights of sleep I have lost since you first made your report of the terrible calamity which took place in Palermo, no one will ever know. How many scores of nights given up in their entirety to praying for the well-being of my episcopal brother enslaved by the vile caliph, only the Lord God Himself knows." The bishop ponderously shook his head. "Knowing of the ranks of self-servers who surround the Holy Father in Rome, I knew it would be a futile thing to send a written communication begging that Christian forces be dispatched to liberate that portion of Sicily in the hands of Saracens. Yet my frail health did not allow me to make the long journey to Rome to offer my petition in person." The bishop sighed. "What to do? What to do? I begged God for guidance and here, today, I have finally gained this guidance.

"I appoint you my emissary, Father John."

Nikon groaned and turned his head away, while a buzz of excitement swept through the rest of the assemblage.

"Your name is not unknown to Rome, Father John. Go to Rome and you will have no difficulty in gaining an audience with the Holy Father. Stay in that city as long as you must — there will be, alas, those who will oppose you. In time, if it is God's will, your eloquence and persistence will gain the results so near and dear to my heart. Go to Rome, young priest, and assure the pontiff that Bishop Nikitas will supply double his quota of troops for the liberation of Palermo, if called upon. Go to Rome, dearest Brother John. And go at once!"

VIII

ROME

$\mathcal{T}$ he ship from Athens carrying Joanna and Marcos entered the estuary of the River Tiber. Scores of gutted stone houses, crumbled fortifications and piles of fire-blackened rubble still stood as stark evidence of the Saracen attack against Rome three years earlier. But as the ship slowly maneuvered up the river and approached Rome, there was less and less evidence remaining of this incursion, for under the benevolent direction of Leo IV, the citizens of Rome, who had much love for this pontiff, had not only repaired most of the damage, but had undertaken the construction of new fortifications.

As Joanna and Marcos finally disembarked, together with the rest of the passengers, they were forced to fight their way through a gauntlet of street hawkers, beggars, and ragged urchins who raised such a din that their seasick-frayed nerves were strained to the limits of their endurance. But unlike the other passengers, whose struggles with these screaming, clutching, shoving men and boys continued well into the city, Joanna and Marcos were quickly freed of this annoyance by a company of armed servants in the employ of the bishop of Porto. Unbeknownst to Joanna, Father Paphnutius had written to his longtime friend, who had gained the reputation as the leading exorcist in all of Christendom, asking that he take the young priest under his personal protection. The servants of the bishop, confident of the power of their master, which some declared was second only to the Pope, made free with their fists and staves as they cleared a path through the rabble. And more than one street hawker whose face was bloodied, instead of showing resentment, saluted the armed men as if the rough treatment was some sort of honorable recognition.

Although the streets they traveled were wide and paved with carefully fitted blocks of stone, the stench that rose from the gutters choked with human excrement, decaying carcasses of dogs and cats, kitchen garbage, and matter so decomposed as to defy identification, was as overpowering as had been the odors of the narrow, twisting streets of Engelheim. And although the houses lining these streets were of grand construction, faced with marble and decorated with intricate carvings, the inhabitants of these fine houses were just as free about throwing their slops unceremoniously out the doors and windows as were the smoke-blackened peasants of the meanest hut of Joanna's native village. As the small procession moved in the direction of the Vatican Hill, where the bishop of Porto maintained his principle residence, it passed other like companies of armed servants that, in respect to the dignity of their masters, refused to give way. There was much shoving and cursing, yet beneath it all, a certain good-naturedness, and no one was injured.

Despite a slight queasiness, stimulated by the combination of stench and heat, Joanna felt exhilarated. To be in the city of the Caesars, the city of St. Peter's martyrdom, of Constantine's conversion, to be in the very heart of Christendom! "I feel as if I have come home, Marcos," she said in an emotion-choked voice. To this, Marcos, who was experiencing none of her elation and who was suffering from a wracking headache, merely shrugged. "If it is God's will I will spend the rest of my life here," said Joanna, her voice trailing off as she remembered that she and Wilma had declared that they would one day return to the convent. Then for a time it was as if a veil lay over her eyes as all of her thoughts were with Wilma.

The day before they boarded the ship for Rome, she had visited Wilma's grave alone. During the three years in Athens, not a month passed without at least one visit to that place part way up on the Acropolis, where she would spend several hours talking to her friend as she tended the grave and planted fresh flowers. During these peaceful hours, it was as if the years dissolved and she was at the grave of the mother she had never known. At times the two dead women became one and then somehow, infused with life from that other woman who was Christ's mother, became a presence with whom she could earnestly converse and from whom flowed understanding and love. "I must go to Rome," she had whispered to the settling mound that last visit to the gravesite. "You understand why I must go, dearest Wilma." The words felt like shards of broken glass, piercing and cutting her chest and throat. Blinded by her tears, she had stumbled against boulders and thorn bushes so that her hands and face were badly scratched by the time she reached the place where Marcos was waiting. And then for the first time since she had met the man that day almost eight years earlier in the city of Palermo, her heart was numbed to him, and this numbing, which he perceived and which caused him deep distress, continued until the ship they boarded the next day was out of sight of land.

Joanna was jolted back into the present by a shouted greeting from a tall, pock-marked man dressed in laborer's clothes who was digging in a large, carefully tended garden they had entered. Throwing down his mattock, the man approached with his dirt-stained, heavily-calloused hand outstretched. Marcos took a step forward and was about to interpose himself between Joanna and the man, who dripped with perspiration, when he noticed the rigid postures of the armed servants, and then saw on the middle finger of the outstretched hand, a thick ring, set with rubies in the form of a cross.

"You are the priest from Athens?" the man addressed Marcos, taking a sudden powerful grip on his hand. Marcos, who was unprepared for this bone grinding hand shake, winced, then shook his head. "Not this one!" The man disengaged his hand and brought it down on Joanna's shoulder, but only with a fraction of the force of which he was capable. "So fine featured, so delicately boned...not at all as I imagined after reading that laudatory letter from Father Paphnutius." With an easy familiarity, he tipped Joanna's face up and stared down into her eyes.

Angered by this familiarity and scarcely aware of what she was doing, Joanna brushed the man's hand away and took a full step backward. "Ho, ho my young priest. Is that a way to treat the Bishop of Porto?" The man released an explosive laugh, then with a sweeping movement of his arm, pulled Joanna forward into a crushing embrace. "From the nature of your deeds, rumors of which have circulated through Rome for the past several years, my expectation was a broad-shouldered wolf with savage fangs. Then after reading the details in that letter sent to me from Geece, the wolf had become a full-maned lion whose roar will terrify every other creature. But here I find the famed priest John, who tamed an entire village of Sicilian bandits, to be neither lion nor wolf, not even so much as a fox." Again the man discharged an explosive laugh. "A ferret. I will risk a thousand years in purgation if you are not a ferret, little priest."

The bishop released Janna from his crushing embrace, during which she had been scarcely able to breathe. "Yet a ferret is no mean fellow. He is quick and sly, is known to have a savage temper, fears no one, and if cornered can prove to be as savage as a beast ten times his size." The bishop stepped backward several paces and openly surveyed Joanna. "I had hoped for a lion I might lead through the streets of Rome, striking fear into the hearts of the multitudes of sinners who live in this wicked city. Although I am still feared," he rolled back his lips, exposing his large, sharp teeth in a frightening grin, "as chief exorcist my eyes have also learned to see the evil hidden in the hearts of men. Yet the populace has grown used to me so that the fear and trembling I once caused when I went abroad amongst them now grows less. But accompanied by that fierce lion from Athens, was my thought, they will sink to their knees in stark terror as before. But to walk the streets with a ferret, little priest, no matter how dangerous that ferret may be if pressed, will, I fear, instead of inspiring terror, cause much laughter."

During all of this, Marcos scowled and several times was on the verge of interrupting the bishop. But there was something about the manner of the man that cautioned him against any hasty action. And then there was that ache in his hand from the crushing handclasp, and the rigid, respectful postures of the armed servants who stood with impassive faces on both sides of him.

"You are angered because you think I insult or mock your priest." The bishop suddenly turned to Marcos. "From the look on your face, it is either anger or that you suffer an excess of gas." Again the explosive laughter. "Well, I suppose if I were this little priest's companion, I too would be angered. But, friend Marcos, I do not mock. It is my habit to speak my mind with as much honesty as I am capable. Already I find myself loving your priest for his fine features please me. And the manner in which he brushed away my hand here in the presence of my servants, who at a signal from me would beat him senseless, proves he has pluck, although there are some who might declare this act as rash. Are you rash, little priest?"

"If defending against rudeness be an act of rashness, then I am rash."

"Very good. Oh, very good. This is a ferret whose sharp teeth are not only in his jaws but in his words." With that, the bishop put his powerful arm around Joanna's shoulders, disregarding her stiffened response, and, chuckling to himself, marched her through the garden to his residence with Marcos, surrounded by the armed servants, following close behind.

Despite the Bishop of Porto's power and prominence, his residence was not half so ornate as had been that of Nikitas, a much lesser bishop. The rooms were smaller and indifferently decorated, the floors were of rough wood covered by rushes instead of marble covered with rugs, even the reception chamber had a feeling of meanness, for it was low-ceilinged and poorly lit.

Scarcely an hour after being shown the room she was to occupy —
from its narrowness and sparse furnishings, more a monk's chamber
than a room for a great bishop's guest — Joanna was ordered into the
bishop's presence.

Not expecting to be summoned so soon, she had made no effort to
freshen up, but had spent the time resting and conversing with Marcos through the almost paper-thin wall which separated his chamber
from hers. Although at first she had attempted to conceal her feelings,
a series of deep sighs followed by a rush of sobs finally gave her away.
Resting her cheek against the wall through which she could almost
feel the warmth of Marcos' cheek, she murmured, "A thousand times
my thoughts turned to Rome. I knew that sooner or later the forces
which control my life would direct me to this place. And when I
thought about this city, there was an excitement, Marcos. My heart
would speed up and the tips of my fingers would tingle. And as we
walked through the streets, despite the terrible odors, my body felt so
light it was as if I walked on air. But now there is a heaviness. And it
was not that exchange with the bishop which caused this heaviness,
dearest friend. Not that. Rather, just being here, at the very heart of
Christ's Holy Church. I feel...I feel, Marcos, the weight of the Church
pressing down on me. And should I fail to hold up my share of this
weight, a terrible calamity will take place."

"Atlas holding up the world," Marcos had murmured through
the thin wall with just a suggestion of a laugh. "My beloved Joanna,
straining under all that great mass."

"You laugh," Joanna had said in a hurt voice.

"I laugh...I laugh not to mock you, dearest love. I laugh to blunt
my feelings. I ache to shoulder a portion of that burden — I understand that burden — yet I am helpless. What sort of a man is he who
will not free the one he loves of a crushing weight? Yet I am helpless.
That is why I laugh, Joanna. I can see what lies ahead of you here in
Rome. Terrible burdens that would crush a dozen like me to extinc-
tion." His words had ended with a hollow groan.

Then, in silence, each had intensely felt the presence of the other
through the thin partition. It was the summons to attend the bishop,
shouted from the passageway outside their rooms, that shattered the
silence.

Still deeply weighted with depression and acutely conscious of
her travel-worn appearance, Joanna followed the bailiff sent to fetch
her in a sort of a shuffle, her head bowed so that her chin rested on her
chest. But the moment she entered the reception chamber with its
scores of clerics milling about, as if a coil of spring steel had been re-

leased within her, she straightened up, squared her shoulders, directed her eyes dead ahead, and marched forward with the firm step of a seasoned soldier. So determined was her step that the others gathered for this audience gave way, making a path directly to the bishop.

The contrast between this robed and mitred personage, who sat beneath a silken canopy on an elaborately carved throne with a cape of the whitest ermine on his lap, and the man who had greeted her in the garden wearing sweat-stained begrimed laborer's clothing, was such that Joanna was unable to conceal her surprise. Then when the bishop addressed her with serious, measured words, his face set in a scowl without the slightest trace of the casual banter he had earlier displayed, there were moments when Joanna was almost convinced that this was a different individual altogether.

"We are honored to receive the servant of Christ about whom we have heard so many favorable reports." The bishop held out his ring and Joanna dropped to one knee as she delivered the required kiss. "Rome is in great need of priests of your dedication, Father John," the bishop continued. "From the communication I received from my learned and holy friend, Father Paphnutius, I know the purpose of your visit to Rome, my brother in Christ."

At this a surprised murmur ran through the audience, for it was the first time they had heard the Bishop of Porto address one of a lower rank as brother.

"Knowing of your eloquence and of the depth of your fervor, my friend, rather than my informing this assemblage of the purpose of your visit, may I request that you share this information in your own words."

A hush fell over the assemblage, which numbered something over a hundred, at least half of whom were present as information gatherers for other bishops, archdeacons, various high-ranked noble men, with several who reported directly to Pope Leo himself.

Conscious again of her travel-stained appearance, Joanna struggled against the urge to wipe the perspiration from her face with her sleeve, to brush the dust clinging to her robe, to lock her grime-encrusted hands behind her. The attention of everyone in the large chamber was directed at her, and she swallowed several times, trying to relieve a tightness in her throat. Then, taking in a deep breath, she allowed her eyes to close for several moments as her mind turned to the day she had entered Marseilles and stood on the platform before that expectant audience. But this time there was no Wilma with whom to share the performance. For Joanna knew that a performance, not a simple statement of her purpose, was required by this waiting audience.

"Armed with curved swords, lusting for the flesh of Christian maidens, the blood of Christian men, with the name of vile prophet Mahamat on their lips, Saracen soldiers descended upon the peaceful populace of Sicily." Joanna's voice rang out. "Swooping down on unprotected coastal villages, these heathen Africans who cursed the name of Christ disemboweled peasants and fisherman." Joanna snatched a staff from one of the bishop's servants and made violent, slashing motions with it in every direction as choking, gasping sounds issued from her open mouth. A number of the clerics pushed backwards. "Their men dead or made prisoner, the Saracens then had their way with the Christian women of these villages."

Joanna sank to her knees, hunched her shoulders together, raised her hands as if in supplication, crying out in a high-pitched voice: "No, no, no!" Rising from this crouch and covering her face with her arm as if in shame, she limped slowly around the open space, uttering a series of deep groans.

"Having established a foothold on this Christian island, the Saracens then determined to capture the great city of Palermo," Joanna reverted to her oratorical stance. "Despite the bravery of this city's inhabitants, the Saracens finally conquered!" Joanna suddenly brought the staff down on the wooden floor with all her strength. The sound caused the audience to stiffen. "The city captured, they then enslaved the bishop."

Joanna laid the staff aside, sank to her knees, clasped her cross in her hands as she bowed her head, her lips forming the words of the Paternoster, her body violently shuddering from time to time as if in response to kicks and blows. Her head still bowed, the cross still held in both hands, Joanna carefully rose and moved slowly around the chamber, the audience giving way before her. "And the Bishop of Palermo is still enslaved." Her voice cracked with emotion. "Chained like a dog at night in the caliph's privy, in the day forced to do that abominable one's bidding as he is spit upon and otherwise reviled in a thousand ways." Moving backwards until she stood to one side of the bishop, Joanna directly faced the audience and extended her arms, palms upward. "I have come to Rome to urge the liberation of Palermo and the rest of Sicily that lies under Saracen control. I have come hoping to gain the ear of the Pontiff, that he may order a holy crusade against the infidel."

"The reports I have gained of your eloquence, my Christian brother, were not exaggerated." The bishop nodded at Joanna, then slowly and elaborately made the sign of the cross. "Nor were the reports of this priest's modesty." The bishop turned to the audience. "Not once during the course of his stirring presentation did Father John make so much as a single mention of his attempt to liberate Palermo and free its martyred bishop." With that the Bishop of Porto gave a detailed account of the attack against the Saracens of Palermo and the events leading up to this attack, exaggerating Joanna's role so that in his account she was put at the head of the attacking forces. Then when she attempted to clarify her role, the bishop, in a fatherly manner, waved her silent as he made additional references regarding the modesty of this young priest.

Having communicated everything he intended to and not wanting to risk any dilution of his fulsome praise which might take place if his guest were subjected to a session of questions and answers, the bishop ordered all to leave in silence with their thoughts and prayers directed toward the enslaved Bishop of Palermo and the many thousands of suffering Sicilian Christians.

When the last of his guests had departed, the bishop dismissed his servants who, at a gesture from him, marched Marcos out of the room with them, leaving Joanna and him alone.

His mouth widening into a wolfish grin exposing the tips of his sharply pointed teeth, the bishop winked at Joanna as he pulled off his mitre, cast aside the ermine robe, then got up from his throne and stretched, releasing a great belch which echoed through the chamber.

"You are no ferret, Father John. With all your pretty features and delicate bones, you are no ferret that can be beaten to death with a stick or driven off by a single hunting dog." The bishop belched again and patted his stomach. "You will not take offense if I now compare you to a certain species of adder that makes its home amidst the rocks of the desert. Delicate-appearing, its finely textured skin reflecting the colors of the rainbow, this fellow's bite is so deadly that death comes in an instant. Yet I understand this adder will bite only when provoked and if treated with love and consideration can prove to be a loyal friend." The bishop winked and grinned again. "It is to my advantage to have the adder as my friend. The adder with his quickness, his skill, his ability to kill when needs be, can, if properly directed, do much for the Church. The Church," the bishop repeated. "As for the adder, he will find more than enough to recommend a sworn friendship with this old wolf." The bishop's thick eyebrows pulled together into a frown. "The very moment you set foot in this city you amassed an awesome number of enemies, my friend."

Joanna made as if to speak, but the bishop waved her silent.

"As long as you were separated from the seat of power which is the Pope, it was easy enough for the hundreds who gain their position and influence from him to admire your piety and your deeds. And had you moved eastward to Byzantium or beyond, this admiration would have grown as your distance from Rome increased. But here in Rome you are a threat. I can count on the fingers of one hand those of the Pope's court who sincerely desire reform."

The bishop's eyes bored into the eyes of Joanna. "Yes, I am one of those." He stroked his jaw with the tips of his fingers as if he had one time worn a beard. "For most of the Pope's court, reform would deny them preference for their bastards whose number must exceed a thousand, for they are vigorous fornicators. Reform would cost many of them their positions, would dry up the considerable income which flows from bribes, would lead to the condemnation, trial and punishment of more than a few. And they know how eager is the populace of Rome for a pious young priest whose chasteness shows in his every gesture, in his angelic expression, as your chasteness shows, Father John. A young priest who will enter the Pope's palace and cleanse it as did that greatest of priests in the courtyard of the temple.

"As for your holy crusade against the Saracens, there is not one admitted to the Pope's court who will declare that he opposes such a crusade. But it is always next year, or the year after, never now. The cost of such a crusade would reduce the flow of gold into their pockets. Besides, they might be called upon to participate and, with few exceptions, they have grown soft and fat from easy living.

"Depart from Rome, Father John, and you will again become revered by those who inhabit the Pope's court. But remain here and you have many deadly enemies who are already conspiring to destroy you. That is why you need this old wolf, this wolf who had inflicted his share of scars on the toadies of the Pope's court; that is why you need the Bishop of Porto as your friend."

Joanna had listened intently during all of this long monologue. And it was as if the words of the bishop were bricks and mortar which, as they issued from his mouth, formed a solid structure on which she took her place alongside the man. There were things about the bishop she did not like: an arrogance which declared a contempt for most other human beings, the ease with which he changed his manner, depending upon his audience. And, she suspected, there were times he could be cruel without a twinge of conscience. Yet she was certain she could trust him and for the moment there was nothing more important.

She was about to ask how best to arrange an audience with the

Pope when the bishop, as if he could hear unspoken words as easily as those given breath, declared: "Your position would be strengthened an incalculable amount, my friend, if the Pope calls you into his presence without you soliciting an audience. There is one who has the close ear of the Pope who, if he learns you solicit an audience, will make certain you are kept waiting for days, even weeks. And your request for an audience will give this one an opportunity to fill the Pontiff's ears with quantities of scurrilous material, and then when you finally appear, there will be nothing to prevent this one from subjecting you to a subtle kind of ridicule of which he is a master."

"I have such a sworn enemy who has the ear of the Pope?" Joanna was bewildered.

"This one would be your enemy even had you journeyed to Byzantium rather than Rome. He is a friend to one with whom you are not unacquainted, my young friend. You are familiar with the name Nikon?" The bishop showed his wolf-like grin. "Bishop Arsenius of Orte has carried on a close correspondence with that so-called hermit for more than twenty years. And I have gained certain information from a man in that bishop's employ who is secretly sworn to me that not less than six communications have been received recently from Athens, all in the hand of Nikon and all primarily concerned with a certain young priest named John who's birthplace was the district of Engelheim. This Arsenius of Orte, although he wears the clerical garb, is a master politician. And, may the Lord preserve us from them, he has two nephews, Ado and Anastasius, who rival their uncle in political acumen and far exceed him in their acuity and the diabolical nature of their thinking. Who is enemy to the uncle is enemy to the nephews, my friend; and these three alone will prove to be troublesome enough. Yet there are others, many others, who will join their ranks, of that you can be certain.

"We will find a retreat for you here in the city of Rome. A scholarly place. A place where you will be safe and where your abilities can be put to use immediately. While you live humbly in this place where no one would dare to molest you, I will do my work with Pope Leo to whom I too have access."

Joanna nodded. "So, we have made our preliminary plans." Again the wolflike grin. "But tell me, Father John, what are your ambitions? After you have urged your crusade against the Saracens, after you have insinuated yourself into the good graces of the Pope, which with my help you will certainly do, then what? Do you seek the bishop's mitre, pious priest? The cardinal's cap? You have no bastards whose fortune you seek to advance. No clamoring clan urging you to gain preferment for them. So, tell me, what are your ambitions? I will declare myself your confessor, thus what you reveal will, excepting God, never be known by another."

Taking in a deep breath and tightening the muscles of her chest and stomach, Joanna looked directly into the bishop's eyes for several long moments. "My confessor. The Bishop of Porto my confessor. A signal honor for a young priest. Then hear my confession, Bishop." Joanna crossed herself. "I am guilty of the sin of holding vile thoughts regarding one who holds high rank in Christ's Holy Church. A bishop. I confess that I must use all the forgiveness of which I am capable to restrain myself from spitting in that one's face for his insinuations. May I be forgiven for this unChristian feeling."

His eyes narrowed into slits, his face in a full scowl, the bishop leaned toward Joanna as if he were about to spring.

"Do I gain absolution for my sins, Your Eminence?"

The bishop cleared his throat several times, then in a dry voice said the words and made the sign of the cross.

"As for my ambitions, Your Eminence, they are to serve the Church in whatever way I am called upon to do. When no longer useful to the Church due to age, infirmity, or some other reason, then to be allowed to return to the district of my birth to spend whatever time that may be left in quiet contemplation. Those are my ambitions, Your Eminence. Nothing else."

The bishop's scowl softened and then turned into a smile. A true smile, not a grin. "Father Paphnutius did not misjudge you, my friend. Forgive me for putting you to this test. I should have accepted the judgement of my dear and most holy friend without question." With that, still smiling, the bishop again held out his ring for the required kiss.

A swirl of thoughts and emotions agitated Joanna's brain so that she could not sleep. She had raced to her room after leaving the bishop, filled to the bursting with things she wanted to say to Marcos. But the soft snores coming from the other side of the thin partition told her she would have to wait til morning.

A half a dozen times she settled herself down to sleep, but each time her eyes would spring open as a portion of what the bishop had told her invaded her thinking: Unknown enemies at the papal court. A powerful bishop who had the pontiff's ear who was a friend of Nikon. The corruption that existed within the ranks of much of the Roman clergy. The need for what amounted to a conspiracy to gain for her an audience with the Pope.

Marcos groaned, mumbled some incomprehensible words, then settled back into a deep sleep. A sheet of wood scarcely the thickness of her thumb separated her from the man. She felt an ache in her throat which gradually descended into her chest, into her belly and finally down into her loins. She had felt this ache before, yet with stern thoughts she had been able to drive it away. But this time the ache took hold of her and would not let go. She dug her nails deep into her thighs until her eyes began to water. She rose from her pallet and started for the door of the chamber — once out in the passageway it was but a single step to Marcos' door — but then she forced herself back down on the pallet, digging her nails deep into the muscles of her thighs again.

Morning found Joanna exhausted and in a state of agitation bordering on confusion. What would have happened had she been forced to remain in that chamber through another day and night there is no way of knowing. But fate so decreed there would be thick stone walls to provide a sufficient separation, for at the bishop's instruction they were taken to the monastery of St. Martino shortly after daybreak. And it had been constructed as a monastic fortress with none of the walls inside or out less than three feet thick.

Joanna's agitation, which at least in part was a reaction to the miasma that arose from the swampland surrounding the city, turned into a fever within hours of her settling down in the cold, damp stone chamber of the monastery. Thus the monks, who had excitedly looked forward to being nourished by the erudition of their renowned guest, were forced to spend the first week supplying nourishment, the nourishment of thick soups and draughts brewed from certain medicinal roots.

During the week of her illness, both day and night, Marcos mounted guard, allowing none of the monks, not excepting the abbot, to enter Joanna's chamber. Even the Bishop of Porto, who visited on the fourth day, found his way barred. A single word from the bishop and his servants would have seized and bound Marcos, but the bishop, after inquiring how the young priest did, and after requesting that his hopes for a speedy recovery be conveyed, departed without attempting to enter Joanna's chamber.

The interest of the monks was heightened by this forced separation from their guest as a treat withheld for a time is further sweetened by anticipation. Thus when Joanna finally emerged from her chamber, wan and unsteady so that she had to be supported by Marcos, the monks, instead of challenging their guest with a barrage of difficult and tricky questions whose purpose was to expose any defects of erudition, any theological inconsistencies, encouraged her to share portions of her history. They did not press when her energy flagged. And those times when they might have disagreed with a given proposition, instead of growing contentious, they sought clarification by politely phrased questions. The week of sickness established Joanna's position in the monastery, which position she would have had to earn by means of intellectual struggle otherwise.

For Marcos the role of guardian which he vigorously exercised provided him with a sense of purpose. He had begun to feel like an appendage to Joanna, at times useful, at times irrelevant, and this had reached its climax when he had been unceremoniously escorted from the Bishop of Porto's reception chamber. Yet this feeling that he was a personage of essentially little value might have returned as Joanna assumed an increasingly commanding role in the monastery during the course of the next several weeks, had not the Saracens determined that this was a most propitious time to again attempt an incursion of Rome.

Two hours before daylight at the end of their fourth week in the monastery, the alarm bells throughout the city of Rome began to clang.

Joanna had conducted a class attended not only by the monks but also by the Bishop of Porto and several of his friends until well after midnight, and then she had spent an additional hour with the bishop, who detailed his efforts thus far in obtaining an audience with the Pope. When she finally retired to her chamber, her exhaustion was greater than usual. It was this unusual exhaustion that caused her to continue to sleep through the alarm and only awaken at Marcos' insistent shaking.

His eyes shining with a brightness not seen in them in many months, a torrent of words rushed from his lips as soon as her eyes were opened.

"The city is in danger, Joanna, great danger! A Saracen fleet of more than a hundred vessels approaches the mouth of the Tiber." Joanna's hand rested on his arm for a moment.

"They say thousands of Saracen soldiers are aboard these vessels. The Pope has personally taken command of the Christian forces. They say the Saracens will be close enough to attempt a landing by mid-morning. A call has gone out to the citizens of Rome for able-bodied men to aid in the city's defense. If the Saracens land and gain a foothold, it is not certain Rome will be able to withstand their attack. If they establish a foothold, Joanna, there will be reinforements sent from Africa, of that I am certain. If they land and are able to mount their attack, the fate of all Christendom hangs in the balance. They must not be allowed to land!"

"Yes, Marcos, yes, I understand," said Joanna, trying to calm the man.

"I am determined to aid in this city's defense, Joanna," Marcos said in a roughened voice as if he expected her to raise an objection. But when she inclined her head and made a sound indicating her agreement, he went on in a softer voice. "I have gained enough skill with arms. I will declare myself a centurion as in the old days and gather a company of a hundred Roman men."

Joanna took hold of his hand and gave it a tight squeeze.

"And you, Joanna, will remain here in the monastery. Do you understand?" Marcos' tone as he gave this order was one allowed only to a lover speaking to the one he loves. "Do not set foot out of this monastery. The tasks you must do are too important for you to risk the streets at a time like this."

Then, after implanting a kiss on her forehead and enfolding her in a tight embrace which left her gasping for breath, he rushed out of the monastery and headed in the direction of the quarter inhabited by blacksmiths, stonemasons, and tanners.

That day and the day following, Joanna spent most of her time on the roof of the monastery in the company of the older monks — the younger, able-bodied monks having joined the defending forces. From this place of vantage — the monastery of St. Martino being located on a hill — Joanna was able to observe a significant portion of the activity taking place within the city and, when the morning mists had burned off and the sun was directly overhead, the movements of horses and men through the countryside west of the city.

She had not been on the roof an hour when a swarm of beggars, pickpockets and petty thieves tore through the northern portion of the city, breaking and looting. This band of desperate men and women were met by a contingent of mounted knights who, after cutting down the leaders, drove the rest back into their hovels and cellars. A fire set by a handful of looters in the southern section of the city broke out and burned until late afternoon. Then again in the north a contingent of looters appeared, but these were quickly driven off. At sunset companies of armed men gathered just outside the western wall of the city where they camped, their fires seen from this distance resembling fireflies that the aristocratic matrons of the city affixed in their hair.

Struggling against an increasing apprehension for the safety of Marcos, Joanna had to force herself away from the roof after dark. Then after spending a fitful night, she rushed back up to the roof at daybreak as if by being there she somehow would add a measure to his safety.

By midmorning of the second day all of the troops had marched out of view in the direction of the mouth of the Tiber. After that until late afternoon there was nothing. Rome lay still as if asleep or dead. The streets were deserted. Even the half wild dogs that were the scourge of the city had retreated to their dens in the sewers.

Although no order had been given, the evening meal on the second day was taken in absolute silence, broken only by the abbot's fervent prayer for the deliverance of the city. This silence continued to be observed after the meal and would have been maintained until morning had not one of the younger monks unexpectedly returned, his head wrapped in a bloody bandage, the fingers of one hand broken, but otherwise in a fair condition.

The gash in his scalp having been sewn up by Joanna, who also splinted his broken fingers, the monk, after being restored with a flagon of spiced wine, was showered with questions.

"The Saracens still stand out to sea," he rasped out, then coughed, his lungs having been singed by hot smoke. "They have lost some of their vessels, but still have enough. Tomorrow will tell the tale. Pope Leo declares they will never set foot on this soil." A fit of coughing interrupted the man for more than a minute. But then after another flagon of wine he went on. "If not for your friend," he nodded at Joanna, "a company of the infidels would have gained foothold this morning and had this happened..." The monk shook his head ominously.

Leaning toward Joanna whose heart was beating wildly, the monk continued. "He calls himself 'Centurion'." The monk was unable to suppress an excited laugh. "He appeared at the mouth of the Tiber leading a company of the strongest and most savage of Rome: blacksmiths, butchers, tanners, others. And all this hundred, who from their appearance will call no man master, saluted this Marcos and when they addressed him it was always as Centurion. Ordered to take up a position just to the south of the river's mouth, this Christian Centurion, seeing a possible weakness in our defense, ordered his men to build rafts and collect a quantity of pitch from the local peasants and boat builders."

The monk reached out and took hold of Joanna's sleeve as if to concentrate her attention on what he was saying. "Instead of having his soldiers make camp on the shore, this Centurion ordered them aboard the rafts, which were anchored a crossbow shot from land. The first night his men may have grumbled at their crowded conditions and at being tossed by the tide — I would have grumbled. But the second night when all the other Christian forces were asleep, because they believed the Saracens still safely out to sea, his hundred intercepted four Saracen galleys loaded with soldiers that came up from the south to attempt a landing. His barges lying low in the water, the Saracens did not see them and only became aware of their presence at the very moment burning pitch, which had been set afire by hot coals kept for that purpose, was hurled onto the decks of their vessels. Three burst into flames, a fourth escaped out to sea. The galley slaves aboard the burning vessels broke free and attacked the Saracen soldiers, driving scores of them into the water where they were easily dispatched by the Christians on the rafts. Then this Centurion led his men aboard the burning vessels to assist the slaves. The Saracens fought savagely, yet they were slaughtered to the last man. Not less than ten score of the infidels, I will give my oath, now sup in hell. We gained half a hundred worthy soldiers from the slaves who survived, but a like number of Romans commanded by this Marcos died."

Unable to restrain herself, Joanna interrupted, asking: "And Marcos, is he one of the half a hundred Christians who died?"

"When I saw him brought into the presence of Pope Leo, who declared him one of his papal knights and who embraced him in front of all the gathered regiments, your friend Marcos was still very much alive. What has happened to him since..." The monk shrugged and let go of Joanna's sleeve. "I received my hurt shortly after and I have no doubt your friend was back in battle. But if nobility and bravery and the blessing of our sainted Pope are any protection, Marcos lives and will yet live a while."

A wave of weakness as if from a recurrence of her fever made Joanna retire, although the monk had by no means completed his account of the events at the mouth of the Tiber. Back in her chamber she lay in the dark, shivering despite the heavy sheepskin covering. Almost as if she had been present, she could see Marcos in the midst of his men, crouching on the raft, watching the Saracen galleys approach. Then the attack with flaming pitch; the slaughter of the Saracen soldiers in the water; the boarding of the vessels. Half a hundred had been killed. He could easily have been one of that half a hundred. A strange fluttering sensation in her chest made her grow short of breath. Perhaps at this very moment... She cut off the thought. The Saracens have not yet been defeated. There will be more battles. She clenched her teeth and shook her head. Her exhaustion deepened so that she sank to the edge of sleep and in that twilight place where dreams and thoughts intertwine, she could see Marcos with his glorious copper hair and finely molded features standing proudly before a man dressed in the most lavish of vestments who must be the Pope. She could see the Pope embracing him to the thundering cheers of the regiments of Christian soldiers and as the soldiers continued to cheer, she could feel herself being dragged out of sleep into full wakefulness. And then, instead of a sense of elation at this glorious occurrence, Joanna felt a heaviness bordering resentment. Forcing herself to refocus on the scene where the Pope delivered his embrace, she murmured: "Well deserved. I am proud to have you as my friend." But these words were hollow and said mechanically while the feeling of resentment increased.

Before she was fully aware of what she was doing, Joanna delivered a vicious pinch to one cheek. As the pain caused tears to form in her eyes, she pinched the other cheek just as viciously. Then, for the moment, she was back in the field beyond her village with the hare-lipped widow's son. He was pulling her down, his breath like decaying meat filling her nostrils, his soot-blackened hands groping under her shift and then his mouth forcing itself up between her thighs — fear, horror and shame. Afraid to struggle against this powerful youth. Hating him. Hating herself. Then later, the villagers hunting the hare-lipped widow's son. This was followed by another and even greater shame, one she had never admitted to herself until this moment.

Although now fully awake, a dullness descended on Joanna as if she had had an excess of drink. It was a state of non-feeling, the way she had been during those hours the villagers hunted the hare-lipped widow's son. In a dry voice, as if she were repeating someone else's words, she asked: "What sort of love is this I have for Marcos? My heart beats fast and I tremble when I see him, but when he gains a great honor, instead of feeling pride and happiness, my teeth are set on edge." She groaned like an old woman. Then she asked herself in a whisper, her words sending shudders through her body, "Are my feelings for Marcos those of love or of lust?" She listened for several moments as if to gain an answer from the darkness of her chamber. She remembered the question of the Bishop of Porto as to what were her ambitions, and her brave answer. "Is my ambition only to selflessly serve the Church?" she whispered to the darkness. "Or are there other things? Other things..."

His face and hands black as those of a Nubian, his eyebrows and hair singed and his clothing reeking of pitch and smoke, Marcos burst into the monastery just before sunset the next day. From early afternoon on reports of a great victory against the Saracens had been filtering into the city; by mid-afternoon these reports were confirmed by the first contingents of returning soldiers; by late afternoon all of Rome exploded into pandemonium as full regiments entered the city led by the Pope and the chief bishop.

For the first several moments after his entrance, Joanna thought Marcos had suffered terrible injuries, so bad was his appearance. But then when he crushed her to his chest and let out a tremendous roar of laughter, she could see that he had escaped without the slightest hurt.

As soon as she was certain he was as sound as when he had left her, Joanna eased backward several paces from the man experiencing twinges of shame.

"You have heard," Marcos cried out. "A great victory! The Pope has led us to a great victory against the Saracens. And they did not land as he foretold. Not one!"

"I heard of your heroic actions," Joanna said, trying to force a note of excitement into her voice. Marcos made a depreciating sound and shrugged. "We have been told you were honored by the Pope — declared one of his personal knights and embraced by him in front of all the regiments."

"I was honored more than I deserved," Marcos answered in a softened voice. "But this honor may enable me to be of some assistance to you..." He started to say Joanna, caught himself, and said: "John, my brother in Christ."

"I would be grateful for your assistance, my dearest friend." Joanna began to feel her resentment dissolving, its place taken by a tenderness that made her lips tremble.

"As a papal knight I am granted access to the court at any time." Marcos held Joanna's eyes with his. Joanna nodded. "Any time," Marcos repeated, and Joanna nodded again showing her white teeth in a full smile.

Although within the monastery Marcos continued to be regarded as a great hero, outside in the streets of Rome he was only one among many heroes — Rome having a surplus of heroes past and present. After the passage of a few days he was scarcely recognized when he went abroad except by the street urchins and by those in the blacksmith and tanners' quarter who were more generous with their marks of honor than the rest of the populace. Even at the papal court, he was accorded only the bare minimum of recognition as the nobility quickly re-established their superior authority over those who had gained a moment of triumph through heroic deeds but were of inferior rank. Yet Joanna's reputation continued to grow as the tales told about her and her skill at preaching (which she did before hundreds every morning and evening in the courtyard of the monastery) caught the fancy of the lesser clergy and much of the populace. And this reputation was further enhanced by her willingness to treat any sufferer who knocked on the door of the monastery. There were days when the stream of sufferers soliciting her attention was so great that as soon as the evening meal had been taken, she collapsed in exhaustion and had to be assisted to her chamber by Marcos. Yet it was not only her past reputation, skill as a preacher and ability as a physician which had gained for Joanna this adoration. It was that Rome was hungry for a personage of unblemished reputation, a selfless servant of Christ, who could be both adored and respected.

Although the Bishop of Porto had been a regular visitor at the monastery during Joanna's first month of residence, for the entire month after the great victory over the Saracens, he did not put in a single appearance. For the first week Joanna scarcely gave a thought to his absence — he had been at the head of one of the regiments and was doubtless exhausted. When a second week passed without a visit, she felt the beginnings of concern. The third week this concern grew into apprehension. And by the fourth week she despaired of his return, assuming that for some reason he had decided to disavow her.

At the beginning of the fifth week of the bishop's continued absence, Joanna began to consider various ways of soliciting an audience with the Pope. She had about decided to discuss this problem with the abbot, who was reputed to have some influence with Pope Leo IV, when, without announcement, the Bishop of Porto appeared.

Drawing Joanna away from the others, he revealed with a minimum of words that he had suffered a severe wound during the battle, that had this been known by his enemies at court, they would have declared him to be a dying man as they tried to usurp his place, that they might even have employed methods to guarantee that he did not recover. Thus he had determined to keep his condition secret from everyone.

Joanna examined the bishop's face, which at first glance had appeared to be as robustly healthy as always, yet under a more careful examination she could see that the features were pinched and the ruddy complexion was from the juices of certain berries carefully applied. "You still suffer?" she asked. The bishop made a depreciating sound. "Perhaps if you allowed me to apply a balm I have prepared..."

"Save your nostrums for the credulous," the bishop interrupted in harsh voice. Then seeing a hurt expression on Joanna's face, he went on less harshly, "Perhaps if the throbbing of my wound continues another week, I will test your healing powers, my friend. But I did not come to talk about the damages to my flesh. Rather that I intend to approach the Pope tomorrow and ask that he grant you an audience." The bishop allowed himself his wolflike grin, but then, in a conspiratorial fashion, winked one eye. "That gentle one whose 'friendship' you share with Nikon has fallen out of favor." The bishop rubbed his hands together and grinned again. "In case your many labors have caused you to forget, I speak of the Bishop Arsenius of Orte. He continues to hang close to the Pope like one of those farmer's dogs who has learned to suck milk from a teat. But he will gain no milk this month or the next. His nephew Anastasius has been conspiring against the Pope and this was just revealed." The bishop raised his eyes in a mock reverential expression. "What is this world coming to when young priests conspire against Christ's vicar here on earth? What ingratitude! Only last year he knelt in front of the Pontiff when appointed priest of St Marcello, declaring with his honeyed words he was unworthy of this honor and swearing eternal loyalty in gratitude." The bishop forced a sigh which contained elements of a snort. "Anastasius has fled and for the moment is beyond the Pope's reach, but his uncle has enjoyed a stream of invective from Leo's lips that has left his ears scorched, his limbs trembling as if he suffered the ague. What better time than this to request your audience, little priest? Yet if I request this audience, there may be others who, for their own reasons, will raise objections. But with Arsenius hobbled, who is there to interfere if I march you directly into the Pontiff's presence?" The bishop drew in a deep breath, held it for several seconds, then let it out explosively. "We will risk it! Before they have a chance to organize any effective opposition, it will be, as they say, an accomplished fact."

The monotonous reading of a communication from Louis King of Italy by Ado, another nephew of Arsenius, was suddenly interrupted as the doors to the papal chamber were flung open over the objections of several of the Pope's lesser retainers. Then the Bishop of Porto, accompanied by all of his servants in full livery and at least two score assorted clerics, marched into the great chamber. An astonished murmur rose from the several hundred who were gathered there. This murmur turned into shouts of anger or exclamations of excitement as they grew aware of Joanna's presence in the midst of this procession. By the time the bishop reached the papal throne, the shouts favoring and opposing the young priest had grown so great that the windows rattled and the Pope, his face crimson with anger, pressed his hands over his ears against the din. It took several minutes before the archdeacon and his bailiff were able to restore order.

"As your most loyal and faithful servant, I humbly request that you grant an audience to this pious priest: John of Engelheim," the Bishop of Porto boomed out. A chorus of Yesses and noes rose from from the assemblage, and this time by way of warning the archdeacon had several who were lowest in rank unceremoniously ushered out of the chamber.

"Is this a proper way to request an audience," the Pope addressed the Bishop of Porto in a stern voice when order had finally been restored. "Only my high esteem for you restrains me from declaring my displeasure at this unseemly occurrence."

"May I beg your forgiveness." The Bishop of Porto sank to his knees, then leaned forward until his forehead rested on the pink silken slippers of the pontiff. "It was the urgency and importance of this priest's communication that compelled me to risk your displeasure," the bishop continued, his forehead still resting on the slippers. "There are times when certain ones who are close to you, your Gracious Eminence, will put obstacles in the way of he who seeks an audience through ordinary means."

At a tap on his shoulder from the Pope, the bishop rose to his feet. "No doubt these obstacles come from a desire to, ah, shield your Gracious Eminence. I would bite my tongue before suggesting there might be other reasons." Bishop Arsenius and his nephew Ado colored deeply at this.

"Shield me you say? Shield me?" The Pope started fingering his ornate golden crucifix. "I need no shielding, although I cannot grant an audience to every chance wanderer who happens to enter Rome. Nor will I have my precious time taken by charlatans, self-seekers, and others of ill-repute."

"It is only from those you just mentioned that we who are your loyal servants try to protect you," Bishop Arsenius said in an oily voice. "No, protect is not the word. The Pope needs no protection from flies and other loathsome insects. It is that we, his loyal servants, brush away these flies to save the Pope an annoyance." Pleased with his flow of words and eager to regain the Pope's good graces, Bishop Arsenius went on: "The Pope's loyal servants gladly risk stings from what at times are hoards of insects so that the Pope's precious time is not contaminated." Rubbing his protruding belly, Arsenius eased closer to the Pope until he stood alongside the Bishop of Porto. Then, nodding at that bishop and pursing his lips into a smile, Arsenius said, "You declared that those who are of ill repute may be properly screened from your presence, your Gracious Eminence. Such a one, I fear, is that so-called priest in the company of my revered friend, the Bishop of Porto." Bishop Arsenius made a series of lip smacks accompanied by several slow head wags. " I am certain that your loyal servant and my dearest friend, the Bishop of Porto, is unaware of that one's unsavory reputation. I am certain he has been gulled by that one's mellifluous words as have so many others. And if I had not received a certain communication from the revered hermit Nikon, I too might fall victim to his reputed eloquence."

"Spit it out, Arsenius, spit it out," the Pope said in a barely civil voice. "If you have an accusation against that one," he nodded at Joanna, "make it. But I beg you, do not drown me in words."

"He conspired against Bishop Nikitas. Nikon, a true Christian who has never uttered a false word, declares that this John so inflamed the populace of Athens that in order to preserve his episcopy Nikitas was forced to use the ruse of an appointment as emissary to Rome to rid himself of this priest."

"Conspired against the Bishop of Athens?" The Pope formed his words slowly and carefully. "I have been hearing much about conspiracy these days. Too much!"

"And there are those, my Pope, who will swear that this priest practices witchcraft," Ado called out. "There are reports — "

"Reports!" Marcos shouted as he elbowed himself in the direction of the Pope. "Vile vilifications of one of this Church's most pious priests. Vicious rumors deliberately invented to cast ugly stains on a reputation which otherwise would be white as snow."

Several bailiffs and subdeacons rushed forward at a signal from the archdeacon and started dragging Marcos out of the chamber. But their actions were brought to a sudden halt by the Pope, who rose from his throne and raised his hand in a commanding gesture.

"Is not that one your bailiffs are handling in such a rough fashion the same one I embraced before all my assembled regiments?" the Pope asked the archdeacon. After several seconds of hesitation during which he studied Marcos' face, the archdeacon inclined his head. "Is this a way to treat a brave soldier who by my personal order was elevated to the rank of papal knight?" The Pope's features had assumed a severe expression. "Bring the knight forward so that we may hear what he has to say. And in the future..." The Pope glowered at

laugh that was almost a cough. "Not that this mortal man is not grateful for your attention and learned advice. But the Pope, who is vastly more than the man, needs to discuss certain matters with the young priest in privacy."

At a nod from the Pope, Joanna sank to her knees next to his couch where she remained for the rest of the time she spent in his chamber.

"You are no stranger to me, John." The Pope reached out and placed his hand on Joanna's head for a moment. "I first became acquainted with your name and your exploits several years before I was elevated to the throne of St. Peter. There may have been some present at the audience today who were unacquainted with your service to the Church in Sicily, but not this one. And if I have received one communication about your stay in Athens, your relationship with Bishop Nikitas, Nikon, Tryphon, and of course your relationship with Father Paphnutius and the hermit Aegidius, I have received half a hundred. Communications from those who love you, those who despise and fear you, and several from my own men. The Pope must be alert to happenings anywhere in Christendom, must be especially alert when a priest such as yourself appears who causes such strong emotions in men."

The Pope paused while his eyes examined Joanna. Then he went on. "A face like one of the cherubim, so slight of build, yet powerful men who command hundreds fear you while thousands, first in Athens, now here in Rome, have come to revere you. Perhaps you have learned some of the arts of sorcery as you learned the arts of the physician in Marseilles from the Jews." The Pope gently waved his hand indicating that he did not expect a response. "When I learned that you had arrived in Rome and had as your patron the Bishop of Porto, I was pleased. Yet knowing that many in my court were uneasy at your arrival, I determined to wait and let matters take their own course — sooner or later with your bishop's help you would gain an audience. Of this I was certain. To show an interest in you before you had a chance to establish yourself in this city and gain the admiration of the populace, might have led to your death by assassination at the hands of any one of a score of men whom I could mention. Men who would not tolerate a pious reformer gaining the ear of their Pope, their Pope who has already instituted too many reforms." The Pope found a more comfortable position on his couch, crossed his arms over his chest, allowed his eyes to partially close, then continued, "Your appearance in my audience chamber today was no surprise to me, Father John. I was certain the Bishop of Porto would take advantage of Bishop Arsenius' loss of favor when I discovered the conspiracy of his nephew Anastasius." Joanna shook her head in wonder as these convolutions of life in the papal court were revealed.

"I have a need for the services of a pious, popular, and loyal priest. Great need. There are very few who crowd my audience chamber I can trust. But, Father John, no more of this business of raising an army to liberate Sicily." The Pope partially arose from his couch and stared hard at Joanna, whose face showed the puzzlement she felt. "Since my elevation to the papacy, not a single day has passed when my thoughts did not turn to the Bishop of Palermo, when my heart did not reach out to the thousands of suffering Christians on that benighted island. I do not need the eloquent words of a young priest to prick my conscience, Father John. My conscience causes me enough suffering..." The Pope's words trailed off and he squeezed his eyes shut for several long moments. "I could raise the necessary forces in two or three months. But once raised, these Christian forces must be led by no lesser personage than the Pope himself. And as I proved at the mouth of the Tiber, I have sufficient skill in commanding men under arms. Yes, it would ease my conscience to lead a force south, to drive the infidel from the Christian lands of Sicily, to free the Bishop of Palermo. But while I am absent from this city, there are scores like that Anastasius who would conspire against me, more than one who would make every effort to usurp my throne. And, my young priest, with all those who love me fighting by my side in Sicily, who would be left here in Rome to protect the papal throne? An usurper, in a single day, could nullify all my reforms. There is so much corruption. So little piety. Such a disdain for learning. In the few years that are left to me, there is much that can be yet accomplished."

The Pope fell silent and his eyes fluttered closed, but from the tension she could see in his body, Joanna knew the man was still awake, deeply occupied with his own thoughts. "No more of your petitions to free Sicily," the Pope finally said as his eyes partially opened. "Such petitions fuel the fires of the enemies of the papacy. Do you understand?" Joanna inclined her head. "Now you may go and within a week I promise to report to you the efficacy of your baths." The Pope smiled as he simulated a shudder.

Exactly a week from the audience, as Joanna was preparing to address the assemblage that crowded into the courtyard of the monastery, shouts arose from the street outside, calling, "The Pope! The Pope!" Then came ringing cheers as different ones cried out: "Our Blessed

Leo!'' "The Savior of Rome!" "Our Beloved Leo!''. Soon the cheering and shouts grew so great, individual words were lost. The gates of
the courtyard of the monastery flew open and as if a magician's wand
had been employed, a passageway wide enough to accommodate
three men walking abreast was formed in the ranks of those in the
courtyard where only moments earlier there had not been room
enough for one more to squeeze in.

Flanked by the archdeacon and by a huge black soldier who carried an unsheathed sword in his massive hands, Pope Leo entered the
courtyard dressed in armor, a pointed helmet on his head, followed by
a score of papal soldiers also armored and fully armed. Joanna bowed
low and made as if to dismount from the platform when the Pope
called out: "I am come as have all these others to listen to your lesson,
Father John."

Knotting her hands tightly together, Joanna again took up a position in the center of the platform, then raised her eyes to the sky,
which was crystal clear except for a roll of silver clouds on the eastern
horizon. Her heart now beat so rapidly she was short of breath and
she struggled to bring it under control.

She had thought of little else other than her public and private
audience with the Pope during the past week, had ached to share her
thoughts with another but when at different times the Bishop of Porto
approached her with guarded questions she had shaken her head.
Had Marcos questioned her, she might have shared some of the
doubts she had about the Pontiff, might have revealed to him details of
the private audience, but Marcos had been so full of himself, so
pleased with his role in securing her papal audience that when they
were together he laughed, joked, and showered words of affection on
her.

She could feel her heart slowing down and was now able to regu-
late her breathing. Not even in her wildest fantasies had she pictured
the Pope, the Vicar of Christ here on earth, coming to hear her
preach. Yet here he was standing directly beneath her, raised face
showing the same expectant expression as the several hundred others.
Her hands unknotted as if they had wills of their own, then they
stretched forth as she delivered the blessing. And then her words
began to flow, her skillfully roughened voice reaching the furthest corners of the courtyard.

"Why do Christians engage in the sacrament of confession?" Her
lesson began with this rhetorical question. "Why is it not enough for
the Christian to detail his sins to God through the medium of prayer?
Why this need for the priest?" Her eyes met those of the Pope. In that

single moment she tried to read what they were saying but they shifted away just a fraction and whatever message they contained was lost. "As God transmitted His thoughts and love for humankind through the person of Jesus Christ, so it is that we show our true love for God, for the gift of His Holy Son, by revealing ourselves, exposing our inmost thoughts, yes, our shame and misdeeds to Christ's priests and through these priests, communicate with God. There can be no love between human beings without the revelation of the inmost self. How then is there to be love shown to the Creator Of All Things without this personal revelation? To confess to God through the medium of the priest is the most intimate act of which mortal man is capable. As intimacy is a proof of love between mortal and mortal, so it is the chief proof of love between mortal and the Divine. And as it is true with those whose love is truly deep, there is always forgiveness after you have openly revealed yourself to the Source Of All Love." With that Joanna turned to the matter of the confessor's sacred responsibility never to reveal any matter entrusted to his ears other than to God.

Now, scarcely aware of the Pope's presence, her voice rose and fell, at times jolting the hundreds of listeners whose faces showed their rapt attention, at times soothing and caressing. Then as if the vessel containing her thoughts and words had been drained to its uttermost drop, her lips parted as if still in speech, Joanna fell silent. And this silence held the hundreds and the young priest in a perfect bond for the space of a hundred heart beats.

To the wild excitement of the monks, the Pope followed Joanna into the monastery. No reigning Pope had ever set foot within the walls of St. Martino. As the monks crowded close, Pope Leo freely bestowed his blessings until all the monks, their eyes running with tears, had been blessed. The Pope then asked the abbot if he might retire to one of the private rooms and the old man, struck dumb by the honor contained in a request by the Pope, could only nod and point with a trembling hand at his own chamber. Ordering Joanna to follow him, the Pope started for the chamber, but stopped for a moment to salute Marcos who was standing to one side. At this mark of recognition, Marcos fell to his knees, his face turning a dead pale while, despite all his efforts at rapid blinking, his eyes filled with tears.

As soon as the door to the chamber had been securely closed, the Pope turned to Joanna, caught her eyes for a moment, and then to her consternation sank slowly to his knees. A wave of unreasoned fear sent icy shudders through her body as she fought the urge to run from the chamber.

"Confess me, Father John," said the Pope and each of his words stabbed at Joanna like needles of ice.

"Confess...me..." The ice needles filled her throat and choked off her words.

"Even the Pope must be confessed. Although supremest among men, he is still a man, and as you so eloquently said out in the courtyard, he too must reveal himself to Christ's priest, that he may declare his love for God and gain from the Eternal One His divine forgiveness. Confess me, Father."

Her heart beating with such force she was certain it would crack her ribs and burst from her chest, Joanna made the sign of the cross over the kneeling Pontiff. Thoughts swirled through her mind as she struggled to gain control over her lips, tongue, and throat: if it is an abomination for a woman to be priest, then is there any greater abomination than for such a priest to take the confession of Christ's vicar here on earth? She remembered the moments of terror she knew as she moved among the kneeling bandits after having been ordained a priest by the Bishop of Palermo.

Was her priesthood sacred despite her sex, or was it Satan's curse.

All the doubts she had ever known congealed into a single twisted claw that tore at her lungs and heart. If her priesthood was an anathema, then standing here before a kneeling pope was a sin of such magnitude that her punishment must be instant death. Joanna struggled for breath, her teeth clenched against the bursting of her heart. But her heart did not burst. Her breath came again. She had not been punished. The Pope, his head bowed, his arms crossed over his chest, awaited her words. And she confessed him as she had scores of others.

The confession over, Joanna hesitated as she considered what penance she should offer. Then she said, "For a pope there can be no ordinary penance." Pope Leo made a questioning sound. "The penance must be textured to the man and, Your Holiness, he that occupies the throne of St. Peter is no ordinary man."

Joanna gently laid her hands on the Pope's bowed head and said, "This shall be your penance: Arise an hour past midnight and, wearing your least adorned robe, mount to the roof of your palace alone. Once there, raise your eyes to the star-filled skies and do not lower them until the first light of morning shows on the eastern horizon."

The Pope made a sound that was almost a sob as he nodded a single time. Then after rising to his feet and brushing the creases from his garments, he ordered Joanna to come to the papal palace each week on the day before the sabbath to receive his confession.

The Pope's hand was already on the latch of the chamber door when he turned back to Joanna, his face twisted into a simulation of a scowl. "Those baths you have forced me to take have come close to causing the death of my chamberlain, young physician. When I first told him I must bathe in the morning and evening, the man turned white and started to shake as if suffering from the ague. And he must kneel in the passageway when I bathe, praying for me — at his age the cold and damp will surely lay him low with the catarrh. My skin rebels at your baths — I am constantly scratching. But I have gained a certain relief, priest-physician. Though this relief is almost certain to cost me my chamberlain."

Unable to sleep, Joanna paced the floor of her chamber that night until after midnight with no other light than the faint luminescence of the quarter moon seeping through the tiny panes of glass of the single narrow window. Like the carefully fashioned pieces of glass all the many pieces of her life were now joining together in a single pattern, yet she could not be certain how the pattern would look upon its completion: an exquisite work of art, or would the pieces score and crack one another if placed under too much pressure? Or was it possible the entire structure would be shattered by an iron blow from an outside source? As she paced her room by turns she felt bubbles of elation then the cold weight of apprehension. But even during those moments of apprehension there was an overriding feeling of excitement. The Pope's Confessor! She was to be the Pope's Confessor and thus his closest confidant.

Joanna had turned to the Bishop of Porto moments after Pope Leo had left the monastery. The bishop had hastened to the monastery to pay his respects to the Pontiff as soon as he learned of his visit, and had arrived just in time to receive, along with all the others, the parting blessing. From her high coloring, from the expression on her face, and from the way she kept her arms tightly crossed over her chest, the bishop gained a suspicion something unusual had taken place before Joanna said a single word. But his suspicion was not enough to prevent him from suffering a shortness of breath and a certain giddiness when she stated that she had been chosen the Pope's Confessor.

"In my wildest dreams I could not have expected such a stroke of good fortune, my friend." The bishop took Joanna's hand and held it tightly in both of his. "Our Pope is the finest of men but I have seen his judgment clouded at times when surrounded by those hordes of toadies and self-seekers who infest his court. How I feared that Anastasius would be the one selected as his confessor." The bishop's flow of words were interrupted by a burst of nervous laughter. Then he went on, "Had that Anastasius been able to contain himself a little longer, he would have gained the Pope's ear to the terrible hurt of our Holy Church. But he must conspire." Another burst of laughter. "And now Anastasius is in exile under the ban of excommunication while one of the most honest and pious priests in all of Christendom has permanent access to the papal ear. I will offer not less than one thousand Pater Nosters in thanks for the guidance the Lord God has given to our Holy Father."

The Bishop of Porto then warned Joanna that she would be bombarded by pleas from important personages to intercede in their behalf, to reveal the Pope's mind on various matters, to attempt to influence his decisions.

"As his confessor you will be privy to the Vicar of Christ's innermost secrets. You will be the one he turns to in moments of desperation. You will have to guard against compromising the Pope not with words, this you would never do, but by an inflection in your voice, a change of expression." Although the bishop had other things to say, he restrained himself as he felt her hand grow cold and saw the young priest's face drain of color.

Exhausted, Joanna sought her chamber and slept through the remainder of the afternoon and into the evening, awakening fully refreshed and charged with excitement just as the others in the monastery were settling down to sleep. Her surges of conflicting emotions started as she rose from her pallet. She felt the weight of her responsibility. This together with a lingering doubt as to the right of one of her sex to be granted this high office, generated feelings of oppression, while a realization of her virtually limitless opportunity to serve the Church and prove her devotion stirred up bursts of elation. Trying to bring her excitement-charged body under control, Joanna knelt for a time before the narrow window, allowing the soft moonlight to bathe her hands, which she held out palms upward in supplication.

She gazed at her hands. Sophia had spoken of these hands, had declared that they would some day rule. How could the old woman have known? Yet she knew. She remembered sitting on the hill that time when she went away alone to seek the experience of solitude. She remembered how she had been filled with some of the same excitement she felt this moment, but then it had been the excitement of imagining herself a princess. "A princess who would rule wisely and justly," Joanna whispered. She remembered her dream of wearing gowns of silken cloth edged with patterns formed of silver threads; gowns worn only by princesses and queens; gowns that would display her womanly figure to its full advantage. But now she would never wear a gown. She was condemned til death to wear the concealing, long robe of a cleric and to hide much of her head under the cloth hood. Her hands, the hands Sophia said would someday rule, felt cold. Her chamber was cold and the light from the quarter moon provided no heat. The hard, cold stone of the floor made her knees ache.

Still holding out her hands in supplication, Joanna arose. She shuddered from the chill in her chamber and from something else, from an apprehension for which she had no words, an apprehension that hovered in the shadows as had those things that had lurked in the dark outside of her childhood hut late at night. She dropped her hands. An urge so powerful she was unable to struggle against it even for a moment drew her out of her chamber into the passageway. There she could hear the muffled sleeping sounds of the monks, each in his bare chamber; sighs and groans, snores and sounds that were almost words.

As if pulled by hempen cords in the hands of a monstrous giant, she was drawn down the dark passageway until she stood before the door to Marcos' chamber. Her hands, drawn by those invisible cords, reached out and stroked the rough wood of the door. Deep, even sounds of a man breathing came from within. A yawning ache filled her loins. Her wildly beating heart rose until it filled her throat. In that room there would be warmth and comfort. Beyond the door was relief from the cold, from stabs of heat deep in her abdomen, for her loneliness. Relief. Step through that door and she could be a woman, could cast off the mask that at times was as oppressive as a suit of heavy chainmail armor. Her hands tightened on the door latch and a tingling ran up her arm into her chest, then down into her abdomen, making her insides churn.

She depressed the handle and there was the soft click of the latch. And it was this sound that caused her body to freeze, caused her hand to fall away from the door handle as if it were a poisonous adder, caused her to slowly back away in the direction of her chamber. The click of the latch had been the same as the sound that warned her of the presence of the assassin years earlier as she had lain, at the edge of sleep, in her chamber in the cathedral of Aachen. The click that had saved her from strangulation at the hands of that assassin. The click that now warned her of the terrible risk, of the dire consequences should she enter that chamber.

She lay on her pallet until morning, sobbing softly. Her tears were for what lay beyond the door to that chamber; for the girl who had sat on the hill dreaming of marrying a prince and becoming a princess; for the woman who hid within the ugly coarse robes of a man, and some of her tears were for things yet unknown awaiting her in the future.

There could have been no better declaration of the change in Joanna's status than the manner in which Bishop Arsenius greeted her upon her next entrance into the reception chamber at the papal palace. His protruding belly quivering, his face a vast, toothy smile, his chubby hands rubbing together, the bishop waddled up before she had taken a dozen steps into the chamber. He inclined his head and moved his shoulders into a partial bow — a full bow would would be inappropriate for a bishop to make to a priest even if this priest were the Pope's Confessor — then he showered her with statements about how delighted he had been to hear of her appointment; how they must become better friends; how he intended to invite her often to dine with him at his residence; how incorrect Nikon had been in his assessment of her and how he intended to write a letter of censure to the hermit; a torrent of words that only ceased when, with just the suggestion of a bow, Joanna turned away from the man and joined the Bishop of Porto, who held out both of his hands in greeting.

She was not certain how she came to take her place on a stool alongside the Pope — perhaps it was the Bishop of Porto who had guided her there, or was it because of a gesture from the Pope? So many people had crowded around her, so many marks of attention — but there she was so close to the Pope she could have reached out her hand and touched him. A communication from Louis, King of Italy was being read in which he urged the elevation of a certain John, a member of one of Ravenna's most noble families, to the rank of archbishop of that city. Several times during the reading Pope Leo turned to Joanna and whispered about King Louis seeking too much power and John of Ravenna being of doubtful loyalty. To each of his comments Joanna inclined her head, acutely aware of the hundreds of pairs of eyes fastened upon her, carefully examining her face for any changes of expression that might serve as clues. There were other communications and more whispered comments from the Pope. Then various petitioners approached who, although they presented their petitions to the Pope and said not a word to Joanna, were aware of her presence, glancing quickly out of the corners of their eyes to assess her reaction.

When The Pope arose at the conclusion of the audience, without being told, she too arose. Again, without being told, she followed the

Pope into his private chamber and the bows from the gathered church dignitaries, Roman nobles, papal knights and scribes were not only to the Pope as he passed but were maintained until the Pope's Confessor had also passed.

Once inside his private chamber, even before he stretched out on the ivory and ebony couch, the Pope started to discourse about the communication from King Louis. He then abruptly shifted to various of the petitioners, moving quickly from one to the other so that at times Joanna lost track of the identity of the one in question. Then the Pope returned to Louis' communication, but before all of his thoughts had been expressed, he veered off to rumors that had been brought to his ears regarding a new Saracen attempt on Rome.

Within a quarter of an hour Joanna clearly understood the nature of this portion of her relationship with the Pope. As his confessor, he could trust her as he could no other human being, yet it was not her advice that he wanted, rather a silent ear against which he could test ideas and differing points of view. That there would come a time when her thoughts would be solicited, she was certain. But for now her task was to store away facts for later analysis and consideration.

His discourse over, the Pope eased from his couch and knelt before Joanna. "I did your penance, Father," he said, a faint smile softening his lips for a moment. "Those hours I spent on the roof of this palace were the longest I have ever known — they might have been a hundred. Those stars piercing down burned through my eyes into my brain. It was a penance too severe for a murderer, yet perhaps not severe enough for a Pope."

With that Joanna confessed the kneeling man. But this time the penance was to say the name of every man for whom he had hatred or fear and for each, find one loving statement.

"If Satan were a priest he would not demand such a penance," the Pope murmured. Then, with rapid shakes of his head, "I did not really mean this, Father. It is a penance of love, one that only a priest who walks in the footsteps of Christ could have offered." The Pope lowered his face into his hands for half a hundred heartbeats and softly murmured, "Yes, a statement of love for each."

The day following this public recognition of Joanna as Pope Leo's Confessor, all of Rome buzzed with rumors regarding the young priest's future. The citizens of Rome celebrated the elevation of one who already was their favorite. Most of the nobles, if not enthusiastic, at least were content, for young John was not allied to any faction, had no relatives, bastards, or mistresses for whom he would attempt to gain preferment. The lesser clergy mentioned Father John's name during their sermons, lectures, or lessons for it was a glorious thing to have one of their rank sitting at the side of the Pope. The higher clergy, for the most part, made polite remarks in public about the new confessor; in private there were expressions of concern, resentment, fear, and anger.

Immediately after it became generally known that she was the Pope's Confessor, Joanna was caught up in a swirl of activity that involved her every moment from the time she arose early in the morning until she collapsed on her pallet into an exhausted, dreamless sleep at night. Everybody in Rome must hear this rising young priest. Such large crowds gathered for her morning lesson that to accommodate them she often had to offer the same lesson two or three times. Hundreds milled outside the walls of the monastery clamoring for her services as physician. Many of these broken and diseased ones would lie on the ground all through the night, suffering the damp and cold in the expectation of gaining a moment of her attention. And the Pope took to calling her into his presence on days other than just the day before the Sabbath. There were weeks when she made the procession to the papal palace three and four times, always accompanied by hundreds of clamoring citizens, many of whom struggled with one another that they might get close enough to touch the garment of the pious priest and beg for his healing touch on diseased and deformed limbs.

Always she took her place on the stool alongside the Pope in the reception hall where the audiences often lasted for hours and then there was always that private time with Pope Leo in his chamber.

For the first few months, Pope Leo asked no advice regarding political or ecclesiastical matters of Joanna although there were always questions from him regarding his health which, despite all her efforts, was slowly deteriorating. But there finally came a time when the Pope, after sharing his thoughts regarding a papal matter, instead of turning at once to another matter, paused and examined Joanna's features. At first it was only from a narrowing of her eyes or a tightening of her mouth that the Pope gained clues as to her opinion. But finally she began to offer not only an opinion but advice as well. And then there was an occasion when Joanna risked criticizing one of the Pope's actions. He had ordered the elevation of John of Ravenna to the rank of archbishop despite all his earlier doubts regarding the loyalty of the man and despite his numerous expressions of concern about how such an act would give King Louis too much power.

"You should have resisted the pressure, Your Holiness," Joanna had said in a stern voice. "You know what harm John of Ravenna can do as archbishop. Why then did you allow yourself to be manipulated into such an act?"

"Manipulated!" The Pope had shouted, shaking his fist at Joanna, his face white with rage. "You go too far." Then he harshly ordered her out of his presence. But a day later she was summoned back by his chamberlain and he rose from his throne when she entered the reception chamber, a mark of honor seldom given to any of lesser rank than that of king. After that Joanna tended the Pope at least several hours every day except the Sabbath. That day she reserved for prayer and contemplation in the monastery, and for a shared hour or two with Marcos whom she scarcely saw during the rest of the week.

Shortly after she entered her third year as Papal Confessor the health of Pope Leo took a marked turn for the worse. His limbs had grown so stiff, he had great difficulty in walking and there were days when he could not cut his meat and had to be fed. Although Pope Leo at first protested, Joanna took to massaging his joints with warm oil and medicinal herbs while they conversed. In time he grew so dependent on these treatments for relief that those days when his suffering was acute he would send his chamberlain for Joanna hours before she was expected. These summonings by the papal chamberlain dressed in his august robes and proceeded by never less than half a score of his servants, always generated great excitement among the masses pressed into the courtyard of the monastery, for these special summonings invariably came while she was preaching. That the Pope would send his chamberlain for their beloved Father John always caused the assemblage to respond with shouts of delight. Instead of resenting this interruption, all who were present assumed a portion of the honor.

As Joanna entered her fourth year of service to the Pope there were days when the Pontiff's illness was such that he could not effectively conduct his audience. On those days Joanna, together with the archdeacon, received petitions, acknowledged communications, then going into the Pope's private chamber, returning with either the papal signature or reasons for rejection. Although often confined to bed for days at a time, the Pope, through Joanna and his archdeacon, superintended the construction of additional fortifications around Rome, and continued his attempt to have Anastasius returned to his jurisdiction for suitable punishment — this nephew of Bishop Arsenius having become the focal point of anti-papal conspiracy. By use of the helping hands of Joanna and the archdeacon, the Pope continued a lively correspondence with various rulers and leading clerics so that there were many in the distant reaches of Christendom who had no suspicion of his deteriorating condition. But in Rome it was the chief topic of conversation.

Again and again during Joanna's first year of intimacy with the Pope, Bishop Arsenius had invited her to be his guest at his residence, one of the most lavish in all Rome. But each time Joanna offered some excuse for not accepting the invitation, until finally they ceased. After that, although the bishop always greeted her with smiles and every mark of affection, he invested an ever increasing amount of energy in organizing a network of higher clerics whose avowed purpose was to deal with this priest quickly and effectively when Pope Leo died. It was rumored that this network, which numbered perhaps half a hundred, favored the excommunicated Anastasius as the next pope. And if the Roman populace, which always had much to say about the election of a pope, could not stomach this enemy of Leo, then John of Ravenna who had King Louis' support would be their man.

These rumors regarding Anastasius and Archbishop John of Ravenna were finally brought to Joanna's ears by the Bishop of Porto who had remained in the shadows much of the time contacting her only on rare occasionally. This was partially because he did not want to compromise the young priest's position, which would happen if it were known that she favored the Bishop of Porto's faction, but part of the reason for the Bishop of Porto's retiring stance was recurring bouts of intense pain from the wound he had suffered. But as time went on and the conspiracy launched by Bishop Arsenius deepened and the condition of the Pope worsened, the Bishop of Porto, despite his pain, began to attend Joanna regularly. This Joanna encouraged for she knew her position with the Pope was now such she could not be compromised. Almost entirely bedridden, he was totally dependent upon her.

The Bishop of Porto had chosen his words carefully when he first approached Joanna with information about the network organized by Arsenius. Had power and his great influence on the Pope effected a change in this young priest? the Bishop of Porto asked himself as Joanna led him to the roof of the monastery where they could talk in privacy. Through years of association with those who had gained power, the bishop had a full appreciation of how much this could alter personalities, distort thinking, and create justification for abominable actions. But from the gentle way the priest looked at him — eyes which were all softness as they met his — from the expressions of friendship, and from other things for which there are no words, the Bishop of Porto knew that power had not left its bitter imprint on this one.

"The intentions of Arsenius and his followers regarding my person, I will not discuss with the Pope," Joanna said when the Bishop of Porto had finished his communication. "He is a desperately sick man and I will not add to his distress concerns regarding my safety. But as to their plans to secure the papacy for Anastasius, or if the Roman populace objects to this, place the Archbishop of Ravenna on the papal throne, this information I cannot withhold from Pope Leo, although hearing it will certainly worsen his condition." Joanna turned away from the bishop for several moments while she gazed over the roof tops of the city, then turned back again. "As long as he still breathes Leo is Pope and must be informed of matters affecting the Church."

"I once called you a ferret, my friend," said the Bishop of Porto. "It has been my habit for many years to find an appropriate beast for each of those with whom I am acquainted. But now for you I can find no beast." The Bishop of Porto smiled his old familiar smile, exposing the tips of his pointed teeth, yet Joanna would no longer have described this smile as wolf-like. "You are a man, John, a man among men. For you only the word man will suit."

When the Bishop of Porto returned the following week, as soon as they had mounted to the privacy of the roof, he asked Joanna what had been the Pope's reaction.

"After I informed him that efforts were being made so that either Anastasius or the Archbishop of Ravenna would be his successor, Pope Leo groaned and turned his face to the wall. Then he lay so still that after the passage of several minutes, I thought the information I had brought had caused him to expire. But then another groan, so I knew he lived. Then another. Finally, after the passage of not less that an hour he turned to me, his eyes showing a deep hurt, and asked for more details." The Bishop of Porto bit his lower lip and squeezed his eyes closed while he continued to listen. "Now all the Pope talks about is the possibility of Anastasius or John of Ravenna securing the papacy. If it should be Anastasius, he is certain that all of his reforms would be nullified and the Church would be plunged into a sink of corruption; should it be John of Ravenna then King Louis would gain authority over Rome, which is that one's ambition and the power of the papacy would be lost."

"My guess it will be the Archbishop of Ravenna," said the Bishop of Porto. "I doubt the Romans would accept Anastasius. Yet if enough bribes are passed out, enough pots of wine... but it is my belief it will be John of Ravenna. Then, as Pope Leo says, King Louis, who holds that black John as if he were a puppet, will rule Rome. Louis dreams of nothing else except becoming another Caesar."

The bishop took Joanna's arm and they walked slowly back and forth across the broad roof. "You are a physician, John, how long does Pope Leo have to live?" the bishop asked.

"One month, two, no more than a quarter of a year," Joanna answered.

"So little time." The muscles in the bishop's arms tightened. "The forces of Arsenius are well organized — if it is to be John of Ravenna all the resources of King Louis will be at his command. Yet what efforts have been made by those who detest Anastasius and Black John? Who will we offer in their place? So little time. Yet Pope Leo still breathes and if I know the man he will fight to hold on for the full quarter of a year."

They continued to walk in silence, stopping for a moment when they reached the end of the roof, both studying the streets of the city, the hills beyond, the sky. Then they turned and walked to the other end.

"There is only one person in all of Rome who has a chance of securing the papacy from those who conspire with Arsenius." They stopped and Joanna turned and looked directly in the bishop's face. "You are that one, John. The people of Rome revere you. And you have many friends and supporters among the clergy. Many." Joanna shook her head, but the bishop paid no attention and continued. "If we can organize a network of our own, can secure declarations of loyalty from certain noblemen, cardinals, and bishops..."

"No, my dear friend, no." Joanna raised both of her hands as if to defend against an attack. "I cannot be the Pope. It is too much."

"That is no more than I would have expected you to say, my friend. No truly pious man believes himself worthy to be Pope. But this determination is made by those who rule the Church with the approval of the citizens of this city and he who is elected Pope must serve."

"But, I am not worthy. There are things..." Joanna broke off.

"There is not a man who lives on this earth who has not acquired certain stains. Only the angels are unblemished." The bishop glared at Joanna as he had years earlier when they first met in his garden. "You will be Pope, John. You will be Pope or I will die in the attempt to fill the throne of St. Peter with a righteous man. My mind is made up. I will do what needs to be done, and I, together with all your many friends, will expect your full cooperation." The bishop's voice had grown harsh and for a moment Joanna felt the same uneasiness she had known when she first met the man. Then the bishop said in a softer voice, "Would you rather have Anastasius on the throne or Black John with King Louis pulling his strings?" At this Joanna turned away and moved to the very edge of the roof where she stared down at the milling people in the courtyard below who were waiting for her appearance.

Each day during the week following her conversation with the Bishop of Porto, Joanna devoted not less than an hour praying for a miracle which would restore Pope Leo. And each day she visited the desperately sick man whose flesh had melted away leaving him little more than a skeleton encased in a bag of skin. A portion of each visit was given over to gently massaging him and then attempting to feed him thick soups she had ordered prepared, the Pope refusing to take food from any hands other than those of his confessor. The treatment and feeding over, the rest of the visit was devoted to papal duties under the direction of the Pope, for Joanna was determined that until he had breathed his last breath, Leo would be Pontiff in fact, not only in name.

Again and again as she sat on her stool next to him, Joanna considered telling Pope Leo of the Bishop of Porto's intentions. But by revealing this, would she not, in fact, be soliciting the Pope's support? She asked herself. And would there not be something base, even unfair, in gaining support from a helpless, dying man, wholly dependent upon her? And, she asked herself, had she really been as reluctant to gain the most exalted rank possible for a mortal being as she had declared to the Bishop of Porto?

Her mind full of these matters, Joanna found it impossible to go to sleep. She had to speak to someone...to Marcos.

During the several years of her rise to power Marcos had devoted much of his time to scholarly pursuits. In many ways their relationship now was that of brother and sister, and the hour or two they spent together each Sabbath contained little of the passion and intensity of earlier years. Yet each would have declared to the other, if asked, that the love they shared was undiminished.

Marcos opened his door at Joanna's knock and was startled. It was not the Sabbath. And they always met in the garden of the monastery when the weather was fair, in the chapel when it was not. Then when she took his hands and held them tightly in both of hers after she entered his chamber he was puzzled.

"I have need of your ear, dearest friend," Joanna hesitated. "Also of your advice."

"Advice?" She had never sought his advice. Other things, yes, but not his advice.

"Pope Leo is close to death." Marcos murmured that he had heard rumors to this effect. Then she told him about the forces allied to Arsenius and their intentions regarding the papacy. After that, choosing her words carefully, she told him about the conspiracy against herself which was to be put into action at the Pope's death.

Marcos reacted as if he had been stabbed. His face turned a dangerous red, his muscles tightened and his eyes flashed anger.

"From this moment I will be at your side at all times. Will sleep in the passageway outside your chamber." Marcos struggled to catch his breath. "I will organize the monks in this monastery so that there are no less than a dozen armed guards. They will have to hack me to pieces before they touch a single hair on your head, Joanna."

"You will be my guardian," Joanna said in a flattened voice. "The risk may not be as great as the Bishop of Porto says. Yet," she hesitated, "when it becomes known that the Bishop of Porto is organizing a faction to secure the papacy for me, attempts may be made against my life."

"The papacy! For you, Joanna? The Pope. You? My God! My God!" The man dug his hands into his coppery hair and pulled, as if by inflicting pain he could force himself back under control. Then he began to shake like one who is burning with fever. And he kept repeating, "My God. My God." Finally, he whispered; "There is no one in all of Christendom more worthy of the office, Joanna. No one. Your mind exceeds any I have ever known. You are pious and pure, my dearest one. But you are a woman."

"Yes, a woman," Joanna said with her eyes closed.

"Can a woman be the Vicar of Christ? Is that not too much? Too much. And if it should ever be found out..." The man shuddered and pulled at his hair again.

"The Bishop of Porto declares that if elected I must serve and he is determined to have me elected. There is nothing I can do to dissuade him. Nothing except revealing who I am."

"He would have you stoned to death. Never forget he is a bishop. A powerful bishop." Marcos walked to the window of his chamber and pressed his forehead against the cool glass panes. Then he said softly, "The one to whose womb God entrusted His Own Son was of your sex, Joanna. Then why should not a woman be His chief earthly servant." He licked his dry lips. "For all of your life you have been under divine protection. I knew it must have been for some great purpose, but now I see it is intended that you rise to the very ultimate. You will be Pope, Joanna. The eighth one with the name John who has held this exalted office.''

"Pope or grave, Marcos. I suspect my chances of sitting on the throne of St. Peter are far less, far, far less than lying beneath the earth, anathematized without so much as a rude cross to mark my final resting place.''

In the several weeks that followed this conversation a depression settled on Joanna that so drained her energies that there were days she was unable to deliver her sermon in the courtyard and had to plead illness. Yet despite this depression she did not fail in her attendance on the Pope, who had grown so weak there were times he could not speak. But the day she learned from the Bishop of Porto that Nikon had arrived in Rome to join with the forces of Arsenius, a burst of rage more violent than she had ever known swept away this depression, swept away all thoughts of death and unmarked graves and left her charged with a wild energy and a determination to do everything possible to secure her future rather than just stand by passively while others decided her fate.

This wild energy completely burst its bonds the following morning when, as she mounted the platform in the courtyard, Joanna saw Nikon's hideous face grinning up at her among the ranks of the hundreds of expectant faces.

It was said that the power of the sermon delivered by Father John that day was such that had Satan heard it, he would have been at once converted and fallen to his knees to worship Christ. It was said that those who were privileged to stand in the courtyard that day were cleansed of all sin and went forth to live the lives of saintly men. But for Nikon this sermon was proof of the priest's power, a warning of what a danger the one he despised above all other men was to the cause he espoused. If all the others left the courtyard determined on a saintly life, Nikon passed through that gate into the city quivering with rage, his mind churning with vicious plans.

The sight of the hermit's hate-filled face among all those others who cared so deeply for her goaded Joanna to approach Pope Leo and ask for his support. The Pope, during his several minutes of lucidity, although he could not speak, nodded his agreement with the Bishop of Porto's plan. So that the Pope's support would become known to the clergy, nobles, and citizens of Rome, Joanna then decided, despite a lingering distaste for taking any action that might advance herself, to gather a representative delegation and bring them into the Pope's presence as witnesses.

For the rest of that afternoon and through the evening, Joanna locked herself in her chamber as she thought deeply about which noblemen, which of the greater clergy she should approach with the request to accompany her into the papal presence. Should she ask Bishop Arsenius to be one of that number? she wondered. He would find it very difficult to refuse this invitation to attend the dying Pope. And then, learning directly from the Pope his preference for his successor, might not this cause the bishop to reconsider his plans — if Arsenius loved Pope Leo as much as he declared, how could he conspire against the one Leo recommended as his successor? Yet bringing Arsenius into the Pope's presence might make events go just the opposite. Realizing the strength of his enemies' position and deciding to disregard the desires of the Pope, might not Arsenius put his plans into immediate action rather than waiting until Leo had breathed his last? So deep was her concentration on these matters that Joanna did not appear for the evening meal. And she was the last one in the monastery to fall asleep, still undecided about Bishop Arsenius, whose features became confused with those of Nikon as she drifted off.

But all of those hours of thought, all of those neatly balanced considerations became irrelevant when just before sunrise the Bishop of Porto, accompanied by all of his servants, burst into the monastery with the announcement that Pope Leo no longer lived.

"He died at midnight and I only gained intelligence two hours since," the Bishop of Porto informed Joanna as he entered her chamber together with Marcos. "Bishop Arsenius must have bribed the Pope's servants. King Louis has already been informed and his forces are preparing to march on Rome. Nikon and others are already at work distributing flasks of wine and silver coins among the citizens of Rome. And my informants tell me Arsenius is gathering a force of armed men whose intention, I am certain, is to seize you, John. You must come with me to my residence at once. Arsenius will hesitate before attacking the residence of the Bishop of Porto."

"Will hesitate, Your Eminence," said Marcos, "but as his hand is strengthened, when the forces of King Louis are ranged outside the walls of Rome, he will no longer hesitate. As I know Christ died for us, I know he will tear down your residence stone from stone to get his hands on Father John." Marcos stared hard at the Bishop. "For a day, no more than two, this one whose destiny it is to be Pope will be safe in your residence. But then he will need soldiers of his own to mount defense until he mounts the throne of St. Peter." He turned to Joanna. "I will become a Centurian for the second time. There are still a few blacksmiths and tanners who remember Marcos. They will come to me at once. Then, when the people learn I recruit for the defense of their pious priest, others will join. With the help of God I will command not one hundred, but five times that number."

Not knowing of Joanna's removal to the Bishop of Porto's residence, a company of seven score heavily armed men recruited by Arsenius but under the command of Nikon attacked the monastery of St. Martino that afternoon. Despite the monks' valiant defense the monastery would have fallen in less than an hour had not a mob of Roman citizens driven the attackers back with showers of stones. But this force of Arsenius was quickly augmented by half a hundred men, a score of whom were mounted, and this time the monastery fell with the loss of more than a dozen of the monks.

When a thorough search failed to produce the young priest, Arsenius, who had appeared on the scene, declared that the Bishop of Porto would know the whereabouts of the hated priest and he, alongside Nikon, led the armed force, which by now numbered almost three hundred in the direction of the bishop's residence.

The time consumed by the two attacks against the monastery enabled Marcos to recruit his army of five hundred. Within minutes of his arrival in that quarter of the city where his name was still known, several of his veteran soldiers left their tanning sheds and anvils and joined him. Then, as the word went out that the Centurian was back to secure soldiers for the defense of John, John whose piety and good works declared him a papal candidate, tens, then scores, and finally hundreds put down their tools, picked up their weapons and joined the swelling ranks.

Although Marcos might have wished for another twenty-four hours in which to ready his army, he started in the direction of the Bishop of Porto's residence as soon as he received the urgent message that it was under siege.

Had it been daylight instead of a moonless night, or even had there been a moon to offer partial illumination, it is almost certain Marcos' forces, despite their greater number, would have been defeated. They were untrained, no captains had been appointed, their weapons were of an inferior quality and mostly rusted, and many of them were staggering from drink. But out in the dark, in alleyways, among the trees of the bishop's garden, and even in the streets, it was man for man with hard muscle more than training, discipline, or fine weapons making the difference.

While the forces clashed out in the dark, their screams, grunts, and curses echoing through that section of the city, Joanna sat opposite the Bishop of Porto in his reception chamber. A ring of a dozen of the bishop's servants, each holding a naked sword in one hand, a dagger in the other, stood guard completely surrounding them. An equal number were stationed in the entranceway to the chamber and at the front and rear entrances to the large residence. "If the need arises, we can escape the city through the sewers and go to my palace in Porto where you will be completely safe," said the bishop with a deep frown. "But once away from Rome, there is little chance you will be elected Pope, my dearest friend." The bishop toyed with his crucifix, then went on, "The Roman populace is fickle. If they do not see you in the flesh, they will turn to another and demand his election. Yet if we must escape we must."

Although Joanna nodded from time to time at the bishop, she scarcely heard his words. The screams and other sounds of the contending forces pounded against her ears, worked their way into her brain, filled her skull until it felt as if it must crack. She had seen so much death; so many had died. Now out there in the dark, men were dying because of her. *If this was the cost of being Pope...* Her thoughts were interrupted by the entrance of the abbot of St. Martino.

His face and hands badly scratched, his robe covered with a reeking filth that could have only come from the sewer, the abbot started speaking as soon as he caught his breath.

"Anastasius is in Rome! He has brought forces of his own; they say as many as eight hundred men. I came through the sewers."

The bishop nodded.

"No other way. The monks of St. Martino have gone out among the populace, each swearing a holy oath that no one supported by Nikon or Arsenius will ever be pope, not after what was done to our monastery — a dozen brothers lie dead. Fires have broken out all over Rome. There are shouts coming from different sections of the city for the appearance of Father John." The abbot sank down on a stool provided for him and emptied a flagon of wine in a series of rapid gulps without removing it from his lips.

"Everything is in wild confusion. If King Louis' soldiers enter the city and join with those of Anastasius, there will be no way of conquering them. But they say King Louis will not enter the city until after the first vote is taken, will not do anything to aid Anastasius. They say he is waiting for just the right moment and then will enter, as if in triumph, and demand the election of that black John of Ravenna." The abbot drained a second flagon of wine. "They clamor for you, Father John. The people clamor for you. If you appear in their midst..."

"Too dangerous!" The bishop said in a voice that was almost a shout. "If he is captured by Arsenius or by Anastasius he will be put to death on the spot. And there are others in this city who may have papal candidates of their own; others who if given the chance would not hesitate to destroy a rival to their man."

"But, Your Eminence," the abbot rose from his stool and took a step toward the bishop, forgetting for the moment his stench, "if we do not seize the opportunity, if Father John fails to appear when the populace clamors for him..."

"I will not risk his life. If it is intended that he be Pope, the Lord God will grant us His assistance."

"But does not the Lord God expect us to do all in our power to assist Him in His divine works?" The abbot took another step forward until scarcely a distance of two spans separated the two men. "While we wait, Nikon is everywhere. He moves about as if he possessed Mercury's winged slippers."

"I thought he was with Arsenius' soldiers," Joanna muttered.

"He may have been. But now he moves among the people." The abbot, suddenly becoming aware of his closeness to the bishop, took several steps backward, much to the bishop's relief.

"Nikon is everywhere," Joanna repeated the abbot's words in a hoarse voice. "And I am here doing nothing." Several moments passed while Joanna, the bishop, and the abbot stared at one another. During these moments they became aware that the sounds of men battling with one another had almost ceased. Except for an occasional high-pitched scream or angry curse, the sounds that now came from the darkness outside the bishop's residence were not those of battle but those of wounded and dying men: moans, cries for help, choking gasps.

Suddenly the ranks of the bishop's servants guarding the passageway opened and Marcos, his face dripping blood, entered the reception chamber. Brushing aside concerns about his condition, he said in a voice that was almost a command, "It is best for Father John to go out amongst the populace. He will be safer in the district of the blacksmiths and tanners than here. I have perhaps as many as two hundred men left to accompany him through the city."

"And if the eight hundred men of Anastasius should attack on the way," the bishop said slowly, with an ugly edge to his voice. "I agree Father John will not be safe here. But he will be safe enough in my palace at Porto. We will escape the city through the sewers."

"I will not leave this city at this time," said Joanna in a voice containing the ring of absolute finality. "If it is my fate to be taken by the forces of Anastasius, so be it. If it is the Almighty's wish that, for reasons of His own, I be placed on the throne of St. Peter, I will not retreat through sewers expecting the Lord God to seek me out from among the swarms of rats." At this the Bishop of Porto, after crossing himself, bowed low as if Father John already wore the papal ring on his forefinger.

Disciplined by their hours of fierce fighting and by the terrible losses they had suffered, the men commanded by Marcos, except for the dozen sent forward as scouts, moved through the city in a tight band with Joanna in their midst. The scores of fires that still raged in different sections of the city reddened the skies, and their light cast grotesque shadows and painted the color of blood on the faces of the battle-soiled soldiers. Looters ran unchecked through the streets, but retreated and melted into the shadows as this company of men appeared. Twice the advance scouts gave warning of the approach of enemy forces. But both times these forces proved to be looters accompanied by mobs of street urchins. But then as they neared the quarter inhabited by blacksmiths and tanners — less than five hundred paces separated them from safety — the forces of Anastasius came at them from an arcade where they had been waiting, crouched in the darkness.

Half of his force, responding to Marcos' shouted command, turned and rushed at the enemy soldiers who outnumbered them more than ten to one. The remainder of his men tightened their cordon around Joanna and started to race in the direction of safety.

Of those who rushed at Anastasius, less than a third escaped death. But this tactic provided a sufficient delay so that the young priest had a chance to disappear in the maze of narrow, twisting streets which by now were choked with hundred shouting: "Pope John! Pope John!"

"Do you hear them? do you hear them?" Marcos gripped Joanna's shoulders with such force it brought tears to her eyes. "The people of Rome declare you will be the Pope. What a glorious day in the history of our blessed Savior's Church. The people of Rome will have no other as their Pope. Do you hear them? Do you see their faces? They will not have Anastasius or the Archbishop of Ravenna, only you."

"If this is a dream, I must awake," Joanna whispered to herself. She stared up at Marcos' half-crazed bloody face, at his opened mouth from which issued bursts of wild, almost insane laughter. All those people reaching out to touch her, kissing the hem of her garment, holding out their children for the holy touch.

Then she was in an open space lit by hundreds of blazing torches. Thousands upon thousands of people. Shouts like a great avalanche of snow coming down off the mountain. And then from ten thousand throats the chant: "Pope John! Pope John! Pope John!" Yes it was real. This was no dream.

By sunrise word of the thousands who had turned out to declare John of Engelheim the new pope had reached every section of Rome and fresh thousands took up the cry until virtually all the working men and artisans of the city were in the streets demanding his election.

Yet the merchants and nobles, the clergy both lesser and greater, and the officials of the city remained indoors, most with their shutters tightly bolted, although many in their hearts favored the young priest. But declaring oneself in favor of an unsuccessful candidate could prove to be costly. The working men and artisans of Rome had little to lose; let them mill about in the streets shouting the name of their favorite, threatening the cardinals with terrible punishments if they should dare elect another. The populace of Rome was known to be fickle. Today the chant is for John of Engelheim, but if the cardinals are able to delay, who is there to say whose name will be shouted by the mob tomorrow?

As the shouts for John of Engelheim spread from the blacksmiths, stonemasons and tanners quarter into other districts of the city, Anastasius withdrew his forces to the area directly adjacent to Bishop Arsenius' residence. Then, as the cry for the new pope reached its crescendo, Anastasius would have retreated from the city in fear of his life had not word been received that King Louis was mobilizing his forces for an invasion of the city. This word was brought by Nikon, who had run to King Louis after Joanna escaped capture by Anastasius, warning the king that if he failed to move at once, all would be lost.

Despite the urging of his uncle, the bishop, to wait until King Louis was inside the city, Anastasius decided to march on the papal palace at once trusting that he would gain reinforcements soon enough and fearing that any delay might result in the election of the favorite of the clamoring mob.

Tightly massed into a juggernaut with each man holding his unsheathed sword at the ready, the soldiers of Anastasius rushed toward the papal palace, cutting down and trampling any who dared stand in their way.

Had the forces commanded by King Louis entered the city at once and joined with those of Anastasius, which now waited for reinforcements a spear throw from the palace, it is likely that the mob surrounding the palace would have been dispersed. But for reasons of his own, King Louis delayed entering the city and the crowd around the papal palace continued to grow.

As this crowd approached ten thousand in number, scores then hundreds scattered through its ranks began to urge an attack on Anastasius' forces. Minutes passed with both sides cursing and hurling threats at one another. Then like a storm-swollen river overflowing its banks, the mob, waving a wild assortment of weapons started across the open space. Anastasius hesitated for several seconds — if his men held their tight formation and rushed forward, it was possible that they could cut through the mob. He looked backwards to see if there was any sign of reinforcements. But the streets to his rear lay empty. Then as stones from the mob began to shower down, he ordered a retreat, which within moments turned into a rout.

As soon as they saw that the forces of Anastasius had been routed and then learned from several messengers that King Louis had not yet moved, the cardinals, at the urging of the Bishop of Porto and several others, acceded to the thundered demands of the populace and elected Joanna Pope.

A silence fell over the crowd, which by now had swollen to more than twenty thousand, as the cardinal archdeacon, dressed in his shimmering robes, stepped out on the balcony of the palace. Raising the papal crucifix in one hand, displaying the papal ring with the other, the archdeacon thundered out: "The blessed Pope Leo IV is dead. By election of the princes of the Church, Pope John VIII now reigns. May the Lord God in His infinite wisdom and boundless compassion guide and protect our Pope. May His only begotten Son, Christ Jesus, be ever at his side."

At a nod from the archdeacon a shout went up from the multitude that was heard in every quarter of Rome and beyond. It reached the ears of King Louis outside the walls of Rome, who now knew what his hesitation had cost.

As if a giant hand had choked it off, the thunderous shout died away as Joanna, accompanied only by Marcos, entered the square from a narrow side street. At the appearance of the new Pope, all the many thousands sank to their knees while the archdeacon shouted out hosannas and streams of blessings. Then descending from the balcony, the archdeacon, closely followed by a score of cardinals and a like number of bishops, met Joanna as she approached the entrance to the papal palace, prostrating himself before her and kissing her feet. Then, rising to his knees, the cardinal archdeacon placed the papal ring on Joanna's finger.

IX

THE VATICAN

*E*very window in the papal palace, not excluding those narrow windows in the highest turret, was ablaze with light, the wide square that lay before the palace was lit by countless torches so that even the remotest corner of the square was bathed in light. Romans stood bareheaded and marveled as a stream of dignitaries from virtually every kingdom in Christendom passed through their ranks and entered the wide-opened portals of the palace.

It was exactly two months since the papal ring had been placed on Pope John's finger, forty days since the required ceremonial dinner had been given by the new Pope for the nobles and greater clergy of Rome, thirty days since communications had been carried to all the major rulers of the western world and every bishop, and now was the time when those with any pretension of power, from kingdoms and dioceses nearby and remote, were gathering to lay eyes upon the new Pontiff, to say their names and declare their ranks, and to make proper obeisance by first kissing the Pope's satin slippers and pressing their lips to his ring.

With Marcos, who had been elevated to the priesthood and declared papal confessor just hours after she had been elected Pope, seated immediately to her left, and with the Bishop of Porto, who was now an archbishop, seated to her right, Joanna received each dignitary with a few carefully chosen words followed by the papal blessing. From reports whispered into her ear by the cardinal archdeacon, the numbers of waiting visitors and those still entering the city was such that this audience must surely last forever. Fatigue such as she had never known had worked its way into Joanna's flesh, into her very bones during the course of the sixty days since that tumultuous night when the citizens of Rome had demanded her election. Other than a few hours snatched for sleep, each of the sixty days, minute by minute, had demanded the maximum of her attention and a significant portion of her energy. An ocean of accumulated correspondence had to be attended to. Decisions which had not been brought to her dying predecessor were now placed before her with urgent requests for answers. Hundreds clamored for a moment of her time, each begging some sort of preferment or advantage. Crises were generated by reports of new movement by Saracen ships and armies. And there were precious portions of already choked days that must be devoted to appeasing King Louis and gaining a show of friendship from this powerful ruler, who had kept his considerable army camped outside the walls of Rome for several weeks after Janna's election. And now this endless audience.

The faces of the men and occasional women who approached, sank to their knees and went through the required ceremony, had become a blur. Although there were words for each, and although Joanna forced her voice to sound full and strong when she gave the blessing, it was as if the speech emanated from another being, another being who was the Pope, who therefore must not flag, who would not deny a particle of the precious experience for which so many of these men and women had traveled great distances. But as the Pope continued on with apparently undiminished energy, Joanna ached for the relief of sleep, hungered for just the smallest portion of time which could be spent alone doing nothing.

Within the first weeks of her papacy Joanna understood why so many popes had been short-lived. She understood in her wearying body, in her choked mind, why Pope Leo, despite his robustness, ended his papacy as a broken and helpless man. It was more than the work, which in itself was enough to drain the resources of ten like herself; it was the leaden weight of the responsibility. Each word uttered had its consequence; an ill-chosen word, even a change of expression, could produce devastating results. Hundreds constantly watched her face, measured not only her words themselves but their intonation. "You are now the spokesman for Christ," the Bishop of Porto had whispered to her as she entered the papal palace after receiving the papal ring. And so she was. For all the many millions who were within the compass of Christ's Church, she now was the Savior's voice. From her edicts there could be no appeal on earth.

Without the constant services of Marcos, who brought food to her lips when she was immobilized by exhaustion, who massaged her hands and feet and bathed her temples with spirits of wine, who stood guard outside her door during those few hours taken for sleep, turning away those who would awaken the Pope for some urgent matter or other; without this constant attention by Marcos, who himself often

reeled from exhaustion, Joanna could not have completed these first
two months of her papacy without total collapse.

"You must eat something — a bit of bread and cheese — something," Marcos urged Joanna, who had briefly retired to her chamber
during that endless audience. To this Joanna shook her head, muttering a few words about her stomach being as heavy as a stone. But she
did accept a flagon of milk into which some wine and honey had been
mixed. "Order today's audience at an end, Joanna, tell the rest to
come back in a day," Marcos begged while she drank. To this Joanna
shook her head. "You are the Pope. One word from you..."

"Many of them have traveled for weeks," said Joanna in a flattened voice. "It is because I am Pope, I cannot send them away. If I
were not," she sighed deeply. "To have them wait for those hours
while I slept...No, Marcos, we will finish with this audience. Then I
will grant myself a full half a day for sleep and for time to spend in
meditation." She gazed at the man's troubled face for several moments. She allowed her eyes to travel quickly over his thick, muscular
torso; if she ony dared, what comfort she could gain embraced by
those arms, her head resting against that chest. If she only dared.

The stench of the reception chamber, filled as it was with
hundreds of sweating human beings, struck Joanna like an iron-
studded club as she emerged from her private chamber. The scores
upon scores of blazing torches, flickering lamps and sputtering
candles dug into her eyes like the talons of a falcon. She had been absent less than half an hour, but was greeted with thunderous shouts,
as though she had just returned from a month's journey.

Seating herself on the throne and smiling faintly at the
Archbishop of Porto, whose face was haggard with fatigue and deeply
lined with the pain he still suffered, Joanna continued with the reception.

A savage-looking personage, dressed in furs despite the heat, his
face bristling with an unkempt beard and a huge mustache, approached, holding in his hands a gift of a finely carved sword made
from what appeared to be the purest ivory. "He is a recently converted
Norse chief, Your Holiness," the cardinal archdeacon whispered in
her ear. "It is rumored that before his conversion this one was not ad-
verse to eating human flesh," he continued with a shudder. "Yet now
as a Christian chief, he must be received."

The Norse chief sank to his knees. Then with his leather fittings
creaking and his huge muscles knotting and bulging, he brought his

lips to her slippers, then raised his head and grinned in such a fashion that Joanna had little doubt as to the accuracy of the archdeacon's suspicions. Muttering something in an incomprehensible tongue, he took her ringed hand in one of his, which was not less than three times its breadth, and implanted the required kiss. Joanna struggled to control a shudder — not one of loathing but of fear. One squeeze of that enormous hand and her hand would be hopelessly crushed. One massive hug from those arms and the very life would be squeezed from her. Crackling like lightning over the surface of her brain was the thought: *if he knew that this one to whom he made obeisance was a woman, if somehow this was suddenly revealed to him, none of my retainers would be able to act quickly enough to save me from his vengeance.* There had not been a single day during the sixty days of her papacy when thoughts of the terrible consequences should her sex be discovered did not gnaw within the darker portions of her mind. But now, for some reason, the gnawing had risen to the surface, had sent out threads of ice to her throat, to her chest, deep into her abdomen. Hers was a dangerous game that at any moment... at any moment... She drove the thought back down into the darkness as she gave the kneeling Norse chief her benediction.

Had her attention not been so fixed on the fierce face and frightening physique of the Norse chief, Joanna would have been aware of who waited next in line and thus would have been able to make certain preparations. Even with her attention fixed on the chief, had her eyes been less fatigued, she might have gained a glimpse of the grinning face made even more hideous by the passage of time. But when she looked down again after following the chief's departure for a moment, she was unable to control her body's recoil as she saw that the hermit Nikon knelt less than an arm's length away.

Gripping the finely carved side rails of the throne with all her strength, Joanna forced her eyes to meet those of the hermit. Never had she been this close to that one. An odor of death rose from the man and filled her nostrils. And from his eyes there came a heat as if they were two pools of molten iron in the caldron of his skull. The fear that she might be discovered she had experienced just moments earlier returned with even greater force. But from the hermit she would not suffer a quick and merciful death from a sudden explosion of rage. No, from him there would be tortures of unimaginable cruelty...

"I am come to declare my loyalty and make my obeisance to Pope John, the Vicar of our Lord Jesus Christ." Nikon's harsh and powerful voice rang out and filled the audience chamber.

"Although there may have been some slight differences at one time between the priest John of Engelheim and this one who now kneels before you, there can never be any differences between a true Christian and his Pope." The hermit sucked in his breath, bent forward in such a manner that it was apparent he was making a supreme effort, and brought his cracked lips down to Joanna's slippers. Then, rising, he went on, "From Nikon, Your Holiness can expect slavish devotion. I give my oath to all here assembled never to be out of sight of the papal palace so that I may be instantly summoned. And should Your Holiness be forced to travel, I will always be in attendance, although my humble rank demands I remain at the outer fringes of your train. And I swear to you, Your Holiness, that to prove my devotion, no task will be too mean, no burden too great to bear in my unswerving support of your papacy."

The death stench which rose from the man was like that of the soldiers killed at the walls of Engelheim. Joanna's eyes locked with those of the hermit. His eyes were no longer molten pools of metal. Now each was like the single eye of the terrible octopus.

"Such is my loyalty, Your Holiness, that I will forswear sleep so that my eyes can either be upon your person or turned in the direction of your place of habitation." Again with a supreme effort, Nikon bent forward, this time bringing his lips to the papal ring, lips whose coldness and roughness, as they brushed her hand, sent waves of fear and revulsion through Joanna's body.

As if some force had seized her and taken control of her voice, Joanna heard herself saying: "I disbelieve all your declarations of loyalty and devotion, Nikon." Gasps of surprise echoed through the papal chamber at this departure from the prescribed form of ceremony. "You have done everything in your power to vilify John the priest. I have sufficient information as to your efforts to take the life of that same John. Now this John, who through the grace of God has become Pope, views you as an enemy to the papacy and orders you, on the pain of death, never to enter the papal presence again." At this there were more gasps and a buzz of whispers.

"From the orders of the Pope there can be no appeal." Nikon's voice cracked with barely suppressed rage. "But I am determined to prove my loyalty and will maintain my vigilance from a distance. From a sufficient distance but never too far away, Your Holiness. Never too far away."

If Joanna saw the faces of the dozen men following Nikon at all, it was only as indistinct blurs — if asked, she could not have been able to state a single thing about them. Although her lips formed the necessary words, although she held out her ring to be kissed and then stretched out her hand during the blessing, her brain continued to seethe with thoughts of Nikon. Would his constant vigilance discover her sex? Was it possible that he already suspected? There was no doubt that his eyes would be constantly on her, that he would gain intelligence of her every movement. Had she been unwise to treat him so harshly — publicly declaring her enmity? Would it be possible to continue her deception through the months and years that lay ahead with eyes such as those of the hermit constantly upon her? The hermit's daring to come into her presence must be viewed as a portent of possible disaster. Then, as if in a diabolical confirmation of the worst that might happen, the face of a person who could reveal her true identity swam into focus.

Head held high, shoulders squared, dressed completely in black except for a silver cross, the abbess Brita knelt before her. For a moment, a single moment, Joanna doubted her identity — the face was so much older, the eyes now hooded and sunk much deeper in the skull, the few tufts of hair which showed now a silvery white — but then she was certain. The one kneeling at her feet awaiting the papal word was the same personage as the one who had offered the ten-year old the choice of the doll or the cross.

Biting her lower lip to keep it from trembling, Joanna forced her eyes to meet those of the woman. They were steady but showed no signs of recognition. Was it possible that the abbess did not recognize her? So many years. So much had happened. She was now grown old. Perhaps the years had dimmed her vision. But how could she not recognize one to whom she had been so close? Joanna bit more deeply into her lip. Any moment the abbess might denounce her, might declare that the one sitting on the throne of St. Peter was a woman. Joanna allowed herself to take in a deep breath and as she did this, released her lower lip and tasted blood.

Feeling the tension draining from her, Joanna smiled faintly and inclined her head a fraction. In response to this permission, the abbess cleared her throat and said, "I am from the land of Saxons, Your Holiness." Her voice was the same, age had not touched it. "I am Mother Superior to a convent of pious nuns. I have come into your presence to declare the loyalty of not only the nuns of my convent but of all the sisters of Christ of Saxony whom I, by their election, also represent."

Making her voice as deep as possible, Joanna said: "I too am from the land of the Saxons, Holy Mother."

"So I have been led to understand, Your Holiness. And as one who is familiar with our land, it is the hope of all the Saxon sisters of Christ that the newly elected Pope will provide us with the means for extending our services to the hundreds of villages without church or priest, where the inhabitants wallow in ignorance of Christian ways that is so deep they are scarcely better than heathens."

"I will consider your words carefully, Holy Mother," said Joanna.

After Joanna had given the papal blessing, just as the abbess Brita was starting to rise from her knees, their eyes again met. Then the abbess said softly, "The companion with whom you traveled for years, Your Holiness, is of my district. How does that one fare?" Joanna's heart pounded violently. Scarcely realizing what she did, she reached out and took Brita's hands.

"My companion...Brother William?" The abbess nodded. "My companion and beloved friend now stands before the throne of our Heavenly Father." A film of moisture clouded the abbess's eyes as she turned away. Then with head held high, back straight as a young oak, she walked slowly out of the papal chamber.

The six months following the great reception were filled with such difficulty and were fraught with such pain for Joanna they might have been a like number of months spent in Purgatory.

Immediately following the great reception, tension and fatigue that had been heightened by the confrontation with Nikon and the appearance of the abbess Brita caused Joanna to come down with a desperate contagion similar to the one that almost took her life after Wilma's death. She had staggered from the audience chamber moments after the last dignitary was received and as soon as she was in her private chamber collapsed into Marcos' arms, shaking and weeping. She had gasped out her fears that Nikon would be the instrument of her ultimate undoing, then revealed those terrible anxious moments as she waited for the abbess to expose her deception; how she had yearned to rush from her throne and enfold her in an embrace as she showered kisses on that deeply wrinkled face. The days that followed were darkened with the struggle against this sickness, which at times threatened to strangle her. The struggle might have failed had Marcos not been in constant attendance, bathing her hands and face, forcing her to take sips of nourishing liquid. Yet even in the depths of this sickness the work of the Pope must go on. Hours that might have restored her if devoted to sleep were spent listening to endless petitions, answering correspondence, granting brief audiences to holy men from remote regions while the fever raged on. And then the day she found sufficient strength to leave her private chamber and take her place on the throne an attempt was made to poison her.

Fearing that just such an attempt would be made, Marcos, using his power as confessor, had taken it upon himself to issue orders to the papal chamberlain that one of his men must always taste any food or drink before it was offered to the Pope. Joanna had ordered a flagon of milk sweetened with honey — scarcely anything else would remain in her unsettled stomach. The flagon had been brought, one of the chamberlain's men had taken a good draught, but the press of business was such that Joanna left the flagon untouched just long enough for the poison to start its work. Grabbing his stomach and crying out that he had been stabbed in the gut, the taster sank to his knees, then vomited blood. Joanna's face went a dead white. She knew what had happened. Within moments the contagion was again upon her with such severity she had to be carried from the chamber.

Her recovery from this second bout was delayed for weeks during which there were days when her delirium was such she could not function, and the work of the papacy came to a halt. During these weeks there were rumors that Anastasius and others would attempt to usurp the papacy. Painful as it was, Marcos could not withhold this information from Joanna and this knowledge inhibited her recovery.

And then when she was finally able to remount her throne, an occurrence took place which brought on another relapse.

The papal audience had just begun, with scores of noblemen and bishops who had waited weeks for this audience crowding the papal chamber, when the doors burst open and a giant of a man, whose features were European although his skin was almost black, forced an entrance together with at least half a hundred other men equally swarthy but of somewhat lesser stature.

"We are from Sicily and we demand to see Pope John," the man thundered as the chamberlain and some of his men tried to bar his way. "If Pope John is the friend of Sicilian Christians as he has so often declared, he will not deny us this audience," the man went on, leveling his thickly muscled arm in Joanna's direction. At a gesture from Joanna, the chamberlain stepped aside and the man forced his way through the crowd.

"I am Antonias of Syracuse and I bring greetings to Your Holiness from all the Christians of Sicily — those already enslaved by the Saracens and those who soon will be." The man ponderously sank to his knees and stared hard at Joanna. His eyebrows were so thick and bushy, his eyes so deep set and dark that it was almost as if his face were covered with some sort of mask. "You who led the bandits down from the hills in an attack against the infidels who occupy Palermo, you who were raised to the priesthood by the Bishop of Palermo and know from the evidence of your own eyes the depth of his plight and that of other Sicilian Christians, you who declared again and again before your election to the papacy that the infidel must be driven from Christian lands, will now not stand idle while with the passage of each day those vile followers of Mahamat move closer and closer to the ancient city of Syracuse, the glorious city of my birth." The man paused while he caught his breath and during this short interval Joanna closed her eyes and lowered her head into her hands as she fought off a wave of dizziness. " 'Pope John will take command of a Christian army and drive the Saracens from this island,' the archdeacon of Syracuse declared the day he ordered me and this company of men to take ship to Rome. Your name is on the lips of every Sicilian, Your Holiness. Little children are taught to lisp your name. Dying ones call out Pope John with their last breaths. There are many who declare you a saint, although you yet live." Snatching Joanna's hand and bringing it to his lips, then bathing the hand with a shower of unashamed tears, the man choked out between sobs: "Declare a holy war against the infidel, Your Holiness! Form a great army! Lead us to Sicily where we may die a glorious death in defense of the Cross! Lead us, Your Holiness, lead us!"

A sickening hollowness spread from beneath Joanna's breastbone down into her abdomen and up to the base of her throat. It was as if this huge dark-skinned man had, with his impassioned words, torn away a portion of her insides.

A hush fell over the papal chamber. For a moment Joanna was transported back to the cathedral of Aachen as Wilma pulled open her tunic and revealed the famed miracle of transformation. Would that she were able to produce such a miracle now to satisfy this man, to satisfy the hundreds of bishops and noblemen whose eyes were turned to her. A miracle to satisfy all the tens of thousands of suffering Sicilians. Then came a helplessness little different than that she had experienced years ago as they fled from their village at Rolf's urging, fled into the forest as the soldiers who had once served the Great Charles approached.

"One word, Your Holiness, just one single word." Tears still flowed from the man's eyes and bathed her hand, held so close she could feel his moist, hot breath. "Give me the word I can take to the Archdeacon of Syracuse, to all the Christians of Sicily. Give me this word, I beg you."

Her tongue so thick she could not speak, her lips trembling despite all of her efforts to control them, Joanna withdrew her hand from the kneeling man. She shifted her eyes — she could no longer look at him. She could not remain in that chamber another moment. The fevered contagion was returning. She must have the privacy of her chamber.

She rose from her throne and started toward her chamber. A sound that was a groan, yet more than a groan came from the open mouth of the kneeling man, a sound she had heard as men were pierced through the heart in battle. She forced her numbing limbs to carry her. Forced her dead hand to open her chamber door, then close it behind her, with that word the Sicilian had begged for unspoken.

She sobbed, as she once had sobbed in Gerberta's arms, all through that afternoon and evening, but this time it was the arms of Marcos that comforted her, his deep chest against which she rested her head. "It is the same with me as it was with Pope Leo," she finally whispered when she had no more tears left for crying. "You understand, Marcos, don't you. If I leave Rome, if I lead an army to Sicily, the papal throne will be usurped. I know with an absolute certainty that within a week of my departure, Anastasius will be vying with that black John of Ravenna for this throne. If I leave Rome, Sicily will not be freed, but all of Christendom will suffer from this usurpation." She shuddered with dry sobs. "Yet how could I reveal all this to that noble Sicilian," she went on. "You understand, Marcos, you understand. Tell me that my remaining here in Rome is the correct thing." Instead of answering Marcos gently stroked her hair with his thick, broad hand.

Another series of dry sobs and the tension started draining from her body. Gerberta had stroked her hair, then Marla, then Wilma. Now this. Her head still resting against the deep chest, Joanna felt her flesh beginning to blend with Marcos' sinews and muscles. Within her being it became all liquid. She could feel the touch of his hands on her hair radiate down to the tips of her fingers. A yearning greater than that she had experienced the night she had almost entered his chamber spread through her body, down into her thighs, into her loins. She smelled the musk of the man's breath and this caused her breathing to grow more rapid. So many years of struggle; years of self-denial; years of hiding her womanhood. Just let it happen...let it happen...why deny herself any longer? So much love that hungered for expression. Just let it happen...Marcos' arms tightened and his hand moved from her hair to her shoulder; then down to her breasts.

With a sudden violent twist of her body, Joanna wrenched herself away. Such was the force of this movement that she fell to her knees on the floor. There she remained for several seconds as if in supplication, her eyes on the hurt features of the man. Then as she started to rise she whispered, "I cannot do it. I am a priest...you also are a priest, dearest Marcos. We can love. Nowhere is it written that priests cannot love. But ours must be a love only of the spirit." She twisted her hands together.

A heavy numbness softened the pain of that period of purgation Joanna had yet to go through. Most days her head throbbed and the muscles of her body ached as if she had been beaten with a heavy stick. Most nights she had difficulty in falling asleep and then her sleep was troubled with frightening dreams, dreams of exposure, of other things. Often she was unable to keep anything on her stomach other than bread soaked in milk, so that as the weeks and months passed she grew dangerously thin.

Acutely aware of what she could and could not do, aware of the subtle yet controlling limitations on the power of the Pope in this decaying time of history, Joanna bent every effort in the direction of instituting those reforms that were possible, in minimizing the abuses of the Church hierarchy when circumstances conspired against effective reform. When the facts were known to her, she rejected self-serving and wicked men who were suggested as candidates for vacant bishoprics. With the help of the Archbishop of Porto and others of his stamp, she attempted to identify those who were of little help when it came to those who lived in the more distant portions of Christendom. From time to time, she was reminded in one way or another of the plight of the Christians in the occupied portions of Sicily, and it was at these times that her suffering was most acute. And it is possible that the condition of a living purgatory would have continued on indefinitely rather than lasting for only six months had not a certain incident taken place, an incident whose effect upon her was like that of a person who survives after being struck by lightning.

Among the bewildering multitude of tasks required of the Pope was hearing appeals from an ecclesiastical court. For the most part, only those of the highest rank had the wealth and sufficient knowledge of canonical law to carry these appeals to the Pope. But now and again there were exceptions. Usually these were holy men of no rank yet with a reputation and a following which demanded they be given special treatment. It was the case of such a one that Joanna was called upon to judge six months, to the day, after the great reception.

His hair matted with dirt, his skin a greyish brown from months if not years of non-bathing, his teeth broken and blackened, his eyes bulging and showing a fierce light, the monk who had been convicted by an ecclesiastical court in Spalato of apostasy was led into the papal chamber. Somewhat shorter than average height, hunched, yet with finely, almost delicately, formed hands, the monk glared at Joanna, his mouth making strange chewing movements.

"This is the monk Edred and he has been judged guilty of apostasy, Your Holiness," the chamberlain announced in a voice loud enough for all who were gathered to hear. "He has declared that certain letters of St. Paul are forgeries: those written to the Thessalonians and the one to the Ephesians. Despite warnings, he has preached to the credulous that no less a one than St. Paul himself appeared while he was walking in the woods and informed him of these forgeries. And, Your Holiness," the chamberlain's face took on a stern expression, "when given the opportunity to recant — in consideration of the many years spent in the East among the heathen — when offered dismissal of all charges if he would only recant, this Edred accused the court of being composed of ill-educated louts. The court, Your Holiness, which included the Bishop of Spalato himself. Then he declared that the least priest in England, his native country, the least priest had a greater erudition than all this court taken together. The bishop included, Your Holiness. The bishop included!"

A chill caused Joanna's hands to stiffen despite the heat of the day, and she had difficulty breathing. Was it possible...?

"I am of the school of the venerable Bede, Your Holiness!" the monk cried out in a reedy voice. "Of the very school founded by the greatest theologian of the past one hundred years. And those ignorant ones, who I doubt have ever read more than a portion of the Holy Testament themselves, they dare to judge me. Those three letters are forgeries! After St. Paul talked to me, I spent a full year in the deepest study making comparisons and, yes, they are forgeries. I have nothing to recant." The monk started his chewing motions again.

Struggling to find sufficient breath, choosing each word carefully, Joanna said, "You served this Church by converting the heathens in the East?"

"First the Saxon heathens, Your Holiness. Then others further to the east. More than a quarter of a century have I devoted to this task. And I have converted thousands, Your Holiness, thousands."

"The Church must take this service into consideration, serious consideration, before rendering a decision." Joanna still had difficulty

breathing. "It is my inclination to set aside the decision of the ecclesiastical court, Holy Father."

"I am not to be called a father, Your Holiness. I am a monk but
not a priest." Joanna made a questioning sound. "Not worthy of the
priesthood," the monk responded. "I have been offered the priesthood
but refused. Refused because I have known a woman in marriage and
have fathered a child."

Joanna gripped the sides of her throne as a wave of dizziness
swept over her that almost caused her to faint. Several long moments
passed in silence with everyone waiting, all eyes on her.

"But before I order you discharged, it is my wish to examine you
further in privacy," Joanna managed to say in a hoarse whisper. She
forced herself to her feet and took in several deep breaths as she attempted to gain control over her limbs, then staggered rather than
walked to her chamber with the monk, escorted by the chamberlain
following.

Dismissing the chamberlain with the promise to call him if
needed — the man had a worried look on his face and his eyes darted
constantly toward the wild-eyed monk — Joanna seated the monk on
the stool next to her couch, the same stool on which she once sat when
Leo first brought her into his chamber. Then she said in a hoarse
voice: "It was not to examine you further regarding those charges of
apostasy that I brought you here." The monk's eyes narrowed and the
chewing motions stopped for several moments, but resumed with increased vigor as Joanna went on. "I am from the district of Engelheim...perhaps you did not know this." The monk made no reply. "I
learned from the priest of Engelheim that a monk, a holy man, lived
for a time in the district." Joanna examined the monk's features for
any clues as to what he was thinking. But there were none. "This
monk, who came from the land of the Ingels, had a wife, a wife who
gave birth to a child in a peasant village." Joanna could not be certain, but she thought she saw a film of moisture forming in the monk's
eyes. "This woman of whom I speak, the wife of the holy monk, died
to give her child life." She waited for the man to speak, her heart
pounding so hard it shook her body.

"I was that monk. The woman, my wife. The child, my
daughter."

"A female child?" Joanna said.

"A female child. Finely formed with features like her mother. Her
mother..." The monk coughed, and the cough turned into a sob. "So
long ago. I have tried to forget. Have dedicated my life to Christ's
Holy Church. I named the child with the name of my dead wife, then

gave her to one of the women of the village to nurse and to keep safe until my return."

"Your dead wife's name?"

"Joanna. A beautiful name. A beautiful, gentle woman." Alternating surges of hot and cold ran through Joanna's body.

"You gave this child to a woman of the village?"

"Gave her to this woman, yes. Together with a silver coin whose value was sufficient to guarantee the child's care until I should return." The monk slowly shook his head.

"And the child, holy man. What of the child?"

"She is dead. Long dead."

"Dead?" Joanna's body was shaking and she made no effort to conceal it.

"I returned after a space of years as I had said I would. Bitter years. Yet years during which I brought many souls to Christ. I returned to that village whose boundaries I found strangely marked with crosses. But all who lived in that village were dead. Slaughtered. A great mound of men and women and children...lying out there in the field covered with a blanket of snow." The scene of that snow-covered mound filled Joanna's vision so that she could no longer see the monk. "They were dead not more than a week. I met a half-burnt, crazed one from another village who said soldiers of the Great Charles had passed through the district just a few days since. Had I reached the village earlier, just a little earlier...had I started my return from the East ten days sooner...but I was too late. All dead. Horribly slaughtered. Horribly slaughtered."

"All dead. Horribly slaughtered." Joanna echoed.

"I knelt by that tragic mound and prayed until forced to rise by the cold. I left that mound of what once had been human beings, that mound containing the hacked remains of my daughter, and returned to my mission in the East."

A period of silence ensued during which Joanna's breathing returned to normal and the monk, who had been openly weeping, dried his tears. The silence was finally broken by Joanna who said, "That coin you gave to the woman was brought to the priest by a peasant who managed to escape that village." Joanna reached inside her garment to the special secret place. "Circumstances finally caused the coin to be given to my care." She opened her hand.

"Yes, that is the one!" the monk cackled. Then without asking permission he snatched the coin from her hand and buried it in the recesses of his filthy garments. The man's eyes were burning as they had when he first entered the papal chamber and his mouth was again making the chewing movements.

"Yes, it is your coin, Holy Father," said Joanna.

"Not Holy Father — I am no priest."

"You are a priest now, Holy Father," Joanna said as she laid her hands on the man's head.

"I do not deserve..."

"I am the Pope. I say you do deserve." At that the monk began to grin and continued to grin as Joanna escorted him out of her chamber, then through the entire length of the reception chamber, with no concern for the startled looks and surprised whispers of the nobles and clergymen gathered there.

When the doors of the papal chamber had closed behind the wild-eyed, grinning monk, Joanna hesitated, then quickly turned to face the assemblage. The eyes of every person in that huge room were riveted upon her. She remained where she was without moving, her vision encompassing everyone.

Time had stopped. It was eternity; it was, in that stoppage of time, as Christ declared it could be: "On earth as it is in heaven."

All of the ache, all the tangled flecks of fear enmeshed in the web of the past, all the cadaverous fingers of loneliness, all of this fell away from her in that moment of eternity. She walked forward toward her throne and her body was as light and free, as free as when she ran through the fields with Magda, her foster sister. Everything had grown so clear — the faces of the nobles and clergymen who watched her with such perplexed expressions, a moth vibrating in a spider's web suspended from a corner of the banner that showed the fish, every detail of that great chamber. And the air, although fouled with the stink of the unwashed scores in attendance, caressed her lungs like the finest velvet as she drew each breath.

"I am Pope, the Vicar of Christ," she whispered to herself as she took her place on the papal throne. Then to the Archbishop of Porto, but in a voice loud enough for all to hear, "I have sat on the throne of St. Peter more than half a year, Your Eminence. I have now gained sufficient mastery of the complexities and awesome responsibilities of this holy office. It is now time for the attention of the Pope to be directed toward the amelioration of those Christians denied the sacrament as they are ground into the earth beneath the Saracen boot. We will recruit an army of sufficient size and readiness." The color drained from the Archbishop's face as he struggled against the almost overwhelming urge to shake his head, to caution the Pope. "We shall take the necessary precautions so that those who conspire to usurp the papacy — and I know the names of those who so conspire — during

Our absence from Rome will not be able to effect this usurpation."

Joanna turned away from the Archbishop of Porto and faced the entire assemblage. "To ensure the safety of this throne, all clergymen except those of the lowest rank will, by my express order, be a part of this army. As will all nobles of Italy of whatever rank. If there should be nobles who will not join this army, let them flee to the most remote regions of the world at once or face arrest and imprisonment. But even escape to the most remote regions will not save any clergyman of Italy above the rank of deacon. For I issue, this day, a bull of excommunication against any Italian priest who will not serve."

Uneasy murmurs passed through the assemblage and there was much stirring about and many long faces.

Joanna turned back to the archbishop, whose features were now composed into a serene expression.

"You see, my noble archbishop, we need have no concern for the safety of the papacy. All of our energies will be directed against those vile and villainous Africans. And we shall allow a sufficient time to build an army whose might cannot be withstood. A year should be enough. Yet if a second year is needed, it will not be denied." Joanna turned back to the assemblage. "It is my single wish that if all else about this papacy is forgotten, it be remembered for one thing: the liberation of those Christian lands now held by Saracens."

As Joanna had finished her speech, the archbishop rose from his seat and with every show of ceremony started slowly clapping his hands. He was quickly joined by Marcos who also rose from his seat. Then by twos and threes, dozens and scores, the assemblage joined the applause until the entire palace echoed with the measured sound.

"I have never seen you as you just were, Joanna," Marcos said as soon as the door to the private chamber was closed behind them.

"I have been reborn," said Joanna, her eyes showing an excited, almost wild luster. Marcos made a questioning sound as he waited for her to go on, but Joanna only tossed her head and flashed a smile that caused a wave of heat to sweep through him.

M   Moving as if in a dance, Joanna brushed by the man and went to the window. "All the world lies before me, Marcos. I have never felt so free." She turned and looked archly at the man, flashed another smile, then turned back to the window. Marcos hesitated several moments as he rubbed his perspiring hands against his robe, then took the several steps and was beside her.

"So beautiful. You are so beautiful, Joanna. So slender." He eased a cautious arm around her waist and, with a sigh, she nestled in his arms. She could feel his breath on her lips, could feel the pounding of her heart. Then their lips met.

And then sighs that were almost gasps came from the woman whose fingers dug wildly into the muscles of his arms. She pressed herself tightly against Marcos as she felt the swelling in his groin. Then she whispered, as the man's eyes asked a question, "I am the Pope. And as Pope I grant permission."

She gasped as Marcos lifted her in his arms and started for the couch. Then as he placed her on the couch and opened her robe, she panted, "As lawful Pope, with the authority of Our Savior...I grant permission..." Her words were cut off by a violent gasp as Marcos with a shuddering moan welded their flesh together.

Declaring that the Pope required the constant services of his confessor, day and night, Joanna ordered that a second couch be placed in her private chamber. But this couch was little used, for their years of denial made them almost insatiable. Often their love-making and impassioned secret sharing between the acts of love left them with little more than two or three hours of sleep. Yet Joanna found herself with greater energy than she had ever known. And the delicacy of her digestion as well as her other complaints vanished so that she quickly filled out and showed a robust complexion. Her every gesture declared her renewed vigor.

As she had announced, she put the program for creating a great army into operation at once. She generated such a storm of correspondence to bishops, archdeacons, kings and princes that it took a full dozen scribes to keep up with her. Ambassadors and visiting theologians, who ordinarily might expect to wait not less than a week, were seen at once, even if this made the papal audience continue late into the night. She personally visited all the fortifications in and around Rome, pouring out a stream of orders for changes and repairs, and then checking to see that these orders had been carried out. Several times, she ventured as much as a day's journey away from Rome. Each time she was aware that the hermit Nikon followed just beyond the farthest reaches of her train. But the furtive actions of this man, instead of causing her concern, produced almost a feeling of sympathy, for there was something pitiful about him.

The energy and vitality of the Pope, whose face now always showed a smile, served to reinforce those who had declared their loyalty from the first, and to bring thousands of less committed ones solidly into the papal camp. This had its effect on King Luis and the Archbishop of Ravenna who began sending regular communications declaring their support. Bishop Arsenias was growing enfeebled by age and thus no longer was a threat. And Anastasius kept his distance. The papal bull of excommunication served to remind him that he was still under the ban of excommunication by Pope Leo — the punishment of death in this new Pope's bull he read as directed at himself.

As the months passed the papacy of Joanna grew stronger and stronger. The nucleus of the army had been formed although it was apparent it would take more than a year before this army was ready to fight the Saracens. Joanna's love and passion for Marcos continued undiminished, satisfying and fortifying her so that even the most difficult of situations (and these regularly arose) instead of being burdens, were interesting and challenging problems for her to solve.

Only one thing marred these months of Joanna's papacy. At first a subtle but noticeable decrease of friendship on the part of the Archbishop of Porto. Then an open coldness, accompanied by a lessening attendance at the papal court, where for the first year he had been in constant attendance. Finally, except when directly summoned by Joanna, he ceased coming altogether. Joanna allowed several months to pass during which she did nothing about this painful situation other than make discreet inquiries that proved to be unproductive. But after suffering a bout of nausea that lasted several days, during which her thoughts constantly turned towards the archbishop (and for this reason she somehow connected her distress with his absence), she sent her chamberlain to escort him into her presence.

"Is it not within the compass of friendship for friends to reveal to one another matters which, if not corrected, may erode this friendship?" said Joanna as soon as they were alone in her private chamber. The nausea, although somewhat diminished, still kept her on her couch where she lay with her arms folded behind her head, while the archbishop stood some five paces distant with his arms folded tightly over his chest.

"Friendship? You speak of friendship, Your Holiness." The corners of the archbishop's mouth turned down as his eyes narrowed. "If there is friendship, yes there is an obligation on the part of the friends. But if friendship no longer exists...has been polluted..." The archbishop's voice was almost a snarl and the wolf-like quality of the man showed itself for a moment as he exposed the tips of his sharp teeth. But then this vicious expression was gone.

"Polluted..." Joanna said the word with a puzzled sound in her voice. "There is no one in all of Christendom I hold in higher respect than you. Ask, and if it is within my power I will satisfy your wishes."

"There is nothing I want, Your Holiness," the archbishop hesitated as he sucked in air between his clenched teeth, "for myself! It was not for personal gain or any sort of preferment that I labored, conspired and risked so that you might be elected Pope. It was for the good of Christ's Holy Church. Only this." The archbishop turned his face partially away and stared at a tapestry on which a likeness of Christ on the cross was stitched in threads of gold and silver. "I would have sacrificed my life gladly that a pious priest of unquestioned reputation might be elevated to the Throne of St. Peter. And how I celebrated when you gained that election — " The archbishop broke off.

"And now?"

"And now I find the one in whom I had such faith, upon whom I and thousands of others placed such hope," the archbishop suddenly faced Joanna directly, "I find the pious priest something less than pious." A stab of fear made Joanna's heart miss a beat. "The one whom I believed to be the purest of all men now, I am certain, regularly engages in abominable acts, engages in those unnatural acts condemned in the book of Leviticus — and with his confessor!"

The fear that Joanna had experienced was replaced with a sense of helpless heaviness.

"The clergy is riddled with this practice of abominable acts." The archbishop lowered his voice and slowly shook his head. "But I had not expected such a thing from you. Not from you." With that, without asking permission, the archbishop turned and, with a sound that might have been a cough or might have been a sob, strode quickly from the chamber.

Within an hour of the archbishop's departure Joanna had made arrangements for Marcos' couch to be removed from her chamber. But from the snickers and grins of the several servants assigned to carry out this task, she was certain the entire palace was aware that her relationship with Marcos was more than that of Pope and confessor. Yet, withal, she was relieved. If it had been discovered that she was a woman, the reaction would have been much different than just snickers and grins.

Exactly one month from the day of her confrontation with the Archbishop of Porto Joanna concluded from certain unmistakable signs that there was to be a consequence of her relationship with Marcos far more devastating in its potential than rumors of unnatural acts.

Other than brief weekly sessions devoted to confession, Joanna, with the concurrence of Marcos, had kept herself strictly separated from him during this month. It had been painful for her — being held at night had become a precious experience — yet there was no other choice. And then, during that month, as she gained the first glimmering suspicion, suspicion she determined to keep to herself until certain, this forced separation from Marcos became a time of agony.

Marcos' hands began to shake as Joanna finally revealed her certainties to him as they knelt in the confession box separated by a thin wooden partition. "Is it possible you are mistaken, Joanna?" said Marcos in a hoarse whisper.

"May the Almighty grant that I am mistaken, Marcos. But I was taught to know the signs when I was a little girl in my village. And I have those signs."

"How long will it be? How long until..." The dryness in his throat choked off Marcos' words.

"I am not certain. I think I have seven more months. But I am not certain."

"Seven more months! We will make plans, Joanna. Yes, we will make plans."

"But if my condition should be discovered?" Joanna fought to conceal the extent of her fear.

"It will not be discovered. No one has the slightest suspicion." He hesitated. "I will drop certain words in certain ears so that those rumors regarding unnatural acts continue to circulate. Your loose papal gowns hide much, my dearest. And you have put on weight during the past year; will continue to put on weight because of robust eating. There will be no suspicion."

"But when it is time, Marcos..." Joanna bit down on her lip.

"Before it is time, a month before it is time, you will announce a period of general meditation and prayer in anticipation of the campaign against the Saracens. During this period, you as supreme leader of the Church will retire to a remote place and will urge other leaders of the Church to do likewise."

Joanna nodded her head in the darkness and then, realizing where she was, murmured her agreement.

"If is it a live birth," Marcos spoke slowly, choosing each word carefully, "and it is my fervent wish that this be the case, I will place the infant in the hands of a good woman."

"As I was placed," Joanna softly whispered.

"I will visit this woman regularly to make certain the child receives the best of care, and when it is the proper time I will find a way to introduce the child to the papal court, as a page or, if a girl, as an assistant to the mistress of the wardrobe." Despite the ring of confidence echoing in Marcos' words, Joanna was unable to control a shudder as a fresh wave of fear passed through her.

"But if in spite of all our cautions we are discovered — they will destroy me. And the infant. And you, Marcos my dearest. If Wilma were only here! Old and ugly as she was, she could have stayed with me in my chamber without exciting the slightest suspicion. And with her skills as midwife when it became time...with her here with me I would feel so much safer."

"You only torture yourself, Joanna, with these thoughts of Wilma. I will take care of you, my beautiful Joanna. I will find a skilled midwife who will not have the slightest suspicion of who you are. I will do everything that needs to be done. All I beg of you, Joanna, is that you do not do anything rash."

"Rash" Joanna sighed deeply. "You suggest this possibility after a life such as I have lived. Is it because I am a woman you suggest this thing?" Without waiting for a reply, she went on. "If all the rashness, the foolishness done by men and done by women in this world were placed on the two sides of a great scale, I fear the foolishness, the rashness of men would be much the heavier." As she said this, Joanna's voice grew stronger. "I am frightened. I have more than sufficient reason to be frightened." She hesitated for several moments. "And I am, in spite of everything I tell myself regarding the preciousness of our love, distressed at my actions which have brought me to this condition. But as for my being rash, being frightened into a foolish rashness, you have nothing to fear, Marcos, as I have nothing to fear from your actions."

With the greatest care of which she was capable, considering the consequences of her every move, Joanna started curtailing her activities, limiting her public appearances, and delegating certain of her responsibilities to the cardinal archdeacon, to her chamberlain and to others. This was done gradually in such a way that it excited little notice within the papal palace and among the ranks of leading clergymen and greater nobles. But the Roman populace, as Joanna's public appearances grew less and less frequent, began to murmur its displeasure.

It is far easier to deny a populace that which it desires from the start than, once given, attempt to withdraw it. Romans viewed as one of their rights those almost daily processions through the city of Rome, when their young Pope could be approached for a blessing, for his touch on the head of an ailing child, for the presentation of a roughly drawn petition. When, after the passage of several months, their Pope only emerged from his palace on important occasions and then only for brief periods of time, groups of angered Romans started to gather in the square before the palace, demanding the appearance of the Pope, and when these demands were not met shouted insults and threw refuse in the direction of the papal guards. Yet on those occasions when Joanna did appear, the mood of the populace shifted and she was greeted with shows of affection. Seeing the delicate build and fine features of their Pope, their resentment was temporarily resolved. But then when another protracted period of non-appearance ensued, their resentment began to build. This rebuilding of resentment was given every assistance by Nikon and others who saw a possible advantage to their cause in what was taking place.

When, by her calculations, she was within six weeks of childbirth, Joanna issued a proclamation of meditation and prayer and isolated herself completely within her chamber, refusing admittance to anyone except her personal servants. Careful arrangements had been made for her to retire to the mountains in the northern part of Italy two weeks hence after a final appearance at the cathedral of St. John Lateran where she was scheduled to say the mass.

Most of each day during the course of these two weeks Joanna devoted to prayer. She would kneel before the tapestry with its representation of the crucified Christ, repeating the Pater Noster again and again, concentrating all of her thoughts on the person of the Christ. These protracted periods of prayer on her knees on the cold stone floor provided her with a certain measure of relief. As she said the name of the Lord over and over Joanna was able to keep her thoughts from herself, from the terrifying possibility of exposure which might happen despite all of Marcos' careful arrangements.

But when the pain of hours of kneeling radiated up her thighs into her back until it was an agony — the weight of the child and its occasional thrashing adding to this — Joanna would be forced to take a temporary respite from prayer. And it was during these short intervals that a depression composed of equal parts of loneliness and despair settled upon her like a close armor of lead whose weight was such she could scarcely move; she had to strain for every breath.

Struggle as she did during these bouts of depression, Joanna was unable to drive away a growing resentment against Marcos. Part of

her yearned for the man, hungered for his comfort, for his safe
embrace; but the rest of her, the greater part, held him responsible for
her condition. Everything had been going so well, her papacy had
been growing stronger day by day; essential reforms were in the process of being instituted, the plans for the reconquest of captured
Christian lands had been moving rapidly forward. Now this. Would it
be possible to reestablish her position, to again move forward after
this period of increasing inactivity? Once-delegated authority is difficult to reassume. And so much of her popularity with the Roman
masses had been eroded. Yet, after the birth of the child, if she
devoted every bit of her energy to repairing the damage and went out
in processions every day, perhaps even gave public sermons as she had
done in the courtyard of St. Martino, was it not possible that in time
her position could be reestablished? So much needed to be done.

Joanna awoke from a troubled sleep with a confused feeling of apprehension the day she was to deliver the mass at St. John Lateran.
Her journey to the retreat in the mountains was to commence that afternoon. Marcos was to travel by another route and they would only
meet when she had reached the deserted monastery which was her
final destination. There was not the slightest indication, so much as a
breath of suspicion had been aroused, yet her apprehension persisted.

She stood at her chamber window and stared out through the un-
even, partially discolored panes of leaded glass. The sky threatened
rain. To the west a bank of blackish clouds was building up. Below, in
the square, lay a scattering of refuse that had been hurled at the papal
guards the day before after a gathering of several thousand had
shouted for the appearance of their Pope with no result.

She turned away from the window and considered occupying the
remaining minutes before the procession was to begin kneeling in
prayer. But her body felt so heavy, so weighted down by the ornate
papal robes and by the living thing that filled her abdomen. She sat on
her couch and rested her head in her hands. It too felt heavy. Perhaps
this apprehension came from a report of one of her servants who had
seen Nikon lurking at the edge of the square the day before, laughing
as the angered crowd hurled its refuse. Or perhaps it was the thought
of walking in procession, being forced to breathe the stench of the
street, to put on a good face as the excited citizenry surrounded her
with their attempts to touch her garment, to gain a word or two of
blessing.

Yet in less than a half a day she would be beyond the walls of

Rome, in the pure sweet air of the countryside. And then...She smiled (her first smile in many weeks) at the thought of the time she would spend with Marcos in the privacy of the deserted monastery.

Although there were occasional splashes of rain and a crackle of lightning to the west of the city which declared that a storm was on its way, the citizens of Rome came by the thousands to view the papal procession. A majority of those who turned out greeted their Pope with cheers — whatever resentment they had was temporarily forgotten as they were caught up in the excitement of the occasion — but there were some in the crowds that lined the way who gave out with hoots and cat calls, with now and again an attempt by someone well to the rear to hurl a bit of offal in the Pope's direction.

"I will give them what they want, they need," Joanna whispered to herself as she dragged her feet over the rough cobblestones, nodding her head and forcing her mouth to smile. "Within half a year of my return from the mountains it will all be as it was before." And then she thought about the campaign against the Saracens, which she had determined to undertake as soon as her strength was restored. If the Saracens could be driven from Sicily...A violent stab of pain deep in her abdomen radiating to her back cut off the thought. She started to stumble but was rescued by the chamberlain who smiled and nodded. Then the pain was gone.

They were approaching St. Clement's Church, and the crowd had grown more dense, so dense in spots that only with difficulty were the chamberlain's men able to open a passage for the procession. A second stab of pain, even more violent than the first, caused Joanna to grab the chamberlain's arm for support. She could feel her knees buckling, could see the surprised, puzzled expression on the chamberlain's face, on the faces of others who were near.

She desperately looked backward for Marcos, who was following a score of paces to the rear. Her eyes met his for a single moment and he hurried to her side.

Supporting her with one arm, shoving back those in his way, he made a path for Joanna to the church door. Slipping inside, he eased her down onto the stone floor and knelt beside her.

"What is it? Is there something wrong?"

"There were pains," she answered, "but now they have gone." Her head rolled slowly from side to side. "It is because I am tired. There are so many people. So many people out there."

Marcos took her hand and pressed it to his lips. "Perhaps it would be better not to continue. Rest here, Joanna. I will explain to them that you are ill. Then we can leave during the night."

A rising noise outside the church door drew Joanna's attention. It was the sound of a huge ocean wave, one she knew she could not escape. She struggled to her feet. "No, they are waiting for me. If you stay by my side I can go on."

Marcos rose to stand beside her, taking her face and cupping it in his hands. He looked deeply into her eyes. "My brave, my courageous Pope John. My beautiful Joanna." He kissed her tenderly on the forehead, on her eyes, then her lips. She smiled and moved resolutely to the door.

Reluctantly, he pushed against the heavy door and helped her out. A roar greeted the pair as they descended the steps of the church. Joanna flinched and wrapped her arms around her belly protectively yet stepped toward the chamberlain and began walking up the street again, Marcos close by, supporting her with his hand. She looked neither to the right nor the left, mechanically taking one step after another, beginning to count them silently to herself, then realizing that she was using her steps to time the intervals between the pains that had begun to shoot through her again.

The mob pushed against her, drowning out her scream as a violent stab of pain seemed to rip her open. Only Marcos heard it, catching her in his arms as she sank to the stony street. He tore off his cloak and covered her with it. But it was too late.

Those nearest to her saw what was happening. They backed away from the figure writhing in the street and stood in total silence, stunned. Those not close enough to see raised a crescendo of questioning shouts.

Then there was a series of high-pitched screams, one after another, and an infant boy was in Marcos's hands.

There were confused shouts, and wild raucous laughs. For several seconds, the mob fell silent as whispered word of what had happened spread through its ranks. Marcos cut the cord and wrapped the child in his cloak. But he was thrust aside as, with an insane shriek, the mob rushed in.

It is said that Nikon was the first to cry out, "Stone her! Stone her!"

But the cry was taken up by others who echoed his demand. "Stone her! She has deceived us! She has betrayed us!" It is certain that Nikon was among the first to cast a stone at the huddled figure on the cold stones.

Too weak to do more than try to shield her head with her arms as the first missiles reached her, Joanna forced her lips to form the words of the Pater Noster. An image of the peasants streaming toward the forest in their hunt for the hare-lipped widow's son rose into her mind. Then it was all darkness.

Exchanging his clerical garb for those of an artisan he had forced to disrobe in an alley, his eyes streaming tears, Marcos left the city and carried the infant north. Then, in the company of a peasant woman whose breasts were filled with milk, he passed out of Italy, found a way through the Alps, and then continued north until he reached the district of Engelheim and the convent that had once been a castle, its tall tower still showing near its summit the ravages of an old fire.

Author's Note

Marianus Scotus, a noted scholar of his era (d. 1086), inserts in his chronicle the following passage: "A.D. 854, Lotharii 14, Joanna, a woman, succeeded Leo, and reigned two years, five months and four days."

In the chronicle of the important medieval historian Sigebert de Gemblours (d. 1112) is the following statement: "It is reported that this John was a female, and that she conceived by one of her servants. The Pope, becoming pregnant, gave birth to a child, wherefore some do not number her among the Pontiffs."